When He
Hollers,
Let Him go

Teresa McClain-Watson

When He Hollers, Let Him Go

sepia™

WHEN HE HOLLERS, LET HIM GO

A Sepia Novel

ISBN 1-58314-664-4

www.kimanipress.com

Printed in U.S.A.

I honor God Almighty for His power and majesty; Jesus Christ His son for His power to love and save someone who was as lost as I once was; and the Holy Spirit of God for the comfort and activity of God's grace.

I wish to thank Evangelist
Dr. Sonia K. Williams, my mentor and teacher, for her refreshing devotion to the unfailing living word of God. As an evangelist at Abyssinia Missionary Baptist Church, she teaches truth and righteousness in the mode of the Apostle Paul. Keep telling the word as the Lord says so, Paulette!

I thank Glenda Howard, my superb editor, an insightful professional who refuses to get in the way of the work, a writer's champion whose suggestions always improve the work, rather than harm it. God bless you indeed!

And, last but never least, I thank
God Almighty for my husband and best friend, John Thomas Watson, for standing by me when I could hardly stand myself.
You are admired indeed!

And, finally, to all those who read my writings, please visit my Web site at www.teresamcclainwatson.com and let me hear from you. Thanks!

Chapter 1

Thelma Wilcox didn't waste time. As soon as she hung up the telephone, as soon as Mary Girl told her news even she found hard to believe, she ran to tell it, too. Out of the kitchen, across the church grounds, and up to the one-story white building on the back side of the main sanctuary, she didn't stop until she was barging into Sister Baker's day-care class. "He's here!" she yelled frantically after she spotted the less than cheerful teacher.

Sister Baker placed a baby in his crib and then glared at the large head poking through her classroom door. "Have you forgotten how to knock, Sister Wilcox?"

"No, ma'am, but I was in the kitchen—"

"Or is it simply too much of a burden for you to show that little consideration?"

"No, ma'am, but I was shelling peas in the kitchen when Mary Girl called and said I was to come straight to your class and tell you he's here."

Sister Baker frowned. "Who's *here?*"

"The new pastor! Mary Girl said he came into the Piggly Wiggly asking for directions to Fountain Hope and he's on his way right this very second!"

"On his way? What are you talking about? He's not due here yet. You sure it's him, Sister Wilcox?"

"Mary Girl said she positive. It's him!"

Stunned was too mild a word to describe Sister Baker. She was shocked. Astounded. Stupefied beyond belief. She looked at Thelma Wilcox and could do nothing but shake her head. Decently and in order, she thought. Things should be done decently and in order or they shouldn't be done at all. Now out of the clear blue sky this new pastor was about to disrupt everybody's day just because he decided to drop on in when he saw fit, never mind all the preparations they made for his arrival tomorrow. "You was in the kitchen, Sister Wilcox?" she asked as she began hurrying toward the classroom door.

"Yes, ma'am. We shelling peas."

"Them peas gon' have to wait. You stay here with the babies. I've got to find Deacon Molt!"

Fountain Hope Baptist Church was a sprawling brick structure on ten acres of land seemingly in the middle of nowhere. Located just beyond the old abandoned train depot in historic Floradale, a small community on the southwestern tip of Georgia near the Flint River banks, it was the largest African American church in town. Although not the oldest in town—the African Methodist Episcopal church had that honor—it was, however, one of the few to boast its very own day-care center and a K–5 Christian School that was supposed to be second to none. Before their pastor died, before Reverend Jeremiah Cobb had a massive stroke that took him away from them without any kind of warning, they'd had plans to expand to middle school grades 6–9. It was a move Sister Baker completely supported, provided she, and not Inez Flachette, would be in charge of that sector of the school. Inez Flachette, the church secretary, treasurer, and currently the school's superintendent, ran enough. Or so it seemed to Sister Baker.

What Sister Baker didn't support, however, was this decision by the national board of the Fountain Hope Baptist Convention to appoint the next pastor of her beloved church, and to do so without any input whatsoever from local leadership. Now some jackleg they knew nothing about was supposed to just crawl up in here and start running things. And he was a day early, too? Just thinking about it made Sister Baker's blood boil. Just thinking about it made her hurry across the church grounds, her high behind and large hips bouncing like layers of waves as she walked, her orderly mind unable to comprehend how some folks just didn't understand; how some folks seemed to have a knack for totally disrupting carefully thought out, well-coordinated plans as if structure meant nothing at all to them.

She slung open the double doors of the main sanctuary and lumbered her big bulk past the choir stand to the back stairs. The church leaders, led by Head Deacon Molt, were meeting in the boardroom on the second floor and that was where she headed. She was leery about this selection from the start, when Bishop Ted Owens, the head of the southern sector of Fountain Hope churches, came to town with the news. He spoke so highly of this new pastor and how he was supposed to be this great man of God, everything they needed, that Sister Baker could smell a rat. Her question was always the same: if this man was as wonderful as Bishop so endearingly proclaimed, then why would he want to come to little Floradale to pastor a church?

But nobody would listen to her, she thought, as she hurried along the narrow hall that led to the boardroom. Nobody would give her concerns the time of day. Now that same great man Bishop couldn't wait to unload on them was a day early. A day early! And she couldn't wait to see their faces when they finally realized just how prophetic her concerns had been.

She threw open the door to the boardroom without so much as attempting to prepare them for her entrance. "He's here and he's early!" she said as soon as she barged in.

It was a small room of paneled walls, high-back chairs, and one large conference table. At the head of the table was Deacon Horace Molt, a short, pudgy man in his mid-fifties with a receding hairline and a stern, almost grim, large round face. He looked up over the rim of his reading glasses and stared at Sister Baker. And although six other people were sitting around the table, all leaders of various auxiliaries in the church, it was understood without debate that if anybody was going to handle the rude interruption, it was going to be Molt.

"Good morning, Sister Baker," he finally said, in his best calm voice.

"Good morning, Head Deacon. You won't believe what wind just blew our way!"

"We're in the midst of a meeting at this particular moment," he reminded her. "I'll talk with you about the weather another time."

Some in the room couldn't hold back smiles. Sister Baker gave them her best insulted look, then nodded her head. "Okay. Fine. Have your meeting. But when that new pastor comes waltzing through this door don't act like I didn't warn y'all."

Sister Mayfield, the head of the usher board, quickly looked at Sister Baker. "What you saying, Baker? You telling us the new pastor here? You telling us he's here *now?*"

"That's what I'm trying to tell y'all!"

Head Deacon Molt, suddenly understanding, bolted from his seat, which led the others to jump up to. "He's *here?*"

"The man is here."

"But he's not due here until tomorrow!"

"You ain't got to tell me that. I know that. That's why it's so outrageous. Mary Girl said he walked into the Piggly Wiggly asking for directions and he's on his way right this very minute! Gonna be pullin' up any second now."

Molt pulled out his handkerchief and began nervously tapping his forehead. "I don't understand," he said. "Why would he just show up like this when we had everything arranged for his arrival tomorrow? He could have called us if he had to show up early, but I didn't get no phone call." Then he shook his head. "This don't make no kind of sense. Wait till Bishop hears about this."

"They trying to catch us unawares, that's what this about," Sister Mayfield said. "Bishop said he would be here tomorrow, I distinctly remember him saying that."

"He said it, all right," Sister Baker agreed.

"This don't make no kind of sense," Molt said again, shaking his head again. But when he realized all eyes were on him, he stood erect and exhaled. "But there's nothing we can do about it now. Let's just try to get organized here. I need the welcoming committee. Who's on the welcoming committee?"

"I am," Sister Inez Flachette said as her large body stepped forward. She was a big, fifty-eight-year-old woman, five-ten in her stocking feet, with small green eyes and a light brown face that seemed fixed in a frowned position. Her husband was the owner of the only black funeral home in town and she wore that badge of distinction as if it were a badge of honor. If Sister Baker was Fountain Hope's by-the-book foot soldier, Sister Inez Flachette was its drill sergeant. "I'm on the welcoming committee and I'm the committee's chairman," she said.

"Good, Sister Inez," Deacon Molt said. "You and your people get on outside so y'all can meet him at his car."

"Ain't no people, Deacon Molt," Sister Inez quickly responded. "The rest of the committee members at work. Didn't nobody tell me he was coming today or I'd have had my people here."

Everybody agreed, Sister Inez was always diligent, and they began talking amongst themselves about the nerve of this new pastor.

"Listen, people," Molt said, to regain order. "I don't like this no better than y'all do. But he's here now, if Sister Baker is to be believed."

"Excuse me?" Sister Baker said, offended, and Molt shook his head.

"I don't mean it like that, Baker," he said. "I'm just... This a mess. Ain't no two ways about it. That's all I'm trying to say. But we've got to get on out there and make the best of this. I want Sister Mayfield, and you, Sister Scott, to go with Sister Inez to meet his car. Sister Baker, you go on back to the day care. The rest of y'all come with me."

Sister Baker watched the group disperse. She watched them scatter like roaches when the light comes on, as if Deacon Molt's orders were inspired by Jesus Christ himself. But she made sure she left last. She wasn't about to jump at his command. "Um," she said when she finally did start leaving, still disgusted by the way the whole thing was being handled. "I warn 'em and what do I get in return? Not even a thank-you!"

But Molt was too worried to give out thank-yous, as he and the remaining leaders made their way into the sanctuary. He didn't like upheaval, and Reverend Cobb's untimely death certainly qualified. But when the national board decided unanimously to take it out of local hands and pick a successor of their own choosing, he knew it was more than upheaval the board was bargaining for. They wanted to shake things up. They wanted to drag this dinosaur of a dying church, kicking and screaming if need be, into the twenty-first century. Nobody Molt or his group could have chosen would have fit that bill, and they knew it. Now Molt felt threatened, because he didn't fit either, and because any fool could see, as he was certain the new pastor was soon to discover, that it was the head deacon, not some handpicked, city-boy reverend, who ran the show around Fountain Hope.

Matty Jolson, his dark shades shielding his eyes from the scorching Georgia sun, drove past the dome-shaped court-house and city hall annex and steered his shiny, bright blue Jaguar down a street with no name. Then he journeyed, as instructed, down a long stretch of highway, some five miles long, to a barber shop called Clem's, where he was then in-structed to make yet another turn onto yet another street with no name. Then he journeyed, again for miles, until he saw a large brick church at the end of the road, a large, white-trimmed, steeple-topped structure with Fountain Hope Baptist Church written on a marble granite in the middle of the well-manicured lawn.

He stopped his Jaguar a good hundred yards from the church's driveway and stared at his new home. He hadn't preached a sermon, let alone pastored a church, in nearly six years. He thought that it would be such a permanent ar-rangement that even he was surprised when an unexpected visit by Bishop Ted Owens caused him to reevaluate. Bishop Owens was very persuasive, Matty now realized as he leaned his head back, his dark shades able to conceal the anguish in his eyes. Bishop knew all the right words to say. He talked about what happened in Chicago and how sorry he was that the church didn't stand by Matty the way they should have. He talked about how this time would be different, and how these country folks, whether they knew it or not, needed Matty's brand of leadership, somebody who would shake things up not for the sake of shaking, but because he knew no other way to lead. The national church would support him one hundred percent as he "straightened out" Fountain

Hope, Bishop insisted. He also insisted that the locals here would understand his mission and, unlike Chicago, not railroad him, too.

It all sounded reasonable then, Matty thought, since he was bored with life in general, his law practice in particular, and was more than anxious to get back to doing what he knew God had called him to do. But that sense of optimism he felt as he prepared to leave all behind for an appointment many former pastors of huge congregations would assuredly reject as too much of a step down, was now being replaced by a sense of impending doom.

Chicago was the problem. When it became clear that the petition to recall him as pastor would succeed and God, whom he thought at the time was surely on his side, would not intervene, his entire faith foundation was shaken. He had been an ordained minister for only a year when Bishop Owens, at the annual Sunday school convention, asked if he would like to pastor a church. Matty didn't object to the idea, expecting to be given some small, upstart church to run. But Bishop Owens campaigned hard for Matty's appointment to head, not some little country church, but Chicago, one of the largest congregations in the Fountain Hope organization. Matty didn't think he stood a chance since his staunchest supporter, Bishop Owens, wasn't even in charge of the northern region, and since Matty himself didn't think he was ready for prime time on that grand a scale. But when the board didn't hesitate to appoint him, and since Bishop Owens had supported him so vigorously, he assumed they knew more than he did.

He assumed wrong. He wasn't ready by a long shot. His penchant for calling a spade a spade and for refusing to follow antiquated traditions that didn't jibe with the real world, put him at odds with church leadership almost from the start. Then the lies came. One lie after another spewed out of the mouths of females in his congregation, out of the mouths of parishioners he thought he knew and could trust. And when all was said and done he was far too devastated to mount any kind of defense. So he didn't. He packed his bags and left Chicago, and, by natural progression, the ministry, for what he just knew at the time would be an eternal parting.

He was thirty-three years old when that trouble first started, and undeniably faithful, even though he was a Johnny-come-lately Christian who many believed was too new to the faith to pastor such a huge congregation and too boastful about how his newfound religion would keep him in good stead no matter what *devils in hell* he had to encounter. Now he was pushing forty, and about as faithful as a philanderer, a man who hadn't even been inside a church in six years, but now was expected to pastor one.

He cranked back up his car's ignition and let out a deep sigh of anguish. He couldn't say with any degree of certainty why he had decided to accept this post, or why they would even offer it to him. He also couldn't stop wondering, as he took one final look at the brick church before him, what in heaven's name he had allowed Bishop Owens to talk him into once again.

"What in heaven's name is he doing?" Sister Inez asked urgently as she looked at the fancy blue car that was stopped down the road from the church. She, Sister Mayfield, and Sister Wanda Scott were standing at the doors of Fountain Hope waiting, with some degree of trepidation, for Matty's arrival.

"How do you know that's him?" Sister Mayfield asked Sister Inez.

"'Course it's him. You ever seen a car like that 'round here before?"

"Judge Marshall's wife drive one of them Mercedes."

"It's an old Mercedes, for your information," Sister Inez

replied. "Real old. And besides, it don't look nothing like that car down yonder. That's our new pastor, all right. Remember Bishop said he was unorthodox. He kept saying it, too. The man unorthodox. Over and over he said that. Like he was trying to prepare us for something. And if you ask me that's exactly what it is. Something, all right. And it's sitting in that car right down yonder."

"You reckon he's waiting for us to come to him?" Sister Scott asked as she, too, stared at the stopped car. She was the youngest of the three women, although she was in her early forties.

"'Course we ain't going to him," Sister Inez snapped. "We'd look like fools running down there, like wild banshees who can't wait to see the great pastor come rescue us poor, backward folk. He'd better come on to us if he's coming."

"I know that's right," Sister Mayfield agreed.

"And he'd better come on soon 'cause I ain't standing out here all day now, I don't care what Deacon Molt say. I got things to do, too."

"He's coming now," Sister Scott said as she pointed at the now-mobile Jaguar.

They looked like three sumo wrestlers guarding the church's front door, Matty thought as he drove slowly toward them. Three hefty, uncompromising women with frowning faces and disapproving stares. Matty shook his head and let out yet another sigh of anguish. How did they even know he'd be here, he wondered. He came a day early on purpose. Just to avoid facing what he knew would be an unfriendly welcome. But he had to remind himself that he wasn't in Chicago any longer, but was in a place where everybody knew everybody and minding your own business was probably only contingent on minding other people's first.

His Jaguar stopped beside the ladies as all three gave each other suspicious glances.

"I'll bet he robbed his congregation blind to be able to afford a car like that," Sister Mayfield said.

"I'll bet you right," Sister Inez agreed. "But I'll betcha he ain't robbing us. I'm the treasurer around here. He ain't robbing us."

"And look at them shades he's wearing, y'all," Sister Scott said with a smile. "Looks like a Blues Brother."

"Ain't that something?" Inez asked, as if she couldn't believe it herself. "A Blues Brother is our new pastor. Shaft and Superfly gonna run our church. Honestly! What was Bishop thinking?"

Matty stepped out of the car quickly, glad to be able to stretch his cramped legs. He was comfortably attired in shirt-sleeves, a pristine white pressed dress shirt that was tucked into a pair of black tailored trousers. His suit coat, a Hugo Boss, was flapped over the front passenger seat, carefully draped to avoid wrinkling. It was easy to see that Matty Jolson was a man of expensive tastes. But what the three ladies didn't know was that Matty was also a man who'd been a hugely successful attorney for the past fourteen years, including full-time once again for the last six, after his brief, two-year stint in Chicago sent him packing back to his home base in Atlanta and the only thing he knew he could do and do well.

"Good afternoon, ladies," he said cheerfully as he stepped from his car. He removed his sunglasses, revealing large, dark gray eyes that were so stunning in their allure that even Sister Inez had to do a double take. He began walking toward them, still smiling greatly, his big hand outstretched as he came. "I'm Matthew Jolson."

Sister Inez, first in line as usual, regained her composure and looked the preacher up and down. "You Reverend Jolson?" she asked him.

"Yes, ma'am," Matty said, withdrawing the hand nobody seemed willing to shake, but refusing to let them shake his smile.

Inez stared at Matty. Even to the less perceptive eye, which Inez's wasn't, there were a few things easily discernible about this man that stood before her. He was very good looking, she decided first and foremost, with a sparkling crop of short, jet-black, naturally curly hair, a narrow, high-cheek-boned face, a beautiful white-toothed smile, and skin that was so velvety brown that it seemed to glisten like silk in the sun. And although his face gave him that lean look of a run-way model, his hard chest and muscle-tight biceps elevated his body into a bigger realm, Inez felt, as if there were some serious weight-lifting workouts in his past.

It was also easy for her to see that he was his own kind of pastor, a man with such an air of arrogance about him and such a fierce impatience to his demeanor that she just knew he was more often mistaken as a man of danger rather than a man of the gospel. And of all those men of the gospel who had come and gone in the fifty-five-year history of Fountain Hope, Inez Flachette sensed in her bones that this Matthew Jolson was different; that this Matthew Jolson would become unlike any they had ever seen or were ever likely to want to see again.

"Hello?" Matty said, waving his hand in front of her, as she seemed unable to break her stare.

"Forgive me, Reverend," she said, upset with herself for appearing so unprepared. "I'm just trying to make sure I'm understanding you. You supposed to be our new pastor?"

"That's what they tell me."

"You don't look like no pastor I've ever seen."

Matty smiled. He wasn't getting any breaks. "I know. I get that all the time."

Inez frowned. "You get what all the time?"

"Prejudgments. And you are?"

Inez hesitated. Was he being smart with her? "I'm Inez Flachette," she finally said. "It rhymes with hatchet, but since folks act like they can't pronounce my name, and since I don't tolerate nobody butchering up my name, everybody just call me Sister Inez."

"Nice to meet you, Sister Inez."

"My husband is the owner and operator of the Ernest Flachette Funeral Home here in town."

"I see."

"You'll hear more about him. Folks be dropping like flies around here and he be right there to scoop 'em up and give them a proper burial."

Matty didn't quite know what to make of that, so he remained silent.

"Besides being the wife of the funeral home director," Inez continued, "I'm also the chairman of the Pulpit Aid Board."

"Chairwoman," Sister Wanda Scott said with a smile as she attempted to politely correct Inez without taking her eyes off the unbelievably handsome stranger.

"I'm *chairman* of the Pulpit Aid Board," Sister Inez repeated, refusing correction, as she glanced at Wanda Scott. "And I'm the church secretary and the church treasurer and I also happen to be the superintendent of the Fountain Hope Christian Academy."

"All those jobs," Matty said. "My."

"Just so you know who you're dealing with. And as fate would have it I also happen to be the head of the welcoming committee, although it ain't much of a welcome since you took it upon yourself to come a whole day early."

Matty smiled and nodded and looked away from her, as if her nastiness didn't bother him at all. Although it did. "And you are?" he asked the younger woman, who at least was smiling at him more than she was snarling at him.

"I'm Wanda Scott," Wanda said. *You are the most deliciously handsome man I've ever seen,* she wanted to say.

"Good to meet you, Sister Scott."

"Wanda, please, Reverend."

Matty smiled. "All right, Wanda. And you may call me Matty."

Wanda's mouth almost gaped open. Inez's did.

"Excuse us?" Inez asked the pastor.

"I said Wanda here could feel free to call me by my Christian name, to call me Matty, or Matthew if she'd like."

"She don't like," Inez said firmly. "You Reverend Jolson whether she *like* or not. Bishop Owens didn't send you here for us to disrespect you, so we aren't gonna do that."

Matty didn't say anything, which prompted Inez to seek confirmation. "You understand?" she said.

"Yes, ma'am," Matty said in a raised voice. He had a sudden urge to place his hand to his forehead and salute her. But he didn't.

"Now that that's settled," Inez said, feeling in control again, "you can come on with us so you can meet the rest of the church leadership that's here today. Mind you, they ain't all here today, because they were expecting you tomorrow. And that's why nothing's set up."

Matty nodded his understanding, and he did understand. He understood that this was shaping up to be the biggest mistake of his life. But he smiled graciously anyway and followed this so-called friendly welcoming committee into a large, cold sanctuary that he just knew, as par for the course, was going to be about as friendly and welcoming as a gorilla in an outhouse.

Chapter 2

Diane Tarver shook her head. No matter how she tried to appreciate the style of the sleek red dress that draped her body, she just couldn't pull it off. "I look like a floozy," she said as she looked at herself, once again, in her bedroom's full-length mirror.

"You do not look like any such thing," Samantha Marshall said as she stood at her best friend's side. "Russell's gonna love it. You look wonderful in this dress."

"No, Sam, you would look wonderful in this dress. You're confusing you with me. I look like a floozy in this dress."

Sam looked at Leah, their other friend in the room, who was lying across the bed talking a mile a minute on her cell phone. "Leah," she said, "will you please get off that phone and come and help?"

"Help do what?" Leah asked.

"Just help, okay?"

Leah rolled her eyes. At thirty-four she was the oldest of the three friends, somebody with more than her share of interesting experiences, but somebody whose love of good times often had her behaving as if she were the youngest. "Let me call you back, Boo," she said into the phone. "Sam didn't take her meds today. Uh-huh, you know it. Later." She turned off her phone and sat up on the bed. "Okay, what is it?"

"Help!"

"Help do what, Sam? You know how Diane is, I don't know why you keep trippin'. That dress looks good on her but she'll never believe it. She's just an old maid who likes acting like an old maid who's gonna die dressing like an old maid. So I say forget it. Why should I waste my time on her?"

Diane glared at Leah in her bedroom mirror. Leah was tall, shapely, always adorned in a stylish hairdo, long nails, and the latest hip-hop fashions more suitable on a teenager than a thirty-four-year-old woman. Although Diane had known her since childhood, watching her play around Floradale with Diane's older sister, Pam, they didn't become friends themselves until two years ago when Sam introduced them. But even now it was a tenuous friendship at best, one defined more by disagreement than agreement and by their innate distrust of one another. If it weren't for Sam, whom they both adored, Diane doubted seriously if she and Leah would have ever been more than casual acquaintances.

"Why don't I put a belt around it?" Diane asked as she looked away from the opinionated Leah and eyed, once again, the sleek red dress Sam had taken upon herself to purchase just for Diane's special night.

"A belt, Diane?"

"Yes, Leah, a belt."

"See," Leah said, shaking her shoulders, "that's why I don't bother. The girl is hopeless."

"But a belt can add something to it."

"No, Diane," Sam said softly. "No belt. Leah's right. You aren't going for the spinster librarian look tonight."

Diane smiled. "But I am a spinster librarian."

"After tonight that'll change. Russell is gonna propose. You want to look sexy on the night he asks you to be his wife."

Diane laughed. "Sexy? Me? Please."

"Amen to that, sister," Leah said.

"Leah!" Sam yelled. "You aren't helping."

"Then you need to stop lying, Sam. I'm very fond of Diane, too, you know I am, but sexy is not the word I'd use to describe her. She's cute, I'll give her that. And her personality, an A-plus. But she'll have to put a lot more meat on those bones before I place her in the sexy department."

"She is sexy," Sam said, placing a scarf around Diane's thin neck. "She's got that youthful, supermodel look men go for."

"A supermodel? We are talking about Diane, right? Awkward Diane?"

Diane laughed. She hadn't been called that name in years, a name Leah wouldn't even know about if Sam hadn't told her.

"Yes, Leah, we're talking about Awkward Diane." Sam looked at Diane in the mirror. "Look at those pretty, big brown eyes," she said, to which Diane playfully batted her eyelashes. "And look at that wonderful white smile, and this beautiful long hair."

"Beautiful hair that she keeps in that irritating plait almost all the time."

Diane looked at Leah. "Lord help her," she said. "How can my hairstyle be irritating, Leah? I like it."

"It's irritating to me," Leah said. "I'm tired of looking at it. Same ol', same ol', practically every single day. Do it differently, that's all I'm saying. I own a beauty salon, I know what I'm talking about."

Diane shook her head. Every day she had to hear Leah mention her ownership of that beauty salon, as if the cold fact that Leah's husband died and left her enough insurance money to rent out a little place somehow said something re-markable about her. But that was Leah. Always the tireless self-promoter.

"Come over to the shop sometimes," Leah said. "I'll hook you up, girl."

Diane, as if suddenly exhausted, plopped down on the chair in front of the mirror. "I don't know why I'm going through all this trouble anyway. Russell likes me just the way I am."

"I'm sure he does," Sam said. "And we do, too. We just want you to dare to be different for once in your life, that's all."

Sam was a jewel, Diane thought as she smiled at her. She was a beautiful woman with a petite body, shoulder length curly hair, and kind auburn eyes so large and endearing that the first thing people often noticed about her were those eyes. Although she was married to Judge Ira Marshall, one of the most successful and revered men in town, she never lost sight of where she came from or who her true friends were. That was why she could still boast that a simple li-brarian like Diane Tarver and a twice divorced, *loose* beauty salon owner like Leah Littleton could be her two best friends.

"Thanks for your concern," Diane said to her. "But being different doesn't interest me, not even for a night. I'm saved, sanctified, filled with God's Holy Spirit. I like being me."

"Don't you get tired?" Leah asked her.

"Tired of what?"

"Being you. Being this Goody Two-shoes who takes care of everybody under the sun without even thinking about taking care of yourself. I mean, look at you. You went away to college, something I never got the chance to do, and what did all that education get you? Nothing. Ab-solutely nothing. You came right on back to jive-behind

Floradale to work in the library. You didn't have to go away to college to do that, girl. And on top of that you still living right here in the same old house you was born in, living right here with your mama and your daddy. Twenty-nine years old, almost thirty, and still living at home. You got to be tired of this, Diane, come on. Don't you need a break?"

Diane stared at Leah. For all of Leah's faults, and she had many, she often hit the nail on the head. Of course she needed a break. Sometimes she felt as if she were wasting away, so busy doing for others while that sensation called living was passing her right by. When she had attended college she often dreamed of getting her degree and never looking back. She thought constantly about moving far away to the big city, getting her own apartment and a good, steady job, meeting new and interesting people who would fulfill her life in ways Floradale never could.

But her parents were aging poorly, as her mother's numerous ailments and her father's crippling arthritis made her certain that she couldn't just leave them. Who'd take care of them? Her brother, Frank, with his drug habit and general irresponsibility? Or maybe her sister, Pam, with her three children and wild living and inability to take care of herself let alone two old people? When Diane looked around, and around again, there was nobody left but her. She had to be the one whether she wanted to or not. And that was why, after graduation, she packed her bags, shoved her dreams deep down beneath her old clothes, and headed right back where she started from.

"You hear me, Diane?" Leah asked her. "Aren't you tired? It should be your time to shine for a change."

Diane smiled, and broke her stare. "I'm fine, Leah. I have Jesus and He's all I need. Besides, if Russell proposes tonight that'll change everything anyway."

"That's another thing," Leah said and Sam and Diane

looked at each other before they looked at her. "Now I know Russell got a job and all that and he's supposed to be cool, but I'm sorry. Russell is not the one, okay? Even you don't seem excited about the man."

Sam glared at Leah. "What is your problem? What's wrong with Russell now?"

Leah laughed. "Yeah, okay. You don't know, I don't either."

"You know, you need to cut that stuff out, Leah," Sam said seriously, pointing at her. "You are so negative about every little thing lately. Diane and Russell make a fine couple. There's absolutely nothing wrong with Russell Scram and you know it."

"Other than his name, you mean? Mrs. Diane Scram just don't have quite the romantic ring, know what I'm saying?"

Sam exhaled. Sometimes Leah made her so mad! "Russell Scram is a hardworking, Christian man—"

"He works at Wal-Mart, Sam."

"I don't care! He still works! And he also happens to attend the church of his choice every Sunday morning, attends Bible study, loves the Lord and, besides all that, he loves Diane. I say he has some mighty fine attributes, especially considering the state of some of these men 'round here. This union will be a blessing."

"It's a blessing, all right," Leah said. "You get Ira Marshall, that gorgeous hunk of a big-time judge. Diane gets Russell Scram, the assistant manager at Wal-Mart. Yeah, I see where she would be the blessed one."

"And who did you get, Leah?" Sam asked this bitterly and Diane, understanding the change in tone all too well, rushed to change the subject.

"Did y'all see T. D. Jakes?" she asked quickly. "I caught him on TV last Sunday morning and ladies, let me tell y'all. He preached up a storm, you hear me? He had that whole congregation on their feet almost the entire time. I've got to get to one of his Women Thou Art Loose conferences, I've just got to get to one."

Leah, still staring at Sam, ignored Diane. "What's that supposed to mean?" she asked Sam.

"You know what it means, Leah. You get on my case all the time because my husband happens to be successful and I happen to be devoted to him. Now you're getting on Diane's case because her man isn't successful enough and she's not falling at his feet. Well, what about your man, Leah? Ebonically speaking, *where he at?* He may be somewhere, but I certainly haven't seen him around here. Have you, Diane?"

Diane smiled tensely. "Now, you know Leah has got way too many menfolk interested in her to even think about narrowing it down to just one. Isn't that right, Leah?"

Leah didn't even bother to smile, the sting of Sam's words still echoing in her ears. "I guess so."

"Yeah, some women don't play that one-man stuff, they just don't see the point of it. But what about T. D. Jakes? Did y'all catch his show last week? That's what I wanna know."

The storm had passed, thank God, Diane thought, because Sam started gathering up her Louis Vuitton clutch as if she were ready to ease the tension, too. "No, I did not catch anybody's show last week," she said. "But anyway, girl, I've got to get the boys from school."

"That's something I never understood, Sam. You don't work, but Judge Marshall still let you keep the boys in after-school care."

"He let me?" Sam asked.

"You know what I mean. Why would they need to be in after-school care if you don't work?"

"Because I need a break, too, Diane, and my husband, thank God, understands that."

Diane shook her head. "You wrangled a good one, girl."

"Praises be to God. And if I can do it, anybody can. You

knew me since childhood, Diane, you knew me back when I was living from one foster home around here to the next. Was in the foster care system from the time I was three until I graduated high school."

"It's amazing we kept in touch."

"Thank the Lord they only had a handful of schools around here or we wouldn't have. So if God can bless some outcast nobody like me, you know He can bless you, too. And that's why I'm gonna be praying that this will be a night you'll never forget, Diane. A blessing. You deserve a good turn, too."

"Thanks."

Sam smiled. "I remember when Ira proposed to me. I was so nervous, girl, I spilled soda all over his good suit."

Diane laughed. "You were so young."

"I know. I was still in college. And he was thirty-eight and fine as pure wine. And still fine as wine if I may say so myself."

Diane nodded heartily. "I concur," she said.

Sam laughed and then looked at Leah, who still looked dejected. "You coming, big mouth?"

That put a weak smile on Leah's face. "I guess so, pigeon toes."

Sam smiled. "Why do you keep calling me that? I am not pigeon-toed."

"If you say so," Leah said, rising.

"I'm not. Diane, am I pigeon-toed?"

Diane looked at Sam. She was actually, but what difference did it make? The truth was, both Sam and Leah were two of the most beautiful women in Floradale and they both knew it. Especially Leah, whose large breasts, hips, and thighs, and almost regally beautiful high-toned face kept her glowing in the adulation of many a Floradale man, although none that she considered worthy of anything other than an occasional good time. But that was why Leah loved to tease

Sam about her looks and Sam loved to tease her. Unlike Diane, they felt certain that no matter what their flaws they would still be placed in the gorgeous category. Diane, with her small body and general awkwardness, knew she was in some category, too, but she doubted if gorgeous was it.

"Well?" Sam asked her. "Am I pigeon-toed to you?"

"Not *really*," Diane replied, and Leah, understanding the qualification of that answer, laughed.

"Told you so," Leah said.

"Y'all gonna burn in hell, keep on teasing Sister Sam, all right?"

They all laughed. Then Sam turned serious. "But for real, Diane, I'm gonna really be praying for you tonight. I want this to be your special night."

"I know."

"Russell may not be your dream man, but he's a good man."

"Here, here," Leah said. "I'll give him that."

Diane smiled. "Thanks, you two. I just hope I don't be too nervous."

"You will be. But you'll live."

"Let's meet tomorrow and talk about it," Leah suggested eagerly, as if her prior dejection were days gone by. "We can meet for breakfast and you can give us the complete lowdown on what went down on this big date of yours."

"That's a great idea," Sam said. "Ira will be gone to work, the boys will be in school. I'll be free."

"But I won't," Diane said.

"Why not?" Leah asked.

"Because I'm a member of the Pulpit Aid Board and Sister Inez—"

"Not that witch."

"Sister Inez, Leah, appointed me to be the one to go over to the new pastor's house tomorrow morning and spruce it up before he arrives tomorrow afternoon."

"That house don't need no sprucing up," Sam said. "Somebody's been over there cleaning it up, filling up the refrigerator with food, doing everything humanly possible every chance they got in anticipation of the new pastor's arrival. You'd think Bishop Owens himself was moving here."

"Now, Sam, you know Sister Inez. That house belongs to the church and she feels it is the duty of the Pulpit Aid Board to make sure it's presentable when the new pastor arrives."

"Then let *her* go clean it up," Leah suggested.

"I don't know why y'all acting like this. She wants me to do a last minute run-through, that's all, to make sure everything's perfect. It's no big deal."

"And you're the only one who can do it?"

"She said I'm the only one she can trust to do it well."

Sam shook her head. "That lady has really got you snowed."

"The point is," Diane said, refusing to get into it about another sister in the faith, "it'll probably take me most of the morning."

"Let's have lunch then," Leah said.

"I don't know about that either. I've got to open up the library tomorrow afternoon."

"You've got to have lunch, too, Diane, come on! We want to hear the news of how your night went with Russell, girl, and straight from the horse's mouth."

Diane smiled. "Oh, all right. We'll meet where? Maxine's?"

"Where else?" Leah asked. "This ain't exactly the big city. It's not like we have all these choices around here."

"Maxine's it is," Sam said, heading for the exit of Diane's small bedroom. "But I've got to get a move on right now. My boys hate when I'm late."

"Yeah," Leah agreed, "it'll be closing time at the shop soon, too. I'd better get over there and make sure those beauticians of mine aren't, how do I say it? Manipulating the till?"

Diane laughed as Leah and Sam left.

But as soon as the door slammed shut, and Diane was alone in her room, that sense of dread, a feeling she'd been unable to shake for weeks now, overtook her once again.

Six-year-old Alan Marshall and seven-year-old Ira Marshall, Jr., sat in the backseat of their mother's Mercedes and talked nonstop about their day at Fountain Hope's school. Alan, as usual, had no complaints, while Junior didn't do anything but complain. From the activities they had to participate in to the food in the cafeteria, everything was mocked or derided or just plain criticized by Junior.

Sam drove leisurely as he talked, listening attentively, but when she pulled into the driveway of their big house on Hill Banks Road and saw her husband's Ford Explorer parked on that driveway, her heart raced with sudden nervousness. Ira rarely ever made it home before nightfall, and just the thought that he had beat her home concerned Sam. She even started wondering if she should make up a lie, maybe claim that she had had a blowout on the road or something else dramatic, because the truth might not be enough. Her husband always seemed to think that her days were loaded with excitement, when nothing could be further from the truth, and she often found herself embellishing what actually did occur just to satisfy him. She hated doing it, but she sometimes felt so boxed in by his persistence that she couldn't see another way. Ira was a wonderful man, she felt, a man who married her and gave her a taste of respectability that she couldn't begin to create for herself. But last year, when he turned forty-five, his entire personality had changed. It was as if forty-five meant the beginning of old age to Ira and he didn't like it. Sam still knew he had his good side, the side that, for most of their marriage, had been nothing but a blessing. But he also had his moments. Her only prayer, as she got out of her car, was that he was in a good enough mood to keep those "moments" at bay.

His boys certainly weren't on their best behavior anymore. They had been playful in their seats as they rode home contentedly, but now they were decidedly aggressive. Especially Junior, who was mocking his brother's speech impediment for no reason, calling him a retard, and then, as Sam opened the back car door, he was snatching off his brother's prescription eyeglasses and throwing them to the floor.

"That's enough, Junior!" Sam yelled with great frustration as she began unlatching their seat belts. Although her heart had started racing as soon as she'd seen her husband's SUV, it was now downright pounding. And Junior, with his over-the-top behavior, wasn't helping.

She picked up little Alan's eyeglasses and handed them to him. She tried to take Junior's hand, but, as usual, he broke away from her and ran toward the house. By the time Sam and Alan had entered the house, Junior was already inside and sitting on his father's lap. His father, Ira Marshall, a forty-six-year-old criminal court judge, was sitting serenely in a wingback chair in the living room, a glass of red wine in his hand.

"You're home early," Sam said cheerfully as she closed the door. Instead of running to his father, however, Alan leaned against his mother. "Nothing's happened, I hope?"

Ira, a tall, lean man with a handsome, dark brown face and small, intense eyes, stared unceasingly at his wife. His stare was harsh; Sam felt as if she suddenly didn't know what to do with her hands. "Why would you ask a question like that?" he finally asked her. "Why should something have happened?"

"I was just wondering why you were home early. I'm glad nothing happened, but that's why I asked the question." That answer didn't seem to satisfy him, as he continued to stare at her. "I was just making a comment, Ira, since you were home early. I didn't mean anything by it."

"You spoke without thinking."

Sam hesitated. That wasn't exactly the way she would have put it. "Yes," she said, however, for the sake of peace.

"Never a good idea, is it, Samantha?"

"No, it's not."

"I thought I told you about that."

"You did."

Ira nodded, as if now satisfied with his wife's response. When he looked away from her and began asking Junior about his day, Sam quietly sighed with relief. She ran her hand through Alan's crop of curly hair and then looked down at him. Alan looked more like a four-year-old, he was so small, with that high-yellowish skin complete with freckles, big, slightly crossed eyes that required spectacles, and curly red hair that, no matter how it was combed, always managed to jumble to the center of his small head, giving it a football shape. His father once said he was the funniest looking kid he'd ever seen, and Alan cried when he said it, and Sam had to spend the balance of the day convincing Alan that his father really didn't mean it, although she knew he did.

When Sam looked down at her sensitive little boy, he didn't return her loving gaze. He was too busy staring at his older brother and his father, who talked like they were friends at a party. A party he was never invited to.

"Want some milk before supper?" Sam asked her son, and Alan looked up at her as if he were going to speak. But tears began to fill his eyes and he couldn't say a word. He, instead, broke away from his mother's side and ran from the room.

Sam began to run after him, to assure him once again that he was just as loved and worthy as his older brother, but Ira suddenly looked at her with such a chillingly cold gaze, a gaze she didn't even have to return to feel its intensity, that she heeded the warning and stopped in her tracks.

Ira, seemingly pleased with Sam's decision to stay, as if his gaze had nothing to do with it, kissed Junior on the forehead. "Go play with your brother," he said to his son. "We'll talk later."

Junior was disappointed and didn't want to leave, but he knew he had no choice. His father was not like his mother. Tears meant nothing to him.

He got down from his father's lap, rolled his eyes at his mother as if it were all her fault, and hurried from the room. Ira looked at Sam and smiled. A warm, caring, compassionate smile. The smile the public got to enjoy every day. "Come here," he said to her.

She moved quickly to him, praying that his smile was an indication that his black mood had lifted, her experience, however, warning her that she could never be quite sure. She sat in a leaning position on the arm of the chair. When that didn't seem to satisfy Ira, and Sam could tell by something as simple as a sudden tightening of his jaw, she sat on his lap. That pleased him. He placed his arm around her waist and leaned her against him, kissing her on the lips. She closed her eyes and enjoyed his kiss. Even after eight years of marriage he still could make her feel as if she were the most important human being in the world to him. But when she opened her eyes she realized his gaze was on her once again, and it could have been a romantic stare or it could have been a malicious stare. The problem with Ira was that Sam never quite knew what she was going to get.

"How was your day?" he asked her.

"Good. Very good."

"What did you do?"

Sam exhaled. She knew she had to tread carefully. "I picked the boys up from school," she said with a smile.

"Before that?"

"I went by Diane's. She's got this really big date tonight with Russell Scram. I think you know him, honey, he's the assistant manager over at Wal-Mart. Always friendly. Well, we believe he's going to propose to her tonight."

"Before that?"

Nervousness overtook Sam again. Nothing she said was going to satisfy Ira. She could feel it. "Before what? Before he proposes to Diane?" She asked him this nonsensical question, not to elicit any answer, but to stall for time.

Bad move. He exhaled. "What did you do before going to Diane's?" he asked as if he were getting tired of her fast. "Now, don't play with me."

Sam could feel her nerves unraveling as she tried hard to stay upbeat. "Oh," she said. "Let me see. I went by Leah's beauty salon, got me a manicure." She nervously showed Ira her freshly done nails.

The muscles of Ira's square jaw tightened, making it clear to Sam that she had given him true, but wrong, answers. "Do I look like a fool, Samantha?" he asked her.

"What?"

"Do I look like I have some kind of brain defect?"

"Of course not, Ira."

"Now you tell me what you did today and stop dripping it out!"

Sam swallowed hard. It was one of the most uneventful days of her life, absolutely nothing of any great moment occurred. But she knew Ira. She wasn't about to tell him that. She therefore began telling, with great care not to leave out one solitary detail, a dramatic, often embellished, blow-by-blow recounting of her entire day.

Chapter 3

It was a century-old three-bedroom house on Haines Street, with concrete steps and a wooden porch, windows with shaded awnings, and a detached one-car garage. Inside the house was a spacious great room with fireplace, a huge dining room and kitchen area, and a parlor/study adjacent to the living room. The house had well-maintained hardwood floors, big sturdy herculean furniture, and didn't smell as closed in and stuffy as Matty had thought it would. He was, in fact, well pleased with the church's selection. Contrary to what he was halfway expecting, given his unceremonious welcome, the church had actually provided him with a decent place to live.

But later that night, after unpacking, he lay on his big poster bed unable to shake the blues. The quietness of the home, not to mention the neighborhood outside, where only the sound of the occasional car driving by could be heard, made for a stark contrast to the lively condominium community he had left behind in Atlanta. And the energy of the town itself. And the bustling law practice he left. And Vicky, his lady.

He sat up on the edge of the bed and pulled out his Bible. He had prayed long and hard before he took this assignment, and he had studied the Bible judiciously. But he never got that word from God. That still, small voice didn't whisper in his ears. Before his fall, he and God used to have regular communication, he felt, and that was why he viewed his faith as strong. But after Chicago everything changed. He felt as if the intertestamental period, those four hundred years between the old testament and the new when God stopped talking to Israel, was now his fate. God had stopped talking to him. Maybe had even turned away from him, as if He were tired of him, too. And Matty knew it. That was why his prayer life always seemed strained. That was why his Bible reading never quite netted any inspiration. And a man like him was expected to shepherd a flock. A man like him was expected to bring God's word to an entire congregation, to tell them what saith the Lord, when the Lord had stopped telling him.

He closed the Bible and placed it on his bedside table. Then he grabbed the pack of cigarettes from that table, pulled one out, and leaned forward as he lit up. It was warm in the room, since he hadn't bothered to turn on the air conditioning, and his bare chest was covered with sweat from heat and fear. What if he blew it? What if he went into that pulpit spouting so much flesh-filled, uninspired garbage that he destroyed his congregation's faith, too, sending them all reeling to hell? What if he wasn't cut out for this pastor stuff after all? Maybe Chicago was right, and he was too boastful a man to do God's work. Maybe he was the wrong man altogether and it was his faith in Bishop Owens, not his faith in God, that had led him back into this lion's den when he himself should have known better not to go.

Bishop Owens, he thought. He should call the man, tell

him that he was sorry but he couldn't do this. He was the wrong person for the job, a cold truth any two-year-old could see. That was why that "welcoming" committee was so hostile to him today, he thought. They could see it, too.

He chain-smoked on the edge of his bed for what seemed like hours. Praying and trying to decide what in the world he should do. Still wavering, however, he reached for the phone to call Bishop Owens. He had to talk to him, to alert him to the real possibility that he might have to disappoint him and resign out of sheer unworthiness, before things really got out of hand. But the phone itself began ringing just as Matty reached for it, which he found so peculiar that he pulled his hand back. Then he answered it. But it wasn't the bishop as he had hoped. It was Vicky.

Matty's heart sank when he heard her voice. "Hey," he said.

"Why haven't you called me?"

Matty didn't say anything.

"You said you were going to call me."

Matty took a slow drag on his cigarette and thought about the last time he saw Vicky. How she laughed when he told her the news. How she cried when he left her. "I guess I forgot," he said.

"We're still friends, Matty, in case you've forgotten that, too. More than friends."

Matty remained silent, knowing full well the import of what she was saying.

"I'm also your law partner," she said.

"Was," he finally spoke. "I'm not practicing anymore, remember?"

"Why didn't you call me when you got there, like you said you would?"

"It just didn't enter my mind, Vicky."

"You mean *I* didn't enter your mind."

"Don't start."

"So when are you coming home?"

"Vicky."

"When are you coming back to Atlanta, Matty? I have a right to know."

"I'm not coming back and you already know it. I told you what I had to do. I explained everything."

"I see. So you plan to keep on with this charade?"

Matty exhaled. "It's not a charade."

"But it's so ridiculous, Matty. It just defies logic. And what about next weekend?"

"Next weekend? What about it?"

"Oh my goodness. I know you didn't just say that. The mayor's annual dinner party is next Saturday, Matthew! Remember? VIP only? He's expecting us to be there."

Matty closed his eyes. How could he forget the mayor's dinner party? He was wrestling with his very salvation, not to mention the awesome task of being responsible for the salvation of an entire congregation, but good old Victoria Avery still expected him to remember, if he remembered nothing else, the mayor's dinner party. He shook his head. He had forgotten, until now, just how much he hated every second of every minute of every hour of his life. "You go on without me, Vick," he finally said. "And have yourself a ball."

"And what am I supposed to tell Mayor Drake? Huh, Matthew? What am I supposed to tell the mayor? That you couldn't come because you're off playing pastor to some backwater church somewhere? He'd laugh in my face if I told him that."

"Then let him laugh."

"Matty! Now I want you to stop this. What's happening to you?"

Matty let out a sigh and began rubbing his forehead with the hand that also held his cigarette. He had no clue what was happening to him. Some might call it an out-of-body experience. Others might call it just plain insanity. "Vicky, I told you before I left Atlanta that I had to do this. I used to pastor a church and you know it."

"But that was years ago. You aren't even a preacher anymore."

"Perhaps I didn't behave as if I were a preacher anymore," Matty said with more than a little regret, "but I was still ordained to preach."

"I thought you said you were excommunicated in Chicago? That you couldn't preach anymore."

"I was asked to submit my resignation as pastor of the Chicago church. That's all."

"But that should tell you something right there, Matty. The first chance you got to be the pastor of a church you blew it. They couldn't wait to get rid of you. That should tell you right there that preaching is not for you, that somebody desperately doesn't want you preaching."

Matty opened his eyes. But it was more than an eye-opener. It felt as if a veil were being lifted. He had thought it was God. All along he thought the fact that his Chicago congregation had succeeded in ousting him was certain proof that God wasn't on his side. He thought his Heavenly Father had allowed those liars to triumph because, although they may not have been telling the truth about most matters, they were right on about him. He was boastful and stubborn, they said, and too high-minded to be anybody's pastor. He thought it was God who muzzled him. He thought it was God who wanted him as far away from His pulpit as his shiftless feet could carry him. He had never considered, not ever, that maybe it wasn't God. Maybe it was the prince of darkness, not the prince of light, who wanted him out of the church and stewing in his own conceit. Maybe it was Satan himself who, as Vicky had just said almost as an aside, desperately didn't want him preaching.

"Am I right, Matty?" Vicky asked, completely oblivious to Matty's epiphany. "Doesn't that fact alone tell you something?"

"Yes, it does," Matty said as he quickly put out his cigarette in the cup on his nightstand. "It tells me that I'd better get off of this phone and start studying my Bible. That's what it tells me. I've got a flock to shepherd."

"Oh for goodness sakes, Matty, what are you trying to prove? I've never even heard you talk about God or anything like that, let alone study a Bible. Now you're all of a sudden holier than thou? You? Give me a break!"

Matty ran his hand through his soft hair. It would take a lifetime to reverse the damage he'd done to God's good name, he thought. "I know exactly what you're talking about, Vicky."

"It's the truth."

"I know it's the truth. I asked you to forgive me before I left town. I begged you to forgive me."

"Well, forgive me if I don't believe it, Matty."

"I'm sorry that you don't, but it's a fact."

"And what about us?"

"Us?"

"Yes, us! You and me. People expect us to be together. Even the mayor expects it. You know how he loves to tell everybody that we make such a cute couple."

"I'm sure you make a cute couple with your other boyfriends, too, Vicky. You never made any commitment to me."

"Oh, and like you made one to me?"

"I never said I did."

"We had an open relationship and you know it."

"I know, Vicky, I know. You don't have to remind me. But what I don't understand is this phone call. I thought we had this settled. I turned over the law practice to you, with no strings attached. Just gave it all to you. And you were thrilled at the time, you know how lucrative our practice is."

"This isn't about that."

"Then what is this about?"

"You left me. You just left me!"

Matty felt a sting in his heart; the emotion in her voice was undeniable. He had never been in love with Vicky, or any of the other females he'd been involved with, for that matter, but he cared deeply for her. The idea that he was responsible for her pain, that he was yet again more darkness than light, kept him in a constant state of regret. He closed his eyes. Of all the holes he'd dug, this one, he felt, might be the deepest. "Honey, I'm sorry," he said.

"I hate you."

"You should."

There was a long pause. "I don't hate you."

"You should," Matty said again.

"So what are we going to do?"

"Vicky."

"Just tell me."

"I told you what I have to do. I told you this is no game."

"I'm not talking about that. I'm talking about next Saturday."

Matty shook his head. She wasn't listening to him anymore. She simply wasn't listening. "What do you want me to do about that? Drive to Atlanta so we can attend the mayor's dinner party and he can comment once again on our cuteness? Is that what you want?"

"That'd be a start."

Matty's anger flared. "Good-bye, Vicky," he said, and hung up the telephone.

The Tarver household was quiet at night as Malveen sat on the plastic-covered antique couch knitting a scarf and Willie James, her husband, sat stretched out in his well-worn La-Z-Boy watching a Braves game. Their daughter Diane came bounding down the stairs that stood near the front door as if she were anxious to get out.

"I'll be back around ten," she said as she landed on the last step and made a beeline for the exit. She had changed from the sleek red dress Sam had given her into a brown skirt suit with matching pumps. Although it was undoubtedly too conservative an outfit for her friends to appreciate, it felt perfect for her.

"Where you going?" Malveen asked as she looked at her. She was a diminutive woman, smaller even than Diane, with a long face and large eyes. Although she was only fifty-five years old, she claimed more ailments than any doctor had ever diagnosed, a fact not lost on her husband, but one completely irrelevant to her daughter.

"I have a date with Russell," Diane said.

"Russell?"

"Yes, Mother, I told you I had a date with Russell tonight."

"That's tonight?"

"Yes."

"But I thought you was gonna take me to bingo tonight?"

Diane exhaled. She was nervous enough. "Frank's upstairs. He can take you. Or Dad."

"Don't put me in," Willie James said quickly. "Them old ladies give me the willies, man. Don't put me in that. Always staring at me."

Malveen looked at her husband. "Who be staring at your ol' fool self?"

"Them church ladies, that's who. Them bingo girls. Every time I come to pick you up they be looking at me like I'm the pork chop and they're the bread."

"They probably be staring at that crazy hairdo of yours, that's what they be staring at."

"Woman, please, this the style." Willie James said this and began patting his wild Afro.

"What style? The caveman style? Be standing all on top of your head like you ain't got no kind of sense? Like Buckwheat or somebody."

"Anyway," Diane said, definitely in no mood for *this,* "good night."

"But who's gonna take me to bingo, Diane? You can't just leave like this."

"I told you I have a date tonight."

"You can take me first."

"I can't. You know how Russell is about tardiness."

"Russell. That's all I hear about. Russell, Russell. What about me?"

Diane sighed and looked at her father. He was still a romantic at heart. Surely he would understand. "Dad, will you please take her over to the hall tonight?"

Willie James looked at his sweet daughter. This was supposed to be her big night, the night of the proposal, and the last thing she needed was to be fooled up with Malveen. He looked back at the game. "I'll take her," he said. "Don't want to, but I'll do it."

Diane smiled. She could always count on her father. "Thanks, Dad. I owe you one."

"You owe me fifty." Then Willie James looked at her. He smiled. "So it's your big night?"

"Hopefully, yes."

"Come over here and let me give you a few pointers."

"Dad!"

"Don't 'Dad' me. Come over here."

Diane could not believe it. She was twenty-nine years old, almost *thirty,* and they still didn't seem to understand that. But she went to him anyway.

"Okay, what is it?" she asked, as she sat on the ottoman by his recliner. Willie James was a short, stout man, who had a long, bulldog face and big, flapjack ears. His hair, wild though it may be, was only in keeping with his absolute commitment to being himself.

He was also committed to the Braves game he was watching, as he could not seem to tear his attention away from a triple play that was being executed.

"Dad, I hate to interrupt you, but it's late. I've got to go."

"Okay," Willie James said, although he was still sneaking peeks at the TV. "Make him get on his knees," he said to her.

Diane quickly stood back up. Her father's hand pulled her back down. "Make him do it, Diane. Then you'll know he respects you."

"Ha!" Malveen said. "You didn't get on no knees when you proposed to me."

"Exactly," Willie James said. "And you see what happened? Made the biggest mistake of my life."

"Right. Is that all?" Diane said as she stood to her feet, this time refusing to let Willie James stop her.

"This all wrong, Diane," Malveen said. Diane looked at her.

"What's all wrong?"

"This marrying Russell Scram. What's supposed to happen to us if you marry that big-headed…"

"That's enough, Mama. And don't worry about it like that. I'll still help y'all."

"Yeah, like you helping me tonight. Just shoving me off on some anybody. How am I supposed to get to bingo?"

"Dad is gonna take you."

"But he don't want to."

"I don't either!"

"See what I mean? You already ain't got no time for me. This is gonna be tragic, I tell you. You gonna rue the day you ever met that Russell Scram."

Diane gave up. Expecting them to understand how badly she needed some happiness in her life was like expecting a baby not to cry. And she knew it. Without saying another word to her mother, who had plenty more words to say to her, she hurried out the front door. By the time she plopped down in her old but reliable Buick Skylark, she felt a sudden sense of urgency. She prayed to God that everything would go well tonight as she started the car and drove hurriedly away from the old wooden two-story house. Russell absolutely had to propose to her. He had to stop his months of hints and suggestions and finally make his move. Because if he didn't, and she was forced to return back to her child-hood home on Clarion Avenue in the same state as she first left, then she would have no choice but to conclude what she had secretly concluded a long time ago: that love and happiness, and the experience of being somebody's chosen one, would, just as life itself had managed to do, find a way of eluding her, too.

The situation, however, didn't look very promising when she arrived at Maxine's restaurant to find Russell Scram looking at his watch rather than her. She swallowed hard. She hated those perfectionist ways of his, but she said a silent prayer and smiled just the same.

"It was my father," she said as she sat down.

Russell Scram, a three-hundred-and-fifty-pound man with a huge chest-span and a small, round head, placed a pen-cil back in his shirt pocket where a pile of pencils stood, and looked at her. He was a nice-looking man, Diane thought, with bright brown eyes and a nice crop of soft brown hair, and although his voice was relatively high pitched and he had some effeminate mannerisms he never bothered to ex-plain, he would still be considered a decent catch around Floradale. Even with his weight.

His weight. His massive bulk. Diane used to feel sorry for him, when people would point and stare and make fat jokes about him, but Russell Scram was such a fastidious man, a man who was too busy finding fault in others to notice what they were finding in him, that her pity was often quickly replaced by sheer annoyance. Why she would even consider this marriage, she thought, proved just how slim the town's pickings were and just how desperate she had really become.

"What does Willie James have to do with it?" Russell asked her.

"That's why I'm late. He was giving me pointers."

"Pointers? On what?"

Diane started to say, but she looked at Russell and realized he was not in the mood to be humored. "Oh, nothing," she said. "It's not important. How are you?"

"I'm fabulous. But that's neither here nor there. This is about us."

Diane exhaled. Sometimes she liked his directness. "Agreed," she said.

"The reason I asked you here tonight, Diane—with some urgency, I'll admit—is because I've been thinking long and hard about things. I've been reflecting about my life, your life, and I felt it was high time, in light of all my reflecting, that we make some changes."

Diane's heart began to soar. "What kind of changes, Russell?"

"There's no other way to say this, except to just say it." He exhaled. "I think we should ease up."

Diane kept looking at him, staring at him. Those words didn't make sense. Those words were inconsistent with what she just knew he was going to say. And her heart, which had been about to soar, dropped. "Ease up?" she asked incredulously. "What do you mean?"

"As a couple we should ease up."

Diane held up her hand. "Wait a minute."

"We, of course, can remain friends. I don't mean a total break."

"Wait a minute, Russell. What are you saying? You want us to *ease up?*"

"Yes. That's what I said. It shouldn't be that shocking to you."

Anger began to bubble inside Diane. He had some nerve, she thought. Some *nerve*. "You're telling me I shouldn't be shocked? Is that what you just said? We've been dating for what, Russell? Two whole years? And I'm not supposed to be shocked by this when every day for the past month you've been hinting that tonight is the night? This is the big night? Forgive me for saying this but easing up on our relationship wasn't quite what I thought you had in mind."

"I know I may have given a different impression earlier."

"You were practically setting a date, Russell! What are you talking about?"

"Settle down, Diane."

"But how can you sit up here and act like this is no big deal to you? How could you think I wouldn't be shocked by all this?"

"I didn't say you wouldn't be shocked. I said you shouldn't be."

"I shouldn't be?"

"No."

"And why's that, Russell?"

"Does it matter?"

"Yes, it matters!"

"Don't push it, Diane."

"Why are you breaking it off, Russell, after all this time? And don't give me that life reflection crap!"

"All right. Okay. You want to know the truth? You want to know the honest truth?"

"Let me think? Yes!"

"Okay. I'll tell you. I didn't want to go there but some people force your hand. The truth is, I can do better than you, Diane. That's the honest truth."

Diane felt as if somebody had just slapped her. She leaned back in her chair and looked at her massive boyfriend, his small head like a pebble on top of a boulder. And even he could do better than her. "You can do better than me?" she asked sadly.

"Yes, I can. I'm sorry, but I can. I am, after all, the assis-

tant manager at Wal–Mart, okay? Which, and I'm not brag-
ging, makes me a BMW—"

"A BMW?"

"A black man working, okay? Which means I can have
my pick of the litter. You're nice enough, and you have a
sweet Christian spirit about you, Diane, which is a wonderful thing, but you're hardly the litter's best. I mean, let's get
real here. So you see, I have to keep my options open. And
being latched on to you doesn't do it for me."

Diane tried to smile, to release the anguish that was
steadily building up inside her like an inflating balloon, but
she couldn't pull it off. "Will you excuse me, Russell?" she
asked, but didn't wait for his response. She instead stood up,
the tears coming like the bursting of a dam, as she ran for
the nearest exit.

Chapter 4

The Marshall household was quiet as Ira ascended the stairs. He bypassed Alan's bedroom but looked into Junior's. He was fast asleep. When he made it into his own bedroom, Sam was still at the dressing table brushing her thick, shoulder-length hair. He watched her as she brushed, as she appeared completely oblivious to his presence, her sheer silk nightgown clinging to her perfectly formed body. He smiled. He was sixteen years her senior, and very much in a different league than her in every way, but he still did not regret the marriage. She gave him Ira, Jr., the son who was his life, and he gave her the freedom to enjoy the lifestyle she dreamed about. He even allowed her to take the boys to after-school care, just to give her even more freedom. Maybe too much, he thought.

He closed the door. As soon as she heard the sound of the door and realized he was in the room, her body tensed as if by reflex and the hairbrush quickly fell from her hands. She moved to pick it up, angry with herself for her nervousness, but Ira came upon her and knelt down to retrieve it instead.

He stared at the brush now in his possession, as Sam's small hand reached out to receive it, and then he looked into her eyes. His look unnerved Sam so that she felt compelled to start talking. "They're asleep?" she quickly asked him.

It worked. That intensity in Ira's eyes, an intensity that sometimes felt like fire to Sam, began to dissipate. "Yeah," he said, and handed her the brush.

As he moved away from her, she continued her nervous babbling as if keeping him engaged in talk were the best way she knew to keep him calmed down. "They have all this energy, all day long, but as soon as night falls you can forget it. They drop like rocks."

Ira smiled weakly and sat on the edge of the bed. Sam looked away from him, as he began to loosen his tie while staring at her, and she was determined not to provoke him tonight.

"Our new pastor will arrive tomorrow," she said with a smile.

"Word around the courthouse is that he's already arrived."

"Already here? No, he's not here yet. Diane's got to go over and finish sprucing up the house for him in the morning and they're planning a big welcome celebration over at the church. It's supposed to be spectacular. Think you'll be able to attend?"

"Nope," Ira said as he laid his long body horizontally on the bed. "I have to preside at trial tomorrow."

"The Wells' trial?"

"Of course."

"I honestly don't think that boy did it, Ira. I'm sorry. I can't see a sweet-faced child like that harming a flea, let alone killing his own grandmother. I just can't see it. You think he did it, Ira?"

"I have no idea."

"I hope he's innocent."

Ira closed his eyes. Presiding over murder trials was the

least favorable part of his job. Although murder trials had the reputation of great glamour and thrill-a-minute excitement, they were, for Ira, some of the most dragged-out, overly technical, boring proceedings imaginable. From DNA to hair fibers, it was like an exercise in tedium for him.

"I heard he wasn't that old," Sam said.

"He's nineteen."

"Not Wells, honey. Reverend Jolson, our new pastor. Sister Loomis said he's no kid, he's forty or somewhere up in there, but he's not ancient like Reverend Cobb was."

Ira's eyes opened. "You saw Sister Loomis today?"

"Yes. At the grocery store. And she seems to think something must be wrong with this new pastor they're sending us. Why else, she wants to know, would Deacon Molt be so unwilling to tell us anything substantive about the man?"

"You didn't mention seeing Sister Loomis today."

"What's that, honey?"

"Earlier, when you were telling me about your day, you didn't mention the fact that you saw Sister Loomis."

Sam, who was brushing her hair, suddenly realized what she had done and froze mid-stroke. It was a minor matter, forgetting to mention Sister Loomis during her earlier blow-by-blow report to Ira, but she also knew Ira, and that minor matter would undoubtedly become a crucial blunder on her part. "Didn't I say something about it?" she asked him nervously.

He looked at her. "No, you didn't."

Further words failed Sam, as fear began to grip her. She just didn't know what else to say.

"What did you discuss with Sister Loomis?" he asked her.

"I told you, honey. The new pastor."

"What else?"

"Nothing else, Ira."

"What did you tell her about me? About us?"

"Good Lord, honey, you know I wouldn't tell that woman anything about our business."

"Did she tell you something?"

"Tell me what?"

"Did she laugh in your face when you told her how you get away with it?"

"Ira! For the love of God! Get away with what? What are you talking about?"

Ira got out of bed with the speed and agility of a man far younger and began walking toward his wife. "Did she advise you to divorce me, the way she divorced Ralph, since I'm so old and feeble and you can have anybody you want?"

"Stop it."

"You stop it!" Ira screamed, his finger pointing accusingly at his wife. "You stop it! You think I'm stupid? You think I don't see the way people look at me now? I feel like some kind of freak! And you're out there messing around with every Tom, Dick, and Harry that comes along. My wife! My *young,* beautiful wife!"

Ira was directly behind Sam now, and pure terror swept through her body. She wanted to stand, for leverage, but she was too terrified to move. "Honey, you know I love you," she said.

"Don't tell me what I know! Tell me why you didn't mention seeing Sister Loomis today. Tell me that, Samantha!"

"I just forgot—"

As if enraged by Sam's sudden claim of a memory lapse, Ira grabbed her by the hair, causing her head to snap back violently. "Don't you lie to me, woman! Don't you dare lie to me!"

"Ira, please, you're hurting me!"

"Who else did you forget to mention seeing today? Who else? Another woman? Or maybe a man?" He slung her up by her hair and threw her toward the bed, causing her to fall onto it. "Is that what this sudden lapse of memory is all about? You're trying to protect some man?"

"There's no man. I don't know what you're talking about!"

He slapped her hard across the face and then grabbed her by the throat. "Didn't I tell you not to lie to me, woman?" He began shaking her violently. "Didn't I tell you not to lie to me!"

The shaking was more than she could take. The look in his intense eyes was too weird, too otherworldly. And she knew she had to fight back. She began kicking wildly and flailing her arms uncontrollably. But when she kicked him in his midsection, causing him to bend over in pain, she knew she had done it now. And she also knew it would be her only chance to get away.

She jumped from the bed in an ill-fated attempt to run from this man she no longer recognized, but he was too swift for her. He grabbed her wrist before she could clear his path and flung her across the room as if she were a weightless feather. She lost her balance almost immediately and stumbled forward, her head just catching the sharp edge of the dressing table, before she fell to the floor.

Ira, angrier than ever, still reeling in pain, hurried toward her with every intention of slinging her up again and teaching her a lesson she wouldn't soon forget. Until he saw the blood. And the stilled face. And the beautiful, still body of his wife. Of the mother of his children.

He fell to his knees.

Willie James was dozing through a *MASH* rerun when Diane came through the front door of their home. He heard the floorboards creak and immediately opened his eyes. Diane shook her head. She had been within seconds of a clean getaway.

"That you, precious?" Willie James asked.

"It's me."

"So how did it go?"

Diane reluctantly walked into the living room and sat on the sofa across from her father's chair. She tried to smile. "Where's Mother?"

"Still at bingo, where else? How come you're back so early?"

Diane didn't say anything.

"How did it go with Russell?"

She exhaled. She was still reeling from what Russell had said. "I turned him down," she said halfheartedly.

"You turned him down?"

"Yes, I did. I'm a librarian, after all. A BWW."

"A what?"

"A black woman working. And I can have my pick of the litter. I mean, Russell's nice enough, and he has a job, but he's hardly the litter's pick."

"You ain't got to tell me that. I doubt if he can fit in the litter."

Diane smiled. Leave it to her father to make her smile. He looked at her. "It's over, then?"

She repressed the tears that were fighting to reappear. "Yes," she said.

"And you're okay with that?"

She nodded.

"So Shamu's out?"

"Yes, Dad," she said with a smile. "Shamu's out."

Willie James nodded. "Good," he said. "I didn't like him anyway. All them pencils in his pocket like he can write with more than one at a time. I see him over at the Wal-Mart sometimes. Trying to play the big man. I wondered what you saw in him anyway. No sir, I ain't got no regrets about Shamu, none at all."

Diane, however, wished she was as heartless. But she

wasn't. She couldn't even lie without hating herself. "He didn't want me, Dad," she finally said sadly. "Truth is, he didn't give me a chance to turn him down." She said this and looked at her father. Willie James was genuinely surprised.

"He didn't want *you?*"

Diane, once again, fought back tears. She hated that it hurt, but it did. "That's what he said. He seems to think he can do better than me."

Willie James was stunned. Poor Diane, he thought. Never seemed to catch a break. "Well, I'm glad he showed his colors before you married him. Thank God for that. He would have crushed you anyhow."

Diane, caught off guard by her father's razor-sharp tongue, suddenly found herself laughing. "You need to quit, you know that?"

"No, he need to quit. Talking about my daughter ain't good enough for him. Who does he think he is? Mr. Wal-Mart? Mr. Big Man? Mr. Jump-in-the-pool-and-all-the-water-disappear? And you ain't good enough for *that?* Child, hush!"

Diane smiled. She may not be at the top of anybody else's list, she thought, but at least her Dad loved her.

Willie James's smiling face suddenly looked concerned. "You gotta be tough in this life, precious," he said. "You can't let people be walking all over you. You can't keep settling for what you can get just because it's convenient. You hear me, child? Stop being so convenient all the time."

"Yes, sir."

"I mean it."

"I know."

The phone rang as Willie James continued his heartfelt talk. Diane allowed him to finish his thought, then answered the phone.

"Hello?" she said.

"Diane?"

"Yeah, Leah, hey. What's up?"

"Can you come out to Memorial?"

"The hospital? Why?"

"There's been an accident and Sam's hurt."

Diane's heart dropped. "My Lord. What happened?"

"I don't know all the details. Can you come?"

"Of course I can come," Diane said, already on her feet.

She arrived at Memorial Hospital in Bainbridge a half hour after Leah had phoned. She was frantic, but when she saw Leah she tried to calm down.

"How is she?" she asked as soon as she rushed into the emergency room. Ira was standing near the nurses' station talking with a doctor, and Junior and Alan sat quietly with Leah. But when Alan saw Diane, he ran to her.

"Aunt Di-tan!" he yelled.

Diane picked him up and smiled. "Hello, sweetheart. How are you?"

"Mammy's tick."

"She's sick?"

"Yes, she's tick."

Diane looked at Leah, who looked worried, too. What a night, she thought. "How is she?"

"They say she'll be fine," Leah said. "But they're running tests now to make sure there are no internal injuries."

"Can we see her?"

"Not yet."

Diane, still holding Alan, sat down on the bench beside Leah and Junior. "How you doing, Junior?" she asked him. Although Junior heard her, he opted to ignore her. Diane, accustomed to his broodiness, looked at Leah. "So what happened?"

"I wasn't there. But Ira says she fell and hit her head."

Junior folded his arms suddenly, as if suddenly angry. Diane looked at him. "You okay, Junior?"

Junior rolled his eyes.

"Junior, I'm talking to you."

"She's ralkin' to you, Junior," Alan added.

But Junior merely got up angrily and walked over by his father.

"What is his problem?" Diane asked Leah.

"He's an angry young man."

"He's not a young man, he's a child."

"Yeah, but he's *Ira's* child." Leah said this and looked at Diane. Diane exhaled. She was well aware of Leah's less-than-flattering opinion of Ira Marshall, although she never explained why she didn't care for the man. And Diane definitely was not in the mood to find out tonight.

"How did it go with Russell?" Leah asked her.

"Don't ask," she said, still unable to shake the pain, not of losing Russell, but of the words he had said to her. "Where did Sam fall?" she decided to ask instead, to at least change the subject.

"Home," Leah said.

"And she hit her head?"

"Yep. Ira claims she had one too many."

"Sam? But I thought she quit. I thought she stopped completely."

"Well, apparently she's started back."

Diane leaned back and began absently playing in Alan's curly hair. Sam was always so in control, so strong, that Diane couldn't even imagine her drinking again. Not that she'd ever seen her drink. She hadn't. Just heard gossip and rumors that she never got around to discussing with Sam.

"How did you find out?" Diane asked Leah. "Judge Marshall called you?"

"Why do you refer to that man as Judge Marshall? His name is Ira, okay? Folks round here act like they got to bow down to his butt like he's some larger-than-life action hero or something. And no, he didn't call me. He can't stand me, why would he call me? One of my customers work here and she knew, from beauty parlor chitchat, that me and Sam were tight. She called me."

"And that's all she knows? That Sam fell and hit her head?"

"That's all Ira's telling."

Diane looked at Leah. "You sound like you don't believe him."

"Let's just say I have my doubts."

"But why would Judge—why would Ira lie? He adores Sam."

"Yeah, okay."

"Leah!"

"Leah nothing! I have a right to my opinion. And all of this great adoration he's supposed to have for Sam, I just don't see it."

"Well, Sam adores him."

"Sam's terrified of him."

"How can you say that?"

"Oh, I can say it. I've been around the block, okay? I can sho' say it."

Diane didn't know what to think. Was Leah trying to insinuate that Sam was some kind of a battered wife? *Sam?* Diane just couldn't believe that. There was absolutely no evidence, for one thing, and Sam was far too strong a woman to let some man beat on her, for another thing. And the idea of Judge Marshall beating on Sam didn't even sound true. Besides, Sam worshiped her husband. She was devoted to that man. And from where Diane sat, irregardless of what Miss Negative Leah Littleton was saying, Ira seemed to return that devotion.

"I'm just glad she's all right," Diane finally said, deciding that this was not the time to argue with Leah.

"I don't know how all right she is," Leah replied. "But at least she survived this round."

Diane looked at Leah, who seemed so certain about everything. Then she watched Judge Marshall, a man she admired, as he laughed heartily with the doctor.

Chapter 5

Matty woke up, two hours after he had fallen asleep, to the sound of music. He was still sitting in the chair in his bedroom where he had prayed most of the night and searched his Bible endlessly for a word, a phrase, a verse of inspiration that he could point to and thereby know for certain he was on the right road. But nothing came. Just a continuing, unable-to-shake feeling of despair, as if life's mockeries had encircled him. That was why he'd thought he was dreaming when he heard the music. He thought he was having himself a heavy-duty dream because that wondrous music, instead of chastising him, too, was soothing him. But as he became fully awake, his Bible still flopped open on his lap, the bright morning sun just beginning to cast its light against the windowpane, he knew this was no dream. Somebody was in his house.

Dressed in a pair of green silk pajamas, and still feeling the effects of another long, near-sleepless night, he set his Bible on the side table and walked swiftly toward the sound, down the hall and through the living room. The sound was coming from the parlor. It was gospel music, Matty discovered as he walked. It was Andre Crouch singing "Soon and Very Soon" in a rich sound that filled the house. But there was another voice, too, a soft, female voice, singing along.

The French doors that led into the parlor were already open, and Matty had only to lean against the doorjamb and watch his intruder. Only he relaxed as he watched. For the intruder was a female, a small, rather boisterous soprano who was dusting the large, fruitwood desk and singing along with Andre, her long hair in an Indian plait, her clothes a pair of loose-fitting jeans and an oversized sweatshirt.

He smiled as he watched her, because she seemed so happy, because every time she sang the word *hallelujah* she'd throw her hands in the air and shake them as if she could only feel the spirit when she mouthed that particular word. Matty looked around for the source of the music, and he found it against the back wall. It was a small boom box CD player that sat on the floor alongside a large pocketbook. Both undoubtedly belonging to his intruder, to that ray of sunshine in his room, he thought, as he turned his attention back to this singing waif of a woman, who, oddly enough, seemed to fascinate him.

Diane had no clue she was being watched, as she dusted and sang and threw her hands in the air. She was trying to counter the effects of last night, when Russell dumped her, when Leah all but said she believed Sam was a victim of spousal abuse. Spousal abuse by one of the most respected men in all of Georgia. Spousal abuse! It didn't make sense. Samantha Marshall was the strongest woman Diane knew. She didn't take guff from anybody. But if it were true, and if Sam were indeed a victim, and one who was willing to deny being so, then Diane could only shudder to think what that meant for the rest of them, for women like Diane herself, who never claimed to be so tough.

"Good morning!" Matty shouted over the sound of the music, deciding it best if he announced his presence rather than scare the poor girl half to death if she had to discover him for herself.

But he still scared her witless as she turned quickly to the sound of his voice. She promptly lost her balance, falling backward in a frightened twirl and landing hard on her rump. Matty rushed to her aid, his hand reaching out quickly to help her to her feet. Diane stared at him as she took his hand, she stared at this beautiful man before her. He was tall and powerfully built, she noticed, and his face had a fierceness about it that should have scared her, too. But it didn't. Because he was so beautiful to look at. From his jet-black, soft curled hair to his dark gray eyes, just the sight of such a man made her want to swoon. And it made her wonder if he were really real, or just a figment of her sometimes-overwrought imagination. But he was touching her. And just his touch sent tremors through her body. He was real, all right. He was perfect, she thought.

She was clumsy, he thought, as he lifted her to her feet. Clumsy and awkward and light as a feather. Perhaps too light, he felt, looking at her narrow waist, although her breasts were hardly sparse and her backside, he'd noticed earlier, wasn't without its girth either. But she was a slip of a woman overall, with big, beautiful almond eyes that seemed so terrified of him that she was literally shaking.

"No need to be afraid, young lady," he felt compelled to blurt out. "I live here."

She continued to stare at him. "You live here?" she asked.

"Yes. I'm Matty Jolson." He said this and extended his hand. She, however, was in too much of a confused stupor to notice that hand.

"*You're* Reverend Jolson?"

Matty hesitated. Was it that bad? Was he so transparent that even this little innocent could tell he wasn't exactly Reverend material? "Yes," he said. "I'm Reverend Jolson."

"Sister Inez said you wouldn't be here until late this afternoon."

"That was the plan, yes."

"What happened?"

Anxiety, Matty wanted to say. "I just came a day early," he said instead. "And you are?"

"Oh, I'm sorry." Diane left his side and hurried to turn off her boom box. "I didn't mean to be so impolite. I hope my loud music didn't wake you." She said this and glanced back at Matty. He, however, didn't want to lie to her, since her music did wake him, and therefore didn't respond. His lack of reaction didn't help ease her nervousness, but she turned off the music just the same. "I was sure nobody was here," she continued as she stood back up and faced him. "I didn't even see a car or anything to indicate..."

"It's in the garage."

"Yes. Of course. It would be, wouldn't it?"

Matty smiled as Diane just stood there, like a raw bag of nerves, he thought, across the room. "And you are?" he asked again.

"Oh," she said, shaking her head. "That's me. Always running my mouth about irrelevancies without answering anybody's question. I'm really bad about that."

But she still just stood there, trying to smile and play nonchalant, although Matty could see the uneasiness all over her. He paused. And then smiled. "Let's try it again, shall we? You are?"

Diane laughed. "I'm really bad about it today." She then hurried back toward him and extended her hand. She felt horrible that she couldn't at least pretend to be more sophisticated. "I'm Diane. Diane Tarver. I'm a member of the Pulpit Aid Board. It's our job to make sure you're comfortable in every avenue of your ministry. Sister Inez, she's our president, had assigned me the task of last-minute sprucing up."

"I see," he said as he placed his large hand into Diane's small hand and kept it there. His subtle refusal to release her hand was so bold, and his stare so unrelenting, that it caused a quiet tension to fill the room. Diane tried to keep her wits about her, to continually remind herself who this man was that stood before her, but his touch and his stare caused such a strong reaction within her that it seemed to cloud all of her good senses.

"Tell me, Sister Tarver," Matty said but she quickly, nervously interrupted him.

"Please call me Diane, Reverend."

"All right, Diane. Are you as surefire as Sister Inez?"

"Oh, God no."

Matty felt oddly relieved. "Good."

"I wish I could be as forthright as she. But I don't seem to have the constitution for such faithfulness."

"Faithfulness? Is that what you call it?"

"Why, yes. What would you call it, Reverend?"

Matty wanted to respond, to unleash his true feelings and let his guest know exactly what he'd call somebody like Inez Flachette. But when he looked into Diane's eyes, those big, sweet, doleful almond eyes, he decided against it. Just his presence in the room has her terrified enough. She'd probably pass out if she had to be subjected to his rage, too.

"I'm not quite sure what I'd call it, Diane," he said honestly and looked at her. And it was an unintentionally prolonged look as he couldn't seem to stop himself from staring at her. From her thick, wavy hair and smooth, unblemished face, to those oversized clothes that draped her body, something about her continued to fascinate him.

She was fascinated, too, by his size and beauty and his sternly defiant spirit. So much so that his stare rendered her too uncomfortable. She felt inadequate, exposed, the truth of those odd feelings that were suddenly bubbling inside her unmasked. And she had to put a stop to it.

"Well," she said, removing her hand from his and moving toward her dusting cloth and cleaning supplies, "I'd better get my stuff and get out of your way. I'm sure you've got lots to do."

Matty watched her as she packed up her furniture polish and Windex, her big eyes riveted on her simple task as if she were afraid of dropping something or spilling something or otherwise messing up. He should have let her go. His mind told him to let her collect up her stuff and go, leaving nothing behind but the memory of her off-key, soprano voice.

But his heart told him something else. By the time she had her supplies, purse, and boom box in hand and was telling him good-bye as she headed for the exit, he called her name.

At first she hesitated before turning, her every instinct telling her to pretend she didn't hear him and just keep walking, but she turned around.

His breath caught when she turned and looked those big, sad eyes at him, and he just stood there, wondering why in the world he was reacting this way, this totally out-of-character way, to this one particular human being. She wasn't even his type, for crying out loud!

Diane felt strange, too, when she looked at him, and she had to swallow before she could speak. "Yes, Reverend?" she finally said.

He sat on the edge of the desk and folded his arms. If he was nervous, if he was having any kind of emotional reaction to her whatsoever, she'd never know it. He seemed almost serene to her, as he sat there, his entire body seeming to relax even more while she was on the verge of emotional collapse.

"Where're you headed?" he asked her.

The question, though simple, seemed somehow odd to her. "Sir?"

"Where are you headed?" Matty said slowly, as if carefully sounding out each word.

"Home," she said, her brain finally catching up with her heart. "To change first. Then I'm going to work."

"Where do you work?"

"The library. I'm a librarian."

Matty smiled. He couldn't believe it. A librarian was fascinating him. And not just any librarian, but one who *looked* like a librarian. She probably was a virgin, too. Maybe even was one of those bitter man haters. Although, frankly, he couldn't imagine her hating anyone.

He was laughing at her, she thought, as she looked at the sudden smile that appeared on his face. He thought being a librarian was funny, some kind of inside joke that undoubtedly ended with how impossible it was for him to ever want to bother with somebody like that.

"Good-bye, Reverend," she said sadly as she turned, once again, to leave. Matty caught that flash of sadness on her face and immediately realized his error. He had offended her.

"How long?" he quickly asked her.

She looked at him, confused. "How long what?"

"Have you been a librarian?"

"Oh. For a few years now. Seven years, actually."

"Straight out of college I would guess."

"That's right."

"Like it?"

"Yes."

"Good. Good for you. What do you like about it?"

Diane just knew this man did not want to know what she liked about being a librarian, and she was inclined to tell him that he didn't need to appease her any, but she didn't even go there. "I like handling the books," she said.

"The accounts?"

"No. The books. The paperback and hardcovers and reference books. I love to touch them and skim them and put them in their proper place. Books can cure anything because reading books keeps you engaged in mankind. You know you're not out here by yourself when you read. Well, having so many books around lets me know it, too."

Matty just sat there, staring at Diane, and his stare was like a sharp blade pricking at her heart. He seemed unable to take his eyes off her and she couldn't understand why. And the look he gave her was unlike any she'd ever seen. It wasn't some hungry, lustful look. It wasn't some kind, gentle look either. He seemed angry to her, upset about something, as he gazed at her with a worried, almost too-intense stare. Then, oddly, his look changed, as if he'd suddenly made a decision.

He stood up and walked toward her, still staring at her but less intensely. "Come with me," he said as he reached her side, not stopping for a response but continuing his walk out of the parlor. Diane, however, just stood there dumbstruck.

Matty, realizing she was not moving at all, stopped walking and turned. He appeared suddenly irritated. "I said come with me. Have you had breakfast yet?"

"Breakfast?"

"Yes. Eggs, bacon, toast. Breakfast."

Diane just stood there. She didn't know what to say.

"I'm talking to you, Diane."

"Yes. I mean, no, I haven't had breakfast yet."

"Then come along. I don't have all day. I've got a meeting at the church this morning."

What did that have to do with her, Diane wondered, but she followed him anyway.

She sat astonished as he cooked bacon and eggs, and made toast, and during the entire meal preparation he wouldn't let her so much as lift a finger to help him. She felt ridiculous letting the pastor do all the work, but he was so insistent.

"I'm here to help, Reverend," she had reminded him.

"I know that."

"Then why won't you let me help?"

He had stopped his cooking and looked at her, as if he were exasperated once again. "You look worn down, Diane," he said. "If I may be so direct. You look like you could use some help."

Such "directness" would have been hurtful to her if it weren't true. But she knew it was true. She was indeed worn down, from Russell's untimely dumping, from staying at the hospital until three in the morning as she refused to leave until Sam assured her that everything was fine and Ira had nothing to do with her fall. But as for needing help, Diane didn't know how to handle help. She'd never been offered it before. So she sat at the small kitchen table and anxiously watched her pastor at work, constantly asking still if she could do something, constantly being told no until he appeared downright annoyed, and she finally got the message.

When he turned his back, Diane tried to smooth her hair in place. She must look horrible to him, she thought, just a straggly old spinster with nothing better to do than to clean up people's houses. And it bothered her that she didn't look better. She wished she would have at least worn a dress, or a skirt suit, something more presentable. But, of course, she had come to clean what she thought was an empty house. She had no idea that a man who appeared as if he'd just stepped out of her dream would be anywhere near it.

But it worried her that she wasn't looking her best, and she didn't understand why it would worry her so desperately. She certainly couldn't be attracted to a man like Pastor Jolson, that would be the height of foolishness on her part. She just knew he'd laugh in her face if he so much as suspected she was thinking about him that way. She was a practical, realistic girl who had enough sense to know that a man who looked like Matty Jolson had little or no use for a woman of her more modest charms. It was simply human nature, she decided, to want to look your best when meeting somebody of Matty's stature for the first time. Attraction, she tried to convince herself, had nothing to do with it.

Matty had, to Diane's relief, put on a robe before he started cooking, but that still didn't stop the unusual feelings that pierced her body every time he came near her. Like now. He was setting a plate of food in front of her and just his nearness made her heartbeat quicken. She couldn't believe it. What in heaven's name was wrong with her? And when he sat down across from her, with only a cup of coffee in front of him, she was actually concerned. "I'll fix your plate," she said as she began to stand up.

"Sit down, Diane," he said tersely, not as if he were touched by her gesture, but were annoyed by it. Then he pulled out a cigarette. "I'm fine," he added in a softer tone.

"You aren't going to eat?" Diane asked him, still feeling confused and uncertain about what exactly was his point.

"I'm fine."

"But why would you cook all this food if you aren't going to eat any of it?"

"Because you're going to eat it. You don't eat enough, it's obvious."

"I'm not as small as you think," Diane said. Matty glanced down at her sizable breasts when she said that. "I mean," she quickly added, feeling a need to clarify, "my bones aren't as frail as they might appear. I'm deceptively strong."

Matty lit his cigarette and immediately noticed that Diane, for a change, was staring at him. "Something wrong?" he asked her.

She hesitated, unsure if she should be so blunt, then deciding to go for it. "You smoke?"

Matty paused, too. "Yes."

"But you're a pastor."

"That's right."

"I've never heard of a pastor with a smoking habit."

"I know," he said. "But I'm also a man. A weak one at that. Pray for me, Sister Tarver, could you do that for me? Pray that God will take this taste from my mouth because Lord knows I haven't been able to shake it on my own."

"How long have you been a smoker?"

"Six years."

"You mean to tell me you started smoking even after it was clear that cigarettes could kill you?"

Matty hesitated. He hadn't cared if they killed him or not at the time. "Yes," he said.

"That doesn't make sense, Pastor."

"Don't call me that."

"Sir?"

"And stop saying sir. I prefer Matty."

Diane smiled. "You can't be serious. What pastor wants his members to call him by his first name? I've never heard of such a thing."

"Well, you're hearing of it now."

"But I can't call my pastor *Matty*."

"Yes, you can." He looked at her. "And you will."

Again Diane was at a loss for words. Reverend Cobb would turn over in his grave if any of his members had ever even thought of calling him by his Christian name, calling him *Jeremiah*. Now this new pastor was insisting upon it. What manner of man, she began to wonder, did they have on their hands? "I'll pray that God will help you quit smoking, Matty," she said.

Matty smiled. Finally he had an ally. "Thank you," he said. Then he found himself staring at her again, long and hard, and his very soul seemed to quake. There was definitely something about this one, he thought, although he was stumped to know what. She had a pretty enough face and was charming in her own awkward way, with a fresh, unscarred youthfulness about her, but she wasn't some irresistible beauty queen by any means. And she certainly was not on par with the type of voluptuous females he'd been attracted to in his day. But he still felt drawn to her. "Why don't you show me around town sometime?" he asked her.

Diane, however, seemed confused. "Show you around town?"

"Yes."

"Me?"

"Yes. Why not you?"

"Well, because, Reverend. That's a deacon's job."

Matty hesitated. "Is it?"

"Yes. I'm thinking that a deacon or somebody senior in the church, somebody important, would want that responsibility."

"You make it sound like a burden, Diane."

"Oh, no, that's not what I meant at all. I just don't see why you would want me to show you around. This is such a small town, is what I mean. There's not much to show."

Matty nodded. She was a timid little thing and apparently aimed to stay that way. "I see."

"I mean, I don't understand how I could be of any benefit to you. I wouldn't know where to begin."

"Forget it," Matty said bluntly. "What time do you have?"

Diane's heart dropped. She felt bad that she wasn't bolder, that she wasn't able to step out of her routine for once in her life and do something daring. He wanted her, for some reason, to be his escort around town. That should have been an honor. But, just as he said, she'd turned it into a burden. Now, from the change in his voice, he probably couldn't wait to get some fearful female like her out of his sight.

"Diane?" he said.

She looked up from her musings to see him staring at her. "Yes? I mean, what? I mean, yes?"

Matty smiled. "The time?"

"The time? Oh." Diane looked down at her small wristwatch. "You asked for the time, I'm sorry. It's nine twenty-two."

"Thank you," Matty said and took a drag on his cigarette.

"You're welcome," she replied, and then hesitated. He looked at her.

"What is it?" he asked her.

"What about breakfast?"

"What about it?"

"Why would you cook all this food if you weren't going to eat?"

"Because you need to eat," he said, pointing his cigarette at her. "Now eat."

Diane's heart swelled. The idea that he would cook all of this food just for her unnerved her. He was probably just a good man with good intentions, she thought, and she was the one who needed to stop overreacting to every little thing he said or did. But why was her heart acting so crazy around him? Her heartbeat never used to quicken when Reverend Cobb came around. And why would he even care if she ate or not? What was it to him? He had work to do, a meeting to attend, he said so himself. But he cared enough to stop from his busy schedule and feed her? She wasn't accustomed to such attention and she certainly didn't know how to handle it. So she stopped trying to handle it, for once in her life. She just ate.

Chapter 6

The meeting in the church's boardroom was headed by
Deacon Molt and attended by many of the leaders in the
church, including Deacon Benford, Sisters Inez, Baker, and
Scott, and, by virtue of being the subject of the meeting,
Pastor Jolson. It was supposed to be informal, according to
Molt, but it felt like a trial to Matty. He sat at one end of
the conference table and Molt sat at the other end. In between were men and women who seemed perfectly content to just stare him down as if he were a carnival act. He
almost felt compelled to pull a rabbit from his hat. Only he
didn't have a hat or a rabbit, just raw nerves that refused to
relax, and the kind of determination that he knew wouldn't
play to a crowd like this.

"Chicago," Molt finally said, after all introductions were
over.

Matty nodded. "Yes."

"What went on there?"

"Bishop Owens didn't explain?"

"He explained. But we wanted to hear it from you. What was so bad up there that them poor folks had to resort to signing petitions to get rid of you?"

Matty smiled. "I guess they didn't like me."

Sister Inez gave a great sigh of exasperation, and Sister Baker threw in a *Jesus.* Deacon Molt frowned at Matty.

"You think this funny?" he asked him. "You think it don't matter to us what they throw our way? We ain't the richest bunch in the world, we know that. And we're backward and country as all get-out. We know that, too. But we ain't stupid. You might have bowled over Bishop Owens with your charm and personality, but excuse us if we don't get the allure of your presence. All we know is that you were kicked out of the only church you ever pastored, and we feel we have a right to know the real reason why. Not just the official version."

Matty leaned forward, his arms resting on the table, his face now stern. "You're absolutely correct. And I apologize for my flippancy. Yes, I was the pastor in Chicago, and yes they did sign a petition to have me removed. As for the reason, well, I'm not quite sure myself. They didn't think I was old enough in the faith to pastor their church, was the first reason, then they didn't like my leadership style, then they didn't like me. You name it."

"We want you to name it."

Matty paused. "There was a woman," he said.

"I thought so!" Sister Baker said, as if she and she alone could have figured that out.

"There were a number of women, actually, all claiming varying degrees of improprieties on my part. But there was one young woman in particular who called herself falling in love with me. I wasn't interested in her or anybody else at that time, but she, unfortunately, sadly, tried to kill herself. She lived, thank God, and I had no involvement with her whatsoever, not ever, but it was another something to throw on the pile of their discontent."

Inez shook her head. "That don't make sense," she said. "That don't make a lick of sense. Why would that girl try to kill herself if there was nothing between y'all?"

"You'll have to ask her that."

"No, I'm sorry, Pastor," Sister Inez said sternly, the drill sergeant in her beginning to rise to the surface. "You got to tell us something better than that. My grandmama used to always say where there's smoke there's fire or fire done been there, and that ain't nothing but the truth. People don't go around trying to kill themselves for nothing. You must of done something to that poor child."

"Nothing he'll admit to," Sister Baker threw in.

Matty continued to stare forward, looking at Deacon Molt. But Molt wasn't in charge of this hanging, Inez was.

"And where you been since you left Chicago?" Inez asked. "Bishop said you went back to Atlanta and started working in the private sector. What he mean by that? And what church did you belong to in Atlanta?"

"I'm an attorney. I went back to practicing law."

"A lawyer?" Deacon Benford asked. "You're a lawyer?"

"Yes."

"Since when?"

"I've been an attorney for years. The only time I wasn't practicing law was the two years I was a pastor in Chicago."

"So you a lawyer now?" Molt asked him.

"I'm pastor of Fountain Hope now."

"But why would a big-city lawyer wanna pastor a church?" Molt asked. "And especially a small-town church like ours? I'm with Inez. This ain't making a whole lot of sense, Reverend."

Matty exhaled. "God will use whom He sees fit to use. Not who you want Him to use."

Sister Baker frowned. "What's that supposed to mean? This ain't about God. This about you and why you would even come to a place like this. A man of your means."

"What church did you belong to up there in Atlanta?" Inez wanted to know.

"I didn't," Matty said honestly.

Everybody looked at Matty. "What did you say?" Molt asked him.

"I said I didn't belong to any particular church during my six years after Chicago."

Inez's gaped-open mouth finally closed. And then it opened again. "And why not?" she asked.

"I just didn't."

"But you went to church," Molt said, as if attempting to rescue Matty.

"Not really, no."

"You didn't even go to church?"

"That's correct."

"But...what did you do?"

"He practiced his law," Inez said. "That's what. Bishop didn't send us no pastor. He sent us a lawyer. What you gon' do, counselor? Make sure all of us stay out of jail? Make sure we following the church constitution right?"

Matty smiled. "No, Sister Inez. That's not what I intend to do."

"Then what are your plans?"

"To do the work while it is day. Now look, I know you have a lot of questions about me. But Bishop Owens and the national board of bishops have a lot of questions about this church."

"Questions about us?" Inez asked. "What kind of questions?"

"Why hasn't your membership increased at all in the past ten years? This church, in fact, has lost nearly thirty percent of its membership in the last five years alone, the only Fountain Hope church to have this reversed trend. The membership is very old and nonprogressive and there doesn't appear to be any community outreach whatsoever. Now I have nothing against older members, that's a great thing. We can learn a lot from their wisdom and insight. But I have a lot against stagnation. And that's what's going on around here. No progress, when we're supposed to be a progressive church."

"We are a progressive church," Sister Baker said. "We have a day-care center and an academy that's second to none. How many churches 'round here can claim that?"

"How many souls have come to Christ in the last decade thanks to this church, Sister Baker?"

Sister Baker stared at Matty. Then she looked at Molt.

"We don't keep a tally, Brother Pastor," Molt said.

"Give me a rough estimate then? A hundred? A thousand? None? Well, Bishop says none. And he's very concerned about that. What good is a church, he feels, if there's no outreach? Salvation is the goal, not day-care centers and schools. And that's what I intend to do. Help to get people saved."

Inez grumbled. "And I guess you just been a pillar of salvation these last six years yourself," she said.

"No," Matty said without hesitation. "I'll never tell that lie. I've perhaps been just the opposite. But this isn't about me, is it? It's about bringing lost souls to Christ. It's about new beginnings for troubled hearts. It's about evangelism and stewardship."

Everybody, once again, looked at Deacon Molt. He exhaled. "I'm gonna be blunt with you, Reverend," he said. "I know people think pastors make a whole lot of money. And I reckon in a place like Chicago that might be true. But let me be clear here. You talk like you got a lot of work you gonna do. You talk like you gon' be on the case day and night. And that's fine. Winning lost souls is a worthy vocation. But I don't think we can afford to pay you what you're expecting for your soul winning."

Matty was offended. It was as certain as the nose on his face. And everybody could see it. "Don't worry about it," he said.

"Oh, we have to worry about it. We need to make it clear to you before you get started on all this soul winning you planning to do. We flat cannot afford you, Reverend."

"You can afford me."

"No, I don't think we can. Our members are wonderful, but they're by and large just hard-working folks living from paycheck to paycheck. Big salaries for the pastor isn't something we can budget."

"That's not an issue."

"I say it's a big issue."

"Amen, Deacon," Sister Baker quickly interjected.

"How much are we expected to pay you for all this great mission work on your agenda? You may not wanna talk about it, but we have to." Molt said this and then stared unceasingly at Matty.

Matty shook his head. Being a misunderstood soul was supposed to be a virtuous thing. But he didn't feel very virtuous. He felt angry. "You pay me nothing," he said.

Molt looked at the leadership and then back at Matty. "What?"

Matty stood up. "Nothing. Not a dime, not a cent, nothing. Zero. Is that all? Is this meeting now adjourned?"

"You mean to tell me you don't wanna get paid?"

"Oh, I'll get paid. But it won't be by you and this humble group of Christians. I wouldn't accept it if offered. Now is there anything else?"

Molt looked around, and then he looked at Matty. "No. I guess that's it."

Matty nodded. "I'll be in my office if you need me," he said.

When he was out of the room, everybody seemed astonished. "What do you make of that?" Inez asked.

"He's a sneaky one, that one," Sister Baker said.

"He's a lawyer," Deacon Benford said. "He's been cheating folks out of their money left and right and he don't need our few pennies, that's what he saying."

"You 'bout right, Brother Deacon," Sister Inez said. "I wouldn't trust him as far as I could throw him. And he's a big joker."

"I think he's honorable," Sister Scott said and everybody looked at her.

"Honorable?" Inez said.

"Yes, Sister Inez. He looked so hurt when y'all accused him of wanting our money."

"We didn't accuse him of nothing. We was just laying down the law. He's a lawyer. He understood that."

"I still say he's honorable."

"And I say you better stay away from him," Inez warned. "Lucifer was pretty, too, you know."

Sister Scott rolled her eyes, and Deacon Molt leaned back. They either had a con man on their hands, the likes of which they'd never seen, or they had a true man of God, a man who was going to shake things up just as Molt suspected. But no matter who this Matthew Jolson was, good man or evil, it was bad news for Molt and, he felt, in the long run, for Fountain Hope.

It was Friday night and the Tarver household was filled with the sound of bats clanging and crowds cheering and announcers screaming hysterically with every successful play. Diane sat on the sofa along with her mother as they reluctantly watched yet another Braves game with Willie James. Willie James, stretched out in his recliner, gave them the play by play, a little color commentary, too, while Malveen complained bitterly about why they always had to watch what he wanted to watch. Willie James countered that it was his house, his TV, and if Malveen didn't like it then she could buy her a TV of her own or, even better, hit the road. Malveen said it was her house, too, and her TV, too, and if anybody was hitting any road it was going to be Willie James. And Diane just sat there shaking her head. Bored beyond words. Knowing their arguments verbatim because they replayed them every week. But when they started going back in time, trying to blame the other for why they married in the first place, Diane excused herself and hurried into the kitchen.

She sat at the kitchen table and ran her hand through her thick, loose, wavy hair. It was a typical Friday night at home with good old Mom and Dad. A typical night in Diane Tarver's life. And she'd had enough. She wanted a break. She needed a break, according to everybody, including that new pastor in so many words, and he didn't even know her. She picked up the telephone and dialed seven numbers.

"Hello?" the strained male voice said on the other end.

Diane breathed hard. "It's me, Russell. It's Diane."

There was a hesitation. Never a good sign. "What is it, Diane?"

"How are you?"

"I'm fabulous." He said this in such a cut and dried way that Diane almost smiled.

"I was just calling to see how things were going with you."

"Things are going just fine with me."

"Good. I'm doing okay myself." No response. "I hope I'm not disturbing anything." When Russell again didn't respond, Diane closed her eyes. "Okay, well, I'd better get going myself. Always so much to do. Bye, Russ." She hung up before he could say, or not say, another word.

She looked at the telephone. Desperation was becoming her middle name. Why else would she even think about fooling up with the likes of Russell Scram again? He dumped her like a bad habit and she was still giving him a call? That was her idea of a break? She wanted to slap her own self. She'd bet Pastor Jolson would never be so rude to a female. He'd know how to treat a lady. Then she shook her head again. She was obsessing about her pastor again. Her pastor! She was the lowest of the low, she thought.

And she phoned Leah Littleton.

"I'm surprised you're home," she said.

"So am I," Leah replied. "This Bainbridge brother stood me up. No phone call, nothing. Just stood me right on up. Wait till I see him again."

"I just finished talking with Russell."

"And you gave him a piece of your mind I hope."

"I don't know why I called him. Maybe I was hoping he was free tonight."

"Free to do what? Oh, Diane, come on. I know better than this. That blob of Jell-O dumped you, and you still wanna go out with him? Are you out of your mind? I already told you you could do better than Russell Scram, even before he proved me right. But you keep trying to prove him wrong. He's already showed you what he was made of."

"I know. It's just that... My parents are at it again and I just got tired of it, that's all."

"Then you call me. Or Sam. But you ain't got to be calling Blimp Boy. I could hook you up."

"No, thanks, Leah. No, thanks. I've got to have a good Christian man, and you don't know any."

"You don't know who I know. And if I may remind you Russell Scram was a, quote unquote, 'good Christian man,' and where did that get you? Maybe the last thing you need is good and Christian."

"Thanks for the offer, but I'm fine. Really."

"Okay, whatever. But the offer still stands. Life has a way of tricking you, girl. Life has a way of cutting you down to size."

"What are you talking about, Leah?"

"I'm talking about your high and mighty Christians who have all of these lofty expectations for people when people are just people. We're all just fleshly beings trying not to mess up too bad before we croak. Some of the best people I ever met never even seen the inside of a church."

"And that's supposed to be the goal? Nobody goes to church, everybody does whatever they want, but because we're good at heart we'll all just mosey on to heaven?"

Leah laughed. "Something like that, yeah."

"And where does the Bible fit into this little scheme?"

"The Bible?"

"Yes! God's word."

"It'll fit."

"I'll bet."

"Anyway, let's talk about something else. I'm depressed enough."

"You brought it up."

"I don't care. Let's still talk about something else."

There was a pause. Then Diane said: "You talked to Sam today?"

"Briefly. She's all hot because I told her how I feel."

"About Judge Marshall having something to do with her fall?"

"Yep."

"She told me he didn't have a thing to do with it, Leah. She seemed offended that I would even think such a thing."

"Yeah, he's got her real snowed, Diane. Practically brainwashed if you ask me."

"But have you ever seen him hit her or even raise his voice at her?"

"Nope."

"Then what's the basis of your accusations? Judge Marshall seems so friendly and kind to everybody. He even lets Sam take the boys to after-school care, when she doesn't even work and could easily care for those boys herself. But he wants her to have some time to herself. That doesn't sound like a controlling wife beater to me, Leah."

"To me either. But this ain't the first time Sam's been out to that emergency room and you know it. And it's always the same excuse. She was drinking and started slippin' and slidin'. I just don't buy that. I've never seen Samantha Marshall drink anything stronger than soda water in the whole time I've known her."

"Which has only been two years."

"You've known her a lot longer than that. Have you ever seen her drinking?"

"No, but that doesn't mean anything. She's the one who admits she has a problem with alcohol. You think she's lying about that, too?"

"I'm just saying I don't put anything past abusers, that's all I'm saying. My father used to whack around my mother pretty bad, and he had the world snowed, too."

Diane exhaled. "So what should we do?"

"There's nothing we can do as long as Sam's in denial. She loves Ira still. She'll die for that joker. Just, I don't know, pray for her. That's the best I can tell you."

Diane nodded. Her prayer list was getting exhaustive. "I met our new pastor today."

"You mean *your* new pastor."

"You're a member of Fountain Hope, too, Leah, don't even try that."

"What's he like?"

Diane smiled. "Unbelievable."

"Terrific. They sent some HNIC didn't they? Some stuck-up clown who wouldn't know how to pastor a congregation any better than I could?"

"No. He's wonderful. He's...very nice actually."

"Really?"

"He cooked me breakfast this morning."

"He cooked you breakfast?"

"Yes."

"Why would the pastor be cooking you breakfast?"

"He thinks I'm too small."

"With all those big clothes you love to wear I don't know how he could tell. Unless..."

"That's enough, Leah."

"Is that why you canceled our lunch date?"

"I canceled lunch because Sam couldn't make it, remember? But if you mean was I full, the answer is yes. The man cooked me a full-course meal, girl. Bacon, eggs, toast. I couldn't believe it."

"Dang. But I thought he didn't come in until the afternoon?"

"He wasn't supposed to. But he came early. He's unlike any pastor I've ever seen, Leah."

"Is he single?"

"Yes."

"Sure about that?"

"Yes, Leah, he's single. Sister Inez told me when she first got the news of his appointment. But guess what? He told me to call him *Matty*."

"Matty?"

"His first name, yes."

"That *is* different. What does he look like, that's what I wanna know."

"Oh, girl, oh, girl, oh, girl! He's gorgeous. I've never seen anybody so beautiful."

Leah laughed. "I'll betcha he looks like a Chia pet."

"Leah!"

"I'm just saying. But, just in case, I guess I'll be making an appearance in church Sunday morning. Just to peek, mind you."

"What a wonderful reason to come out of your hibernation and attend church service."

"It's as good a reason as some of those so-called Christians have. At least I ain't no hypocrite about it."

"No, Leah, you're no hypocrite."

"Thank you!"

"You know what he asked me? He asked me if I wanted to show him around town."

"You?"

"Yep."

"Now that's a switch. What did you say?"

"I said no. What was I gonna say? I don't know him like that."

"Have mercy."

"Well, I don't."

"You are hopeless, Diane Tarver. Hopeless!"

"Anyway," Diane said, to end that line of discussion, "what are you gonna do tonight?"

"I'm doing something, that's for sure. I'll probably fly solo to a club, check out somebody's set."

"Wanna go to the movies?"

"The movies? To see what?"

"This movie about the last days of Christ playing at the dollar show."

"Yeah, I thought you would pick that one."

"What do you mean?"

"You're a saint, Diane. That's what I mean. You're consistently good, you hear what I'm saying? In my whole life I've met one real Christian, I mean in the truest sense of that word, and you're it."

"Oh, Leah, I've met plenty. You just aren't looking hard enough. And if I'm your example of a great Christian then you're in a pretty pathetic state."

Leah laughed. "I hear that."

"But wanna go to the movies?"

"Why not? I don't exactly have anything else on my plate. Holler when you're ready."

"Deal," Diane said. Just as she hung up the telephone, however, the doorbell started ringing.

"I'll get it!" Diane yelled as she hurried out of the kitchen and up to the front door.

"Who is it?" Malveen asked.

"She ain't even at the door yet," Willie James said. "Give

her a chance to get to the door, Malveen. She ain't psychic."

"She might be."

"I wish I was before I married you."

Diane looked out of the peephole. When she saw that blond hair and those big, contact-blue eyes, she shook her head. "It's Pam," she said as she opened the door.

As soon as she opened the door Pam's three children flew into the house and began running hysterically. Pam, Diane's older sister, came in behind them.

Willie James looked at his wild grandchildren and braced himself. "The demons are here! The demons are here!" he started yelling.

"Don't you call my children no demons, Willie James!" Pam yelled back.

"And don't you call Daddy by his first name," Diane said to Pam as she closed the door.

"When he starts actin' like a daddy then I'll call him Daddy," Pam replied, then she started yelling at her children. "Stop running around like y'all ain't got no sense! Sit down! Kirsten, you and Tia get on over by MaDear. And Bobby Ross, where you think you at? I'll put a hickey on your head so fast, boy, if you don't sit your narrow butt down!"

The children, accustomed to their mother's wrath, kept on running anyway, prompting Willie James to hold up his cane just in case. Diane, however, knowing her sister all too well, still stood at the door. "What is it this time, Pamela?"

"Well, dang. Can't I come visit my mama, too? Everybody ain't able to still be living at home rent free and all."

"You wanna trade places? You and your children come here and I take your place?"

"Over my dead body," Willie James said.

"That can be arranged, old man," Pam replied. "I got me some connections."

"And I got me a nine. So I want yo' connections to come

up in here. I can't wait for them to come! Be leavin' with a
bullet up their butts!"

Pam looked at Diane and shook her head. "How do you
put up with that?"

"You're not answering my question, Pam. Now what is it
that you want?"

"How do you know I want anything?"

Diane folded her arms and stared at her dark-skinned,
flamboyant sister, who wore leopard skin and blond weave
as if they were made for her and her alone.

"Okay," she said. "I need you to keep the kids for a few
hours."

"No way, Pam."

"Just a few hours, Diane, dang! Just so I can get a little time
away, that's all."

"No, Pam."

"Why not? They'll behave."

"Oh, please."

"They will!"

"Number one," Diane said, "they never behave so I'm cer-
tain as soon as you dart through that door they won't tonight.
Number two, you never come back in the time you claim.
And number three, I've got my own plans for this evening."

"You?"

"Yes, me."

"But MaDear said Russell dumped you."

Diane shook her head. Her pain seemed so insignificant
to her family. "Russell isn't the only human being I know,
Pam."

"Just for a few hours, Diane! That's all I'm asking. I never
get to go anywhere. I'm always saddled with them kids day
and night. I'm under so much pressure lately, D., you just don't
know. All I want is a time-out for me. Just a little time away.
And I promise I'll be right back. I promise you I will. You
can do your thing anytime. This is the only chance I'll have."

Her argument was about as genuine as that blond hair on her head, but she knew Diane well enough to say all the right words. Just for a little while, she said. She'll be right back, she said. Diane would never deny her a small break, she knew.

"Okay," Diane finally said and Pam hugged her baby sister. "But if you don't come back like you said, Pam, this will be the last time I do you any favors."

"Oh, I'll be back," Pam said, hurrying to open the front door. "That ain't nothing but a thing. I'll be back. And thank you so much, Diane. Thank you!"

And she left, without even thinking about telling her little ones good-bye. Diane looked at the children, who always looked thrown away and pathetic to her, although they were trouble on legs, and she closed the door. At least Leah will be glad to know the movie's off, Diane thought, as she headed for the telephone. At least Leah will have a chance to salvage a perfectly fine, ripe-for-the-taking Friday night.

Chapter 7

The church parking lot began to fill as late arrivals scurried for the few remaining spots. Diane was among this group, her Buick Skylark finding a spot just behind the church bus and settling there. It was a warm day in Floradale, with a breeze just calm enough to keep it humid and just fierce enough to ruffle hairdos, especially for those like Diane who were driving cars with no air conditioning.

She flipped down the mirror on her visor and began finger-combing her long hair back in place. It was still in its customary plait, but for some reason, on this particular Sunday morning, she wanted it perfect. She was dressed her best, too, she felt, in a light blue belted dress that brought out the soft brown tone of her skin. She even had on makeup, just a dab of powder and lipstick, but to many observers it would be a considerable step forward for Diane. She tried constantly to convince herself that the presence of this beautiful new pastor had nothing to do with it, that it was only natural that she would want to spruce herself up every now and then, but she was too honest to tell that lie. That new pastor had everything to do with her sudden vanity. She didn't understand why, since any fool could see she was nowhere near in his league, but there it was. An attraction. An out-of-the-blue, can't-stop-thinking-about-him, complete and uncharacteristic turn-on.

She exhaled before getting out of her car. She was exhausted, having kept Pam's three unruly kids for two nights. Pam never did show back up, so Diane had to drive them all the way to Pam's apartment in Bainbridge before coming on to church. That was why she was late. That was why, even though she was a member of the church choir, she would not be allowed to participate in the singing but had to sit in the congregation and watch from the pews just like everybody else—church bylaw #149.

And the choir was already singing as Diane got out of her car. The song, "Can't Nobody Do Me Like Jesus," she knew by heart. She even started humming the chorus as she stepped lively across the parking lot's graveled drive.

Inside, almost everybody in the half-filled church was on their feet, singing along with the choir and turning an already rhythmic tune into a fast, almost-out-of-control shouting beat. Sister Wanda Scott was so into it, in fact, that she was stomping her feet and swaying from side to side and knocking whomever happened to be in her way out of her way. Unfortunately for her, Sister Inez was in her way, and after a few such knock-arounds Inez completely stopped clapping and looked at Wanda Scott.

"What are you doing, woman?" she asked Sister Scott, her tone making clear how fed up she was.

"I'm praising God, Sister Inez! I'm stomping that devil right under my feet!"

"You step on my toes one more time and that devil ain't the only one gon' get stomped!"

"Oh, Sister Inez! Just praise the Lord! Can't you feel the Spirit moving?"

Sister Inez, however, wasn't interested in feeling the movement of the Spirit. She was more interested in keeping that wild Wanda Scott, who was always up and stomping every time anybody had a song to sing, from harming her brand-new, forty-nine-dollar-and-ninety-nine-cent pair of shoes.

Sister Mayfield didn't care about Inez's or anybody else's shoes, however, because hers had flown off her feet as soon as she ran up to the front of the church and started her weekly holy dance. The choir, in her mind, were nothing more than background singers as she managed to take center stage. Not to be outdone, however, Sister Baker was taking the stage, too, out-muscling Sister Mayfield on the already crowded field. Both ladies were shouting lively, dancing and dancing and getting merry like Christmas, until they collided and fell to the floor.

Matty, who was seated in the pulpit, quickly stood up to make sure they were all right. Sister Baker looked as though she were slain in the Spirit the way she was laid out like a big whale, while Sister Mayfield was sitting and rubbing her own large head. But the ushers seemed to have it under control, as if they were well acquainted with Mayfield and Baker's *I can praise God better than you* Sunday morning contest, and Deacon Molt, who stood in the amen corner beating a tambourine, gestured to Matty that the sisters would be all right. To Matty, however, the sisters appeared to be growling at each other as they spread out on the floor, and both seemed angry that the ushers would even deign to assist them, but he left it alone as Deacon Molt suggested, and sat back down.

Matty was dressed elegantly; at least that was what he heard some members of the choir comment when they first saw him, his double-breasted Armani suit and shiny leather shoes seemingly a class above what they were accustomed to expecting in a pastor's wardrobe. And not just them, but most everybody in the church, it seemed to Matty, looked on him with sheer amazement, as if they were absolutely unable to comprehend how an easily ostentatious man like that could be their new leader. Matty, however, tried hard to ignore their stares. He leaned back in the pulpit's high pastor's chair and thought on good things, like delivering God's word, like learning to live with the background noise as long as God be glorified.

At least the songs from the choir were soothing. The choir members were a stiff bunch, with a disproportionate number over sixty, most wearing eyeglasses, and their songs of choice were decidedly old-fashioned, too. But he loved that old music and the way it could energize an entire church and bring everybody to their feet. He even started tapping his feet, his expensive shoes sparkling like diamonds in the pulpit, shoes Deacon Molt had said could probably fetch enough money alone to pay for the needed renovations to the church's cafeteria. Matty had smiled at the time, and took it as the joke it was meant to be, but he knew now that it was yet another indication of the awesome task he had before him. How could they hear him give a word from the Lord, he wondered, when they couldn't even get over his shoes?

As he thought about it, however, Diane walked into the church. Diane Tarver. His little intruder. To his own astonishment his heart pounded faster when he saw her, as if he were seeing someone near and dear to him when he barely knew the woman. But there was no denying his reaction to her, as he watched her enter, her small body walking with a kind of graceful, gazellelike glide down the center aisle to her seat. She wore a dress that appeared to be two sizes too big for her, it seemed to Matty, as if she were determined not to reveal an inch of the nice shape he already knew she had. Many women, especially the kind Matty was accustomed to, gave themselves too much credit. But some, like Diane, didn't give themselves enough. And she looked tired to Matty, with that same kind of unhealthy exhaustion that had compelled him to prepare a full breakfast for her when he first met her, and he wondered what her problem was that she couldn't take better care of herself. He was even troubled by her frail appearance, a reaction that stunned him.

But by the time she waved to one friend and sat down beside another one, he closed his eyes to dismiss her and everybody else from his mind. He had a sermon to preach. He had souls in need of a word from the Lord. He had work to do.

And when the choir finally stopped singing, the congregation finally took their seats, Sisters Mayfield and Baker finally gave up the limelight and took theirs, a hush came over the church. It was then and only then that Matty stood up slowly and walked to the glass podium.

"Good morning, saints," he said in a lively voice. The reply, however, was very muted, with only a handful of members even bothering to respond, and even then only tepidly. But Matty, to his credit, Deacon Molt noted, did not appear ruffled in the least. "My name, for those of you who don't know, is Matthew Albert Jolson."

Diane, who was seated in the pew beside Leah, smiled when he said his full name. *Matthew Albert Jolson.* What a lovely name, she said to herself. Leah smiled, too, but not because of the man's name, but because she couldn't get over the man's amazing looks. Diane, for once, she thought, had it right. He was beautiful.

"Simply put," Matty went on, "and I believe in simplicity, I'm Matty Jolson. The national board of bishops of the Fountain Hope organization of churches appointed me to be your pastor. And if you're shocked, don't be, because so am I." Matty said this with a smile. The silence in the room, however, was deafening. "But however shocked I may be, or you may be, is irrelevant. God is still on the throne. And He will use whom He sees fit to use, amen." They couldn't exactly argue with that, Matty thought, and they didn't. The church as a whole mouthed "Amen."

"And now that the introduction's over," Matty said with a smile, ready to get on with it, "those of you who have your Bibles, please turn with me to the book of Luke, chapter one, verses 60 through 64." Matty waited, as the sound of turning pages could be heard throughout the sanctuary, and he drank from the glass of water on the podium. The butterflies in his stomach were fierce, and his nerves raw, but he kept praying that he wouldn't fall prey to the flesh, although he was already questioning why he would choose this particular passage of scripture as his very first sermon anyway.

But when the sounds settled and the congregation appeared ready for the word, he forged ahead and began reading the verses aloud: "Verse 60, 'And his mother answered and said, "Not so; but he shall be called John."' Verse 61, 'And they said unto her, "There is none of thy kindred that is called by this name."' Verse 62, 'And they made signs to his father, how he would have him called.' Verse 63, 'And he asked for a writing table, and wrote, saying, "His name is John." And they marveled all.' Verse 64, 'And his mouth was opened immediately, and his tongue loosed, and he spake, and praised God.'"

Matty looked up from the podium. The quiet audience stared back at him. "I don't, as many ministers do, give subjects to my sermons. But I would like to speak on this train of thought: every devil in hell may say yes, you're the bad apple, you're the one accused, and they may even seek to destroy your very life. But God says, 'Not so. This one is mine.'" More than a few members shouted amen to that and Matty felt, at least for the time being, that he had somehow crossed a threshold.

And he had. His sermon, he felt, was Spirit-filled and

Bible-based as he sought to use the Biblical examples of Zacharias and Elizabeth in showing how sometimes God muzzles his own people if they would seek to get in the way of the work of the kingdom. And it is only when they get back in step with the word, as Zacharias did when he agreed that his son should be named John—not because of the traditions of man who would have given him a family name, but because God said so—that the muzzle was removed. And his voice returned.

Matty even told his congregation that he was a living witness, that he had "lost his voice" for six years and when his voice returned he knew what he had to do. He had to do as Zacharias did when his tongue was loosed, and praise God.

The sermon was well received by the congregation, who didn't shout about it, but they at least appeared to listen throughout. But at the end of the sermon, after the fruitless altar call, he had an announcement. And any goodwill his straightforward sermon seemed to garner, flew like a ship made of paper out of the window.

"Effective immediately," Matty said sternly, "church service will take place each and every Sunday. Not every other Sunday as I understand is currently the case."

Before Matty could finish speaking, the shock reverberated throughout the entire congregation. Sister Inez stood up on one side of the church ready to correct the pastor. Sister Baker stood up on the other side of the church ready to concur. Sister Mayfield stood up in the middle of the church ready to second both their motions. Sister Scott headed for the exit in case a fight broke out when they lobbed that pastor from the pulpit. And Deacon Horace Molt stood up in the amen corner ready to make it clear to *his* congregation that the fifty-five-year tradition of church service only on the first and third Sundays of the month—and fifth Sunday when applicable—was not about to be altered by some upstart who wouldn't understand tradition if it bit him in the butt.

Matty had expected resistance, but nothing this fierce.

"Excuse me, Brother Pastor," Deacon Molt said over the murmurs. Everybody looked his way, looked to the real leader of their church. "I understand your enthusiasm. We all do. But church service at Fountain Hope is always on the first and third Sundays and, Brother Pastor, with all due respect, it is a tried and true tradition that we're not going to alter."

The congregation, satisfied that Molt said it exactly the way they would have, nodded their agreement and looked at the pastor for his response. Matty, however, seemed oddly preoccupied, looking down at some notes he had scribbled on a piece of paper, rather than at his congregation. They, therefore, looked back to Molt.

"The reason for this way of doing things," Molt continued, "was because, well, many reasons. It has always been done, for one thing. It started back when the very first pastor of this church, a Godly man by the name of Hezekiel Cooper, was also the pastor of the church in Columbus. There were no board of bishops back then or no host of ministers waiting in the wings to pastor our churches. So Reverend Cooper did as any industrious man would have done and divided his time. One Sunday he pastored this church, the next Sunday he pastored the Columbus church. And even years later, when Columbus had their own full-time pastor, the practice remained. Not because of necessary circumstances anymore, but because it had become a convenient way of doing things for our congregation. Now I don't know how it was in Chicago, but these are hard-working Georgia folks down here, folks who deserve a chance to unwind and spend time with their families every other Sunday. They can even visit other churches if they like. It's an arrangement that works beautifully for our congregation. And that's why, for fifty-five years, fifty-five *long* years, we have done it this way."

When Molt concluded his polite but firm refrain, Matty finally looked away from his notes and looked at his head deacon. "Thank you, Deacon Molt," he said. Molt smiled and nodded. Matty looked at his congregation. "Church will convene every Sunday from this day forward. God does not bless us part time and we will not worship Him part time. That being all, let's rise for the benediction."

It was the talk of the church. Everybody had an opinion. When they stood to their feet and waited for the pastor to make his way outside to meet and greet parishioners as they left the sanctuary, they were talking amongst themselves even then. Including Leah, who hardly ever went to church at all, let alone every other Sunday. But even she was offended.

"Who does he think he is?" she asked Diane. "I ain't never seen nobody so bossy."

"You think he means it?" Diane asked.

"Of course he means it! He said it, didn't he? Now he may be cute—and he is cute, I'll give him that—but he's going just a little too far. Church every Sunday? I can barely get here as it is."

"It'll take some getting used to, that's for sure," Diane said. "But I just don't see Deacon Molt going for that."

"What Deacon Molt gon' do?" Leah asked. "Same thing he always does. Talk. That's all. This man the pastor. He don't care nothing about what Deacon Molt thinks. Please. It's gonna happen. Unfortunately, it's surely gonna happen. Not only will I be feeling guilty for missing two Sundays every month, now I got to feel guilty for missing all four! Let me go talk to this man. Let me let him know this ain't right, that this is some serious come-on here."

Leah hurried off, heading for the exit. Diane started to follow behind her, not to confront the pastor, but to see him again. She had been thinking nonstop about his suggestion that she show him around sometime and had decided just this morning, while taking Pam's rowdy children home, to be daring for once in her life and take him up on his request. But Sam's voice interrupted her.

Diane turned and saw her, looking gorgeous in a beautiful white suit, with little Alan, as usual, by her side. But Diane was saddened when she saw her. Although Sam wore dark glasses, the bruise on the side of her face from her fall was still partly visible. What if Leah was right, Diane thought as she watched her friend approach. What if Judge Marshall was beating on Sam, and Sam was too terrified to admit it? Diane could only hope not. She could only pray that Sam was still Sam and wouldn't stand for such treatment, and Leah was just being Leah and starting up trouble where none really existed.

"Hey, Aunt Di-tan!" Alan said with a smile and Diane leaned down and ruffled his curly hair.

"Hey, little man. How you doing?"

"The church got a new rastor. Brand-new rastor."

"Yeah, he's a rastor all right," Sam said.

Diane smiled and stood erect. "I take it you aren't too crazy about this having church every Sunday business?"

"It's just strange, that's all. I've been going to Fountain Hope for years and I've never heard anybody so much as question the way service is conducted."

"I know."

"I don't see how he can get away with this. Sister Inez is already 90-hot."

"She was hot before service ended. Deacon Molt, too."

"Yeah but you know Inez. She and some of the others already gone in the upper room to plot their strategy."

"Oh, Lord. I hope they don't give the man a hard time."

"Well, what you think he's giving us, Diane? We're the ones who'll have to be here every Sunday. Every Sunday, girl? That's what I call a hardship."

"Most churches meet every Sunday, Sam, now come on. We're the oddballs."

"That might be true, but I still say it's the right way to do it. That's the reason I like it here. They don't pressure you."

Diane looked at Sam. What did she mean by that? Was she getting too much pressure at home? "You okay, Sam?"

"Yes." But Diane continued staring at her. "Diane, I'm fine. What?"

"You took a pretty nasty fall."

"I know that. And I also know you're still wondering if what Leah said was true. I told you it's not."

"But—"

"No but, Diane. Ira beating on me? Come on. Even Leah knows better than that."

"But she sounded so definite."

Sam gave Diane a cross look. "Has Leah Littleton ever sounded indefinite about anything, girl? Especially stuff she knows nothing about?"

Diane laughed. "You got a point."

"Thank you!"

"Hello, Sister Tarver," a strong, male voice said behind them and Ira, along with Junior, were upon them. Sam stiffened, but she kept smiling. Diane smiled, too.

"Hello, Judge Marshall," she said. "We didn't hear you coming up."

"It would appear."

Diane always thought of Ira Marshall as a kind man, somebody with great warmth and charm to go along with his mature good looks. The idea of him as a batterer seemed crazy even to her, but she was no fool either. Nowadays anything was possible.

Diane looked down at Junior. "Hey, Junior," she said with a smile, but Junior looked away from her and didn't respond. Alan, however, did.

"Hey, Aunt Di-tan," he said again.

"Ira, Jr.," Sam said, "didn't you hear Aunt Diane speaking to you?"

Junior frowned and pushed closer to his father.

"I declare sometimes," Sam said, ready to tell Junior a thing or two, but Ira gave her a look that, although laced with a smile, was loaded with too much chill for her to keep talking.

Ira looked at Diane. "How have you been keeping yourself, Sister Tarver?"

"Very well, thank you. I'm just a little concerned about this having church every Sunday thing our new pastor wants to institute."

"It'll be over Molt's dead body."

Diane laughed. "That's what I told Leah. But she doesn't believe me."

"Yes, well, my advice is that you watch out for that Leah Littleton. She talks a lot but with very little to say, if you understand my meaning."

"I've heard something to that effect. By your wife, for starters."

Sam smiled weakly. Ira looked at her. "And that's good. Samantha is always thoughtful, as you know, and fair, and she wouldn't say it if it wasn't true."

"Amen to that," Diane said.

Ira placed his arm around Sam's waist. "Yes, I'm blessed to have somebody like her, and somebody like my boy Junior here, in my life."

"And Alan, too, of course," Diane said smilingly as she looked down at the quiet youngest son.

"Yes, of course," Ira said. "And Alan, too. Now who could forget Alan?" Ira said this and laughed, with Sam reluctantly joining in, and Diane, although unable to understand why he would have forgotten to mention Alan in the first place, eventually laughed, too. Alan, however, may have had a speech impediment, and he may have appeared small for his age, but he wasn't stupid by a long shot. He pushed his glasses up on his nose and moved closer to his mother.

Matty and Deacon Molt had already shaken the hands of most of the members by the time Leah made her way up the line. They were standing on the steps of the church, meeting and greeting and enjoying the fresh Floradale sun. When Leah appeared, Deacon Molt, as he had done with all of the other parishioners, whispered in Matty's ear. "This is Sister Littleton coming up now. She owns a beauty salon in town."

"Hello, Sister Littleton," Matty said gaily as he extended his hand at the approaching young woman. She wore a tight red dress and matching heels, and although her makeup was excessive, Matty thought, it nonetheless could not impugn her beautifully sculptured face.

"It's nice to meet you, Reverend," Leah said as she shook his strong hand. Up close he was even more daring looking, she thought, even more the incredible hunk. And more, Leah decided right then and there, her type. "Your sermon was off the chain, Rev."

"Why thank you, young lady."

Young, Leah thought. Yeah, definitely her type. "What you said about God running the show and all," she said, "and how all these hypocrites around here need to just step back and let the man do his job, I agree one hundred percent. Some of these so-called saints just don't never shut up."

"Yes, ma'am."

"Well, nice seeing you again, Sister Littleton," Deacon Molt said to hurry her along.

Leah, however, gave him an evil eye and then smiled back at Matty. "Listen, Reverend, I understand you're new in town."

Molt rolled his eyes. Matty smiled. "Yes, ma'am, I am."

"Would you like me to show you around?" Leah asked this too eagerly, even to herself. "I'd love to do it."

"We'll take care of that," Molt interjected, but Matty continued staring at the lovely Leah.

"No, I think she'll do just fine, Brother Deacon," Matty said.

Leah smiled greatly. "Wonderful!"

"Next Saturday?"

"Okay. That'll be perfect." It was the busiest day at her salon, but she wasn't about to lose this opportunity. "We can work out the details later in the week."

It sounded like a deal to Matty, and he nodded his head. "Sure thing," he said, and Leah, totally forgetting her earlier disagreement with Matty's new church-every-Sunday policy, hurried along. Molt, however, wasn't pleased at all. He leaned toward Matty.

"She's fast," he said. "She ain't saved."

"I know," Matty replied. "That's why I'm taking her up on her offer. Winning souls is why I'm here. Hello, ma'am," Matty said to the next saint in line before Molt could even introduce her.

And it continued this way as more members stopped by to meet and greet the new pastor, with Molt setting aside his outrage and giving Matty a bit of information about each one as they arrived. Including Ira and Sam and the boys, as they approached.

"Judge Marshall's family," Molt whispered to Matty. "Judge Ira Marshall is by far our most prominent member."

"Brother Marshall," Matty said gaily as he extended his hand to Ira. "How are you, sir?"

"Excellent," Ira said just as cheerfully as he shook Matty's hand. "Thank you. And this is my wife, Samantha, and our two angels, Alan and Ira, Jr."

Matty almost hesitated in extending his hand to Sam, as he found himself staring at her bruised face. "Mrs. Marshall."

"I heard about your unfortunate accident, Sister Marshall," Deacon Molt said. "I hope everything's all right."

"Other than looking like Frankenstein," Sam said with a smile, "I'm fine."

"Good to hear it." Then Molt turned to Matty. "Sister Marshall took a terrible tumble at her home Thursday night, Pastor. It was just awful from what I understand. But thank God Judge Marshall was at home at the time to help her because she was unconscious there for a while."

Matty nodded, still staring at Sam. "I'm sorry to hear that, Mrs. Marshall."

"But I'm fine now, Pastor, thank you. It was just an accidental fall."

"I understand you're from Chicago," Ira said to Matty. Matty, however, continued staring at Sam.

"No," he said.

"No?"

"No."

Ira looked from Molt back to Matty. He seemed disturbed that he would be given wrong information. "But I distinctly understood that you pastored a church in Chicago."

"Yes, I did. But I'm from Atlanta and was living in Atlanta when I came here."

"I see. But you are an attorney, now did I hear that correctly?"

"Yes."

"Excellent! Another brother of the bar. Good to know it."

Matty, seemingly bored by Ira's little show, knelt down to the boys. "Hello, boys," he said.

"You're our new rastor," Alan said, pointing at Matty.

"I'm your new pastor, yes, I am. And what's your name?"

"Ralan."

Junior rolled his eyes. "Your name is Alan, stupid. Not Ralan. Goodness!"

"That's enough, Junior," Sam said.

"Well, he shouldn't be so stupid."

"I said that's enough."

Matty looked at Alan, who appeared distraught by his brother's correction. "Alan's not stupid, Junior," Matty said, and then looked at Junior. "He's got what my mama used to call plenty good sense." Matty said this and patted Alan's hair, causing Alan to smile. Matty stood erect.

"Anyway, Reverend, we won't keep you," Ira said and extended his hand again. "Nice meeting you. And come over to the courthouse sometime. Say hello."

"Thank you," Matty said as he shook Ira's hand then watched him and his beautiful family leave.

"He's a fair man," Molt said to Matty. "Not uppity with his success. That's why everybody loves him. He's as good as it gets."

"I'll bet he is," Matty said with little enthusiasm as he continued watching Ira.

"Diane Tarver," Molt said and Matty, surprised to hear that name, turned quickly.

"What?"

"The young lady coming out of the church now is Diane Tarver. She's our local librarian."

Matty looked at Diane, and as soon as he did, his heart throbbed.

"Good afternoon, Deacon Molt," she said as she approached. Then she looked at Matty. "Reverend."

"That's Matty to you," he said and Diane smiled. He extended his hand. "How are you, Diane?"

"I'm doing well, thank you," she said as she nervously shook his hand.

"You don't look so well," he said, studying her face. "What have you eaten today?"

"Today?"

Matty didn't respond.

"I haven't had anything to eat today. Not yet."

"You need to eat more."

"Oh, she's fine just the way she is, Brother Pastor," Molt said with a smile. "We got enough big women in this church. It's refreshing to see somebody with some stopping sense."

Matty, however, ignored Molt and continued to stare at Diane, his hand still unable to let hers go. "I want you to take better care of yourself, Diane. I've only seen you twice and I haven't liked what I've seen either time. You understand me?"

Diane suddenly felt uncomfortable with his unusual sense of concern. He couldn't possibly care *that* much. "Yes, I understand," she said. "I'm going to eat as soon as I leave here."

Matty relaxed, and let go of her hand. "Good," he said.

And she just stood there. She wanted desperately to tell him that she'd changed her mind and would be honored to show him around town, even thought she had worked up the nerve to say it, but she just couldn't bring the words to her mouth. Not now. Not with Deacon Molt staring down her throat. Not with Matty being so concerned about her welfare. It would seem as if she were playing a seduction game or something equally awful with her own pastor, a man who was obviously interested only in her well being. But watching Matty, who she sensed was perfectly in tune with her for some reason, made her decide to go for it anyway.

"I'm free tomorrow," she said and almost immediately regretted saying it. Matty just stared at her.

"Are you?" he asked.

"I mean, the library, where I work, isn't open on Mondays. And if you'd like I can show you around town."

"Too late," Molt said. "Sister Littleton's already volunteered for that assignment and Pastor Jolson's already eagerly accepted."

Diane's heart nearly skipped a beat. Embarrassment gripped every fiber of her being. Of course he would prefer somebody like Leah escorting him around! She was exciting and full of life and matched him perfectly. He wouldn't have to explain anything to her, because she was just as experienced as he appeared to be. Diane wanted to find a hole and crawl into it. But since there were no holes around Fountain Hope, except, perhaps, the one now piercing her heart, she decided to smile. "Leah's taking you around then?" she said cheerfully. "Good choice. She's an excellent escort. I mean, she's very knowledgeable about the different historical landmarks around town."

"Is she?" Matty asked, still staring at her, the concerned look on his handsome face seeming to void Diane's gaiety.

"Oh, yes, she is. Very knowledgeable. She owns one of the busiest beauty shops in town and everybody will tell you that Leah, Sister Littleton, is a good one to have on your side."

"Well, nice seeing you again, Diane," Molt said, to get Diane out of the way so the next group of members exiting the church could meet and greet their new pastor.

Diane felt like a piece of plywood being slapped up on a brick building. Completely out of place. Out of *her* place, that is. "Nice seeing you again, too, Deacon Molt," Diane said. "And you, too, Rev—I mean, Matty. Have a nice day."

Matty smiled. "You have a nice day yourself, Diane," he said. "And make sure you don't neglect to put some nourishment in your body as soon as you make it home."

Diane smiled as she walked away. She didn't think she could eat a crumb right about now.

Matty watched her leave, watched her small frame head down the steps and hurry across the parking lot. His heart dropped watching Diane Tarver, as if a part of him were leaving with her. And that soul-wrenching reaction of hers when she realized somebody else had already asked to take him around, worried him. She was smiling and putting her best foot forward, but she was devastated. He could feel it even if he couldn't see it. But he didn't say a word. He let the only woman ever able to make his heart leap for joy just by showing up, leave brokenhearted. But he felt he had to.

He was not the man she needed. He came with too much baggage, too many old clothes unsorted and unwashed, a man with the kind of past a woman like her couldn't begin to understand. Besides, the Lord didn't bring him all this way to meet a woman, he felt, but to preach His gospel. And nobody, not even sweet Diane Tarver, was going to distract him from fulfilling that awesome calling that carried enough drama all its own.

Chapter 8

It looked like a labor-pool pickup, Sister Baker thought, as a motley crew of twelve men stood aimlessly around the Fountain Hope parking lot. Some were smoking, some were drinking what she could only assume was beer out of brown paper bags, all appeared to be street corner thugs looking for whatever trouble might come along next. At least that was Sister Baker's assessment as she looked out of the window of her day-care classroom and saw the assembled group. Stunned and angered by the display, she immediately called for Thelma Wilcox and urged her to drop everything and go and get Deacon Molt. She would have addressed the matter herself, she was quick to tell Sister Wilcox—just in case Molt asked—but those men looked too dangerous even for her.

Deacon Molt, to Sister Baker's surprise, was swift in coming. So swift that he was still putting on his suit coat as he walked out of the sanctuary doors and headed for the parking lot, his face flushed with annoyance.

"May I help y'all?" he shouted out to the assembled men as soon as he walked near them.

Joe Dobson, a forty-year-old chronically unemployed laborer who still lived at home with his parents, was the only one willing to speak up. "Hey, Deacon Molt," he said with a smile. "I'm Joe Dobson. Remember me?"

"Of course I remember you," Molt said testily. "I just saw you yesterday, Joe. Remember that?"

"Oh yeah, that's right. In church."

Molt wanted to roll his eyes. He, instead, decided on empty niceties. "How your mama doing?" he asked, looking more at the other men than at Joe. "I meant to ask you after service. I heard she had surgery."

"Yes, sir, she did. And she doing good. Thank the Lord."

"So tell me, brother," Molt asked, getting to the point, "what y'all doing out here?"

"Pastor called us—"

"Who?"

"Pastor Jolson. The new pastor. He called me last night and asked if I was working now, if I had a job. I told him jobs are so hard to come by nowadays and what with Mama being sick and all, so I told him no, I didn't have no job right now. That's when he told me to meet him up here this morning because he had some work for me. And from what I'm hearing that's what he told all these others, too. The job suppose to pay ten dollars an hour, he claim. And if'n it's true, that's more money than any of us ever made, Deacon Molt. That's why we here. Trying to get paid."

Molt exhaled. Was Jolson out of his mind? Ten dollars an hour? He must be mad! The church could barely fund its current outlay; how in the world were they going to pay these men ten dollars an hour? He started to head back into the church, to give *Pastor* a call, but before he could even think about making a move, *Pastor* arrived. In his dark sunglasses and shiny blue Jaguar. Looking like a drug dealer, if you asked Molt.

The men all stood in rapt attention as Matty stepped out of his car in his double-breasted, charcoal-gray suit and expensive black shoes, his shades not worn for style, as Molt seemed to think, but to conceal the effects of another long, near-sleepless night. He had prayed and read his Bible most of the night hoping for sleep to come, but even when it came he managed only to get a couple of hours tops of good, sound rest. Now he was exhausted, but he had work to do.

"Good morning," he said jovially to the men, a clipboard and a stack of flyers in his hand. "I called nearly forty guys last night and truly wasn't expecting more than a handful. So this is good. I'm counting twelve men. Excellent turn-out!"

"The job still pays ten dollars, right?" Tiny Lincoln, the tallest of the men, asked.

Matty smiled. "Absolutely, doc," he said.

"That's all I need to know."

"Good. Because the job is as simple as it is complex. I'll explain what I mean."

"Ah, Pastor Jolson," Molt said, and walked over to him, surprised that he didn't so much as acknowledge his presence. "May I see you for a moment?"

Matty, not at all in the mood for Molt's negativism this morning, nonetheless respected his head deacon enough to walk with him out of earshot of the men. "What's up?" he asked when they were standing alone.

"I'm thinking I need to ask you that."

Matty pushed his shades further up on his face, the bright sun not helping his exhaustion at all. "I asked Sister Scott to compile me a list of the men in the church, mainly those who appear to be having some hard times, those she knew to be in need of employment, complete with their home phone numbers if she had them on record. She did as I asked and I phoned each and every man on the list last night."

"You promised them ten dollars an hour."

"That's right."

"To do what, if I may ask?"

"Pass out flyers. Encourage their peers to come to church. Talk to their peers about the Lord."

Molt laughed. It was too incredible. "Are you serious?"

"I usually am."

"Pastor Jolson, I don't know if you're aware of this but these brothers here, and I'm not trying to put them down, but they're some of the sorriest, laziest, most unreliable men I've ever met."

Matty slid his glasses down on the bridge of his nose and looked at Molt. "And you don't call that a putdown?" he asked.

"They don't attend Sunday school, don't tithe, rarely come to church themselves, and can't even hold down a job for more than a month at a time. And we're gonna pay them ten dollars an hour to be a witness for *this* church? *Them?*"

"God will use whom He sees fit to use, Deacon Molt. Now is that all?"

"But ten dollars an hour, Pastor? The church don't have ten cents an hour to be giving away like this."

"I'm paying these men. It's my money, not the church's. Now is there anything else?"

"But ten dollars an hour?"

Matty sighed. Trouble on every hand, it seemed to him. "A laborer is worthy of his hire, Brother Deacon. I need help and I'm willing to pay for it. Now if you'll excuse me."

"But why these men?"

"Because they're available, and could use the work, and they'll be more inclined to understand the alcoholic on the street corner than those who've never been a part of soci-

ety's underbelly. Why not these men, Deacon Molt? Everyone's a king and a champion, if somebody believes he is."

"And you believe these men, these particular men who
have been nothing but a burden on their families since the
day they were born, are champions?"

"Yes, I do."

"Them?"

"The Lord will use whom He sees fit to use, Deacon
Molt, not who you think He should use."

"I understand that. But this don't make no sense, Reverend."

"Is that so bad?"

Molt shook his head. He was wasting his time and he
knew it. "What about your other duties?" he decided to ask.

Matty smiled. "Winning souls to Christ is my first and last
duty, Deacon Molt."

"No, sir, that's not true," Molt said firmly. "Learning the
church's bylaws and other rules and regulations is your first
responsibility right now. How can we expect the members
to obey the rules when their leader don't even know what
the rules are? It'll be anarchy up in here. You have to take
care of home first."

"And that's why Jesus came, to heal those who are well?"

Molt hesitated. "What?"

"And that's why Jesus commanded his disciples *not* to go
and preach the gospel to all the nations of the world, but
just to *their* nation?"

"Don't you twist around no scripture on me."

"Then stop telling me my job. Worry about yours. Okay?"

Molt exhaled. He knew Jolson would be a handful; that
Jaguar and those expensive clothes he loved to wear were
the first indication. But he never expected it to be this bad.
"So let me get this straight," he said to Matty. "You're telling me, considering everything else you've got to do, that
you still have enough time on your hands to be running

around town supervising these men, these so-called church workers?"

"No. I don't have time to supervise anybody. I've got to be out winning souls myself. I'm going to let Brother Dobson handle the supervision duties."

"Brother Dobson? Joe Dobson is going to be their supervisor?"

"Yes."

Molt shook his head. "But Pastor, again, I don't mean to rain on your parade, and I don't mean to put nobody down, but Joe Dobson can't even read or write!"

"He told me."

"And he's gonna be the supervisor?"

"Yes. A man like that is gonna be their leader. Ain't God good?" Matty said this with a sarcastic smile that he immediately cut off, and then went back to the men who anxiously awaited his instructions. Most of them had been praying for a chance to earn a little money, although they barely had skills enough to even apply for a job, and when Pastor Jolson had called last night it was like the voice of God to them. They weren't about to mess this up.

But Deacon Molt thought the mess was already done. He was livid. He couldn't believe the nerve of Jolson sending these thugs out to represent their church. It didn't make sense on any kind of level. And whoever heard of paying people to witness anyway? That was the craziest thing Molt had ever heard. Members volunteered their time for witnessing, that's what true stewardship is all about. Of course, Fountain Hope didn't participate in witnessing at present, as he tried to explain to Matty over the weekend, not because they didn't believe in it, but because their members were already too busy trying to live their lives and take care of their own affairs than to be running up and down the road minding somebody else's. Matty, at the time, didn't say anything to Deacon Molt. He just stared at him as if he were dumbfounded.

A church that didn't win souls, to Matty, was a church of no earthly good.

But he'd taken it too far now, Molt felt, because instead of abiding by the needs of the church, which was the pastor's duty, he had, in the same way he instituted weekly services, subverted the church's needs. He just took it upon himself to go out and get his own foot soldiers to witness, never minding the fact that they probably needed somebody to be witnessing to them! Molt threw his hands in the air and walked away. *Monumental foolishness,* he thought. Wait until Bishop hears about this!

By the end of the day, when Matty finally made it home, and showered, and threw himself across his bed, his every limb screamed exhaustion. It had been like Murphy's Law out there, where everything that could have gone wrong, went wrong, and Molt and Inez and all those other naysayers were shaking their heads with their *I told you so*'s as soon as the church bus returned the men to the parking lot.

Matty, driving the big blue-and-white bus himself, had dropped the men off at various locations around town and given them their assignments. They were to pass out flyers to everybody they encountered, flyers that described new programs the church would be instituting, such as an addictions support group and a job skills class. They were also supposed to talk compassionately to them about God's grace and mercy and how they needed to be in somebody's church, and then they'd meet the bus, at the end of the day, at their designated pick-up spots. As simple as that.

But as Matty circled back later that day to check on his men, after doing some witnessing of his own, it was obvious that it wasn't simple at all. Of the twelve men in the group, five had tossed their flyers in the trash as soon as they got to their designated witnessing assignments, and they joined in with the brothers drinking and laughing on the corners. Matty had to round up the men, give them more flyers, and restate the aim. Two of the twelve men had gotten arrested for fighting when the people they were witnessing to didn't want to hear anybody's sermon or receive anybody's flyer. Matty, though upset by this unnecessary violence, did go downtown and bail the men out. And three of the twelve got off the church bus at their designated locations, went home, and returned at the end of the day as if they'd been working their hearts out. Only Brother Dobson and Tiny Lincoln stayed on task all day.

Molt, who literally met the bus as they pulled back into the church parking lot, seemed so pleased by the reported difficult day that it angered Matty. And instead of simply paying the men, which he did, he also told every one of them to report back to the church first thing tomorrow morning where they would be trained first and then sent out. He took full responsibility for the debacle of a day, making it clear to the men and Molt and anybody else in earshot that he should have better prepared them for the task at hand before he sent them out. And yes, Tiny, he said before Tiny could ask it, they would be paid ten dollars an hour for the training, too.

The men were elated. It was the easiest money they'd ever made. Molt, however, was dumbstruck. He fully expected Matty to admit failure and throw in the towel on what any fool could see was a crazy idea. But Matty apparently had money to burn, it seemed to Molt, because he wasn't throwing in anything.

And he was paying dearly for that stubborn streak of his, Matty thought, as he laid across his bed. Any other man would do as Molt wanted and call it a day. But not Matty. Those men were kings and champions and he wasn't stopping until they knew it, too. He would teach them basic job skills first, for longer-term use, and witnessing skills later. Those who couldn't read, he would teach them to read.

Those who couldn't add, he would show them the trick. It wasn't because he was some great saint with a heart of gold. He just hated, absolutely hated, to lose.

His phone rang, as he began to drift off to sleep, the tiredness wearing on his body like a weight pulling on his soul. And when he realized the voice on the other end of the phone was Vicky's, his body sank deeper into the abyss of loneliness and despair that he had been working hard to ignore.

"Hey," he said with little enthusiasm.

"You hung up in my face."

"We didn't have any more to talk about, Vicky."

"Oh. So it's over now?"

"Vicky."

"Is it over now?"

"Whatever 'it' is, yes, it's over!" Matty snapped. Then he calmed back down. "I told you it was over before I left Atlanta, Vicky. I told you it was over when you called me my first night here."

"I called you because I thought you would have come to your senses by now. But I guess you still haven't."

"That would be a fair assumption."

"Oh, Matty! Why don't you quit this nonsense and come back home?" She said this with a tinge of desperation in her voice. Then she paused. "I can make you feel real good."

Matty closed his eyes. He had a lot of regrets in his life, a lot he had to give penance for, and fooling around with Vicky Avery, a woman who hated to lose, too, was top of the list. "I don't swing like that anymore."

Vicky laughed. "Since when? Look, you can fool those country bumpkins with your holy man act all you want. I'm not mad at that. But I know you. Including in the Biblical sense, if you dig my drift. So you can cut the con with me, okay? This is Victoria Avery here. Good old Vicky? And she knows a playa when she sees one and Matty, brother, you the man when it comes to play. So don't even go there with me, all right? You don't swing like that? Yeah, right."

"Why don't we pray together, Vicky?" Matty asked with all sincerity, as his heart ached to make amends. But she broke out in laughter again.

"Will you stop?" she said between laughs. "People don't change overnight, Matthew. That's why this has got to be a scam you're running. But what I don't understand is why you trying to run it on me?"

"Because maybe it's not a scam," Matty said, praying that this woman would finally understand.

It seemed to work. There was a pause on the line. A long, agonizing pause. Then Vicky's voice again. "So you're serious about this?"

"Yes!"

"But what about..." She didn't finish her question. The anguish in her voice ripped at Matty. "Just forget you, all right?" she finally said, and then hung up in Matty's face.

He hung up, too. And fell on his knees. He had begged for forgiveness probably a hundred times, and he'd prayed for Vicky even more than that. Not because he wanted her; he didn't. They had zero in common except an enjoyment of something neither one of them had any business engaging in. But Vicky needed the Lord. She needed stability and calm in her life, a sense of purpose and meaning. That was why she kept calling Matty, he was beginning to realize. Not because she was so in love with him and had to hear his voice again. He wouldn't believe that for a second. But because she wanted what he had. She didn't know it yet, but it was his prayer that she eventually would.

After praying, he threw on a pair of jeans and a T-shirt, grabbed his Bible and cigarettes, and went out onto the porch. The traffic was sparse along Haines Street, and the air outside was breezy and cool—much cooler, he felt, than indoors. He leaned back in one of the two wrought-iron chairs that sat on the porch, lit up a cigarette, and found himself thinking, not about Vicky, but about Diane Tarver. He wondered if she were taking better care of herself or still running on empty. She'd looked awful Sunday, as if she'd been caught in a whirlwind of activity and didn't have time to even notice how rundown she was becoming. And he was angry that she hadn't noticed. His only hope was that she'd heed his advice and slow her behind down.

He rather doubted it, however, considering what kind of woman she probably was. Anybody as young as Diane and on the Pulpit Aid Board with Sister Inez Flachette had serious issues, he concluded, somebody who probably had no real life of her own. But everybody expected her to be there for them. Everybody expected her to listen to their hard-luck stories and hear them sing the blues and whenever she felt blue or had a story to tell, nobody cared. And they used her and abused her until, Matty feared, there was going to be nothing left. That was Diane Tarver. He'd bet the farm on it.

He flicked the ash of his cigarette over the porch rail and smiled when he thought about her in his parlor that morning, the way she was singing in that out-of-tune soprano voice of hers, the way she shook her slim little hips in time with the beat. There was unquestionably something about the woman, something about everything about her, but for the life of him he couldn't figure out what.

And he couldn't stop thinking about her. All day long she was on his mind. He'd see a petite female around town and he'd have to look twice to make sure it wasn't Diane. Even when he went into the bar to witness to the patrons, and many of the females tried to hit on him, he found himself comparing every one of them, not to beautiful Vicky, but to Diane. Diane had a better temperament, he'd say to himself, or a friendlier smile, or she'd never lie to him the way those females seemed conditioned to do. It was all Diane, all day. His little intruder. And there was no way, he knew, that he could wait until Sunday before he saw that face again.

A green-and-black Subaru Outback stopped in front of his house just as he had ended his musings on Diane and was opening his Bible. The woman who stepped out of the vehicle was familiar, but he couldn't quite place her. She was pretty enough, he thought, in her skintight jeans and stiletto heels, and when he saw that she had a bowl of something in her hands, he assumed she was from the church. It wasn't until she walked up the steps of his front porch and smiled at him, however, that he remembered her. She was that hot mama from Sunday. The female who had volunteered to be his guide. Sister something or other.

"Good evening, Pastor," she said grandly, revealing a nice, warm smile. "How are you doing this evening?"

"I'm doing good. How about yourself?"

"I'm real good," Leah said and laughed.

Matty, however, only smiled mildly. "Why don't you have a seat?" he asked as he stood up. "And let me take that from you."

"I'll just put it in the kitchen," Leah said as she headed for his front door, anxious to see for herself what the house looked like. "It's soup."

"Thank you," Matty said as she went inside. Soup in ninety-degree weather, he thought as he sat back down. Great choice.

By the time Leah returned from the kitchen and sat in the chair across from Matty, he had put out his cigarette. Leah found this humorous, too.

"You didn't have to do that on my account," she said. "I don't see nothing wrong with a man enjoying a cigarette in the comfort of his own home."

"It's a bad habit," Matty said. "Bad habits are always wrong. But what brings you this way, young lady? What's up with you? And please forgive me but I don't remember your name."

"It's Leah. And nothing's up with me. That's the problem. Ain't nothing never up 'round here."

Matty smiled weakly. Then he looked at her. "Let me see. You're the one with her own beauty salon, right?"

"Right," Leah said proudly.

"I remember you."

"I'm surprised you didn't at first. I'm hardly forgettable, Reverend."

Matty laughed lightly, but enough to embolden Leah. She could tell he was a playa. She could tell it by the way he shook her hand after Sunday service and stared into her eyes. All she needed to do now, she felt, was get him to admit it. "Yes, I have my own business, thank the Lord. And like you, I'm single." Leah said this and looked down at her body, then back up at Matty.

She was seducing him, he could see that himself, and she was doing a sorry job of it, too. She even crossed her legs and smiled a deceptive smile at him. He wanted to laugh.

"You've never married, Pastor?" she asked him.

It seemed like too personal a question, and he should have cut it off right then and there, but he didn't want to scare her away. If the only reason she was coming to church was to charm him, then fine. At least she was coming. One day she might even hear a word from the Lord. "Once," he said.

"Divorced?"

"Yep."

"When?"

"Long ago. When I was in my late twenties."

"Your late twenties? And that was a long time ago? Dang. Just how old are you, Reverend?" Leah asked this unabashedly as she was suddenly worried that he might be too old for her. He did have those lines around his eyes. And during his sermon Sunday, when he talked about how God had silenced him for years when he was disobedient, she got the distinct impression that the man had been around the block far more times than she'd ever been. That was why, when he didn't respond, she pressed. This was one answer she had to have.

"Pastor?" she said.

"Yes, Leah?"

"How old are you?"

"I'm old."

"But how old?"

"Old."

"What? Fifty?"

Matty smiled. "No, but I'm almost forty."

Leah sighed relief. "You're thirty-nine, that's not too bad. I'm thirty-four, although I've been told I don't look a day over twenty-four."

She didn't at that, Matty decided, looking at her. And he also decided that this was becoming an inappropriate conversation. "How long have you been a member of Fountain Hope?" he asked her.

"Too long."

Matty laughed.

"I'm sorry, Reverend, but sometimes those church folks can be so phony, you know?"

"You can only account for yourself, Leah. You don't get to heaven in a group."

"I know, but..."

"No 'but.' You go to church because you need God. You go to church because your spirit will die without the Lord in your life. You go to church for you. It's purely a selfish matter."

Leah nodded. "Understood," she said, more to end that line of talk than to demonstrate any real understanding.

Silence ensued. A long, tense silence. Leah began shaking her crossed leg and staring at him, her motives as obvious as the lust in her eyes. When Matty finally decided to return her stare, she smiled. "Aren't you curious about me?" she asked him.

"Curious how?"

"Don't you want to know if I'm hooked up with anybody right now?"

Matty frowned. "Why would I be curious about that, Leah?"

"Because."

"Because why? I'm your pastor."

"And that's exactly why. Because you're my pastor. You should want to know everything there is to know about me."

Matty wanted to smile. This was the *loudest* seduction he'd ever encountered. "All right, Leah. Are you hooked up with anybody right now?" he asked her.

"No, as a matter of fact. But I was married before."

"Were you?"

"Twice. But even my husbands didn't have nothing I really wanted. They were too trifling for me, know what I'm saying? That's why I'm flying solo these days. I'm holding out for the real deal, for the real thing."

"Good for you. I hope you find what you're looking for."

"I think I have." She said this with another one of those smirks on her face, but Matty ignored her. Women were falling at his feet in Chicago, too, doing everything they could to distract him from his work at hand. But it didn't work then, and it wasn't going to work now.

He stood up, forcing Leah to stand, too. "Well, it is getting late, Miss Leah, and I've got some Bible reading to do."

"I understand that. I'd better get on home anyway. We're still on for Saturday though, right?"

Matty hesitated. What was he getting himself into, he wondered. "Yes," he finally said.

"That's all I wanted to know. I'm gonna make certain you enjoy your little tour."

"Thanks for agreeing to show me around."

"No problem at all, Reverend. It'll be my pleasure, trust me. Good night!" She said this with too grand a smile and walked off of the porch and back to her vehicle. Matty waved at her as she drove off, then he sat back down.

Leah couldn't stop smiling as she drove away. He was perfect, she thought, a brother every female in Fountain Hope would want to get their hands on if she didn't move fast. He was tall and powerful and beyond great looking, and so obviously rolling in the big bucks that just the prospect of being with a man like him was exciting Leah. She knew he talked a good talk about the Lord and the church and whatever else pastors were supposed to talk about. But she also saw the way he looked at her, the way those luscious dark gray eyes trailed down the length of her, and she knew she could have him. And come Saturday morning, she decided, when all of his soul talk was going to end up in pillow talk, she would have him. She'd have him so wrapped up into her heart that he wouldn't be able to bear the thought of ever letting her go.

Chapter 9

Diane stamped the book's back cover with a return date and handed it to the older man. "Have a nice day now," she said to him.

"You, too, dear," he replied, smiling as he accepted the book and made his way to the exit. Diane sighed with relief when he left, as his departure made it possible for her to finally get off of her feet. It was always busier than normal after the long three-day weekend (the library did not open on Mondays), but this particular Tuesday seemed especially hectic. And then Miss Wheeler, her aide, didn't show up at all—no phone call, no note dropped by, not a word. And then the local elementary school had a field trip planned to their beloved public library, something they remembered to tell sixty students, but somehow forgot to tell Diane. So she was anxious and exhausted and about ready to pull a disappearing act like her assistant, and it was only mid-morning.

She picked up her coffee mug from the countertop and

leaned back in her tall chair. She sipped her coffee and re-laxed, thrilled for the break, when, out of her periphery, she saw a car pull to the curb in front of the library. She took a quick glance and was about to swirl back around, as her eyes were too tired to focus on anything at that particular mo-ment, but when she saw that it was a blue Jaguar, the same car everybody in church was talking about Sunday and won-dering collectively how a preacher of the gospel could af-ford, she looked again. And her heart nearly skipped a beat. It was Pastor Jolson. The one man she couldn't seem to get off her mind was making an appearance at her job.

He stepped out looking around, obviously unfamiliar with the south side of town, she thought. He wore a white, long-sleeved dress shirt, a pair of snugly fitting blue dress pants, and dark sunglasses on his handsome face as he looked up toward the harsh Georgia sun. He was a big man, as Diane remembered from the two times she'd seen him previously, with a wide chest and large, muscular arms, and the shirt he wore today only highlighted that point. He looked like a model in a workout video, she thought, just a beautiful man with a beautiful body whose taste probably tended toward beautiful people, which made her wonder why he would be coming anywhere near her today.

But he was. He walked around to the passenger side of his car, his expensive watch and dress shoes both reflecting the sun as if they were made of diamonds and the purest of gold, and he reached into his car and pulled out his suit coat. To Diane's shock, given the heat, he put on the coat before closing the car door and heading her way.

She swirled back around in her seat and tried to regulate her breathing. He was her pastor, after all, and it was foolish and wrong for her to be carrying on so. Just get it together, Diane, she kept telling herself. Don't get all crazy about this man and make a fool of yourself again. He was probably still laughing from Sunday when she had offered to show him around town but had been beaten to the punch by Leah. Leah, Diane thought. The queen of seduction. A woman she knew she couldn't compete with and wasn't about to try.

"There she is!" Matty said as he entered the small library's revolving door and smiled at the little lady behind the large checkout counter. He'd never been happier to see anybody before, he thought, as he moved toward her, as her small, narrow face lit up into a great smile that pleased him even more.

"Hello, Pastor Jolson," Diane said, trying her best not to appear overly excited.

"I told you about that pastor stuff," he replied gruffly as he stood in front of her desk. "It's Matty to you."

"I stand corrected. Hello, Matty. How are you this fine Georgia morning?"

"Hot," he said with a smile.

"That suit coat doesn't help."

"It does not."

Then why are you wearing it, she wanted to ask, but didn't bother. "I heard you've got a job-training class going on at the church today."

"My, how quickly word travels around here. Faster than the speed of light, in my opinion. But yes, in response to your comment, yes, I do. Sister Scott's helping me out even as we speak. She's teaching the men how to complete job applications."

"That basic?"

"Yes, I'm afraid so."

"Is it for men only?"

"No. They just happened to be as good a place to start as any."

Diane nodded.

"So," Matty asked, still smiling, still surprisingly cheerful, "how are *you* this fine Georgia morning?"

"I'm good. It's been busy around here, but it's settled down considerably now."

Matty nodded, but found himself studying her face. She felt uncomfortable, the way he couldn't seem to stop those big gray eyes of his from staring at her, and what really kept her uneasy was that he appeared very displeased by what he was seeing. His smile was gone and that cheerfulness he'd walked in with was slowly fading into a kind of gloomy disappointment. What did he expect? she wondered. Miss America?

"So, Pastor," Diane said, to change his focus, "what brings you out this way?"

He exhaled, as if he were angry. "What is it, Diane? You don't care?"

The oddity of the question wasn't lost on Diane. "I don't care about what?"

"You."

"Me? Why wouldn't I care about myself?"

"Have you been taking care of yourself?"

"Of course I have."

"Really, now?"

"Yes!"

In a move so swift that it startled Diane, Matty lifted up the sideboard and was behind the desk and, consequently, in her face, before she could say another word. His large hand touched her by the chin and turned her face toward his. "Those are bags under your eyes, Diane. Bags. And what about these dark circles? And your face looks drawn and your color is almost pale. Now don't tell me that this is the face of a young lady who takes care of herself, because it's not." He said this and then released her chin, causing her head to jerk slightly upon his release. He slung open his suit coat and placed both hands on his hips, as if he couldn't wait to hear her explanation this time.

Diane looked at him, at those fierce gray eyes of his, but quickly looked away. She'd admit she wasn't taking great care of herself, but so what? It was *her*self.

"What's your excuse this time, Diane?" he asked her. "Why are you so exhausted and it's not even twelve o'clock yet?"

Diane sighed. Who did he think he was? But being combative was not a part of her makeup. "I told you I had a busy morning."

"You work here alone?"

"No."

"Where's your staff?"

"My staff consists of one assistant and she couldn't make it today."

"Why not?"

"I don't know."

"You haven't heard from her?"

Diane hesitated. "I haven't."

"I'd bet she rarely ever makes it to work. Am I right?"

"She's not very consistent, no."

"Then why hasn't she been fired and replaced with somebody you can rely on?"

Because Miss Wheeler may not have been the world's best worker, but she needed her job, Diane thought to say. But she didn't say anything.

"It's because Miss Helpful Diane just can't put it in her heart to fire anybody, isn't that why?"

"She needs her job," Diane finally said.

"Then she should be here. You shouldn't have to run this place all alone."

"It's not a problem, okay?"

"And don't you get cute with me. Okay?" Matty said this and immediately regretted his tone. Diane, surprised by his tone, stood up. He was just like everybody else in her life, she thought. Just another somebody to talk to her any kind of way, and boss her around, and tell her what she was and wasn't going to do. Only she was disappointed in Matty. She never took him to be that kind of man.

"Diane, I'm sorry," he said as she began stacking books.

"Meaning no disrespect, Pastor," she said, "but I have work to do." She said this and looked him dead in the eyes. Her heart quivered when she did, but she refused to release her stare.

He tried to smile, but even she could see it was a fake display. He was still too angry for amusement. "When's your lunch break?"

"I don't know if I'm taking one today."

"Diane!"

"Yes?"

Matty threw his hands in the air and shook his head. "You know what? Fine. Do whatever you want."

"Funny you should say that because I've been doing just that very thing for the past twenty-nine years now. And guess what? I've actually managed to survive without you or anybody else dictating my every move. Could it be possible?"

She knew she had done it now, but she didn't care. He just stared at her, as if he were surprised by something. And she knew that could mean anything. She wasn't the sweet little innocent he thought, maybe? Or maybe he was disappointed in her as well. Maybe he now thought, as she had concluded about him, that she was just like the rest of them, too.

But before he could break his stare to say or do anything, the library's side door swung open and Frank Tarver, Diane's younger brother, came storming in. "What's the problem, Diane?" he asked, his arms flailed out, his face flushed with dismay.

Diane rolled her eyes. All she needed. "I'm at work, Frank."

"You told me you was gonna do that for me, sis. You told me you was gonna get it done today."

"Is the day over yet, Frank?" Diane snapped. She hated that Matty had to see her like this, but it couldn't be helped.

"This ain't right, though. I'm depending on you."

"This is my pastor," Diane said when Frank finally made it up to the desk. "Pastor Jolson, this is my brother, Frank."

"Hello, Frank," Matty said, extending his hand, his eyes fixed on Frank's. He was a tall man with uncombed nappy hair and a scraggly beard. But oddly charming, Matty thought.

"Hey," Frank said reluctantly and shook the hand. "You the brother with the Jag."

Diane could have died. But Matty seemed unmoved. "Yes," he said.

"Everybody ain't able."

"Frank, I am at work," Diane reminded him. "I'll go take care of that on my lunch break."

"But he don't wanna wait no more. He said I either do this in the next hour or the whole deal off. This my life, sis, my future. You have got to come through for me."

"And I told you I will."

"But what if he calls the deal off?"

"What's this deal about?" Matty asked and both Diane and Frank looked at him.

"What?" Frank asked, stunned that Matty would dare to get up in his business.

"You heard me," Matty replied, not the least intimidated.

"Oh, so this got something to do with you now?"

"That's enough, Frank," Diane said.

"Nall, sis, he wanna mind our business. Standing up there in his fancy suit. Driving around in his fancy car. Gonna save us poor country folk. Well, who gon' save you, preacher, 'cause from what I hear you need it worst of all."

Matty smiled. "You've got a point there." Then he looked at Diane. "What's this deal about?" he asked her.

"It's about none of your business," Frank replied.

"I said that's enough, Frank," Diane said, and then shook

her head. "Here," she said, pulling her purse from the desk drawer and then pulling out an envelope. She handed it to Frank. "Take it. Just go on and give it to him."

Frank smiled. "Ah, sis, I knew I could count on you!" He gladly accepted the envelope.

"And Frank," Diane said as he was about to leave, "mess up if you want. It may be my money, but just as you said it's your life, your future."

Frank nodded. "Yeah," he said. "I hear ya'." He looked disapprovingly at Matty one more time, and then hurriedly left the building. Matty looked at Diane, his face stern, intensely disappointed.

"What was that about?" he asked her.

"A friend of his is supposed to be starting a car-washing business."

"A car wash?"

"Yes. You know, a detailing business. And Frank wanted to go in on the deal."

"How much money did you give him?"

"It was just a little capital for him to—"

"How much money did you give him?"

Diane exhaled. "A thousand dollars," she said.

Matty frowned. "You just gave a thousand dollars to a *crackhead?*"

Diane, stunned by Matty's words, frowned herself. "Frank is not a crackhead, Pastor Jolson. Yes, he had some rough days but he's doing much better now. This business opportunity may be just what he needs to get back on his feet again."

"Has he ever been on his feet, Diane? Or have you been too busy carrying him to notice?"

Diane didn't respond. How could he possibly know all of this? He'd only seen Frank for two minutes, how could he know anything about him? His prior drug problems couldn't be that obvious.

"I've got to go," Matty said with some frustration. He

looked at Diane with what seemed to her to be a distressing, worried look. "Eat lunch today, okay? Even if you don't want to eat it with me."

Don't want to eat with him? Diane was floored. Was he kidding? She'd love to have lunch with him, if he'd only ask. She, however, didn't recall him asking. "I'll eat lunch," she said.

He smiled. A beautiful smile, she thought. Then after a moment of just standing there he walked up to her, looked deep into her eyes, and then placed his hand on her cheek. His touch was like fire against her skin, and it was searing every inch of her, and the way he looked at her, the way his eyes trailed over her face as if he saw something remarkable, made her heart throb. This man was unlike any she'd ever met, and the way he made her feel was unlike any other man ever could, and she didn't know if she could handle it. But then his look turned more earnest, more concerned, as if his hopefulness was now tinged with reluctance. That gave her some relief, knowing that he, too, didn't know if he could handle these feelings either, but her relief was premature. Despite his obvious misgivings, despite the questionable wisdom of two Christians going down this kind of emotional road, he pulled her against him and then wrapped her in a warm bear hug anyway.

He held her, he held her tightly, and a great well of emotion bubbled up inside of her as she first resisted, then could not stop herself from holding on to him, too. She'd never been this close to a man before in her life, and it was a pitiful testament, she felt, but it was the truth. Russell had hugged her a few times in their two-year relationship, but his body was so big and his belly so protruding that the intimacy was never there. This was different. The intimacy she felt as she stood in Matty's arms was overwhelming. And the strong scent of his cologne, so masculine yet so fresh and clean, made her feel like dancing. Was this it? Was this that wonderful, sweet, electrifying feeling she'd been missing all her life? She could have died in his arms, without experiencing any more than this, and felt as if she were a fortunate lady.

Matty didn't know what he felt as he held her, or why he was holding her at all. He was even upset with her, because she was so thin and her body felt frail, but he was also pleased because she was in his arms, and protected. She didn't wear perfume, but had a sweet, fresh soap smell to her skin, and as he found himself pulling her closer against him, he felt an urge to touch her long, wavy hair. He knew it would be soft. But he didn't touch it. He, instead, released her. She almost staggered when his grip of support was gone.

"You take care of yourself," he said, staring at her, as if he were studying her response.

Diane was uncomfortable with his stare but she managed to smile just the same. "I will."

He was about to walk away, to get back to the numerous duties he had awaiting him, but he couldn't seem to break his stare. Diane started to ask if there was something wrong, but he spoke instead. "Diane, sometimes I'm too blunt," he said. "And much too insensitive. And a general jerk when I wanna be." Both he and Diane smiled. Then he turned serious again. "But I'll never lead you wrong," he said. "You've got to take better care of yourself. I know you don't wanna hear it, I know I'm becoming a Johnny-one-note about this, but it's a fact. You've got to do better than you're doing. Eat your lunch. Take your breaks. And fire that darn aide if she's not doing her job. Get you some real help up in here."

Diane laughed. Was he really this concerned about her? "Yes, sir," she said.

Matty smiled, too, and found himself, once again, staring at her. "You're in the choir, aren't you?"

How did he know that? she wondered. Because of her tardiness she hadn't been permitted to sing Sunday. "Yes," she said.

"Rehearsal's Thursday night."

"I know. It's every Thursday, now that we're having service every Sunday."

"I'll see you then."

"At choir rehearsal? Have you joined the choir?"

Matty laughed. "No, but I'll be at the church. So I'll see you there."

Diane's heart soared. "Okay. Sure thing." Matty turned to leave. "Oh, and Pastor?"

"It's Matty to you," he said, as he turned back around. "Yes?"

"Why haven't you asked me my opinion about your new policy?"

"What new policy?"

"Your service-every-Sunday policy, the one everybody's talking about? Why haven't you asked what I thought about it?"

"Honestly?"

"Of course."

"Because I don't care what you think. Not about that. I'm not taking a poll to see if it's popular to worship the Lord. It doesn't matter if it's popular or not. It's the right thing to do."

Diane nodded. "Amen."

"Take care of yourself, Diane," he said again as he began to leave. "And I'll see you Thursday night."

"Yes, you will," Diane said as he left, barely able to contain her excitement. She even shouted a hallelujah when he left. Because just like that she was happy. Just like that she was looking forward to something again, something as simple as going to choir rehearsal, something she, just moments before, had viewed more as her duty than her pleasure.

Sam didn't know what to say. He claimed it was a courtesy call, a way for him to get to know all of his members up close and personal, but her every instinct told her differently. The good Reverend was snooping. No other way to put it. He'd seen the bruise on her face at church Sunday and was apparently not at all satisfied with the explanations. Well, she thought, as she placed the teacups on the tray and headed for the living room, she'd just have to satisfy him. Nobody—not the Reverend, not anybody—was going to break up her happy home.

"Here we are," she said as she set the tray on the cocktail table and began pouring Matty a drink. Matty was seated in the massive high-back chair that Ira favored, his legs crossed, his pristine suit a perfect match for the Victorian motif of the Marshall living room.

"You have a lovely home, Sister Marshall," Matty said as he looked around.

"Thank you," Sam replied, handing him a cup of tea. "I certainly work hard at it."

"No interior designer or—"

"Oh, no. This is all me. There are certain things Ira will tolerate, but strangers in his home isn't one of them."

A warning. Matty sensed that his welcome was limited. "Yes, he seems like a pretty cut-and-dried brother," Matty said.

"He is. But always fair."

Sam took her cup of tea and sat back on the sofa. The Reverend was smooth if he was anything, and he was hanging onto her every word. This was the time, she thought, where she had to be very careful.

"Where did you guys meet?" Matty asked her.

She sipped from her tea first, and then responded. "In Albany," she said. "Ira was a visiting professor at Albany State. I was a student. I didn't take any of his classes, of course—he taught on the graduate level—but he saw me walking across campus one day and the rest, as they say, is history."

Matty smiled. "You married your teacher."

"I married *a* teacher. Not mine. Which wasn't bad for an F.C. girl like me, let me tell you."

"F.C.? What's F.C.? Future Christian?"

Sam laughed. "No. It's Foster Care. I was brought up in the foster-care system."

"I see. Your parents died or…"

"No, they just didn't want me. Or the state didn't want them to have me, I don't know. I was three at the time."

"Young."

"Yes."

"Did you stay with one family?"

"I wish. More like fifty families over the whole time I stayed in the system. Of course, I was on adoption status for most of those years, but I had no takers."

"That's unfortunate, Sister Marshall. Thank God you kept your spirit."

"I did. I was all I had and I was determined to do right by me. Nobody else did, so I had to."

"Thus college."

"Right. I don't know if you've met Diane Tarver yet?"

Matty's heart quivered. "Yes, I have."

"Well, we were in high school together, we were in every school together actually, and she kept telling me about this college she had been accepted to and all of these dreams she had. But I didn't think it could be for me so I just concentrated on graduating high school. I'm a year older than Diane but I was behind by a year, which meant we graduated together. But when I got out of foster care, I found nothing but emptiness. I had nothing else to do. Or nowhere else to go, really. So I followed Diane. We weren't what you would call close but she was the only somebody who ever treated me kindly, you know? So I figured she'd look out for me."

Matty smiled. "Little Diane looking out for you."

Sam laughed. "Yes. She was all I had. And then Ira came along and gave me what I wanted most."

"A family."

"Right."

"He's older than you."

"Oh, yes. Sixteen years. But it doesn't matter. We love each other dearly. He really comes through for me, you know? Sometimes I can't believe how good God's been to me."

Matty nodded. Then he set his cup on the table and leaned forward. "What happened Thursday night, Sister Marshall?"

Sam swallowed hard. She knew she had to be convincing. "I told you, Reverend," she said with a smile. "I fell. It was an unfortunate accident."

"How?"

"How what?"

"How did you fall?"

Sam paused, unnerved by the intensity in Matty's eyes. Then she exhaled. "I have a slight problem, all right? It's occasional but it's still a problem." She waited for Matty to encourage her to go on, but he didn't say a word. He just continued staring at her. "I had a little too much to drink."

"Too much?"

"Right. And I get kind of, shall we say, active, when I drink. I was quite active last Thursday night." She said this with a little laugh. When she realized Matty wasn't playing along, she turned serious. "But thank the Lord I'm beyond that now."

"What's your brand?"

"Excuse me?"

"Of drink."

Sam hesitated. "My brand?"

"Yes. What do you like to drink?"

"Oh! Well, I don't have a specific brand name or anything that I rely on. I just like brandy, bourbon, stuff like that. And I know I shouldn't drink at all, I know it's not ladylike and it's definitely not Christian, but as I told you I've stopped now."

"Completely?"

"Completely."

"Certain about that?"

"Oh, yes. I have no intentions of taking another sip."

"Until another Thursday night rolls around and you're in the emergency room again. But maybe it'll be another excuse."

"Another excuse? What's that supposed to mean?"

"Alcoholics. They rarely blame it on the booze."

Sam felt lost in the conversation, as if the Reverend was in the game tossing curveballs while she was still trying to figure out the game itself. "I don't think I follow you," she decided to say.

"Sure you do," Matty said as he stood up. He then extended his hand. Sam stood up to shake it. "Thank you for allowing me to visit with you, Sister Marshall."

"My pleasure, Reverend," Sam said, trying to smile. "You're always welcome here."

"Good. I still can't get over this home. It's just beautiful. Almost...perfect. You've made it right comfortable for yourself, haven't you?"

"Yes, I have."

"No more F.C. for you."

Sam laughed. "That's right."

"No matter what."

Sam's smile began to fade, but she wouldn't allow it to disappear. "That's right," she said less gaily.

"Well. Tell your husband I said hello." Matty said this as he began walking toward the front door. "He's the judge on the Wells' case, isn't he?"

"Yes," Sam replied, following him to the door. "Quite a big case, too. Reporters from everywhere, even Atlanta, are covering it."

"Such a tragic situation."

"I know. That poor boy."

Matty, at the front door, turned and faced Sam. "That poor grandmother," he said.

"Oh," Sam said and couldn't help but smile. "Of course."

"I mean she's the one who was murdered."

"That's very true."

"And I believe in reserving judgment, I really do. But it's never a good idea to turn a cold-blooded, cold-hearted maniac into a victim."

Sam hesitated. "True," she said.

"Not that the young man is a maniac. But we'll see. It'll all come out eventually." Matty said this and stared at Sam in such a way that she couldn't help but understand what he was really saying. But she wasn't about to let him know that she understood it. "Yes, it will," she replied.

"Well," Matty said, extending his hand again. "Thanks again for your hospitality."

"And again you're welcome," Sam said, smiling as she shook his hand, relieved that he was leaving. "But tell me, Reverend," she decided to ask, unable to let well enough alone, "does our little family life meet with your approval?"

Matty stared at Sam. Too long, she felt. "No," he said. Then he stared at her a little longer, and left.

Sam closed the door and fell against it. And her heart began to pound. Could he know? she wondered. He didn't know a thing, he couldn't. But he seemed so sure that he knew it all. Her life wasn't perfect, he was right about that, but at least it wasn't hell either, unlike it had been before she met Ira. And then she thought about Ira and how furious he was going to be if he found out. That preacher was well intentioned, she knew, but he didn't know what ground he was upturning. It wasn't the yelling that worried Sam. Or even the beatings. She was tough, she could handle both. She *had* handled both. But Ira would leave her, and take her sons, and that was what she couldn't abide.

She knew the system. She knew how rigged it was against

her. She knew no court on the face of this earth would even consider giving her visitation rights when Ira was through. Because he'd destroy her. He'd make certain she was penniless and on the street, just as she was the day she turned eighteen and the state was done raising her. And just like then she could fall off the face of the earth and not only would nobody care, but Ira would make sure that nobody would even notice. That Reverend had to be stopped, she decided. He had to be put in his place before all hell broke loose. Because Ira would ruin her, and take away the only hold she had on life, if anybody ever questioned his humanity.

Chapter 10

Diane arrived early, which surprised many of her fellow choir members. They stared at her as she made her way up the center aisle to the choir stand, moving to her favorite seat in the dead back. Some even commented as they watched her, amazed by this first-time event.

"Diane here already? The end of the world is near, y'all."

"Ain't no way that's Sister Tarver. We're usually twenty minutes into rehearsal before she shows up. What's going on here?"

"Now I seen it all. Diane early. Wait till Sister Inez hears about this."

Sister Inez wasn't in the choir, thank God, Diane thought, but she was her leader on the Pulpit Aid Board and she was always on Diane's case about coming late to meetings. This would shock her, no doubt about it, but Diane wasn't interested in shocking Inez or anybody else. She wanted to see Matty. He was the only person on her mind. She'd thought about him all day Tuesday after he left the library, thought about the way he held her, the way he became so angry because she wasn't taking better care of herself. She'd never seen such fire in a man concerned about her. They'd usually notice that she wasn't looking her best, but, like Russell for two straight years, wouldn't even care enough to comment.

But Matty seemed to care enough. More than enough. And it was confounding the daylights out of Diane. She asked herself why a million times. Asked the Lord why a zillion times. Why would a man like that, of such unquestionably great looks and style, want somebody like her? It didn't make sense. Yes, he was a Christian who should be more interested in a woman's heart rather than her waistline, but this was the real world. And Christian men, like anybody else, had to see the woman before they got to know the woman and Matty, it seemed to Diane, didn't really know her at all.

She exhaled and looked at the choir members as they lumbered to their seats in anticipation of getting started. They were all older than Diane, and larger in every way, and their mere presence in the stands seemed to swallow up her small frame in the back. She usually didn't care. She wanted it that way. Inconspicuous, that was Diane. But tonight was different. Matty had specifically said he'd see her tonight, as if he were looking forward to it, too, and she wanted to be seen. She couldn't stop thinking about him, and the way he'd held her, unlike any man ever had, his strong, sweet scent still in her nostrils two whole days later. Maybe Matty was different after all. Maybe Matty was man enough not to need a trophy girl on his arm but a woman he could really get to know, and cherish, and love.

Diane and the rest of the members stood as Brother Maurice, the choir director, lifted his baton and began directing them in his version of Walter Hawkins "Going Up Yonder." Diane shrugged off the idea of Matty *loving* her. It seemed almost sacrilegious for her to even think it. He was a preacher of the gospel, after all, a pastor no less. He didn't have time for that.

And after nearly thirty minutes of rehearsing and still no sign of Matty, Diane began to realize it even more. What if he didn't show up? Pastor Cobb never attended any choir rehearsals unless he just happened to be passing through the sanctuary on his way to or from his office. But Matty had said he'd be here. He said he'd see her here. So she continued to hope. She didn't look her best; she wore the same skirt suit she had worn to work, a two-piece brown number with a short jacket and a just-above-her-knee skirt. But if she had gone home to change first she would have had to listen to Malveen and Willie James go on and on about whatever problems they encountered today, and she would have been late for sure. Now she realized it wouldn't have mattered, since Matty wouldn't have been here anyway.

He didn't show up, in fact, until rehearsal was a full hour old and not all that far from wrapping up. Diane had even resigned herself to the fact that he wasn't coming. And when he did show it wasn't like he searched her out. He didn't even look her way. He walked in from the rooms behind the choir stand as if he were wandering in because of the sound of the music, not because of her. But it still felt odd, Diane thought, to see him again. He was in shirtsleeves, in yet another white shirt that looked brand new and that did wonders to highlight his beautiful brown skin and big gray eyes. But when Matty saw a deacon in the pews, one who had been watching the choir rehearse, he acted as if he'd found who he was looking for and hurried to his side. They talked briefly, with Matty doing the lion's share, and then they left almost leisurely out of the sanctuary and into the back rooms.

Although Diane's heart dropped, she kept on singing. She even closed her eyes and swayed to the music, determined to blot out Matty and all other distractions. She should have been here to serve the Lord anyway, not to pick up some man, and the more she understood that fact, the easier it became for her to cope. And by the time they rehearsed the last song of the evening, a rather upbeat version of "Precious Lord," Diane had her eyes closed and had all but forgotten her earlier disappointment. The Lord was precious indeed, she thought, and He deserved to be praised.

But when she opened her eyes, as she occasionally did when her balance seemed lacking, she was stunned to see that Matty had returned and was seated in a chair just beyond Maurice. He was facing the back of the chair, straddling the seat, and was staring straight at her. Her heart nearly stopped. Her swaying did stop, which made her even more conspicuous since everybody else still moved to the beat, and she quickly recovered her step and continued moving, too. He had a rolled-up sheet of paper in his hand and wore reading glasses, the first time she'd ever seen him in those, and his stare was so penetrating that it seemed trance-like. But when he realized that her eyes were now open and she was returning his gaze, he immediately unrolled the sheet of paper in his hand and began looking it over. That gave Diane a chance to breathe again. And get excited again. And forget, once again, the movement of the choir, forcing her to get back in step again.

Matty exhaled, too, as he looked over the list of things he had to do, including finding a teacher for the support group he was starting in the church, a group devoted to helping addicts and other sinners come to Jesus and seek God's help to break the habit. A recovered addict would be ideal, but no such person had turned up yet. But he was prayerful. Sister Wanda Scott, an angel in Matty's eyes, had been gracious enough to take over the job-training/witnessing class for him, and the men, who were still getting paid for showing up, seemed to love it. But there was more to do. Much more. And Matty was determined not to slow down until every human being within any distance of the greater Fountain Hope community had every opportunity to give their lives to Christ. As the largest African American church in town, it was their duty, and even their privilege, to be a light. And not one hidden as had been the case for the last five decades, but bright as day.

Matty looked up from his list and removed his glasses. Diane's eyes were still open and she was in better step with the other choir members, but she still looked out of place to him. Something about a woman her age in a choir where the median age had to be sixty-plus made her stand out. Why would she even want to be in such a choir? he wondered. But he knew. It was the same reason she was on the Pulpit Aid Board with that Sister Inez. Or giving her crack-addicted brother a thousand dollars of her hard-earned money for yet another one of his pipe dreams, literally, money Matty just knew she couldn't afford to give away like that. But they asked and Diane, who probably never learned to say no, said yes. He knew he had to break her of that. He didn't know how, or why he even wanted to, but he knew he was going to.

Rehearsal broke up shortly thereafter and Matty stood up and began a thoughtful conversation about song selection with the choir director. Matty kept glancing over at Diane, as Brother Maurice bent his ear about this very long, drawn-out process he used when deciding on which songs the choir would sing. Diane was talking with other members, including one of only three men in the choir. When that man laughed and touched Diane's shoulder, an understandably friendly gesture, a wave of jealousy ripped through Matty. But he continued to nod and listen to Maurice, without moving, without giving any hint to anyone but himself that his eyes were watching Diane.

Diane didn't realize it either. Every time she took a peek at Matty he was watching and listening attentively to Maurice. She felt robbed in some way, and scared that her hopes might once again be dashed by his lack of interest. Yet when her fellow choir members began deserting the stands and preparing to go home, Diane felt compelled to stay. But she didn't quite know how to approach Matty. He looked stern when he was serious, making him appear unapproachable. So she just stood near him, hoping that he would notice her, but not once did he look her way.

"We've going over to Maxine's, Diane," one of the older, female choir members yelled to her. The older woman and a small group were about to head out. "You coming?"

Matty, seemingly out of the blue, turned from the talkative Maurice and looked at Diane. "No," he said to her.

Diane, stunned that he would have even heard the question, looked at her fellow choir members with a kind of quiet excitement. "No, but thanks for asking," she yelled to them.

Diane looked back at Matty, ready to smile and say something clever, like thanking him for saving her from that group, but he had returned his full attention to Maurice. So she just stood there quietly and let them talk, feeling awkward. Just because he had nixed the idea of her going to dinner with the other members didn't mean he wanted her hanging around him.

She wished she weren't so inhibited. She wished to God she had more experience with life and understood how these things worked. Sam and Leah would know what to do. You'd never see them standing here like some bump on a log waiting for somebody to pay attention to them. They'd tell him to forget it, if he'd rather talk to some boring choir director then fine, talk to him. And they'd go home. It wasn't what Diane wanted to do, but she felt compelled to do it. So she began to leave. If he wanted her to stay, he'd speak up. If not—God forbid—at least she wouldn't have embarrassed herself any longer.

He apparently didn't want her to stay because he didn't say a word. She stepped loudly as she walked, and he had to have heard her movement, but he didn't make a sound. Her heart felt battered, as if it had pumped up then pumped down, and she moved swiftly to get away. Why did he intervene if he wasn't going to at least hold a conversation with her? That didn't make sense. And he was always telling her how she needed to eat, but when her friends offered to take her to eat, he said no. None of it made sense.

But as Diane made it out of the sanctuary and across the parking lot to her car, she stopped trying to make sense of it. Maybe the man was just toying with her, seeing just how weak a woman she was before he went in for the kill. Virtue wasn't honored anymore. Or humility. But strength was. And independence. And those who believed that the go-getter gospel was written just as surely for women as it was for men. Traditional women with traditional values were like jokes now. Thought weak when weakness had nothing to do with it. Thought dumb when intelligence wasn't even an issue. Diane felt inadequate. She knew she was no role model for today's modern woman, but what was she to do? Make a man love her? Step out on the town and make somebody pay her attention? She shuddered at the thought. She'd step out, all right. And fall on her face.

She got into her car and just sat there, buried in her less-than-flattering thoughts, when a knock suddenly came upon her window. Startled by the sound alone, she turned quickly. And she was astonished. It was Matty, standing there looking gorgeous, but decidedly ill tempered. She rolled down her window.

"What do you think you're doing?" he asked with a frown on his face.

"I'm sitting in my car."

"You planned to just leave, didn't you? You were going to just get in this car and drive on off."

"There was no reason for me to stay."

"I was the reason."

"You? You seemed pretty busy to me."

"Cut it out, Diane, you hear me? If I wanted a woman like that, trust me I could get one."

Diane frowned. "What are you talking about?"

He exhaled. "Let's go get something to eat."

"But what are you talking about? If you wanted a woman like what?"

"The kind that play games."

Diane paused. She couldn't believe how much the Reverend had misunderstood her. "I wasn't playing a game."

"Good. Because I'll be very disappointed if you were. And you don't want to disappoint me, do you, Diane?"

He sounded so smooth, so certain of his power over her, that she began to wonder if it was she who was being played. But she wasn't going to lie. "No," she said.

"Now, can we go get something to eat? I'm starving here."

Diane couldn't help but smile. And relax. "Okay," she said.

"You can follow me in your car. Let me go get my coat first."

But as he went back into the church to retrieve his coat, her usually reliable Buick Skylark wouldn't cooperate. It wouldn't start. She tried while he was inside the church and continued trying when he came back up to her car. But it wouldn't start. Not once.

"I don't know what's wrong with it," she said, seemingly frantic.

Matty looked at the car. "It's old, Diane," he said.

"But it's never given me any trouble before. It's probably just the battery."

"Come ride with me. We'll worry about that later."

And Diane agreed. And she didn't worry about it either. Not when he put her in his beautiful Jaguar, the leather seats and sweet smell clogging her very senses, and not while they drove slowly along the streets of Floradale to a small diner far away from Maxine's and any other place Diane had ventured.

"Where did you find this one?" she asked as he opened the car door for her.

"Deacon Molt and I had lunch here the other day. The food was wonderful."

Most of the patrons were long-haul truckers and Diane was surprised that a man of Matty's obvious tastes would go for a place like this. But he seemed excited about it, as he walked her into the restaurant, his large hand pressed against her lower back as he ushered her through the entrance doors. He was the only somebody wearing a suit in the place, that was for sure, and they were the only blacks, but by the time the food was served and Diane had eaten heartily, she was satisfied, too. She dabbed her mouth again as the waitress removed her near-empty plate. She was careful not to have a crumb anywhere on her as she was now ready to impress Matty. It was a tall order, but as they'd been driving to the restaurant, she had become determined to try. Russell didn't want her. Nobody else was breaking into any phone booths to give her a call. Maybe the best man she could ever hope to have, a man of such integrity and personality and great looks, was the one God wanted to give to her. It would be some gift, she knew, and maybe her desire was overshadowing the reality of the thing, but wouldn't it be something, she thought. And that thought alone kept her determination high.

"You weren't joking, Matty," she said. "The food was wonderful."

"I'm glad you liked it," Matty said as he leaned back, his voice sounding bored, his face showing little enthusiasm. Then he pulled out a cigarette and held it up to her. "You mind?" he asked.

"No," she said. "Although I'm still praying for you."

"Excuse me?"

"The smoking. I'm still praying that you will allow God to help you quit."

Matty lit his cigarette and leaned back. He could use all the prayers he could get, he thought. "So tell me about yourself, Diane Tarver. Were you born and raised here in little Floradale? No, let me guess. You were."

Diane smiled. "Yes, I was. Although I spent four years away at college."

"Albany State, right?"

"Right. How did you know that?"

"I know everything."

"Oh, yeah?" Diane asked and folded her arms. "What was my minor?"

Matty smiled. "Almost everything."

"That's more like it."

"And after college you, the dutiful citizen that you are, returned to your good old hometown."

"I had no choice, really. My parents needed me."

Matty took a slow drag on his cigarette and stared at Diane. He'd figured as much. The good daughter wasn't about to go live her life until everybody said it was okay. Of course, nobody was going to say that, not as long as they could keep riding such a willing horse. And poor Diane never understood. She was living a catch-22 and didn't even know it. "I take it you still live with your parents?"

"Yes."

"Like it? Hate it?"

"What do you mean?"

"I mean what I said. Do you like living with your folks or do you hate it?"

"I never, I don't know, I never thought about it. I have no choice."

"Come on," Matty said with a frown. "Of course you have

a choice. It's your life. If you don't want to do something you don't have to do it."

Diane smiled. "It's not that simple, Pastor. My mother has so many ailments and my father, well, I think he just likes having me around."

"And what do you like? Do you like being there?"

Diane shook her head. "You don't understand. What else am I supposed to do? Abandon my parents?"

"They aren't children, Diane. I suspect they'll get along just fine without you."

"You don't know my parents."

"Enlighten me. Are they invalids?"

"Well...no."

"Can they walk, talk, use the bathroom on their own?"

Diane smiled. "Yes, Pastor, but—"

"Have they lost their sense of reason?"

"If they ever had it, no."

"That's what I thought," Matty said as he tapped the ash off his cigarette.

"They still need my help, you just don't understand."

"Is this about your parents, Diane, or is it more about you?"

"What?"

"Are you afraid of abandoning your parents, or is it the other way around?"

Diane felt suddenly frightened. What was he talking about? Why would he even say such a thing? "I'm not afraid," she said.

"Sure?"

"Positive."

"A bird stays under the mother's wing so long, she forgets how to fly. Or at least that's everybody's impression."

"Can we talk about something else, please?"

Matty looked at Diane. Afraid my foot, he thought. She was terrified. "So what was it?" he asked her.

Lord knows she was having a hard time following this man's train of thought. "What was what?"

"Your minor."

"Oh! It was...psychology."

Matty smiled, and then he laughed. "And here I am analyzing you."

"Right."

"But every preacher's a closet psychologist. Didn't you know that?"

"I'm beginning to suspect it now."

Matty laughed again. "You're all right, Diane," he said, and then looked at her.

Diane didn't know what to say. She was wholly unaccustomed to compliments. So she smiled. "What about you?"

"What about me?"

"Tell me all there is to know about you."

"Oh, honey, I'm not about to bore you with my life story."

"I doubt if you'd bore me."

He exhaled. "What do you want to know?"

"How old are you?"

"Forty, or very nearly. You?"

"Twenty-nine. Old."

"Watch it now. If you're old then I'm ancient."

Diane laughed. "Good point. So tell me, Mr. Ancient, were you one of those child preachers who heard the voice of the Lord when he was two and went on to travel the world spreading the gospel?"

"In a word? No. I was right around your age before I even gave my life to Christ."

"Really? So you weren't born preaching?"

Matty gave a one-syllable laugh. "Hardly."

"When did you start preaching?"

"A year after my conversion."

"That was quick."

"Yeah. But there it was. I was visiting a Fountain Hope church in Florida at that time."

"Bishop Owens' church."

"Right. I was about to tell him that I believed the Lord was calling me to preach the gospel, but he told me before I could open my mouth. I eventually had my ordination service right there at that same church. Thought I'd get my preaching credentials and finish out my days as just another minister in somebody's crowded pulpit. But Bishop and the board had other ideas."

"They saw the potential in you to shepherd a flock."

"They saw something. Next thing I knew I was the brand-new pastor of the Fountain Hope Baptist Church of Chicago, Illinois. A promotion if ever there was one."

"That's one of our bigger churches, isn't it?"

"The second largest, behind the church in Philadelphia. And I was about as ready for it as a child is ready to oversee a million dollars."

Diane desperately wanted to know what happened, she had heard so many rumors. But she was hesitant to ask.

Matty studied her. He could see her apprehension. "What is it?"

"There are rumors," she said.

Matty paused. The only thing he disliked worse than rumors were the people spreading them. "And what are these rumors, Diane?"

"That you were kicked out of the Chicago church because you…"

Matty braced himself. "Because I what?"

Diane swallowed hard. "Because you were sleeping around."

Matty smiled. Coming from Diane it almost sounded cute. "To put it mildly."

Diane looked at him. "Was it true?"

Matty looked at her. "What do you think?"

"How would I know? I wasn't there."

"Neither were the ones spreading the rumors. I want you to always keep that in mind."

"I do."

"Good."

She paused. "Is it true?"

Matty shook his head angrily. "No, Diane, it isn't true. Not a word of it. I had creative differences with the powers that be in the Chicago church. They thought I was arrogant and brash and they wanted me out of there. And they succeeded beyond their wildest dreams."

Matty could feel the bitterness build back up just thinking about Chicago. He quickly took a slow drag on his cigarette.

Silence tried to come and settle, but Diane wouldn't let it. "What did you do before you went into the ministry? I mean, did you have a profession or..."

"I was an attorney."

"A lawyer? Really?"

"'Fraid so."

"What kind of law did you practice?"

"I did some property law, a little corporate law, then eventually I mainly handled personal-injury lawsuits."

"I see. The whiplash attorney."

Matty smiled. "Right."

"Is that what you did after Chicago?"

"Yep. Moved back to my hometown, Atlanta, and practiced law up until a few weeks before I came here."

"Have you ever been married?" Diane looked away when she said this. She couldn't believe those words had just come out of her mouth. She didn't mean to ask him that. Not yet anyway.

"Yes," he said as if it were no big deal. "Once. She divorced me eleven years ago."

"Just before you got saved?"

"Yep. Upheaval has a way of taking you to your knees."

"I hear that. But I'm sorry it didn't work out."

"Yeah, well, that's life."

"What's her name?"

Matty hesitated. Talking about the past wasn't something he relished at all. "Anastasia."

"Oh. Sophisticated name."

That was Annie, he thought.

"Was she a professional person, too?"

"You can say that. I paid her way through med school. She was completing her residency when we divorced."

"A doctor? Really? My." Diane began to feel that sense of inadequacy again. He was a lawyer and his wife was well on her way to becoming a doctor. A doctor! And Diane could barely handle the library crowd. "You must have been very proud of her."

"She was a good kid."

"So what happened? I mean..." Diane immediately regretted asking such a personal question. And when Matty looked at her with such a stern, almost angry stare, she knew then that he didn't appreciate it either.

"Rumors happened, Diane," he said. "Ugly, vicious, nasty rumors."

Diane waited for more, waited for some clearer explanation, but that was all Matty planned to say about it.

They talked quietly after that, about far less emotional matters, such as his new church-every-Sunday rule and local politics, and by the time he had paid for dinner and escorted Diane back to his car, they both felt a sense of relief. Diane leaned her head back on the headrest and watched him drive. He was the pastor of a not-too-shabby church, and a trained lawyer, but even he had issues. It made her feel better. It made her feel that she wasn't the only one who didn't have it all together. Because digging into the past only conjured up ghosts, and she now knew that they both had too many skeletons in their closets to be conjuring up anything.

It took a jump from Matty's Jaguar in the dark church parking lot but Diane's Buick finally cranked up. To be on the safe side, however, Matty insisted on following her all the way to her home on Clarion Avenue. She waved at him as she pulled up in the narrow driveway, behind her daddy's Sanford-and-Son-looking, beat-up pickup truck, expecting him to wave, too, and keep on driving, but he stopped at the curb. By the time she got out with her keys in hand, he was already out of his car and coming her way. Her heart dropped. Please don't let him ask to meet the parents, she prayed.

"Thanks again, Matty," she said, "for following me home."

"No problem at all."

"Okay. Well. I'll see you Sunday then."

"Why don't you invite me in, Diane? I could use a soda right about now."

Diane's stomach tightened. No, he didn't ask it, she thought. "Oh, I'm so sorry, Matty," she said, "but I don't think we have any sodas to drink."

"Then I'll take whatever you have."

"I'm serious."

"So am I."

Diane exhaled. If he wanted an excuse not to have anything more to do with her, he was about to get it. "Follow me, then," she said, seemingly upbeat, although her insides were churning.

The house was lit up to the max as they stepped up onto the porch, which was the first bad sign because it generally meant that everybody was probably at home. And when she unlocked the front door and entered, and saw, not just her dad sitting in his recliner, or her mother sitting on the couch, but Frank downstairs, too, sprawled like a hungover bum in the chair, she wanted to turn back around and run for cover. But of course it was too late. Her father, who was always the one watching some dreadful baseball game on TV, never missed a thing.

"That you, baby girl?" he yelled.

Diane sighed and immediately began walking farther into the room, with Matty, to her dismay, closely behind her. "Yes, Dad, it's me."

"Where you been?" Malveen asked without looking up from her knitting. "Rehearsal don't be lasting this late. I could have needed something and you out somewhere runnin' the street."

"I want y'all to meet my pastor," Diane said before her mother could get any further, and Matty moved from behind her. All three family members looked up, suddenly very interested in this unexpected guest in their home.

"Yo' pastor?" Malveen asked.

"Yes, Mama. This is Matthew Jolson. He's the new pastor at Fountain Hope."

"He don't look like no pastor to me," Malveen said.

"Don't act like one either," Frank said, his uncombed hair and unshaven face putting years on him since a few days ago, when Matty first laid eyes on him.

"You must be Mrs. Tarver," Matty said cheerfully as he moved from Diane's side and walked over to Malveen, his hand extended as he came. Malveen shook his hand, although her displeasure was obvious. "It's so nice to meet you, ma'am."

"How do," was all Malveen cared to say in reply to Matty.

Matty turned his attention to Willie James, who was staring at him. "Mr. Tarver," Matty said as he again extended his hand.

Willie James shook it, but his eyes were on Matty's suit. "Fine piece of threads you got yourself there," he said, and Diane rolled her eyes.

"Thank you."

"Folks don't dress up no more, you know? Back in my day we wore our fine suits and big hats and you couldn't tell us nothin'. Nowadays everybody pants falling off they rump and hair standing all up like somebody threw them in the electric chair and pulled the switch, and they teeth so loaded with gold, you'd think Fort Knox had a warrant out on them. But at least you look like a man. At least you dress like you got some sense. More than I can say for that Russell Scram—"

"Dad!" Diane said quickly, to forestall any further embarrassment. "Why don't you offer Pastor a seat."

"Why don't you offer it? What's wrong with you?"

"I was going to fix him something to drink."

"Ain't nothing in there but Kool-Aid," Willie James said, to warn her.

"Kool-Aid's fine," Matty said.

"Okay, good. You can just sit anywhere, Matty, and I shall make you a tall glass of Kool-Aid."

"Don't you give it all away either, Diane!" Frank yelled as Diane headed for the kitchen. "I ain't had none yet."

"Yes, Frank," Diane yelled back as she shook her head and disappeared around the dining room and through the arched doorway that led into the kitchen.

Matty sat down on the couch beside Malveen. It was obviously very upsetting to Malveen, as she quickly moved over.

"Them shoes ain't bad either," Willie James said, looking down at Matty's shoes. "Now they look good. How much them shoes cost?"

Matty almost smiled. "I don't think I remember," he said.

"You don't remember?" Willie James practically yelled. "How is somebody gonna forget how much shoes like them cost? I been around, boy. Wal-Mart don't sell them kind of shoes."

"He drive a Jaguar, Dad," Frank said. "Like a drug dealer."

Matty looked at Frank. Frank gladly returned the look.

"Uh-huh," Malveen said. "I knew something wasn't right. I ain't never seen no preacher looking like that."

"You ain't never seen no preacher, Malveen," Willie James

quickly said. "What you talking about? Last time you was in somebody church was 1959. And they kicked you out even then."

"I still know what I know," Malveen said. "And ain't no preacher be looking like that. Reverend Cobb came around here a time or two. You ever seen him with them kind of shoes on?"

"Reverend Cobb wore brogans, woman. That man was old as you. You can't compare him to no young buck like this."

"He don't look all that young to me."

"I'm almost forty," Matty said to Malveen. "Which isn't normally the definition of youth."

Frank laughed. "True that."

"So tell me, Frank," Matty said, "did the deal work out for you?"

"What deal?" Willie James asked, then looked at his only son.

"That ain't none of your business," Frank said to Matty.

"Diane did give you a thousand dollars. It's certainly her business," Matty said.

"A thousand dollars!" Willie James said again in a near yell. "Who in they right mind gon' give you a thousand dollars?"

"Frank told Diane it was a once-in-a-lifetime business deal," Matty said. "Isn't that what it was, Frank? A once-in-a-lifetime deal?"

"Man, whatever," Frank replied in a dismissive tone.

"What kind of deal?" Willie James asked, concerned.

"He was supposed to put a thousand dollars into this car-washing business some buddy of his was getting started," Matty said. "He had Diane convinced it was a great deal."

Willie James shook his head. "The only deal that boy gon' put money in is a drug deal, and Diane should know that by now." Willie James then looked toward the kitchen. "Diane!" he yelled.

"Coming!" Diane yelled back.

"Just using that child," Willie James said to Frank. "That's all you doing. Using your own sister."

"That's between me and Diane," Frank said. "It ain't got nothing to do with you, old man, and it certainly ain't got nothing to do with you, preacher man. So both of y'all better step back and keep your noses up out of my affairs."

Willie James grabbed the cane that sat beside his recliner. "I'll put my fist up your affairs if I want to, boy, don't you talk to me like that. Ain't been nothing but a big fat disappointment since the day you was born—"

"Man," Frank said, rising quickly, "I ain't about to sit up here listening to this tonight."

"Then leave."

And Frank did just that. He headed straight for the front door and left. Matty leaned back. He hadn't meant to confront Frank this way, but it at least confirmed something he had suspected all along, something Diane would never admit to him. Frank had blown Diane's money. And apparently in just two days. If that didn't wake her up, Matty thought, he wasn't sure if anything could.

"I had to make more," Diane said as she entered the living room, a tall glass of strawberry Kool-Aid in her hand. "There wasn't enough left to fill a glass."

"Sorry to trouble you," Matty said as he stood and accepted the drink.

"No trouble at all," Diane said and moved to sit in the chair once occupied by her brother, but Matty grabbed her by the elbow. "Sit here," he said, as he stepped aside and allowed her to sit next to her mother and, consequently, to him.

They were close, shoulder to shoulder, and Diane felt oddly relaxed this way. Her only hope was that her parents somehow would call it an early night and scram. Because if they didn't, she knew more embarrassment was just a word away.

"Did you want me, Dad?" she asked her father. "Or were you just yelling for me to hurry up?"

"You gave that blockheaded brother of yours a thousand dollars?" Willie James asked her.

Diane glanced at Matty, who was sipping from his glass. "I was just helping him out, that's all."

"Diane! You don't give dopeheads money like that, what's wrong with you? And where you get a thousand dollars from anyway?"

"I saved it."

"You gave a bum like that your savings? Money for your retirement? You done lost yo' mind."

"She called it helping a brother out," Matty said. "Which is admirable," he added, then looked at her. "And foolish."

"Big-time foolish," Willie James said. "The whopper of foolish!"

"Can we talk about something else?" Diane asked, understanding now that such a conversation was the reason Frank was no longer in the room.

"At least you got sense, Pastor," Willie James said to Matty. "At least you ain't gonna let folks be taking advantage of Diane, and that's a good thing."

Diane couldn't believe he went there. "Dad, what are you talking about?"

"And you look good, too, you look really upstanding in the community. Which is more than I can say for that whale she was gonna marry."

"Dad!"

Matty, however, was keenly interested. He looked at Willie James. "Marry?"

"Oh, yeah. His name was Russell Scram. And boy, was he a big 'un."

"I really don't think my pastor is interested in Russell, Dad."

"Looked like two Fat Alberts put together," Willie James

continued. "Sometimes three, depending on what he ate that day. I said, 'Diane, baby, I know you want a man, but good grief!'"

Diane quickly flew to her feet, her heart barely catching up. "I'm really tired, Matty," she said. "I think we should call it a night."

Matty hesitated, he couldn't blame her. Willie James was blunt. To the point. Wasn't about to sugarcoat the truth for anybody. Few people, and Diane especially, could deal with that. He placed his glass on the small, magazine-loaded coffee table, and stood to his feet. "Yeah, it has been a long day," he said. "Nice meeting you, Mrs. Tarver. Mr. Tarver."

"Call me Willie James, Reverend, everybody do. And nice meetin' you. You welcome here anytime. Anytime!"

Matty smiled. Diane was his first ally. Now Willie James. Not bad, he thought. "Thank you, sir," he said, and then allowed an anxious Diane to hurry him on out of the house.

Outside, she walked him to his car. She tried to apologize for her folks, saying over and over how they didn't mean any harm, but Matty remained silent. They weren't the ones hiding behind contentment and safety. They weren't the ones deferring their dreams and blaming it on fate. They weren't the ones scared to death of change. Diane's parents, Matty thought, had nothing whatsoever to apologize for. At least they were being true to their natures, even if their behavior was out in left field half the time.

As they stood at his car door, Diane folded her arms to the chill of the night breeze surrounding them. And Matty finally shushed her. "Stop apologizing," he said. "They're all right."

"And Frank. I hope he wasn't too cruel."

"Just don't give him any more money."

"Don't worry."

"I mean it, Diane. Stop being a sucker."

Those words hit her hard. A sucker, was that how he saw

her? Some doormat for everybody to step on? Was that why he was so willing to hang out with her tonight? Because he *pitied* her? She unfolded her arms. "Good night, Pastor," she said and turned to leave.

"What's the matter?"

"Nothing."

"What is it?" he asked as he grabbed her by the arm and stopped her progress, his face unable to conceal his bafflement.

Diane just stood there at the catch of his big hand, unable to do anything but silently fight against the emotion welling up inside her. Matty seemed to sense it, too, or he saw it on her face, she didn't know which, but he pulled her against him and then draped her in his arms. Her face burrowed into his broad shoulder and she let out a sob she had been holding in too long. Every muscle in his body clenched when she cried, and he ran his hand up and down her narrow back to soothe her.

"It's all right, darling," he said, wrapping her tighter in his arms and pulling her closer against him. "It's all right."

"I'm sorry," Diane said, pulling away from him. "I'm just so…"

Matty pulled out his handkerchief and handed it to her. She blew her nose and wiped her eyes. "What is it, Diane?"

"Nothing. That's what's so funny about it. Everything's fine."

Even she didn't believe that, he thought. But he left it alone. "What are you doing Saturday?" he asked her.

"This Saturday?"

Matty smiled. "Yep. This Saturday."

"Well, I don't know. I hadn't thought about it. The library's closed on Saturdays."

"Good. I'm going to get a tour of the area Saturday and I want you with me."

It sounded wonderful, Diane thought. A chance to spend

a whole day with Matty. But was it because she lost herself and cried in front of him that fueled this sudden invitation? Was it *pity* again?

"I enjoy your company, Diane," Matty said, as if sensing her apprehension. "Sometimes it's a good idea not to question everything."

Diane relaxed. He was so right. "In that case," she said, "I'll be glad to show you around Saturday."

Matty smiled. "That's my girl," he said. Then he leaned over and kissed her on the cheek. "We'll get an early start," he said as he opened his car door. "But not too early because I want you good and rested. Around nine?"

"That's good," Diane said with a grand smile of her own. "And thanks again for dinner."

"You're welcome. Good night."

Diane said her good nights and had planned to wave at him as he drove away. But he wouldn't leave until she made her way back inside the safe confines of her house. She waved from the door, and he blew his horn and left. When she did make it inside, she was officially on cloud nine.

"You need to hold on to that one, Diane," her father yelled as she ran up the stairs.

"I aim to," Diane replied, surprising her own self, as the thrill of the night carried her along. He had held her, kissed her, and wanted to spend an entire day with her. Maybe Leah wasn't his type after all. Maybe he was going to call Leah and tell her never mind, he found himself a new guide, one who didn't have to campaign for the job because he chose her himself.

Diane entered her room and fell on her bed. She stared at the high ceiling of the old home unable to stop smiling. "Mrs. Diane Jolson," she said aloud. It had a certain ring to it, she thought.

Chapter 11

Matty tossed a big box of Raisin Bran into his shopping cart and moved swiftly down the aisle. He hated going to the grocery store, but there were certain foods he needed that the fully stocked pantry at his home didn't provide. Like snacks, for instance. And sodas. And cigarettes.

He rounded the corner in search of more fun food, looking at the display of corn chips, when his cart collided with another cart and caused sunglasses to fly onto the floor.

"I am so sorry, Miss," Matty said regrettably, hurrying for the sunglasses, and then handing them back to the woman who stood behind the cart. The woman quickly took the glasses and placed them back on her face. But not so fast that Matty couldn't see that the woman was Samantha Marshall and the dark sunglasses were covering a new bruise, this one the size of a Kennedy fifty-cent piece, over her left eye.

Although she placed the glasses on quickly, Matty just as quickly snatched them back off.

"It's nothing at all, Reverend," Sam said, to minimize

Matty's stare. "I was feeling a little down in the dumps so, I know I said I had stopped, but I took a little sip. Yes, I did. Too many little sips. And the next thing you know I'm washing clothes and decided to let them dry naturally, you know, not in the dryer all the time, but on the clothesline outside. And before I knew it I just ran into the line. That's it. I had too much to drink and I got clumsy. Clumsy me." She said this with a smile.

Matty stared at her with a glare that could cut through steel. Then tossed her sunglasses at her. She caught them and tried to explain more, but he wasn't interested in listening. He left his shopping cart where it stood and hurried out of the store. His face was as grim as his dark mood as he walked swiftly across the parking lot, jumped into his Jaguar, and drove straight to the Jerrison County Courthouse in downtown Floradale, Georgia.

"You can't go in there!" the secretary said urgently as Matty walked into the outer sanctum of Judge Ira Marshall's chambers and headed for the door. He wanted to bust in, he felt like busting in, but he knew he had to think about Sam and those children. He couldn't endanger her any more than she obviously already was. He looked at Ira's secretary. And calmed down.

"I need to see Judge Marshall," he said.

"He's preparing for trial and—"

"I'm his pastor. I need to see him now."

"His...pastor?" The secretary seemed surprised. "Oh. Well, I'll let him know you're here, Reverend."

Matty was hardly dressed in his normal wear of choice. He had on jeans this time, and a sweatshirt, and a pair of Jordan's that made him look more like an aging ballplayer than a reverend. And his manner was hardly congenial either. But how could it be? he thought. He wanted to bash somebody's skull in, not smile and play nice and pretend everything was fine and dandy. That was why he began pacing the room.

What was wrong with the brother? he wondered. Sister Marshall was a beautiful woman: smart, articulate, somebody who'd easily stand by her man. And he was beating on her like she was his physical equal. His personal punching bag. A *thing* rather than his wife.

"You may go in now, Reverend," the secretary announced, causing Matty to drop his angry thoughts, attempt to calm down again, as he walked into Ira's private chambers.

Ira was seated in a wingback chair away from his desk reading over a stack of papers, but he smiled and stood when Matty walked into the room.

"Pastor Jolson!" he said gaily. "How wonderful to see you again." He extended his hand and Matty shook it. But Matty also immediately began an eye contact that he was not about to relinquish. Although Ira was smiling and as friendly as could be, Matty could see, as he had seen Sunday when he first met the man, the terrifying coldness in those eyes of his.

"Have a seat," Ira said. "Please. It's not every day I'm honored with a visit from my pastor."

Matty sat down in the chair across from Ira's. He then crossed his legs and continued staring at him. Ira, however, showed no discernible signs of concern. He wore a black suit and tie and appeared perfectly groomed, Matty thought, even though his wife had looked like Rocky in the grocery store.

"My secretary seemed reluctant to believe you were my pastor. I see why." Ira said this with a smile.

"She caught me on one of my dress-down days."

"Nothing wrong with dressing down."

"But I get that all the time anyway."

"Get what? Disbelief?"

"Prejudgment. People tend to look at me and see what they want to see. And what they see is usually not very flattering."

"I hear you, Reverend. People would believe I'm an undertaker before they believe I'm a criminal court judge. Especially in this neck of the woods."

"All about perception."

"Indeed."

"Like me, for instance," Matty said. "I tell people all the time I'm a control freak. But they don't believe it."

Ira hesitated slightly. But he kept on smiling. "You don't seem like the type, I guess," he said.

"I guess not. But I am. I always have to be in control. I'm domineering, too."

"No."

"Oh, yes. Very domineering. I have that *my way or the highway* syndrome bad. Always have to be in control. Of course, I regulate it now. I must. The key to life is knowing the problem and regulating it, wouldn't you agree, Judge Marshall?"

Ira didn't know what to make of this line of conversation. Where was he going with this? he wondered. And why was he here at all? "It's certainly one key to life. But it's also a rather simple philosophy."

"I knew a man once," Matty said, as if Ira hadn't said a word. "He was a seemingly good, decent man. Yet, like me, he had a dominant personality, too. But unlike me, he never regulated it. Which is fine if that's his choice. Problem was, he liked to beat up on women."

Ira's heart dropped. He continued smiling, continued looking Matty dead in the eye, but his heart was in his shoe. "Is that right?" he said.

"That's right. Loved to beat women. Never a man, mind you, but he could hold his own and then some against any woman. Especially a small, delicate woman." Matty leaned forward, his legs uncrossed, his elbows resting on his thighs. "But you know what I did?"

Ira didn't respond.

"You know what I did, Judge?"

Ira sighed in frustration. "No, Reverend, what did you do?"

"Every time he beat the crap out of a woman, I beat the crap out of him." Matty said this and continued staring at Ira, continued sizing him up and cutting him down to size. And Ira could barely breathe.

Matty stood up, to Ira's relief. "I won't keep you, Judge."

Ira stood up, too, and his smile returned. "I wish I had more time, but I'm afraid I don't."

"I saw your wife today."

Ira hesitated. "Did you?"

"Yes. At the grocery store. She had a bad bruise on her face. She tried to conceal it, of course, but there's nothing that doesn't eventually come to light."

Ira smiled. "My wife tends to have little accidents. She has a problem, you see."

"Yes," Matty said. "I'm looking at it."

"Excuse me?"

"She declares you're a kind, loving husband to her. The greatest man ever created. And she loves you dearly. But the problem is, Judge, I'm nobody's fool. I know a battered woman when I see one."

"You're out of line, Pastor."

"Am I?"

"Way out. My wife, as everybody knows, has a drinking problem. I am doing all I can to help her. But if you continue to tread on territory you know nothing about I'll have no choice but to take some drastic action. Including legal action. You're an attorney, you know what the remedies are. So I would strongly suggest that you take my wife at her word and reconsider your erroneous position."

There was a pause, as Matty continued staring at Ira.

"And besides," Ira added, "I'm sure the board of bishops would not take too kindly to their new pastor scandalizing the good name of one of their most faithful, not to mention charitable, members. In fact, I'm positive they wouldn't."

Matty nodded. A not-so-veiled threat, as if Matty could

be threatened. He nevertheless began walking toward the door. But then, as if he were in a scene right out of *Columbo*, he quickly turned back around. "You know what else about me, Judge, and I'll let you get back to your work after this?"

Matty waited for a response from Ira. Ira sighed and shook his head.

"What else about you, Reverend?"

"I'm also very badly underestimated. You ever had that problem?"

The rage began to build in Ira, but he contained it. "No."

"People say I'm a reverend, a pastor no less. I wouldn't get in the gutter the way they would." Matty paused. "Or would I?" he asked. Then he smiled and began nodding his head. "You'd be surprised, Judge Marshall. Really surprised. Shocked, even."

Matty continued staring at Ira, to make it absolutely clear by eye contact alone that Ira's game was up, and then he left the office.

At first Ira stood there in a fog of bewilderment, as if the idea that Jolson knew his deepest secret was distressing him greatly. Then he took a stack of papers and threw them violently against the wall.

Diane didn't see him drive up, nor did she see him walk into the library. She was busy in one of the aisles, showing two school-age girls where the best information on pop stars could be found. Matty saw her, however, after he entered; her crumpled, light green skirt hard to ignore amongst the rows and rows of drab books. She was near the back of the library talking like a teacher to two young ladies, and Matty stood momentarily at the head of the aisle watching her. She loved her job, it seemed to him, and she seemed passionate about it, and when the two girls smiled or nodded or gave any kind of indication that they understood what she was telling them, she beamed.

By the time Diane felt confident that the girls would forever understand the concept of library browsing, and made it back to the checkout counter, Matty was already seated on the stool behind it.

She couldn't believe it when she saw him, and she was unable to contain her grandest smile. She knew she'd see him Saturday, and she hadn't stopped thinking about spending an entire day with him, but the idea that he would drop by today as if he just had to see her before then, thrilled her. He looked so casual behind the counter, she thought, in his jeans and sweatshirt, he looked younger than a man pushing forty, and even more fit. It made her proud to know that he was interested in her. But it also stunned her. This man, this epitome of male perfection, was interested in her? She smiled again. Of course he was interested. Why else would he be here? she decided.

"Well, hello there, Matty," she said cheerfully, careful to keep their relationship as personal as he seemed to want it to be.

"Afternoon," Matty said in that bored voice he sometimes displayed. He was twirling around in her chair and flipping through a magazine, his eyes not even looking up at her, until he tossed the magazine on the counter. And when he did look her way, a shiver went through her entire body. He never just looked at her, it seemed to Diane, but his dark gray eyes always seemed too aware, too alert to her every mood, as if he were looking through her, beyond her, *into* her.

He folded his arms, his big, muscular arms, Diane noted. "How are you, kiddo?" he asked her.

Diane smiled. Perfect when you're around, she wanted to say. "I'm well," she said instead.

She did look better, Matty thought as he eyed her. She may have even been gaining a few inches, although you couldn't really tell it for those oversized, easy-to-wrinkle rayon skirt suits she loved to wear. "You look pretty today," he said.

"I do?" Diane said, caught off guard. "I mean, thank you."

"You're welcome. Whatever you're doing, keep it up."

Diane smiled. "I'm sleeping better," she said.

"Are you?"

"Oh, yes. Much. Last night I slept like a baby."

Matty stared at her as if he didn't like where the conversation was leading, and then he looked away. Diane could have kicked herself. Why did she have to get so personal with the man? He didn't need to know what kind of night she spent in bed. He obviously didn't even like to go there with a female, he was a *reverend* after all. He probably thought she was the biggest flirt around. She started to tell him to pardon her manners, she didn't mean to sound so forward, but she decided against it. She hadn't exactly said anything wrong or untruthful, she noted. Just commented on the kind of night she had. It was his problem if he couldn't handle that.

She lifted up the side bar and stepped behind the counter where Matty sat. He watched her as she stood inches away from him stacking the pile of books that covered the counter. He looked down at her hair that hung like a long, thick plait of silk, at her thin back, her narrow waist, her firm backside. He quickly looked away.

Silence filled the space between them, as neither seemed interested in carrying the conversation further. Diane wanted to say something desperately; she just couldn't think of anything to say. Matty was still thinking about his encounter with Ira Marshall.

"So," Diane said as she turned toward him, afraid that the silence could be some indication of his growing disinterest with her, "what brings you to the south side today?"

"Many reasons and no reason."

"Oh, that's real clear."

Matty gave a slight, half-second smile. "You know Sister Marshall, don't you?"

"Sam? Sure. She's my best friend."

"And her husband?"

"I know him, of course, but not on any great personal level or anything. Why?"

"What kind of marriage would you say they have?"

Marriage, Diane thought. And her heart began to leap. Was this really about the Marshalls, or her and Matty, she wondered in a way even she took as fanciful. The man was almost forty after all. Maybe he was ready to settle down and felt a sense of urgency about it. Maybe so urgent that he was willing to grab the first thing that came along. And she was it. And she would take it, too. "They have a wonderful marriage. Well, let me preface that. At least that was what I used to think."

Her response piqued Matty's curiosity. "But you don't anymore?"

"I do but, well, after Sam's latest accident where she fell and hit her head, I don't know if you know about that."

"I know about it."

"After that night a friend of mine started making comments about how she thought it might not have been an accident."

"What did she think it might have been?"

Diane smiled. "This is so crazy, I mean really farfetched. And you have to know this friend I'm talking about to understand that she's a conspiracy theorist at heart. I mean, sometimes the girl is so far out there."

"Diane," Matty said with some degree of impatience, "answer my question. What did she think might have happened?"

Diane hesitated. He could be almost harsh at times, she thought. She didn't know if she liked *that* side of him. "She believes Judge Marshall might have done it."

"Beat his wife?"

"Yes. It's crazy. Sam herself denies it. She's like, 'there's no way in this world Ira would ever beat on me.'"

"Does this friend have any proof?"

"Of course not. Just running off at the mouth the way she always does." Diane wanted desperately for Matty to ask the friend's name, so that she could say Leah Littleton proudly and he could see that she wasn't the Miss Perfect she undoubtedly put herself out to be. But he wasn't interested in that. He seemed too deep in thought, as if he were planning and strategizing and suddenly miles away from Diane.

"But it's a good marriage," Diane said with some confidence. "It always has been, even though the Judge is a lot older than Sam."

"She blamed it on the booze," Matty said almost absently.

"She...what?"

"An alcoholic never blames it on the booze. But she did. Like it was rehearsed. And she had no favorite brand." He looked at Diane. "Does Sister Marshall have a lot of these falling accidents like the one she had that night, Diane?"

"No. I mean, how much is a lot? I've never fallen and had to go to the emergency room. Sam's been there, what, three or four times."

"In the last few years?"

Diane thought about it. "In the last couple of years, yeah, I think that's right. Never before. But that's probably because she..."

Matty looked at Diane. "She started drinking."

"Yes."

"Have you ever seen her drink, Diane?"

"I've never seen her drunk, but from my readings on the subject alcoholics can be really good about covering their tracks."

"I didn't ask you if you ever saw her drunk. I asked if you ever saw her drink."

Again Diane didn't like his tone. "No," she said. "I've never seen her touch the stuff."

Matty nodded, as if his suspicions were confirmed. He stood up.

"You're leaving?" Diane asked in a tone even she didn't like. It had a desperate ring to it, she felt.

"Afraid so," Matty said, as if her desperation wasn't lost on him either. "I've got a lot to do today. But listen, I want you to stay away from Ira Marshall for a while."

Diane smiled, astonished that he would say such a thing. "Why? He would never harm me."

"Just do it, Diane."

"But why?"

"Because I said so! Don't argue with me."

Argue with him? She couldn't believe he would call asking why arguing. She started to take umbrage with his unnecessary bluntness. She wasn't some child, after all, that he could just waltz in and push around like this. But she wasn't about to mess up her budding relationship over a little bluntness. "Okay," she said. "I'll stay away from the Marshalls."

"Don't stay away from Sister Marshall, that's not what I'm telling you to do. Just keep away from the Judge. In fact, I want you to talk to Sister Marshall more, try to get her to open up to you."

"What are you saying, Matty? You believe it, too? You believe Ira's beating on Sam?"

"I believe she's in more pain than she's letting on. Talk to her about it. But don't be too tough on her. She'll think she's looking out for her family. And she'll probably never believe otherwise."

Diane nodded, and felt horrible. She was so into her own feelings, her own longing for Matty, that she hadn't even taken his concerns about Sam seriously. He wasn't blunt with her because of some character flaw, he was trying to impress upon her the gravity of Sam's situation. Because if it were true, if Judge Marshall was indeed beating on his wife, it would be devastating. And the children, Lord. They were probably witnessing it, too. No wonder Junior was always so hostile. Maybe they should call the authorities?

"And tell them what?" Matty said as quickly as Diane asked it.

"They could at least talk to the doctor and see if he suspected spousal abuse."

"I already talked with the doctor. He says no. He believes Sam fell and hit her head. Period."

"Then why would you still believe it's not true?"

"Ira Marshall has a presumption of deity around here, Diane. Which is the problem. You just keep an eye on your friend, okay? Let me handle the rest."

"Okay," Diane said, although she still found it all hard to believe.

Matty looked at her. He was too hard on her and he knew it. "You okay?" he asked her.

"I guess," Diane said, unable to hide her concern.

Matty stared at her momentarily, as if he suddenly saw something, and then he walked closer to her and placed his hands on her shoulders. His closeness and touch made Diane feel as though her legs were going to wobble and she would just drop where she stood, but they rallied and didn't fail her. She was even able to stand erect and look him in the eye. In his gorgeous, dark gray eyes. He smiled, as if he could sense her surrender.

He began rubbing her shoulders, as if he were trying to decide if he should make his next move, then he looked into her eyes. She was lovely, he thought, and so very sweet. Far too sweet for a man like him. "How's Willie James?" he finally asked when it appeared as if Diane would crumble if he didn't do or say something.

She smiled. Her father did have a way of growing on people. Like a mole, according to her mother. "He's doing all right," she said. "Watching his baseball and doing just fine."

"Glad to hear it. He's a good man."

"That's not normally the way he's described, but thanks."

Matty nodded. His look turned serious once again, as he moved even closer and gripped her shoulders tighter. Diane could feel his warm, sweet breath, smell his cologne, hear his suddenly deeper breathing, until his face was in her face and, after staring deep into her eyes, his mouth covered hers in a short, but heart-stopping, kiss. She thought she would die right then and there, as his lips touched hers, and when he finally stopped kissing her and looked once again into her eyes, with a now drowsy, hungry look, her breath caught. She wanted to step back, for balance, but he kept her close. And he just stood there, breathing heavier and heavier, his forehead eventually resting against hers, and then he stepped back.

"I'll see you tomorrow," he said in a voice huskily soft.

"I'm looking forward to it," she said with a great smile, barely able to contain her sense of delirium.

He started to walk away, but he turned back toward her. "And Diane," he said, and she immediately looked his way.

"Yes?" she said, virtually out of breath.

He leaned over and whispered in her ear, as if he were about to tell her a profound secret only they could share. "Wear pants," he said. "And not baggy ones, either."

He looked at her again, as if she should know exactly why he was making such an odd request, and then he walked away.

Diane, however, was clueless. Maybe they were going to do some hiking or a lot of walking when she showed him around, and he wanted her to be prepared. Maybe he just liked seeing women in pants, which, she conceded, would be a strange thing for a preacher to like. Or maybe, just maybe, she thought, he just wanted her to be comfortable tomorrow. Relaxed.

Whatever the reason, however, Diane aimed to obey. She even started looking at the clock on the wall, hoping for six o'clock to hurry up and come. Then she'd close up the library and drive over to one of those shops in Bainbridge, and purchase such a pair of pants. And not just any pants. Tight-fitting, one size too small, unlike any Diane had ever worn, but just the kind Matty wanted her to wear.

Friday night dinner at the Marshalls and you could hear a pin drop. The boys ate everything on their plates, as they knew they had to do when their father was around, and Sam was careful to continually ask Ira if he had everything he needed before he had to complain that he didn't. A typical night around the table.

What wasn't typical about it, Sam thought, was Ira's mood. He didn't laugh or smile or even talk, but he appeared upbeat, too upbeat, as if everything were going his way. She didn't quite know how to take this new Ira, and she didn't try to learn either. His mood could turn dark and foreboding at any second, and she was experienced enough to know it. So she did as she normally did and let it all play out.

And it was all good for most of the evening. After dinner she was able to put away the dishes and tidy up the dining area and yell at Ira, Jr., and Alan only a handful of times, and she and the boys even felt relaxed enough to sing songs while she helped prepare their bath. Junior wasn't very excited about singing, however, calling it sissy stuff, but little Alan was having a ball. And Junior wasn't picking on his brother or rejecting the merriment and that, in and of itself, Sam thought, was a triumph.

But then she heard Ira's calm voice behind her.

"Come here, Samantha," he said.

Her heart dropped. Alan, who had been singing loudest of all, stopped suddenly and looked at his mother, the terror on his face breaking her heart.

"It's all right," she said to him with a smile as she stood

up. She instructed Junior to bathe his brother's back, and then she hurried to the bedroom where Ira had gone.

He was sitting on the bed, looking glum now, the upbeat mood she was earlier suspicious of no longer in sight.

"Close the door," he said.

Sam nervously closed it. "What's the matter, baby?" she asked him.

He looked at her. "Pastor Jolson, that's what."

Sam leaned against the door. Her black eye was still recovering from their last "conversation," when he didn't like the food she had cooked, and she wondered if she should make a run for it this time. Maybe just lock herself and the boys in the bathroom until he calmed back down. "What about Pastor?" she asked.

"As if you don't know," he said. Then he stood up quickly and hurried toward her. Her breath caught. He slung her away from the door and pulled her until he could fling her onto the bed.

"Ira, what's wrong?" she asked quickly, frightfully, as she bounced from the force of her landing.

He got on the bed over her, straddling her, his large body towering over her. "What did you tell him?" he asked her, still deceptively calm, still so certain of his beliefs that it sickened Sam.

"Nothing," she said, so tired of this ritual that she didn't know what to do.

"What did you tell him, Samantha?" he asked again, this time more demandingly.

"Nothing, Ira! I didn't tell him anything."

"But you talked to him?"

"No!"

"Don't you lie to me!" he said and lifted his hand to slap her. But he stopped midway. It was the voice. The voice of Reverend Jolson. *But you know what I did? Every time he beat the crap out of a woman, I beat the crap out of him.* Over and over it echoed in Ira's head, making him dizzy, flustered. *I wouldn't get in the gutter the way they would. Or would I?* It was like a mantra, and one he couldn't shake. *You'd be surprised, Judge Marshall. Really surprised. Shocked, even.*

Ira withdrew his hand.

He stared at Sam, who was terrified of him, and then stood up. "Keep talking," he said to her. "Keep running and telling the news. You'll be the one ruined, not me. You'll be the one alone in this world, Samantha, I promise you that. So you keep right on doing what you're doing, okay? Keep talking."

Ira said this with every intention of threatening her. Then he left the room, headed down the stairs, and slammed the door shut to his study. He sat behind his desk and pulled a green book from the desk drawer. He leaned back and closed his eyes after dialing a phone number. When the line picked up, he opened his eyes. "It's Ira Marshall," he said.

There was a pause. "Hello, Judge Marshall."

"I need you to check somebody out for me."

"I'm booked solid, man, I couldn't help my own grand-mama out right now."

"Make room, Benny. This is vital."

Benny sighed. He was still paying back Marshall for reducing his sentence from five years to probation during his drug bust conviction last year and the old judge never failed to take full advantage of that fact every time he needed some dirty work done. He had long wanted to tell him to take a hike, he'd take his chances in prison, but he knew not to tempt Ira Marshall. "I can't make no promises on when I can get to it, Judge."

"Just so long you get it done."

"All right. Let me get a pen." After a pause, the voice returned. "Shoot."

"The name's Jolson. Matthew Jolson. He spent some time in Chicago and he hails from Atlanta. He's currently the pastor of the Fountain Hope Baptist Church here in Floradale."

"Now hold up, Judge. I don't be messing up no man of God."

"This guy's no man of God. He's too dangerous. Too streetwise. A slick brother like that in a backwater town like this tells me something's wrong. That's why I'm certain there's something on him, and I'll bet you it's big. I want all the dirt you can turn up."

"Dirt on a preacher of the gospel. Oh, well. It's your soul."

"Got that right."

"I'll see what I can see."

"And Benny, don't mail it to me. Especially if it's bad. Mail it directly to the Fountain Hope Baptist Church. And I don't care how long it takes either. When you get it, mail it. I want them to see it for themselves."

"Fountain Hope. Will do. So you think the dude's a fake?"

"Of course he's a fake. If this guy's legit then I'll be a monkey's uncle. I want this one bad. I need you to get the kind of filth on that so-called preacher that would turn *your* stomach, that's the kind of dirt I'm talking about. Understand?"

There was a pause. "Understood," Benny said.

Chapter 12

Diane waited on the front porch of her parents' home for that now familiar blue Jaguar to appear. She felt like a kid waiting for Christmas morning as anticipation rose deep within her with every passing moment. She also felt extremely blessed that her family, late sleepers every one, had not risen to see her in this unusual condition.

The "condition," at least that was the best way Diane could describe it, wasn't only the fact that she was excited to a point of giddiness, but also that she was dressed in a manner and style that no one had ever seen on her. She wouldn't hear the end of it from her mother, or father for that matter, if they could see her now. She wore a white, tunic-style cotton blouse that was so snug it fit her like a glove, and a pair of brand-new stonewashed jeans she could barely slip into this morning. She had to lay on the bed and pull and tug breathlessly before they finally stretched enough to let her in. And to top it all off she had on tennis shoes, for the first time in her life, and although they weren't any fancy name brand, but were of the Wal-Mart variety, Diane couldn't stop staring at them and marveling how cute and comfortable they were on her feet. She even had plans for her hair, to ruffle it up and let it drop in thick waves down her back, showing a totally different side of herself, but, as her nephew loved to say, she chickened out. Her wardrobe was enough of a shocker for one day, she felt. So she gathered up all of her thick hair and placed it in a ponytail, held in place by a beautiful pin, and smiled at herself in the mirror for the first time in a long time, studying what she saw and declaring that it was good.

She felt young again, she looked young again, and by the time Matty's Jaguar turned onto Clarion Avenue and began lumbering toward her old house, the youthful exuberance that rolled like a river all over every inch of her caused her to jump from her seat.

Unbeknownst to Diane, however, Leah Littleton sat in the front seat of Matty's car. Leah was preoccupied, too, as she tried hard to figure out why they would be going this way. Clarion Avenue wasn't anywhere near where she'd planned to take Matty, and the closer they began to get to Diane's house—the only member of Fountain Hope, to Leah's knowledge, who lived on this street—the more concerned she became. She had taken it upon herself to drive over to Matty's house earlier that morning, before he could come and pick her up, too excited about the day they would share together to wait. She had no idea, however, that he had planned to share that day with Diane Tarver, too.

"Where are we going?" she finally asked him as his car began to slow down.

Matty, however, didn't answer, his entire attention seemingly riveted on the house they were approaching. Leah then decided to be more direct. "Matty, I don't mean to pry," she said, "but why are we stopping at Diane Tarver's house?"

Matty's Jaguar came to a stop at the curb and he finally

looked away from the house and at his passenger. Leah looked deceptively radiant to him today, as she wore with great style a pair of white capri pants and a sleeveless pink blouse, her hair a short, curly bob around her well-formed head, her big, expressive eyes hidden from sight behind a pair of ocean-blue designer sunglasses. She was a woman who reminded him so much of his ex-wife. For she, too, was somebody who knew what she wanted and went after it, no matter what the cost. A strong, determined woman. A dangerous woman, he thought. "I invited her to come along, too," he said.

"Really?" Leah said with a smile, as if it were a happy surprise, although she couldn't believe her ears. She was going to kill Diane Tarver when she got her alone. Matty Jolson was her territory, she thought, and she certainly didn't need a chaperone. And for Diane of all people to try and worm her way into this, to try and compete with her, defied logic.

But from the looks of Matty, who was now leaning over his steering wheel staring at Diane as she walked down the steps and headed for his car, it wasn't all that clear just who had wormed into what. Matty, who wore dark shades over his beautiful eyes, still behaved as if he were starstruck, Leah thought, as he seemed unable to take his eyes off Diane. He, in fact, appeared so transfixed by what he was seeing that Leah looked away from him and at Diane, too. And even she was stunned. Diane, in jeans? And they weren't just tight, they were skintight, revealing a perfect, petite body Leah would die to have, and one she had no idea Diane possessed. All of those big clothes she loved to wear, all of those oversized pilgrim suits, were hiding *that* body? Leah couldn't believe it. How could Diane Tarver look this good? Almost as good as her. And jealousy came rushing like a mighty wind, blowing all over Leah's best-laid plans.

Matty was dressed casually, too, in a dark green polo shirt tucked neatly inside a pair of freshly starched khakis, his attire, as Leah herself had noted when she first saw him, doing nothing to conceal his muscular arms and muscled thighs. Add to the mix those sunglasses that covered his eyes and he had what Leah concluded was the unmistakable look of a successful, well-built athlete rather than some meek and mild country pastor.

He got out of his car swiftly, too swiftly if you asked Leah, as he seemed unable to stop staring at Diane. She looked so differently to Matty, so vivacious, that he didn't know how to react. Gone was that button-down, hands-off, matronly look. Now she looked happy and relaxed, comfortable in her own skin, a woman who could hold her own against the best of any female around. She also looked, he found himself unable to deny, sexy. Very sexy. Sexy beyond his wildest imagination. The legs, the thighs, the narrow waist, the breasts, everything about her was as right on as it could possibly get. He should have looked away. He needed to just look away. But he couldn't.

And when she arrived at his side, smelling as if she'd just stepped out of a bath, feelings began to ripple through his body that he knew he had to keep under control. He even began praying for strength, for willpower from on high, because this little librarian was absolutely turning him on when he had been determined to stay turned off. And consecrated. And free of all the drama that could distract him from his purpose. Diane, he had thought, was safe, because she wasn't a flirt and therefore wouldn't be throwing herself at him like many did. But now, on this warm Saturday morning, just seeing her made it clear that safe wasn't what she was at all; that anybody on the face of this earth would be a safer choice of guide for him than Diane Tarver.

"Good morning!" she said to Matty with a great smile, a beaming, infectious smile he was beginning to love.

But his feelings weren't evident to her. He seemed angry,

repulsed even, as if he were seeing something he didn't like at all. Her heart sank.

"Good morning," he said grimly, the ache in his body a soothing but harsh reminder that he couldn't get carried away. He was just tired and lonely, he decided, burdened by the weight of too much responsibility, and that was why he was having all of these crazy feelings for Diane. Besides, it was his fault anyway. If he hadn't told her to wear pants that weren't too big for her, then she would have put on one of those wrinkly rayon suits of hers and be done with it. But nooo. He had suggested she wear pants, and pants that fit, and that was exactly what she wore. Only they didn't just fit, they appeared as if they'd been stitched on, and made especially for his pleasure, and, he noted with some trepidation, any other man's, too.

He opened the back passenger door, still staring at her with that harsh, stern look of his, a look that made her smile dry up like a leaf on a withered vine as she got into his car. And talk about disappointment. He didn't even return her smile. He didn't even comment on this bold new look she had gone to so much trouble to pull together for him. And he spoke to her as if he were angry with her, as if he were embarrassed that she would dress this *worldly* when it was exactly, at least in her interpretation, how he wanted her to dress. But to top it off, as if insult needed to be added to her injury, good old Leah was in the car, sitting in the front seat as if Diane, not she, was the third wheel. Diane wanted to forget this drama and run back into the safety of her own home.

And she very well might have if Matty hadn't leaned over and began buckling her seat belt, as if she were some invalid who couldn't even be trusted to do something as simple as that, as if he knew she was seconds away from getting away from him. He kept staring those sunglass-covered eyes at her as he fumbled with the buckle, his smell a combination of tobacco and cologne that was too close for her to ignore. And *he* was too close to ignore. And just having him near almost made her stop worrying and relax. This was Matty, she thought. He didn't dislike her. Just the opposite. He sometimes seemed outright infatuated with her. Maybe he was grim because he was just that way in the mornings. Maybe it had nothing to do with her. Besides, it was his idea that she come along in the first place. Why would he invite her along and then be upset that she came?

But when his big body pressed against hers—unnecessarily, she felt—and he glanced at Leah to make sure she was not looking before he leaned over and gave Diane a kiss on her lips, a kiss that was so sudden and so quick that it felt *wrong,* her disappointment rolled into anger. She wanted to lash out, to ask him just what kind of hussy he thought she was, but before she could say a word he closed the door, walked around, and got back into the driver's seat. She felt like a fool. She felt as if she were some easy old maid he could play around with anytime he wished while he wined and dined beauty queens like Leah. Leah was his woman, obviously, she was the one sitting beside him. Did he kiss Leah this morning, too? she wondered. Did he press against her? Did he do more than that?! And here she was thinking he was going to tell Leah to take a hike, that his choice, Diane, would be his guide. Just the idea of such naivete made Diane shake her head. They didn't come any dumber than her, she thought.

Leah turned around and looked at Diane only after Matty had gotten back into the car, as if she wanted him to see how big she could be about such matters. "Hello, Diane," she said with a big smile. "You're looking tight this morning." Leah laughed when she said this. Diane couldn't even manage a smile. Matty looked in the rearview mirror at her.

"Ah, come on, girl," Leah said. "I'm just playing. You know you ain't never worn no pants that tight before in your life! But them jeans look good on you, girl, yes, they do. Gotta give you your props. You gonna make a few hoochies look religious when you step out in them jeans!"

Diane had to smile, not because of anything Leah was saying, but because of the absurdity of this situation. Her earlier excitement seemed light-years away now. Reality had set in. And the reality was harsh, and painful, and yet another reminder of why Diane had played it safe all these years. She didn't need this. She could have stayed home and washed her hair, then driven her mother to the grocery store and flea market, and then driven over to the church to help with the fish fry and car wash. And tonight, instead of feeling awful about the events of the day and how naive she was to even think that somebody like Matty Jolson could want her, she'd read a good book, watch the news and go to bed. But now she was stuck. Buckled in, Matty himself saw to that, as if it were his pleasure to keep her in misery.

"Where to, Diane?" he asked her as he cranked up, the smooth sound of his expensive car engine drowning out Diane's thoughts and making her suddenly aware of his question. Even Leah seemed surprised that he would want Diane's suggestions first, since any fool could see she knew next to nothing about culture.

"Where to?" Diane asked, confused.

"Yes," Matty said, looking at her through his rearview mirror. "You're my tour guide. Guide me." His heart pounded when he said this. He needed her to be stronger than him. Her, little Diane, to guide him in more ways than she'd ever know.

Diane, however, didn't get the nuance. She was too busy trying to remember the great plans she had made for their day before everything went wrong. And when Leah looked back at her, smiling as if she knew Diane had no clue, the uneasiness returned. She wanted them to just leave her alone, to forget she was even there. But since that seemed unlikely, she exhaled.

"I thought showing you the old houses on Baker Street would be nice," she said.

"Oh, Diane, come on," Leah said incredulously. "What's there to show?"

"It's Floradale's historic district, Leah."

"It's a street of old houses, Diane! Houses that ain't no different than your house, my house, and his house. White folks live in those particular homes so the city makes it the historic district. Please."

That wasn't it at all, and Diane knew it wasn't. Those homes were historic because they were the oldest in the city, not because of the owners' skin tone. But she didn't say a word. He should have let Leah pick the place anyway.

Matty, however, placed his Jaguar in drive and began to pull off from the curb. "Baker Street it is," he said.

The drive to Baker Street was quiet for Diane, with Leah and Matty doing all of the talking. Leah was even pointing out where Matty should turn to get to their destination, leaving Diane with absolutely nothing to do. Leah seemed so sure of herself when it came to Matty, and so relaxed around him, that even Diane could see a future for them. And when they arrived on Baker Street and it became clear that Leah was right, that there really wasn't anything to do but drive by the big old houses, Diane acquiesced. She had planned to point out the architectural designs and the history of the area, hoped to bowl Matty over with her intellect, but now she wasn't about to even try. Matty was her pastor and nothing more than that. Just a nice man who treated everybody as if they were somebody special to him. Diane knew now that she had misread his intentions. She was a librarian after all. Maybe she was searching for hidden meanings where there were none to be found. And that was why, when Matty asked her this time where she wanted them to go next, as if it didn't bother him at all that her first suggestion sucked, she didn't even pretend to have a clue.

"Where do you think would be a good next place, Leah?" she asked as she leaned slightly forward in her seat.

Leah beamed. "Out of Floradale first of all," Leah said. "We'll start in Bainbridge. At least they have a mall and a carnival's going on over there and they have real stuff to do. Ain't nothing here in Floradale but old houses and old folks. Let's go, Matty!"

Matty looked, once again, at Diane through his rearview. It didn't take a genius to see that she was disappointed with the day, a day, knowing Diane, she had planned in detail, down to the food they'd eat. But he drove on anyway, thanking God that Leah was there, the kind of aggressive woman he needed right now to help keep his mind—and eyes—off of Diane.

The balance of the day had Leah written all over it. They did "fun" things, or at least the kind of activities that most people would consider enjoyable. For Diane, however, it wasn't so much enjoyment as tolerance. She tolerated the day. She allowed herself to remember that this man was her pastor, not some potential husband slipping from her grasp, and that outlook gave her the courage to at least pretend to be upbeat.

They arrived in Bainbridge as if they were tourists in some grand foreign land. They took strolls around Lake Seminole and through Willis Park, and casually walked along the busy town square. Leah kept her arm wrapped around Matty's, as if he were hers and hers alone. Diane purposely walked slightly behind the couple, disappointed that Matty wasn't protesting Leah's obvious flirtations. He'd glance back at Diane when Leah would say something clearly over the top, like when she called him a *sweetie pie,* but for the most part he didn't seem to mind.

He also didn't seem to mind that he pretty much ignored Diane until later that day, when they were at the Bainbridge Mall and he declared that their shopping trip would be on him. Leah was beside herself with excitement, as she quickly left Matty's side and hurried into a chic clothing store a few doors away from where they stood. Matty even went into a men's store to glance around. When he came back out with a bag that seemed to contain a pair of shoes, Diane was sitting on a bench in the mall as if she'd been there the entire time.

Matty was stuffing his thick wallet back into his pants pocket when he spotted her. His chest squeezed when he saw her, as she sat there looking as if she were some lost puppy nobody wanted to claim, when she was easily the pick of the litter. He sighed in frustration. He was willing to buy her anything in the mall, anything, really, her heart desired, but was she, like Leah, breaking down doors to take him up on his offer? Of course not. He would have to be the last man standing before she'd accept a dime from him.

He had been avoiding her all day, and successfully, he thought, but now she was unavoidable. Anger more than anything else forced him to walk over to the bench and sit beside her.

"What did you buy?" he asked, knowing full well the answer.

"Nothing," she replied. "I don't need anything."

"You don't?"

She hesitated. He didn't exactly sound as if he believed her. "No."

"Could have fooled me."

She looked at him. With his shades now removed and sitting on the top tip of his shirt, his eyes were dark and glowering, as if he were highly upset with her. "What's that supposed to mean?"

"Librarians get a bad rap, you know that?" Matty said.

"Many think they're nothing more than a group of four-eyed geeks who love books more than people; who don't take care of themselves because they don't care. And you're doing everything in your power to make sure the perception holds."

Diane's anger flared, and before she knew it, she was lashing back. "Well, excuse me, Pastor Jolson, if I don't live up to your image of some exotic librarian who can lift up her skirt and dance a jig for you on the tabletop! Yes, I'm a librarian. I'm sorry if you're disappointed that I'm not more than that, but that sounds like your personal problem to me. I'm a quiet, hardworking, unglamorous librarian. And contrary to what you might think, I like me just the way I am!"

Matty almost did a double take. Where did that come from? he thought. Such forcefulness, such wonderful sense of purpose, of who she was, of high self-esteem.

If only it were true.

"Even you don't believe that, Diane," he said.

Diane looked at him. What was it? Stomp on Diane day? "Even I don't believe what?" she asked him.

Matty leaned back and crossed his legs. He exhaled and began looking around, at the people in the mall, at the shoes on his feet. He even took one arm and placed it over the back of Diane's bench, as if hugging her without touching her. He did everything except answer her.

"Pastor, could you please answer my question?"

Matty finally looked her way. At her thighs first, and then into her eyes. "You're confusing contentment with happiness," he said.

Diane paused. "What do you mean?"

"You don't like the way you are. You've resigned yourself to being that way. I'd go as far as saying you hate being that way. But you're just Diane Tarver, right? And Diane Tarver doesn't deserve any good turns."

Diane's heart dropped. Tears wanted to well up in her eyes

but she straightened her back and refused to let them. "That's ridiculous," she said weakly, almost proving by her tone that it wasn't.

"If you say so."

"I know so. Why wouldn't I feel that I deserve to have good things happen to me?"

Matty placed his hand on her shoulder, now hugging her by touching her. "It's all in the treatment, Diane," he said, sorry to have to go there with her, but also knowing that he wasn't about to lie to her.

"The treatment?"

"You've been treated as if you don't matter, as if your life's purpose is to serve others, not yourself, and now you believe it. You believe the treatment. You believe that everybody's got a right to happiness except Diane. Your family, your library aide, even your friends have always dismissed your happiness, your needs, your feelings, because it's not about you. It's about them and what they need and want and feel. You were born to serve their needs. And that's how they treat you. As their servant. It's all in the treatment. Because action, as I'm sure you know, speaks a whole lot louder than people saying that it's not so, when it obviously is."

Diane looked away from Matty. His words always stung her for some reason, as if they were too true to be heard. He didn't know her that well, but he sounded as though he did, to listen to him. And it was so ironic, she thought. It was all in the treatment, he said, when he treated her maybe worst of all. It was Matty, after all, she thought, who made her feel as if she were a queen one day, a nuisance the next. But *his* treatment, she guessed, didn't count.

She didn't say anything after that. What could she say? That it wasn't true? It was true. She was everybody's doormat. She was everybody's servant. And she didn't feel she deserved much, if anything, out of this life. She was just grateful to get through it, knowing that she had a home not made by hands, a place of refuge where she'd eventually get her reward. Not that she felt as if she deserved one. But wouldn't it be grand if she, for once, got it anyway?

Matty didn't continue the conversation either. He kept his hand on her shoulder, squeezing it occasionally as if he had to remind her that he was with her, and when she finally looked his way after a long time of looking everywhere else, she caught him staring at her jeans-covered thighs. It seemed like an odd place to stare, she thought, but then Leah came out of the store.

"There you are!" she said gaily. Matty, knowing females better than most, immediately removed his arm from Diane and began reaching for his wallet. How much, he wondered, had she set him back?

"It's four-twenty," she said. "Is that too much?"

"How can it be too much, Leah," he asked her, with some degree of testiness, she thought, "when I told you to help yourself?" He pulled out bills totaling five hundred dollars and handed them to her. She beamed.

"I'll be right back," she said. "What did you get, Diane?" she asked as she hurried away, not bothering to hear a response. Since she didn't bother, Diane didn't respond.

They left the mall after lunch and after Leah had visited two more stores, costing Matty even more money, and Diane wondered if he were as wealthy as he was letting on. She'd heard Sister Inez say that he was *filthy rich,* in her words, that he'd won a lot of frivolous lawsuits and made a lot of shrewd investments *up there in Atlanta,* but Diane had figured that was just Inez running her mouth. How would she know anything about Matty's financial situation anyway? But he did drive a Jaguar. And did wear expensive clothes. And he did hand money to Leah as if he had it to burn.

They drove around town, with Leah pointing out to Matty all of the hot spots, including nightclubs and bars, which Diane found completely inappropriate, but Matty didn't seem to mind. They had also planned to check out the carnival, too, but it was getting late and Matty had decided he'd seen enough for one day. And to Diane's shock, Leah wasn't even disappointed. She was too excited about all the fancy new clothes he'd bankrolled for her. Clothes she kept showing off even as they rode from Bainbridge back into Floradale, as if the fact that he had bought her clothes, and had obviously bought Diane nothing, somehow elevated their relationship.

But when they arrived at Matty's house so that Leah could retrieve her car, even Leah began to be concerned. A burgundy-colored Lexus was parked in the driveway, and a woman was sitting on Matty's porch. The concern escalated not only on Leah's face, but Diane's as well when Matty's Jaguar drove in behind the Lexus and the woman, every unbelievably beautiful inch of her, stood up.

To say that Matty was uncomfortable would be an understatement. He seemed mortified all of a sudden, as if he'd seen a ghost. He sat behind the steering wheel staring at the woman on the porch. When he finally did step out of the car, he opened the back car door for Diane but would not take his eyes off that woman on his porch. He forgot all about opening the door for Leah, which surprised Diane, but Leah got out on her own. She wouldn't miss this for the world.

The woman began walking down the steps, or marching down as Diane saw it, and she walked up to Matty. She was tall and elegantly dressed in a tan pantsuit. She had that deep, dark black skin that elevated her high cheekboned good looks into something far more exotic than a run-of-the-mill beauty. Her hair was long and straight and brushed under in a wave of curls at the middle of her back, and her lips were full and sexy, eternally posed in a wicked half-smile. If Diane thought she didn't stand a chance with Leah as her competition, she knew she had no chance against this woman.

"Hello, Victoria," Matty said as soon as the woman approached them. His voice was calm, showing no signs of agitation or delight. The woman, however, smiled a complete smile when he said her name.

"I had to see it to believe it," she said.

"Well, now you see it, Vicky. And I hope now you understand."

"Oh, I always understood. Understood better than you did. You play to the jury in the courtroom, that's why you're such a successful attorney, Matty. Now you're just playing to a different jury, a different audience. A more, shall we say, down home audience?" Vicky said this and laughed. Matty frowned.

"Is that why you came all this way, Vick?" he asked. "To get a good laugh at my expense? Well, fine. You've had your laugh."

Vicky stopped smiling, at least for the most part. "We need to talk, Matty."

Matty exhaled. Will she ever get it? "I told you there's nothing to talk about."

"There's plenty to talk about and you know it. And I'm not going anywhere until I say what I need to say. You owe me that much."

Matty looked at Vicky, and he could see the devastation all over her pretty face. Their relationship was never built on love or trust, or any of those virtuous things. The devil was busy today, he thought.

He handed Vicky his keys. "Go on inside," he said to her. "I'll be there."

Vicky smiled, as if she'd just won some prize, and then she exhaled. "Matthew Jolson, church pastor. I thought I'd seen it all. And in true Jolson fashion, you aren't just any old pastor, are you? Oh, no. You're the pastor with style. You're the church pastor with a lady on each arm."

Vicky laughed when she said this and looked at Diane

first, then Leah. Then she looked back at Diane. "Hardly your type, Matty, if I must say. But I guess you have to take what you can get in this God-forsaken land."

Vicky, satisfied with her putdown, began walking back toward the house.

Diane sighed with great disappointment, and Matty had a sudden urge to pull her into his arms. He wished to God he had taken her home first, before coming to get Leah's car, but he couldn't get himself to do it. He had even flirted with the dangerous idea of inviting her inside once Leah was out of the picture. Now all he wanted was to get her as far away from Vicky as fast as he could.

"Leah," he turned and said, as all three of them watched the beautiful woman make her way into Matty's house, "you think you can take Diane home for me?"

It sounded like a slap in the face to Leah. "Only if you let me come back," she said, as if attempting to imitate Vicky. "Part of my plan for you today was that I be allowed to cook you dinner, give you a taste of home cooking for a change."

Another headache, Matty thought. But he wasn't worried about Leah. She and her seductiveness had no power over him whatsoever. It was Diane he worried about. It was Diane he wanted away from this mess. "Yes," he said. "You can definitely cook dinner for me. Say, around six or so?"

"That'll work," Leah said, although she knew such a late hour would provide him with far too much time with that Victoria woman. But she had great confidence in her abilities. Whatever that woman could do to him, she decided, she could do better.

Matty had a plan, too, however. And his plan hinged upon his being able to get rid of Vicky well before six p.m.

He looked at Diane. His dear Diane. "You come back with her," he said to her in what sounded like an order.

"I can't, not this evening," Diane said, stunned that he would even dare ask her. All of this drama. All of these different women wanting him. What kind of pastor was he? It made her wonder if those rumors were true about his time in that Chicago church. One woman even attempted to kill herself over him, or so she had heard. And he expected her to come back to *this?* He expected her to willingly be a party to this sin-filled train wreck? She tried not to show it, but she was royally offended.

"Why can't you?" he asked, as if his request weren't unreasonable at all.

"Because she has other things to do, Matty," Leah answered for her. "I think we've taken up enough of Diane's time as it is. You don't know her. She isn't like us. She doesn't hang like we do. So come on, Diane. Help me get my bags out of Matty's car and I'll take you home, girl."

Diane dutifully followed Leah around to the opposite side of Matty's car. Matty watched her carefully, his mind a torrent of emotions, and he wondered if his past were scaring her away. Vicky always had a way of drying up the competition. Just by her presence other hopefuls would throw up their hands and flee the scene. And if he knew Diane, he knew she wasn't about to even try and compete against the likes of Vicky Avery. Maybe it was a good thing, Matty thought. He didn't need the distraction anyway. But it didn't feel good.

Later that night, when it seemed as if the pain of that awful day were becoming too much for Diane to endure, she heard knocks at her front door. She went to her bedroom window, figuring it was probably Pam trying to dump the kids on her again, but when she saw the blue Jaguar in front of the house her entire body shook. It was Matty, or Pastor Jolson, as she had already decided she would call him from here on out. Their relationship had become a little too casual, with the hugging and kissing, and she knew that had to change. He may not take his salvation seriously, but she took hers seriously. And all of that flirting and teasing was playing with fire.

"Diane!" her father's voice yelled up to her bedroom. "Your pastor's here to see you!"

"Tell him I'm busy," Diane yelled back down. "I'll see him tomorrow at church!"

Willie James Tarver heard his daughter's reply but he didn't believe it. She was claiming just two days ago that she aimed to snatch this one; now she didn't want to see him? He shook his head and walked with the aid of his cane back to the front door. *Women,* he thought.

Matty was standing on the porch, the screen door the only barrier to him and Diane. When Willie James returned to the door, he knew it was going to be bad news.

"She said she'll see you tomorrow in church."

Matty exhaled. He was flustered and frustrated and about ready to scream if something didn't start going right before this day was out. Willie James, a man after Matty's own heart if he could say so himself, sensed it, too. He opened the screen door to Matty, although Malveen had already told him not to let that "so-called" pastor into her home.

"She's upstairs," Willie James said. "Second door on the right."

Matty shook Willie James's hand and then hurried up the stairs, three steps at a time. The second door on the right, to his surprise, was open.

Diane, who was sitting on the edge of her bed, her eyes swollen from too much crying, a tissue in her hand in case she cried more, nearly choked when she saw Matty. She was in an old nightgown she wore around the house. Her hair was loose and hanging unprotected down her back. She looked and felt a mess. And the way Matty just stood there staring at her, his big body leaning against the doorjamb, didn't help matters at all.

"May I help you, Pastor Jolson?" she decided to ask, her

need to be formal in stark contrast to the fact that she was in a gown, in her bedroom, looking, from her point of view, as bad as she could look. But Matty's stare remained unbroken.

"She used to be my girlfriend," he said bluntly.

Diane stared back at him, confused.

He pushed his body away from the doorjamb and began walking toward Diane. Just seeing her made his heart pound.

He sat on the bed beside her. Her breath caught. "Victoria Avery is her name. Everybody calls her Vicky. After Chicago I returned to Atlanta, and Vicky, who had just left the DA's office, became my law partner." He hesitated. And looked at Diane. "And my lover."

Diane looked down, at her small hands. "You were still a preacher," she said. "What do you mean your lover?"

It needed no explanation, and Matty was certain Diane understood that. They sat in silence moments longer, the closeness of their bodies keeping both of them hyper-tense, until Matty finally felt it necessary to say: "I'm not perfect, Diane."

Diane quickly looked at him, as if she were offended by that remark. "Neither am I," she said. "You didn't have to tell me that. Nobody's perfect."

"I broke it off with Vicky before I came here. I want you to understand that."

"Where is she now?"

"She left. Earlier."

"Back to Atlanta?"

"Yes."

"Did you and she..." Diane looked at Matty and was unable to finish her sentence. He exhaled.

"No, Diane," he said. "It's over between me and Vick and that's what I told her. Again."

Diane nodded her head, relieved that she didn't have to say more. Then she thought about it. "What about Leah?"

she asked. "I thought you were going to have dinner with her."

Matty smiled. "I canceled on her."

"Oh, no. I'll bet she didn't like that."

"No, she certainly didn't. But what can I say? I had to come see you."

Those words stunned even Matty. And as for Diane, she felt as if she were on a roller-coaster ride. Down one minute, up the next. Then up one minute, down the next. Up and down, over and over. But that was what you got, she felt, for falling in love with your pastor.

In love? Was she truly in love with this man? She barely knew him. And even the little she did know about him wasn't exactly a glowing testimony. He was a man, first and last, a man with a lot of issues. Too many, perhaps, for a pastor. But even that knowledge didn't change her feelings. She loved Matty Jolson. She loved the way he talked and walked and smelled and tasted. She loved the way he looked so bewildered when she said something wrong, or looked so concerned when he felt she wasn't taking proper care of herself. She cared about Matty Jolson. She wanted him to be happy. She wanted him to be a success. She *loved* Matty Jolson.

Matty's emotions, however, weren't quite so cut and dried. He couldn't afford to be in love with anybody. Not now. Not when he had so much work, so much on his plate as it was. But he couldn't stop thinking about this woman. All day, even when he and Vicky had their little talk and she finally got the message that he wasn't playing games with God, he couldn't get Diane off his mind. And tonight, when Leah came over two minutes after Vicky's departure, as if she'd been watching the house, he couldn't get rid of her fast enough. He had to get to Diane. He had to let her know that no matter how it looked, and he knew it looked bad, he still had enough sense to want her.

He wanted her. That was it, he thought, as he sat beside

her. He'd wanted her from the first moment he saw her singing in his parlor. He wanted to hold her and protect her and make sure nobody else would hurt her. But wanting somebody, even caring about somebody, didn't automatically translate into being in love with somebody. Being in love was the deepest of deep emotions he felt. And he wasn't prepared to go that far with anybody. And that included Diane.

But even with all of that in mind, he still wanted her. He even did something daring, considering the kind of day they'd had, and placed his hand on the small of her back. He could feel her entire body clench as he touched her, and he began to massage her as if that would help calm her down.

It did no such thing. Diane began to breathe heavily as he rubbed her, as his hand pressed hard into material that was already too thin, and she knew she should stand up and put an end to this once and for all. But she loved him and his touch, and her heart wanted to cry with joy, not leap up with indignation.

So she allowed his touch. She even allowed him to pull her closer and place both arms around her. She didn't think she would have allowed more, but she felt so weak under Matty's spell that she couldn't be sure of that at all. She fully expected him to try more, however. He never came across to her as a man who understood restraint. But, to her gratitude, he didn't go any farther than he already had. He, in fact, removed his arms from around her, and stood up.

"Coming to church tomorrow?" he asked, knowing full well he had better get away from her now or he might not be able to.

"Yes," she said, trying her best to regain her composure.

"I'll see you then," he said.

"Okay."

He looked at her longer, at the beautiful hair he was dying

to touch, at the lips he could barely pull himself away from kissing, and he left. He hurried out of her room, down the stairs, and away from that house on Clarion Avenue. Better to marry than to burn. But marriage was out of the question. And he was already burning bad.

Chapter 13

She could not get over the insult. All Saturday night she played it over and over in her head. "I'm going to have to take a rain check on dinner, Leah," he had said. As if that said something. As if that wonderful meal he promised she could prepare for him meant nothing to him. Then, to top it off, he barely gave her a chance to drive away from his house before he was hopping in his car and flying like a madman up the road. Leah couldn't believe it when his Jaguar flew past her Subaru as if he didn't even see her. And she followed him. She put the pedal to the metal just like he had, and followed.

She was stunned when he turned onto Clarion Avenue. She was absolutely livid when he went into Diane Tarver's house, as if he couldn't wait to get to her, as if she had told him not to have dinner with Leah, but come to her. Diane was her betrayer. Diane, of all people. She'd wormed her way into going with them on Matty's guided tour earlier that day, but Leah thought the events of that day had easily trumped any notions Diane might have had. Matty was Leah's man and Leah felt she had proved it in every way. She had sat beside him in the car during their tour of the area, walked arm-in-arm with him while Diane walked behind them as if she were their pet. And when it came to their little shopping spree it was Leah who had hundreds of dollars' worth of clothes and jewels to show for it, while Diane had nothing.

Now Leah was beginning to wonder if that was all planned, too. Diane wanted Matty to think she didn't want him for his money, so she refused to let him buy her anything. Whereas Leah, on the other hand, would have bankrupted the man if he weren't careful. What a slick witch, Leah thought, the more she thought about it. Innocent Diane wasn't so innocent after all.

The fact could not have been clearer than on Sunday, the next day, when Leah made a point of walking out of church with Diane just to see with her own eyes what was really going on between her and Matty. And she saw an eyeful. Matty was in his usual position greeting his parishioners on the steps of the church. Looking delicious in his pinstriped suit, Leah couldn't help but notice. He smiled and was nice to everyone he greeted, but when Diane walked up to him he could hardly contain himself. He held her hand way too long, Leah felt, and she even thought she saw his thumb rubbing across Diane's knuckles. He didn't just want to know how she was doing, which was all he asked of his other parishioners. Oh, no. He wanted to know if she ate breakfast before she came to church, if she slept okay the night before, everything about her. And then, to add insult to injury, Leah felt, he kissed her on the cheek—still holding her hand, mind you. Still rubbing her hand!

Leah, however, still wasn't fully convinced. She just couldn't bring herself to believe that a plain Jane, Goody Two-shoes like Diane Tarver could ever take a man away from her. That was why, when Matty finally released Diane from his grasp and sent her on her way, his dark gray eyes staring lovingly at her as she walked away, Leah made her move. She put on that innocent smile routine, too, just as Diane had done, but the results were dramatically different. He treated Leah as if she were just another one of his members. He shook her hand and released it quickly, asked how she was doing, and then moved on to the next in line. No rub across her knuckles. No kiss on her cheek! That simpleton Diane Tarver had managed to do what not even that hot mama from Atlanta could do: she'd managed to beat Leah at her own game. Diane was the queen of seduction now. She'd won. She'd won the grand prize in a contest Leah was willing to bet no female in Fountain Hope had a clue she had even entered. But Diane, of all the females Matty could have chosen, had won.

"At least she thinks she has," Leah said out loud. She was in a motel room just on the outskirts of town, and she looked at her longtime lover and smiled. They had these little trysts virtually every week, an affair so clandestine even Leah couldn't believe she had kept the secret. But she had. For well over a year. She enjoyed their time together. He could calm her and help her in ways no other man could. It was nine a.m. Tuesday morning, the earliest they'd ever met on any day, but she needed him this day. All day Monday she couldn't get it off her mind, replaying how grandly Diane Tarver had triumphed this past weekend. She just had to unload her anger or else, as she told her lover before he agreed to meet her, she just might hurt somebody.

They both were now dressed and sitting at the motel's small, round table near the window, the sound of traffic whirling by on the busy highway echoing throughout the sparse room. The oddity of the twosome was immediately apparent. Leah, in her skimpy halter top, short skirt, and heels, and he in his tailored suit, made for a stark contrast in styles. And even more startling was the fact that Leah's companion wasn't some obscure local man with no connection whatsoever to her inner circle, but was, in fact, her best friend's husband.

Ira Marshall, with his suit coat still off and flapped across the back of the motel chair he sat in, crossed his legs. "I still don't understand the problem," he said, staring across the table at Leah.

"The problem is she took my man. That's the problem, Ira."

Ira smiled. "I thought I was your man."

"You know what I'm talking about."

"No, I don't know. You think I want to sit up here and hear about your exploits with Matty Jolson?"

Leah laughed. "Why should you care? You told me a year ago you was gonna leave Sam and marry me—a year ago, Ira—and you ain't even thought about doing it. I can't keep waiting on you. Until you get your divorce it's wide open for me. And Matty will do just fine in the meantime."

"You think life is so simple."

"I think you could divorce that woman if you really wanted to, that's what I think."

"Here we go again."

"Yeah, here we go. You can get rid of her, Ira, and you know it. You ain't gonna tell me you so in love with that witch that you can't leave her."

"Love has nothing to do with it, how many times do I have to tell you that? She's the mother of my children. That's the point. It's not as simple as just leaving. Besides," he said, exhaling, growing increasingly bored with this every-week, dead-end conversation, "you and I have an open relationship."

Leah hesitated. Ira was never leaving Sam without a push. Without a scandal that would rock their sleepy little town to its core. And one day, if he weren't careful, if she couldn't persuade him with her undercover tactics to get his act together, she was going to get the rocking started. "You're right," she said, inwardly wondering why she ever got hooked up with a joker like him in the first place, "so why you acting like you all jealous of Matty Jolson? Since our relationship's so open and all?"

"I'm not jealous. I just don't know why you're telling me about it."

"Because you're the smartest dude I know, and I need help. That Diane Tarver not gonna take my man and I just sit back and let her."

"I told you about Diane Tarver. I told you to leave that one alone, didn't I?"

"Yes, Ira, you told me."

"I told you not to trust her. I told you she was not a trust-worthy soul, didn't I?"

"Yes, yes, you did. Now what's the point?"

"The point is you didn't listen to me. You were too busy trying to convince Diane not to trust *me,* that I was some kind of monster, some kind of wife beater or something."

Leah smiled. "Was I lying?"

"She's my wife. I do whatever I want with her. You just better watch it, Leah, that's all I'm saying. I've got enough going on with that Matty Jolson. I don't need you up in my business, too."

"Then forget your business and get up in mine. What am I gonna do, Ira?"

Ira smiled. "Sometimes I wonder if the only reason you wanted to have this affair with me was to pick my brain."

"And glow in the aura of your name and power," Leah said and Ira laughed. "I'm serious," she added. "When Sam started coming to the shop two years ago and she told me her husband was a judge, was you, I knew then I was gonna have you. And when we met and you showed that little twinkle of interest, I knew I had you. And I did."

"Yeah, you got me."

"Now let me use you. What can I do to win Matty back and get Diane Tarver out of his system?"

Ira thought about this. Then he smiled. "Take him," he said. "The way you took me."

"You're talking, Ira, but it sounds like French to me."

"Diane is apparently wooing him with her sweetness. You can't compete in that game because she's a natural at it. So you've got to woo him with what you have plenty of but Diane doesn't have at all."

Leah thought for a moment. Then she looked at Ira. "Experience."

"Exactly. The kind every man wants but every woman just doesn't have. And trust me, Leah, you have it and know how to flaunt it better than any female I've ever run across."

Leah laughed. "You got that right," she said. "But how in the world can I lure him? That's been the problem. I thought I had him Saturday night. That was supposed to be the topper for me. But he wouldn't even let me in his house. And now he's acting like he's all in love with Diane. I don't see how I could ever entice that man now."

"Give him an offer he can't refuse," Ira said, standing to his feet, not the least bit interested in Leah or her love life. His thoughts were on Sam, his wife, and where she might be on this bright Tuesday morning. He'd swing by the house on his way back to the courthouse, he decided. And if she wasn't home, if she wasn't where she was supposed to be, she'd better have a darn good explanation. But if she came up with some lame excuse about a sudden urge for ice cream or car trouble or some other nonsense she'd tried on him in the past, she'd have hell to pay when he was done.

"What kind of offer he can't refuse?" Leah asked him.

Ira smiled as he put on his suit coat. "You'll think of something," he said.

★ ★ ★

Sam was so beside herself with fear that she practically jumped from her Mercedes and ran to the front door. What was he doing home? she wondered as she ran. It wasn't even noon yet and he was home? She couldn't believe it. She just couldn't believe it. Nobody, she felt, could be this unlucky.

She opened the door and hurried inside, but he wasn't in his favorite chair where she thought she'd find him. Maybe he wasn't home at all. But he had to be. His SUV was parked on the driveway. Of course he was home. But why? And *where?*

"I'm in here," he said as soon as she thought to begin looking for him, and her heart dropped. His voice came from the study and she moved in that direction. What was she going to tell him? That she dropped the boys off at school and then treated herself to a big breakfast at Maxine's? That was exactly what had happened. But he wouldn't believe it. The idea of her eating breakfast alone, something she loved doing, wouldn't make sense to him. He wasn't going to believe her.

He was not sitting behind the desk as she had imagined, but on top of the desk's front end. He looked big and beautiful, as he looked at her, and the smile on his face made her nervousness calm down.

"I didn't expect to find you here," she said, smiling, too.

"That's obvious. Where were you?"

She swallowed hard, her nervousness returning like an ache in her throat. "I took the boys to school."

"And?"

"And," Sam said, cautiously, a woman never able to lie without great guilt, "I went over to Leah's. To see how she was doing. And time just flew by. I didn't realize how long I'd been over there." Leah didn't like Ira, Sam knew. She'd back up any tale she told to keep Ira off her case.

Ira, however, continued smiling and staring at her. He'd

just been with Leah himself, had been quite intimate with Leah, and the idea that Sam would use her for an alibi only confirmed his suspicions. She was cheating on him. He'd never been more certain of it than he was right now. He wished he was wrong. He had prayed he was wrong. But he wasn't. His wife, the mother of his children, was cheating on him.

He stood up and began walking toward her. Her heart pounded as he came. He could have hurt her right then and there. He could have really hurt her. But that irritating voice of Matty Jolson's kept playing with his mind. Reminding him that he was being watched. Chiding him of what could happen if he ever tried to harm Sam again. The man was already too suspicious. Ira therefore couldn't just knock her around; that would be easy bait for Jolson. He couldn't leave a bruise. At least, he smiled even more broadly as he thought about it, not one that Jolson could see.

He grabbed his wife by the hand and walked her out of the study and slowly up the stairs. She was talking to him a mile a minute, trying to calm him down although he showed no outward signs of anxiousness. He was, in fact, smiling. But she knew him. She knew him too well. It was always calm before the storm with Ira. And he was way too calm for her comfort zone.

So she kept talking. She kept nervously rattling on as if he could possibly care about what she was saying. All he could think about was his goal. He had to teach her a lesson. One she would never forget. A lesson so definitive in its principles that whomever she was seeing, when Ira was finished with her, she was going to wish she'd never met.

Inez Flachette could not believe her eyes as she drove her late model, pearl-white Cadillac into the parking lot of Fountain Hope and saw the swirl of activity around her. It was a Tuesday morning, a regular Tuesday morning, but folks were standing all over the church grounds talking and laughing and carrying on as if they were on some street corner hangout. Others were coming in and out of the sanctuary, dressed any kind of way, as if the holy of holies wasn't a place of worship but a popular juke joint. And still others were standing in a long line outside the kitchen area complaining about the slow service, as if Fountain Hope was there for no other reason than to serve them.

She parked her big Cadillac in the space reserved for the church's day-care director, and she couldn't pull her big old body out fast enough. She'd seen a lot of strange happenings in her day, but this day took the prize. Normally on a Tuesday morning the church was as quiet as a graveyard, with the only activity coming from the school area. Now it was roiling with activity, all over the place; everywhere Sister Inez looked she saw activity. She momentarily just stood at her car staring, as she literally didn't know where to begin. When she finally saw Sister Baker's high behind walk past a window in the kitchen, her arms folded as if she were as hot as Inez, she decided that was as good a place to start as any.

The kitchen was near capacity with volunteers Inez had never seen before. And they were a lively bunch, feeding the people of the community with smiles and chitchat, one lady even singing them a song. Inez couldn't believe it. She looked around for Sister Baker, and found her near the big, stainless-steel sink.

"Will you please tell me what's going on?" Inez asked her.

"Madness, that's what," Sister Baker replied. "Pure madness. I came in this morning and nearly drove on by."

"All these strangers."

"I ain't never seen nothing like it. They were just starting to form when I got here early this morning. Now it's like a madhouse 'round here."

It was still early, only ten a.m., but soon the children from the day care would be coming into the area for lunch. And that concerned Sister Baker the most. What if this crowd wasn't cleared out by then? What if her precious babies had to witness something like *this?*

"Where's Deacon Molt?" Inez asked Sister Baker.

"Nowhere to be found. I called him at home but his wife said he was already on his way. That was two hours ago."

"Lord knows. What about Pastor? I seen that car of his in the parking lot."

"He's upstairs in his office."

"Didn't you go to him, Baker? Tell him what was going on?"

"I sure didn't. He knows what's going on. All this his doing anyway, ain't no doubt in my mind about that. Whoever seen all these strangers laughing and talking and all merry out here 'round Fountain Hope before he come along? Like this the party house. Reverend Cobb probably turning over in his grave."

"God bless the dead."

"Amen." Sister Baker then exhaled. "But we gonna be all right. Once Deacon Molt gets here and we all get together on this. Because the will of God will not be altered, I don't care what man wants."

"Amen, Sister Baker."

"God is good now."

"All the time."

"All the time God is good. And He's gonna straighten this mess out, or get rid of the one responsible for the mess. One of the two."

Although Sister Inez nodded her agreement, she couldn't disagree more. They'd been sitting back far too long. Now was the time for this new pastor to be called to account. He hadn't been in charge for a month yet and already he was making a shipwreck of everything they'd been trying to do, as if he were hellbent on destroying everything they stood for. They were just old hags to him after all. Just old church folk. Well, it was high time, it seemed to Inez, that the old church folk started standing up, too.

She left the kitchen area, walked through the cafeteria, and entered the sanctuary. She shook her head in disgust at what she saw. There were classes going on, all right, but none of them were appropriate for a sanctuary. There were no Bible studies classes or usher board meetings or choir rehearsals. Instead a job skills class was being taught at one end of the big hall and a support group for recovering addicts was being held at the opposite end. Looked like a communist commune, if you asked Inez. Or one of those crazy cults. Nothing about the Lord was being discussed. Nothing about souls being saved was being mentioned. Just touchy-feely, it's-all-about-me nonsense that had no place in a house of worship.

And Inez aimed to give that pastor a piece of her mind about it, too. Somebody had to. Deacon Molt was too scared of losing his position to speak up to the pastor. He was content to sit back and let it all happen. He even told Inez on many occasions not to worry, that the best way to catch a devil was to let that devil catch himself, but that wasn't good enough for Inez. And she told Molt, too. She told him he had to do better than that. Molt felt enough pressure from Inez to at least call Bishop Owens and complain, but when Bishop told him that Reverend Jolson had his complete support, Molt felt vindicated. At least he tried. If they still wanted to be angry, then they would have to be angry at Bishop, not him. Because Bishop's word of support for the pastor was the end of it to Molt.

But it didn't end a thing to Sister Inez. Somebody had to stop this man before he ruined everything associated with Fountain Hope. They were already becoming the laughingstock of the community, what with all of these classes going on and church every Sunday. He was going too far.

He had to be stopped, it seemed to Inez, and it looked like she was the only somebody with enough courage of conviction, enough Jesus in her, to stop him.

He was sitting behind his desk reading over some papers when Inez finally made it upstairs to his office. She knocked once, and then entered without waiting for permission. He had reading glasses on his stern face and he wore a brown suit, looking far too prosperous, she felt, for a man of God.

"There's a problem downstairs, Pastor," she said as soon as she entered.

Matty kept reading a moment longer, then he looked up at her. Her wide face was tight, ready to explode with indignation. "What sort of problem?" he asked. His every instinct told him to hear her out before he made a move.

"I can't believe you would sanction this."

"Sanction what, Sister Inez?"

"What's going on downstairs."

"What's going on downstairs?"

"They're feedin' the hungry, that's what!"

Matty paused before he responded. She had to be joking. She just had to be. "That's the problem?" he asked her.

"Yes! Don't you understand? We feed the hungry on Thursdays. This Tuesday."

"And?"

"And this ain't Thursday. We feed the hungry on Thursdays from eight to ten."

"What if they're hungry on Wednesday from ten to twelve?"

Such a response sounded ridiculous to Inez. She frowned. "What?"

"What difference does it make, Sister Inez? Tuesday, Wednesday, Thursday, what's the difference? Is it not the point that the hungry are being fed?"

"No, that's not the point, for your information. We have rules and regulations. We have bylaws. We have a very specific way of doing things 'round here."

"There was a need in the community and we're filling that need."

"What need? Feeding people who should get themselves a job and feed themselves? It certainly ain't no spiritual need we filling. You got drug addicts and prostitutes and some of everything known to man in our sanctuary this morning. You got folks hanging out in our parking lot laughing and talking like this the hangout corner. You got volunteers in our kitchen, folks I never even seen before in my whole life, singing songs and chitchatting with riffraff. We always been taught by Reverend Cobb to just feed 'em, don't be trying to get all up in their business. But that don't mean nothing to you. You've taken the house of God and turned it into a den of thieves!"

"A den of thieves? Because sinners are seeking refuge in the church it's a den of thieves?"

"Them kind of sinners, yes."

Matty shook his head. A conversation couldn't get any more idiotic, he thought. "Well, I must respectfully disagree, Sister Inez," he said. "Jesus didn't come to heal the well. He came to bring sinners to repentance. Those already saved, already healed, don't need a physician."

"You don't have to crawl down in the bottom of the barrel to find sick folk, Reverend Jolson, that's where you're wrong. The church got plenty of sick folk already on the rolls."

"Of course it does. But they don't believe they're sick. Those in the bottom of the barrel, as you put it, know they are. And what I've found in life is this: if you offer people help, by and large they will accept that offer. That's why we have that job skills class. Those men want to help their families. Those ladies want to get off of welfare. They just need a little helping hand. And yes, there's always some who don't want anything out of life, whose motives aren't honorable, but it's been my experience that people like that are few and far between."

"That ain't been my experience," Inez said forcefully. "People get in these bad situations because they're lazy and shiftless and don't have enough get up and go to get up and do better. You work at it, God will reward your effort. You wallow on the ground, why should He?"

Matty wasn't about to argue with her. They were going to agree to disagree whether she wanted to or not. "Is there anything else?" he asked her.

Inez sighed with great frustration. The man was hopeless, she thought. But she wasn't backing down. "Now that you mention it," she said, "yes, there is one other thing."

Matty braced himself for this one. "Okay, shoot," he said, then thought the better of it. The way she looked she just might take him up on the offer. "I mean, go ahead," he said in correction.

"About that car," Inez said.

Matty waited for more. When no further explanation came, he frowned. "What car?"

"That Jaguar you be driving."

Matty's lips curled into a smile. This could not possibly be about his *car*. "Yes, what about it?" he asked.

"I can't tell you the folks who've come up to me about that car."

"Again, what about it?"

"They feel, and I have to admit I do, too, that it's an inappropriate style of transportation for the pastor of such an esteemed church as our Fountain Hope."

Matty wanted to laugh. "Is it, now?"

"If you was a gangster, it would be appropriate. If you was a drug dealer, it would be appropriate. But you're a pastor. Least that's what you're saying you are."

Matty leaned back. "Let me get this straight. You want me to get rid of my car?"

"We think you should trade it in for something more appropriate for your job. You ain't no slick lawyer no more."

Matty smiled. A successful lawyer had to be a slick one, he supposed. "Okay. So what kind of automobile do you want me to get?"

Inez frowned. "I don't know. But something less flashy."

"Like a Cadillac? What if I drove a Cadillac?"

"A Cadillac?"

"Yeah. A big, white caddy. Like that big, beautiful white Cadillac you drive, for instance. Would that be less flashy?"

Sister Inez's mouth turned into a harsh line. She knew an insult when she heard one. "I was just telling you what folks saying. That's all I was doing. Trying to give you a little advice. You can take it or leave it, far as I'm concerned."

"I'll leave it, thank you. Now, is there anything else, Sister Inez?"

Inez stared at Matty. What an arrogant so-and-so, she thought. "That's all," she reluctantly said.

"Good," Matty said as he stood up. Inez, taking the cue, began to leave. "And Sister Inez?" he said, and she immediately turned around.

"Yes?"

"Stop being so judgmental."

"Excuse me?"

"You're hurting, not helping. Stop being so judgmental."

Inez sucked in an angry breath. The nerve of him, she thought. "I've been saved since before you was born, I'll have you know," she said, without holding back. "How dare you question my walk with God! I'm gonna tell it no matter what you say. I'm gonna tell it just like it I-S, is. Wrong is wrong and all the talk in this world ain't gonna make it right. Them folks in the sanctuary don't have bit more business being there than Lucifer does. But that don't matter to you.

If we say white, you say black. If we say it's left, you say it's right. Just to aggravate us!"

"When were you ordained?" Matty asked her.

Inez hesitated. What was he talking about now? "When... what?"

"I've never heard of a secretary—excuse me, a secretary-slash-treasurer-slash-day-care-director—ordained to lead a church. So I would love to know when were you ordained to be the pastor of this church and who gave you such an ordination?"

The fire in Inez was simmering. There was a time, back in the day, when she would have told that pastor a thing or two. But she kept her fire to herself and left his presence, although she made a particular point of slamming the door as she went.

Matty smiled and plopped back down in his chair. Oh, well, he thought. Nobody said it was going to be easy.

Less than thirty minutes later, however, when Matty thought this day couldn't get any stranger, it did. Leah Littleton phoned with a voice so weak he could barely hear her. She had taken ill while driving to the grocery store and by the time she made it home she had taken a turn for the worse. She didn't need a doctor, she insisted, she just needed him to come pray for her. And given the desperation in her voice, he agreed. But when he hung up the phone and checked out the time, he realized he had only about an hour before the stewardship/witnessing class he taught, so he thought about sending one of the sisters instead. But Leah sounded so bad, and she had asked specifically that he come, so he told Sister Scott to take over the class in his stead.

He drove slowly the short distance from the church to Leah's small house on Juniper Street, stepping out into a neighborhood that was one of the poorest in town. Stray dogs, dirt roads, shanty houses, and grown men hanging around when they should be on somebody's job. A prime neighborhood, Matty thought, for his next crusade.

On Leah's earlier instructions, Matty did not knock on her front door but walked on in. She was feeling too bad, she had told him, to answer a door. So she left it unlocked. He entered, however, calling her name. It was a small but well-furnished abode, with all of the trappings of a woman who did her best to stay connected to the people while doing all she could to prove that she had risen above them. She lived in the 'hood, her small house looked right in place, but inside it had the look and feel of a well-adorned, rather ostentatious cottage.

"Sister Littleton!" he yelled again.

"I'm back here, Pastor!" she yelled back in what sounded to Matty to be a weak, frail voice. He followed the sound of that voice down a dark, narrow hallway that led to a large, impressively arrayed master bedroom. Leah was lying in the middle of the posh sleigh bed, her pillows and decked-out dolls propped all around her. She looked beautiful, Matty thought, in her pink, silk negligee and makeup. Too beautiful to be as gravely ill as he'd been led to believe.

"Hello, Leah," he said suspiciously as he moved slowly toward her bed.

"Reverend," Leah said, barely audible. "I'm so glad you came." She said this purposely too low. Just looking at Matty, in his beautiful brown suit, made her more determined than ever to make this work.

And it was working, as Matty could barely understand her. "What did you say?" he asked.

"I'm glad you came," she said again, only her voice this time was even more muffled. Matty began to wonder if he had misjudged her. He moved closer to her.

"I can't understand what you're saying, dear," he said and knelt down in a crouched position beside her bed, as close to her as he could get.

The whiff of his cologne alone, as he knelt down, made Leah want to smile inside. She had him right where she needed him to be, she felt. Little Diane Tarver may have won for a moment, but Leah Littleton was about to make certain that she snatched victory back.

"I feel so bad, Matty," she said, near tears. "I don't know what's wrong with me."

"Where are you hurting?"

"All over," Leah said, moving her hands all over her body. When she saw that Matty's eyes were following the movement, she continued to demonstrate. "Oh, Matty," she said. "I just wanna feel better. Help me feel better!"

She grabbed Matty around the neck and pulled his upper body on top of hers. Matty quickly pulled away and stood up. He knew better than this.

"What do you think you're doing?" he asked angrily.

"Matty, please."

"Don't you 'Matty' me. What's going on, Leah?"

"I need you, Matty. I just feel so bad."

"You called me away from church to play *games* with me?"

"Oh, no," Leah said, leaning up on one elbow. She was losing him just that fast. "Goodness, no. I just wanted to see you, that's all. I just wanted you near me. Don't you see, Matty? Look at my home. I'll be so good to you. You think Diane Tarver is the one but she's not. She's nothing like you think. But I'll be so good to you!"

Leah had, once again, conjured up fake tears. Matty just stood there, staring at her, amazed that a woman as talented as Leah would try something this lame. She even tried to smear Diane's good name to achieve her end, which wasn't surprising to Matty—he'd been around a long time—but it was certainly disappointing.

"Give me your hand, Leah," he said, his eyes still riveted on her as if he could see right through her. And Leah, all too willing to comply, did as he had asked.

With her hand in his, he then moved to a praying position, down on his knees. He closed his eyes, not knowing or even caring what Leah thought. "Oh Heavenly Father," he began praying, "forgive us for our sins, oh Lord, for we have sinned against Thee. Cleanse us, Lord, of all unrighteousness and help us to be the son and daughter You are calling for in these last and evil days."

He continued, for nearly five more minutes, praying for forgiveness, strength, understanding, wisdom, compassion, you name it. Leah had never seen a man pray that hard. At first she was overwhelmed. Could he really be as holy as this? she wondered. Was her first impression of him as a playa that far off? Then she shook her head. She knew better. Matty was a playa from way back, she knew it the moment she had laid eyes on him. He was the one playing games. And the more she thought about it, the angrier she became. She felt as if he were mocking her, by taking her hand, by praying so long as if she were some hopeless case. And when he did stop and began talking about how disappointed he was with her behavior, looking at her as if she were a child, her anger flared. He was disappointed, she thought. *She* was disappointed!

She got out of bed. Matty continued to lecture her on the attributes of a virtuous woman, attributes he apparently didn't think she had, and she began to smile as if agreeing with him.

But Matty saw something else in that smile. It was so chilling, so beguiling, that he suddenly stopped speaking. He was wasting his time. That spirit of seduction was still on Leah as if it were cloaked deep within her soul. At this moment in time she was no more interested in changing her ways than an addict would be as cocaine shot through her body. The devil was busy, Matty thought.

Leah wasn't thinking about the devil or anybody else. She thought she had him again. He had stopped his sermonizing and was staring at her, staring with that heavy-lidded look of his she loved, and she just knew she had him again. So she decided to take full advantage of the rare opportunity and began to untie her negligee. Matty, hurt that he had apparently not reached her at all, just shook his head and began to leave.

"Matty, wait," Leah said desperately, stunned by his reaction. She had thought she had him. Why was he leaving? She quickly threw her arms around his neck in a last-ditch effort to break him, a last-ditch effort to seal the deal for good. She pushed herself against him. Matty, however, just as quickly slung her arms away from him and stepped back.

"Knock it off, Leah," he said angrily, pointing at her. "Now I'm warning you to just knock it off!"

Leah, however, couldn't believe her ears. Her smile that she thought had won the day, the smile he'd seen for what it really was, vanished. And an almost unreadable expression appeared on her face. "Warning me?" she asked incredulously. "You're *warning* me? Who the hell are you?"

Matty didn't wait to tell her. He just kept walking down the hall, through her living room, and then out of her door. Leah was yelling at him nonstop, walking behind him yelling and threatening and demanding that he stop and listen before she really lost it. But as soon as her front door slammed shut and it was obvious that her little scheme had backfired mightily, ensuring only that she was the last female on earth he would ever want to be with, her fit of hysterical yelling stopped. He'd won. First Diane. Now him. Two jokers who couldn't hold a candle to her on her worst day had bested her at every turn. And it was too much. Just plain and simply too much.

Something happened to her as she stood in the middle of her living room. Something so strange that even she, at first, was leery of it. Something so subtle that she barely noticed the difference. But there was a definite difference. She could see Matty now, running back to that horrible church and telling all of those hypocrites how she tried to come on to him. And how he rebuffed her. And how he tried to pray those demons up out of her. And they'd all laugh. Laugh at Leah.

Then he'd tell Diane. And she'd get a good laugh at Leah's expense, too. Leah was no fool. She knew Diane never really trusted her. She just put on that phony baloney Christian friendship act for Sam's sake. And she'd love to know that Matty had put her in her place. She'd just love it. They'd all love it and have a good laugh on Leah. And what was she supposed to do about that? Just stand here and take it? Just let that Matty Jolson make her a laughingstock?

No, a booming voice she'd never heard before yelled in her ear.

No!

Then a warm, airy sensation came over her. A calming, serene warmth. And she smiled that beguiling smile again. She stared forward, as if in a sudden trance, and then she began to rip her negligee, stripping that beautiful garment into ugly, horrible shreds. The more she ripped the greater her smile became, as if she were giddy now, as if she had finally figured out the riddle to life and it had been right in front of her all the time. She began laughing as she moved gracefully to her bedroom, gliding as if she were being pulled there. At first she stood at the room's entrance still unable to stop laughing. They thought she was down for the count, a doormat strategically placed for their own use. "But they thought wrong," she said aloud as she started destroying her room, slinging everything off her dresser onto the floor, grabbing her bedding and tossing that, too.

But she wasn't done yet. She had to have proof. Something visible. Something so immediately obvious that everything else would seem like a natural progression of truth. She braced herself. Inhaled, then exhaled. And ran, face first, into the full-length mirror on her bedroom wall.

Chapter 14

The Jaguar stopped in front of the library's revolving doors and Diane came outside just as Matty was getting out of his car. He was dressed smartly, she thought, in his brown suit and shades, the mild weather much more accommodating to his unyielding, professional style. She felt blessed to have somebody like him in her life, a man so wondrously handsome, so captivating in every way that just seeing him standing there made her smile broadly as she waved and walked across the sidewalk toward him.

He smiled, too, when he saw her, as he buttoned his suit coat and moved slowly around his car to the passenger-side door. She wore a pretty sheath-style dress in a solid pale yellow, and, to his astonishment and delight, it actually fit her, revealing her nice, slim figure. He removed his shades when he realized the fit, pleased to get a better look. She had on her standard low heel, jet-black shoes, the kind of shoes more befitting either a child or an old lady—Matty couldn't decide which—but there was still something refreshing about her appearance. When she made it to his side, and just as he was about to open the car door for her, he realized why. It wasn't the nice-fitting dress as he had, at first glance, thought. "It's your hair," he said.

Diane smiled. "Excuse me?"

"Your hair," Matty said, looking at the long, flowing waves of hair no longer in a plait but loose down her back. "You've let it down."

"Oh, that," Diane said as if it were no big deal, as if it weren't the monumental decision it had been for her earlier that day. "I just decided against plaiting it."

"And I'm sure it's grateful," Matty said and Diane laughed.

She got into the car feeling wonderful. So wonderful that she did not mind at all when he reached over to buckle her in, his big body pressed against hers. And when he gave her a soft peck on the lips she didn't mind that either. Their eyes locked into a stare, a long stare, and Matty ran his hand through her hair to feel its softness. He then gave her another one of his scrutinizing looks, closed the door, and began walking around to the driver's side of the car.

Diane couldn't stop smiling, thrilled that her decision to make a few changes to her appearance was pleasing to Matty. She had debated with herself all morning. She would wear her new dress or she'd wear her hair down. But not both, she'd decided. Both would be too brazen, too obviously a play for his affections. She wanted to please him slowly, not bum-rush the man. She loved him, she knew it now deep within herself, but if her time with him Saturday taught her anything, it was that he didn't like the bum-rush. He didn't like a woman who appeared too anxious to get his attention. But by the time she decided on the dress, it was too late to plait her hair. So she let it hang down. Brushing it quickly and forgetting it. Going out in public without the aid of a clamp or pin or bow in her hair for the first time in her adulthood. And if the early returns were accurate, that unplanned, hasty decision was the best one she'd ever made.

He got into the car and cranked it up. When he looked at her this time he didn't appear as upbeat as he had at first, but that didn't weaken Diane's smile. "Where are we going for lunch?" she asked him.

"I had planned to take you over to that truck stop café."

"The place you took me after choir rehearsal? That'll be nice. I like their food."

"But I changed my mind," he said, looking at her. "You look like you could use a home-cooked meal."

"Don't tell me I look anorexic to you again."

"No," he said, looking over the length of her, "not at all. You look fine. Very fine." He said this with an unreadable expression on his face. Then he looked away from her and began to pull away from the curb. "I just don't want to share you," he said. "How's that?"

Diane smiled broader. Could this hard-as-stone man be speaking to her affectionately? She could hardly believe it. "That's cool with me," she said, causing him to laugh slightly as he drove out into the traffic and headed for Haines Street.

Diane plopped down on his sofa and held her stomach. She shook her head vigorously when he asked her again if she wanted some dessert, prompting him to laugh once again.

"What's so funny?" she asked as he sat down in the chair flanking the sofa in his living room. He now had his suit coat off and his shirtsleeves rolled up. Diane was barefoot. Both were totally comfortable. "I'm so full I feel like I'm going to explode," she added, "and you're laughing."

"Can't help it, babe," he said, quickly lighting a cigarette then tossing the match in the ashtray on the low table. "You barely ate anything and you're bent over as if you're filled to the brim."

"I ate way too much, and I am filled to the brim. Rice and peas and chicken, too? For lunch? Goodness!"

"You ate one chicken wing, a handful of rice, and a few peas, Diane, come on."

"I ate two chicken wings, for your information, and a lot more rice than a handful."

Matty shook his head, still smiling. "If you say so."

"I say so," she said as she drew her feet up underneath her and leaned her head back, her eyes easily closing. She suddenly felt sleepy and, oddly enough, relaxed, as if Matty's positive reaction to her new look had emboldened her. Matty took a slow drag on his cigarette and stared at her, her eyelashes long against her smooth skin, her hair draped over her shoulders like a cat's fur. She wasn't the grandest woman in the world, he was certain many would feel. She was just too small and bright-eyed to be considered a great beauty. She would, in fact, rank dead last on his own list of the most beautiful women he'd been involved with, past girlfriends who were big, voluptuous, well-experienced seductresses who were so full of themselves that they just knew they had it going on.

Diane, on the other hand, wasn't big or voluptuous, but was more cute and cuddly, a woman who'd be stunned by the ways of the world rather than well experienced with them; a woman who never pretended to be anything more than what she was. Perhaps it was that very innocence of Diane, and lack of pretense, that drew Matty to her in the first place. He wasn't certain yet. But he was certain that his feelings for Diane were different; that for the first time in his life there was more than just a physical attraction that kept him interested. He cared about Diane. Deeply. Far more deeply, he feared, than he ever thought possible for a man like him.

"Sleepy?" he asked as her head began to lean to the side. She quickly opened her eyes and smiled when she saw him. Then she stretched and yawned. "I guess I am," she said. "Food does that to me, you know." Then she put her feet on the floor and sat erect. "But of course, I can't very well just go to sleep. I left Miss Wheeler in charge of the library and she doesn't like it when I take too long."

"She doesn't like anything."

"I know."

"I still say you should find you a more reliable aide. Miss Wheeler seems to be taking advantage of your kindness. Always complaining about what you're doing but still doing whatever she wants to do. And that's only when she bothers to show up for work at all."

Diane didn't say anything. Matty was telling the truth about her assistant, she knew it was the truth. But Miss Wheeler was an old woman now, who didn't just work for a paycheck, but mainly just to feel as if she still had a reason to get up in the mornings. She wasn't trying to do a good job. She'd paid her dues, working nearly forty years in housekeeping and retiring to no pension and very little social security. She deserved to take it easy, Diane believed. And she wasn't about to fire her.

Matty, however, continued to stare at her, and his gaze, it seemed to Diane, was searching. When it appeared as though his searching was never ending, she smiled. "What?" she asked, hoping that he would say she's pretty today, or something flattering like that.

"How long have you known Leah Littleton?" he asked her.

Her heart dropped, and her smile as well. Was that it? she wondered. Was he thinking about Leah, and not her? Was Leah the one who was really dominating his thoughts? Diane almost shook her head. She should have known. "About two years now," she said dejectedly.

"Know her well?" Matty asked, sensing her changed mood but deciding against acknowledging it.

Diane wanted to ask him why, or what difference did it make, but she kept her cool. "I wouldn't say I know her well. I know her."

Matty nodded. He seemed lost in thought. Then he seemed resigned to whatever conclusion he had reached as he puffed on his cigarette.

"Why?" Diane asked, unable to refrain any longer when it was obvious he wasn't going to explain himself.

"Just curious," he said.

"Curious?"

He looked at her. "Yes."

"But why would you be curious about how well I know Leah?"

Matty did not respond. He stared at her as if he were suddenly upset with her, or disappointed in her, and his reaction—his strange reaction, if you asked Diane—only helped to strip her of her gaiety and begin to unnerve her.

Matty seemed to realize his negative effect on her because he smiled. Just like that. "Sing for me," he said to her.

Diane knew she didn't hear him correctly. She knew that Negro didn't just sit up there and ask her to sing. *Her?* "Excuse me?" she asked.

Matty laughed. "Don't look so distraught, Diane. I just want you to sing a little song for me. The way you were singing that morning when we first met."

He remembered, she thought, and that alone almost lifted her spirits. But what did that mean? she wondered. He probably remembered the first time he met Leah, too. "Contrary to your belief, Reverend," she said, "I cannot sing. Not even a little bit."

"I didn't ask you that," Matty said. "I asked you to sing for me."

Diane shook her head. "You're serious?" She was unable to suppress a smile. "Matty, you can't be serious. I sing in the choir, that's true, but being able to sing isn't a prerequisite to sing in the choir. Just wanting to sing is all it takes. And I can't sing!"

Matty didn't respond. His stare was serious, resolute. Diane gave up, she literally threw her hands in the air and stood to her feet. He told her he wanted her to sing, period, regardless of her voice, regardless of how she felt about it. Just sing. So she did. She stood in his living room, barefoot, and bellowed out a tune. The first song that came to mind, Albertina Walker's "Please Be Patient With Me," was the song she decided to sing.

Matty watched her. He watched her with fierce attention as she started out very nervous and shaky, maybe even annoyed that he would ask her to do something like this, her weak soprano voice barely able to keep time, let alone stay in tune. She looked everywhere as she sang: at the ceiling, the floor, the walls, everywhere but at Matty.

But he looked at her. He couldn't take his eyes off her. And he wasn't smiling or showing his appreciation that she would do this for him. His look was intense. She was a jewel, he thought, so precious to his heart that he could hardly believe it.

He continued staring intensely at this odd lady he now had on his hands, until, in the middle of the song, she began rocking her body from side to side and attempted to sing, way too high, the chorus as well as the lead parts. He smiled then. He couldn't help but smile. She was right. She was the worst singer in the world, no doubt about it. But who said she wasn't the most beautiful woman in the world? he wanted to know. Who said she couldn't compete with any female on the face of this earth? In Matty's eyes, right here, right now, Diane was the most beautiful, the most enchanting creature he'd ever met. And she could more than compete against anybody. In his eyes there was no competition. Just Diane.

Before she could finish her song, before she completed her

booming, off-key, high-pitched finale, Matty doused his cigarette, stood from his chair, and walked to her. Her heart began to pound as he came near, but she kept singing, determined not to be distracted, determined to finish this ridiculous exercise he insisted she begin.

But she had no choice but to stop. For he was upon her, his massive body overwhelming hers, as he gently pulled her into his arms, gave her a humorless, probing look, and then kissed her. She felt as if she were floating when their lips touched. And to her surprise it wasn't a peck. It was the longest kiss they'd shared, as he seemed determined to endure, to make her feel for him the way he felt about her. And she did feel it. Deep within her. So deep, in fact, that she knew, at that very moment, that she could never feel for anyone the way deep down, good feeling she felt for Matty.

When their lips finally parted, when the sensation didn't ease up, but his pressure did, he didn't back away an inch. He, instead, stared once more deep into her eyes. A piercing, desperate stare. Then he spoke. "You're my precious gem, Diane," he said, "and don't you ever forget it."

Her heart seemed to slam against her chest as those words came out of his mouth. And when he pulled her tighter into his embrace, holding her as if he'd never let her go, she wanted to cry. He was the precious one, she thought. He was the one who just made her dream come true. She loved him, she knew even more how much she loved him, and maybe, just maybe, she felt, he cared deeply for her, too. She opened her eyes wide at the thought, her arms gripping him tighter as she pondered the implication. If he did have strong feelings for her it would be wonderful. If he did care just half as much for her as she cared for him it could very well be the most excellent gift anybody, anytime, anywhere, had ever given her.

Matty's eyes shut tightly as he held her. He was falling for this woman, falling hard, and it wasn't right. She deserved a good man, he felt, somebody without all of his baggage. A man who didn't seem consumed by mood swings and arrogance and domineering stubbornness. A kind-hearted, meek and humble, good Christian man.

Matty's past was like a noose around his neck and his future wasn't all that promising either. And he knew Diane. She'd cling to him and be the best woman in this world for him. If he'd only let her. She was always faithful, no matter what she was asked to do, and he knew without a shred of a doubt that she'd be completely, unequivocally faithful to him. Somebody he could trust and depend on. He knew it, as he held her in his arms.

But it wouldn't be right. He had too many enemies, too many storms to withstand, too many devils in hell anxious to consume him. His life was a battlefield, not a paradise. A low-lying, low-down valley everywhere he turned. And he couldn't, he wouldn't, take Diane down, too.

He lifted his head and looked at her. There was so much hope in her almond eyes, so much promise, that he almost broke. He needed her. As badly as darkness needed light. But she didn't need him.

"I'd better get you back to work, young lady," he said sadly, then attempted to smile.

Diane touched the lines on the sides of his eyes and smiled, too. "No rush," she said.

"Oh, yes it is," Matty said. "I don't want Miss Wheeler mad at me."

"Don't worry," she replied with laughter in her voice, "I won't let her get you."

Matty's breath caught when she said that, as the idea of Diane protecting *him* was remarkable. Not because she would think it possible. But because he would.

He kissed her on her forehead, then released her from his grasp.

★ ★ ★

He didn't kiss her again when he dropped her off at the library. He told her to stay sweet and he would see her later. Then he waved and drove away. Diane wanted him to hold her again, and kiss her, almost as if she were craving his touch, but she knew his way was best. Her emotions were like a ball. They were bouncing all over the place. She needed time to regroup. She needed time to fully accept that Matty Jolson, of all people, could feel something special for her, too. It wasn't love—she wasn't so far gone to go that far—but he cared. Nobody, not after the way he kissed her so desperately, could ever tell her that he didn't care.

Miss Wheeler, to Diane's shock, was waiting at the door when she walked into the library. She, in fact, had to squeeze past the heavyset, elderly woman just to get inside.

"Him again?" Miss Wheeler asked as soon as Diane squeezed past.

"Excuse me?"

"You was with him all day Saturday, least that's what you told me."

"That's right."

"And now you're with him again today?"

Diane stared at her assistant. "What are you getting at, Miss Wheeler?"

"You said he was your pastor."

"He is my pastor."

"Why would your pastor be taking you off all the time like this?"

Diane hesitated. She really couldn't believe this conversation. "He also happens to be a friend of mine," she said, and then began walking toward the checkout counter. She understood fully what her assistant was insinuating, and she could see how she would think such things, but she wasn't about to discuss Matty with her or anybody else. Nobody was going to mess up this opportunity for happiness, this opportunity of a lifetime, she didn't care who they were.

Miss Wheeler, however, followed Diane, not at all ready to mind her own business. "That's a fancy car he drives," she said.

Diane didn't respond. She walked behind the desk and began stacking the books that needed reshelving, hoping that her sudden activity would change the conversation's course. They complained that Jesus rode a donkey, which, in their minds, wasn't fit for a king. Now they were complaining that Matty drove a Jaguar, which, they felt, was too much for a church pastor. No matter how you sliced it, Diane decided, you just can't satisfy people.

"I said he drives a fancy car," Miss Wheeler repeated. Diane nodded.

"Yes, Miss Wheeler, he drives a rather fancy car."

"And he always be wearing them shades."

Diane almost smiled. "Yep, that's true. Did Mary Girl drop off that cookbook while I was gone?"

"If she did I didn't see it," Miss Wheeler said. "But about this so-called pastor of yours—"

"Miss Wheeler," Diane said, unable to suppress her displeasure any longer, "I really think we need to get to work."

"Then get to work. I'm not stopping you. I'm just trying to help you."

"Help me?"

"That preacher ain't for you, Diane."

Diane couldn't believe she'd go there. And it angered her. "What?"

"He ain't your type. I see the way he look in that fancy car, all leaned to the side with them shades on. What kind of pastor is that? He find a nice, pretty girl like you and he figure he done caught the lottery. All he got to do is give you some wine then he can have his way with you."

Diane couldn't help but laugh. "Wine, Miss Wheeler?"

"Yes, wine. And you keep laughing if you want. I know what I'm talkin 'bout. He wanna pour that stuff in you then have his way!"

"And I suppose I'm helpless in the situation?"

"What?"

"I can't decline to drink the wine, or decline to let him, as you put it, have his way with me."

"You can try."

"Oh, I'll more than try, Miss Wheeler, trust me. So there. You have nothing more to worry about. No wine for Diane, okay? Now will you take these books and reshelve them, please, ma'am?"

Miss Wheeler looked at the stack of books Diane had pushed toward the end of the counter, then she looked at Diane. There was more she had to say, lots more, but she reluctantly, maybe even angrily, grabbed the books.

It had been nearly three hours. Leah got out of her stripped-down bed in a fog. She looked at her torn and tattered negligee draped like a ripped rag around her body, the mirror cracked but not shattered, her room destroyed as if a tornado had blown by. And she was pleased.

She hurried into her bathroom to survey the damage. She looked expectantly into the small mirror above her sink. The side of her face was swollen now, and a bruise the size of an apple with small cuts around it glared back at her as if it were a Godsend. And that chilling smile of hers returned. A big, bright smile. Who was going to be laughing now, she thought. Then she went back into her bedroom, picked up her telephone, and gladly, almost unable to contain her glee, dialed 911. When the operator answered she suddenly screamed, from the top of her lungs, that her pastor, that's right, her pastor, had beaten her and tried to rape her.

Chapter 15

Deacon Molt removed his reading glasses and sighed. This was not going well. They had already decided on the budget, already decided which auxiliaries were going to get increases and which ones had to suffer a loss. But Sister Mayfield felt cheated. She was the last auxiliary leader of the day in Molt's office. The last one to hear the news. And she was highly upset.

Molt looked at Inez. Inez sighed, too. "We did all we can do," she said to Sister Mayfield. "We went over this budget a hundred times and this is the best we can do."

"The ushers are the most vital part of this church family," Mayfield said, as if she didn't hear Inez. "We meet, we greet, we do everything in our power to keep this church running smoothly. But we're always the ones to get shortchanged."

"Now look, Sister Mayfield," Molt said slowly, tired from too many headaches for one day. "I understand how you feel. Everybody's upset. Everybody want more. But there *is* no more."

Mayfield exhaled. "What about the day care?" she asked. Inez looked at her. "What about it?"

"The day care got an increase. Another increase."

"And?"

"And I don't think it's fair. That day care has its own self-sustaining budget, what with the parents paying for the service. The church shouldn't have to give it a dime. But if the usher board wanna go somewhere as simple as the annual convention out of state we got to have a fish fry. We got to have a bake sale. We got to raise funds like we ain't connected to this church at all, and I don't think that's fair."

"Whether you think it's fair or not," Molt finally said, annoyed, "you can't get blood from a turnip. It's just not here."

Inez smiled. Mayfield fumed. "It may not be here, Brother Deacon," she said, "but all of my ushers, beautifully dressed in white, just may not be here Sunday morning either!" Mayfield said this with sting, meaning every word, and then she left Molt's small office, nearly knocking down Wanda Scott, who was coming in as she was going out.

Molt and Inez looked at each other, and were about to discuss Sister Mayfield's boycott threat, but the frantic look on Wanda's face demanded their attention.

"What is it now?" Molt asked with more than a small degree of frustration.

"Sheriff Crane downstairs," Wanda said, nearly out of breath.

"Sheriff Crane?" Molt asked as he stood up, baffled. Inez stood up, too. "What Lucious Crane doing here?"

"He says he come to arrest Pastor," Wanda said as if she still couldn't believe it. "He said he came here to arrest Pastor Jolson, Deacon Molt!"

Inez looked at Molt and neither one of them could believe it. They hurried downstairs, both nervous and confused, and Wanda Scott's cries of anguish behind them didn't help the situation at all. To Inez, the idea that a sheriff would be in their church to arrest their pastor shouldn't be surprising at all, given who their pastor was. But to Molt it was shocking. Jolson was a maverick all right, but he wasn't a criminal. Molt was so shocked, in fact, that he prayed Wanda Scott had got it wrong. He prayed that this wasn't real.

But it was real. Sheriff Lucious Crane, a tall, big-bellied man with icy blue eyes and a grim, round face, was standing in the sanctuary along with two of his deputies reading Matty his rights. The students in the job skills class Matty had been teaching were on their feet, reeling with agitation, demanding to know what Lucious Crane was up to. Molt demanded to know, too, coming into the sanctuary amazed by this display. To keep the peace Crane had no choice but to stop giving Matty his Miranda warnings and tell all in earshot just why it was necessary for this arrest to go forward.

When he had finished, you could hear a pin drop.

Even Inez was stunned. "Rape?" she finally asked, astounded by what she had heard.

Crane nodded his head. "The allegation is that he attempted to rape a young lady, yes. When she fought back he physically assaulted her."

"But that can't be," Joe Dobson, a member of Matty's class, stepped forward and said. "Rev would never beat no woman."

"Somebody beat her, and that's a fact. She says it was Reverend Jolson."

"But I tell you that can't be," Dobson said again.

"It can, Joe, and it is," Crane replied. "We interviewed the victim extensively. We've seen the bruises on her face and the disarray in her home. We have neighbors willing to testify that they saw Reverend Jolson leave her house earlier today as if he couldn't get away from there fast enough. We believe that an assault did occur, that an attempted rape did occur, that the allegations are credible. And that's why we're here."

The room fell silent again. Molt looked at Matty, who wasn't saying a word, then he looked at Crane. "Who was the victim?" he asked him somberly. The gravity of this situation was mind-boggling. The damage something like this could do to Fountain Hope was staggering.

Crane exhaled. "It's Leah, Horace," he said.

"Leah Littleton?" Molt asked, amazed.

"That's right. Jolson assaulted one of his own church members."

It seemed too unbelievable for words. Even Molt, who'd seen a lot in his day, couldn't believe it either. Crane, realizing that the scene was getting too tense, looked at the largest of his two deputies and nodded his head. "Cuff him," he said.

Molt frowned. "Now wait just one minute, Lucious," he said, his frustration unable to be suppressed. "Handcuffs aren't necessary."

"Let me do my job, Horace," Crane replied. "These are some serious charges your pastor is facing. This ain't no jaywalking arrest. You should see the bruises on that woman. He beat the crap out of her, and attempted to rape her besides. So don't tell me what's necessary. This a terrible crime that's been committed."

And those words seemed like the last nail in the coffin. Everybody—Molt, Inez, Wanda, and especially the students—looked to Matty for the answer.

Matty, however, was numb. He stood mute, his hands behind his back ready to be cuffed, his face as blank and unreadable as anybody had ever seen on the face of a man who was normally so expressive. He seemed resigned to his fate, as if the fix were in and there was nothing he could do about it. Each deputy grabbed an arm and the normally feisty Matty let them, moving with the flow of their pull as if it were his pleasure to be their prisoner. He wasn't demanding, he wasn't fighting, he wasn't screaming from the rafters that they had the wrong brother. He wasn't doing anything, as if they did have the right brother, as if his guilt had rendered him speechless.

But it couldn't be. All the men in his class looked up to Matty, whom they knew to be a caring, compassionate preacher unlike any they'd ever seen. They were men who wouldn't have given the idea of attending a church a second thought if it had not been for Matty's tenacity, and bullheadedness, and faith. They were stupefied by all of this. If somebody like Matty couldn't stand, if a great Christian man like him couldn't hold out, what did that mean for them? And they looked to Matty, once again, for the answer. He always had the answer.

But Matty could not rise to the occasion this day. He could not even look them in the eye. He stared straight ahead. Just when he'd thought he was getting his footing back; just when he thought the pain of Chicago was finally easing out of his life for good and he could breathe a sigh of relief again, another pain, another heartache, another mountain for him to climb had crept in. He had sensed Leah was up to something when he left her house earlier, but nothing like this. And contrary to what it looked like, contrary to what those eyes around him saw, he was fighting, all right. He was fighting anger. And bitterness. And the shock of another lie. Another public humiliation. Another reminder to him of just how much he dreaded every second of this mass of confusion they laughingly called his life.

They dipped their own plates as the large pot of spaghetti quickly dwindled to a spoonful. They all sat at the dining room table and ate, even Frank, who rarely had supper with his family. But he needed a favor. Three hundred dollars by Friday or he was through.

"Then you're through," Willie James said, eating vigorously, his son's new predicament not bothering him in the least. "Especially if you think I'm giving you a dime."

Frank, however, ignored his father and appealed to Malveen. "Mama—"

"Don't 'Mama' me," Malveen said. "I ain't got it either."

"But I'm not lying this time! This serious, Mama. Them boys can mess me up real good if I don't have they money."

"Then you just gonna get messed up," Willie James said, so flustered with his only son that he started moving around in his chair.

"I'm talking to Mama," Frank said.

"I don't care who you talking to. Ain't nobody got no three hundred dollars to be giving to you."

"Mama, please," Frank said. "I wouldn't ask if it wasn't serious."

"Why is it so serious?" Malveen asked. "And who are these people that they would harm you over money?"

"Dope people, who else?" Willie James said. "Drug runners. Always the dope man."

But Frank denied it. Diane ate slowly, only half listening to his denial, her heart and mind still consumed by the day she had spent with Matty. He had phoned her yesterday evening and told her he had wanted to take her to lunch today. And she had dropped everything, driven to Bainbridge, and purchased herself a new dress. A dress he couldn't seem to take his eyes off. It was glorious being with him. The most special time she'd ever had with anyone. And the way he kissed her. And held her. And the way he called her a precious gem, *his* precious gem, floored her. For some great, wonderful reason he had picked her out of the crowd. *Her.* Awkward Diane. It was enough to make a girl blush. It was enough to make a girl like Diane blush so gaily, so excitedly that even Frank had to stop his insistent denials and say something to her. "What's wrong with you?" he asked her.

Diane looked at him as if just discovering that he was in the room. "What?"

"What you smiling at? I'm bleeding here, Diane. These dudes won't hesitate to break both my legs if I don't get their money up, and you over there smiling? The least you can do is lend it to me."

Diane would have. Any other day and the fear of somebody hurting her brother would be enough to make her help him. But Matty's voice was in her ear. Telling her to stop being a sucker. Telling her to stop letting people use her so easily, because she wasn't helping them at all, and was only hurting herself. "I can't help you," she said to Frank.

The doorbell rang. Malveen, just to get out of Frank's presence for a few seconds, rose gingerly and went to answer it herself. Frank, however, was too busy staring at Diane to even notice his mother's movements.

"What do you mean you can't help me?" he asked her.

"I can't help you, Frank. Even if I had it to spare, which I don't, I wouldn't give it to you."

Even Willie James had to look at Diane. He'd never heard his daughter speak so bluntly. It was about time.

"Why not, Diane?" Frank asked. "What I ever done to you?"

"I gave you a thousand dollars on some investment scheme that you declared was supposed to change your life. A thousand dollars, Frank! I believed in you. I believed I was actually helping you to make your dream come true. And what did you do? Got yourself and every dopehead in this town high for days. That's what you did. On my hard-earned money!"

"I did invest that cash, don't even try that. But it didn't work out. Is it my fault that it didn't work out?"

"Regardless, Frank," Diane said, stopping his lies before they got started again, "I don't have any more money to lend you. All right?"

"But what about those dudes, Diane? They'll break my legs."

"I can't help you."

"But what about my legs?"

"She can't help your legs either," Willie James said. "And having no legs may be a good thing in your case anyway. Maybe you'll stop running up and down the road like a dope-fiend fool, embarrassing this family every time you step out that door."

"Wanda's here!" Malveen announced as she reentered the dining room, feeling a need to warn them of company, and Wanda Scott followed nervously behind her.

"And maybe you'll mind your own business, old man!" Frank shouted back at his father, ignoring his mother's announcement and Wanda's sudden appearance.

"Have a seat, Wanda," Malveen said, sitting down herself. "Don't mind them. They always arguing about something. Get you a plate."

"Oh, Miss Malveen, thanks, but I can't stay. I just needed to talk with Diane."

Diane had already detected that something wasn't right. Wanda was smiling, all right, but there was no cheerfulness in her eyes. "What's wrong, Sister Scott?" Diane asked her.

And, sure enough, Wanda's smile vanished. She exhaled. "I didn't think you heard the news. That's why I came by here first."

"What news?" Diane asked and by now everybody, including Frank, was looking at Wanda.

Wanda exhaled again. "Pastor Jolson's been arrested," she said.

Diane immediately flew to her feet, stunned witless. *"What?"* she asked.

"He's been arrested, Diane. Earlier today. For beating on Leah and trying to rape her."

"For beating, for raping…*Leah?*"

"Yes! Sheriff Crane said Leah told him Pastor done it."

Diane felt the floor shift beneath her and she held on to her chair for balance. Malveen leaned back, stunned. Willie James hesitated for a moment, but kept on eating. And Frank laughed. He let out a great, booming laugh.

"I knew it!" he yelled. "I knew that dude wasn't right! Trying to handle me while he's running around raping his own church members!" Frank laughed again. "I knew he wasn't right!"

"I never trusted him either," Malveen said. "No preacher I know of wear shoes like that. I never trusted him from the second I saw him."

"Huh!" Willie James said. "It's that Leah Littleton I never trusted. Before y'all go runnin' off condemning that preacher y'all better check out that Leah Littleton."

"I'm on my way over to her house now, Brother Tarver," Wanda said. "I hear she's taking it really hard. Even Judge Marshall and his wife gone over there. It's just awful. This is all just so awful."

"That poor child," Malveen said. "A preacher hurting her like that. And her family ain't worth sweeping out the door. She gon' need all the support she can get."

"The church will support her," Wanda said. "She needn't worry about that. Won't we, Diane?" She said this and looked at Diane, who, to Wanda's amazement, looked frozen in place.

"Diane," Wanda said, "are you all right? Diane?" Wanda literally had to shake her. A shake that caused Diane to finally break her stare and look at her. "Are you all right?"

"Where's Pastor?" Diane asked, still dazed by the news, still unable to even understand what she had just heard. "He's still in jail?"

"No, honey, no," Wanda said, feeling a need to reassure her. "He bailed himself out. He's home now."

"Have you spoken to him?"

Wanda shook her head. "No. He's not answering his phone."

Diane felt as if her world were crashing before her very eyes and she didn't know what she could do about it. Wanda could feel her anguish.

"Why don't you come with me, Diane," she said. "I'm going over to Leah's. It'll do you good to hear her side of things."

Diane almost said something harsh to Wanda. Leah's was the last place on earth she wanted to go. "Can't," she said.

"I know how you feel, Sister," Wanda replied. "This is all so awful." Then she shook her head. "Lord help us, Lord help us, Jesus help us!" She looked at Diane. "It is so unbelievable. Can you believe all this?"

That question did it for Diane. She stiffened her shoulders and stood completely erect. "No," she said, the first clear thought she'd had since Wanda arrived. "I can't believe any of it."

And she didn't waste another moment. As soon as Wanda was gone, as soon as Wanda's SUV left her curbside, she got into her own car and drove as quickly as she could to Matty's house. An awful miscarriage of justice was occurring, she knew it as sure as she knew her name. Matty wouldn't hurt anybody. He wouldn't try to rape anybody. All those times he could have taken advantage of Diane, all those passionate moments they shared, and he never did. Not ever. He was the one who always pulled back. He was the one who'd shown nothing but kindness and consideration and Godly love and concern to every one who'd ever met him. Why would a man like that rape Leah? And why would Leah suddenly be so unwilling when she'd never turned anybody else down before?

Diane prayed mightily as she stopped her car in front of Matty's house, jumped out, and ran up to his front door. She knew him. He was a proud man, a man who hated evil. This kind of lie was probably killing him. It was these same kind of tall tales they told on him in Chicago. The same kind of nonsense. And it stunk, to Diane. It all stunk to high heaven, to Diane. This was that rumor mill that had sunk Matty before. This was the kind of lie Matty wanted to shield her heart from. But he didn't have to worry, she wanted to tell him. It would take a lot more than Leah Littleton's word to get Diane to lose faith in him.

She knocked on the door and rang the doorbell and called his name over and over. But there was no response. His car was in his driveway, his Jaguar sat quietly in place, so she knew he was at home. "Don't shut me out, too, Matty," she wanted to say. And she would. If he'd only open the door.

But he couldn't. He was inside the house, lying on his bed, listening to Diane's yells and pleas and he was aching all the more. He was not about to drive her down this road with him. It would be humiliating enough. His name would be in all the papers. Maybe his mug shot, too. *Preacher accused of attempted rape on parishioner.* And in the court of public opinion he would be guilty as charged. Hung out to dry again.

That was why he lay there. He heard the pain in her voice and the persistence in her knocking, but he still didn't move. He wasn't about to allow it. He wasn't letting sweet Diane become part and parcel of this hell called his life, no matter how badly she thought she wanted in. Because now she would be fine. She'd survive this round. But what about the other rounds? There was certain to be many more. What about the cumulative effect? It would be too much. And she wouldn't make it. She couldn't. He was barely hanging on, himself.

So he lay there and listened, every inch of his body dying to go to her, to explain everything, to hold her. But it couldn't be. This was a walk he had to walk alone.

He thought about Leah. He divorced the noise around him from his mind and thought hard about Leah Littleton.

She was the real victim here. Although she thought she knew exactly what she was doing, that her little scheme was her concoction and hers alone, he knew better than that. She was a victim. Another victim of the wiles of the devil. Another human soul unable to distinguish the dark side from the light.

He dragged himself out of bed and fell on his knees, his heart lifting up Leah Littleton in his prayers.

Only God could help them now.

But Diane would not give up. By the time his prayer was over and he was getting off his knees, she was banging on his bedroom window. Then his back door. By the time he walked into the living room, just to get away from the sound, she was back up front, too, banging on his door again. He hurried to it, and threw it open. He had hoped to avoid this, but she left him no choice.

"Go home, Diane!" he yelled as soon as he opened the door.

Diane was frantic, her face flushed with unbearable pain and concern. Matty's heart dropped.

"I know you didn't hurt anyone," she said, she pleaded.

"Diane, don't."

"I believe you, Matty. Leah's lying. I know she is!"

"Diane," Matty said, his heart a torrent of pain, "just go, all right? This is not your fight. Now just go on home and stay out of this."

"But Matty, I can help you."

"Didn't you hear me? Just leave, Diane! I don't want your help!"

His anger was palpable. And Diane couldn't bear it. Tears streamed down her face and her heart pounded against her chest. Why was he behaving like this? Why was he behaving as if—as if it were true! He hadn't hurt Leah. He hadn't tried to rape Leah. Why was he acting as though he had? She stared at him for some kind of answer. He had to tell her more than this.

But his anger wouldn't subside, and no other words came. The hate all over his face didn't abate for one solitary second. And she couldn't bear it. She left his sight. She turned and walked away, looking back at him, to be certain that it was true. When she saw him still glaring at her, the look on his intense face still filled with disgust for her, as if it were all her fault, she ran.

"I'm fine," Leah said as she accepted another cup of coffee from Sam. She and Ira had come over that evening, sitting so close together like the perfect married couple, fooling everybody except Leah, because she knew the brother.

Wanda Scott was also there, and Sister Mayfield, and a few other members. All were sitting in Leah's small living room talking quietly, everyone voicing their amazement that a man who put himself out as a preacher of the gospel could do such a horrible thing.

Leah, however, was almost bored. It wasn't the kind of triumph she'd thought it would be. She, in fact, didn't feel triumphant at all. All she could think about was what Wanda had said. They put Matty in handcuffs like a common criminal and carted him off to jail, she said. Matty in jail? For some reason Leah hadn't even considered that consequence. All she wanted was for him to feel humiliated the way he had humiliated her. But jail and prison and all of this talk about how much time he might get was making her far more uncomfortable than she ever thought she'd be. Matty was such a proud man, such an impatient, almost strident man. The idea that he would take this lying down didn't seem plausible to Leah. But according to Wanda that was exactly what he had done. Matty didn't say a word, she said, when they were taking him away. Not one mumbling word. And he wouldn't even look any of them in the face. "He was acting so guilty," Wanda had said. But Leah knew he wasn't. Why would an innocent man act guilty? That was the question for Leah. And it was gnawing at her.

She also didn't like the attention she was getting. Everybody was calling or dropping by, from Deacon Molt to Sister Inez, Sister Baker to Deacon Benford. Everybody seemed so ready to jump on the bandwagon of a woman who rarely even darkened the doors of their church, against a man who was supposed to be their church leader. A man of God. A *true* man of God. *What hypocrites,* Leah thought, and she found herself dwelling on the faults of the saints rather than her own maliciousness.

"I never really trusted him, to be honest with you," Sam said, sitting down gingerly beside her husband. Ira quickly placed his arm around her. Their little lovey-dovey act wasn't fooling Leah for a second, however, as she watched Sam wince every time she moved, and all Leah could do was shake her head. He had beat Sam again. So much so that it was painful for Sam to even sit down. But Ira Marshall was supposed to be this great Christian man. He was supposed to be this bastion of Christian morality. He was moral all right, Leah thought. Just another churchgoing hypocrite, if you asked her.

"From day one," Sam continued, "when he instituted that church-every-Sunday policy, I knew we'd better keep our eyes on him." Sam had her own reasons not to mourn Matty's downfall. He knew too much, she felt, about Ira, about their life in general, and he had to be stopped before he ruined everything she had fought so hard to hold on to. This, she was certain, would slow him down if not completely stop him in his tracks.

"And the way he let just anybody join our church," Sister Mayfield said. "Folks that ain't saved, ain't thinking about getting saved, just coming to church just to come somewhere."

"Well, ladies," Ira said, "I certainly hate to see a man fall, but I believe he's one who deserves it. Like my wife, I never trusted him either."

"But he does so much good," Wanda said and everybody looked at her. "He's helping the men take care of their responsibilities. He brings new blood into the church, young people and such. And what about those folks who had houses in foreclosures and he helped them without blaming them? He didn't just say he'd pray for their misfortune, which was the most they were hoping for, but he actually pulled out his checkbook and wrote checks to their mortgage companies. And these weren't foolish young people who didn't know how to budget. These were old folks who had let some swindlers connive them into expensive second mortgages to pay for repair work they didn't need and never could afford in the first place. Pastor Jolson helped every one of them. He helped you, too, Sister Mayfield, remember that?"

Mayfield rolled her eyes. She remembered his help, but she didn't want to hear about that right now. But Wanda was going to tell it. "When you needed to get to Cincinnati to see about your people," she continued, "it was Pastor Jolson who took care of everything. All at a great cost to him. And yes, he does go into the bars and nightclubs and encourage those unsaved folks to come to church. Pastor knows they're sinners, he never tried to say they weren't. He just believes that if they come to church often enough then they'll eventually hear a word from the Lord and turn their lives over to Christ."

"Not if he's the one got to deliver that word," Sam said. "And he may have done all those things you said, Wanda. But look at Leah. Look at that bruise on the side of her face. He could have killed her!"

Leah cringed. Why didn't they just leave that alone? she wanted to know. It was over with now, as far as she was concerned, and she didn't see the point of continually rehashing it. If she didn't hear Matty Jolson's name again for as long as she lived, that would be all right with her.

But the doorbell rang. And when Wanda opened the door and Diane walked in, she knew her wish was not about to come true. The look all over Diane's face said it all. She didn't believe a word of Leah's allegation.

"Sit down, Diane," Sam said smilingly. "I know you're as shocked as the rest of us."

"I need to talk with Leah," Diane said, her large eyes staring at Leah and Leah alone.

"We all need to talk with Leah," Sam said, "and in time we all will. But right now she's still traumatized, as you can imagine."

"Yes, I can imagine," Diane said, her voice purposely sarcastic.

Leah exhaled. Either Diane was going to make a scene in front of everybody or she would get her private audience with Leah and make a scene with her alone. Either way, Leah knew, Diane was going to have her say.

"Sam's right, y'all," Leah said, sitting the cup of coffee on her cocktail table. "I am tired and still traumatized and all that. But Diane is very close to the pastor so maybe spending some time alone with her is a good idea."

"Are you sure?" Sam asked.

"I'm positive. I need Diane to understand exactly what happened."

Ira, suddenly, became upset. Jolson was dropping like a rock and he didn't want the likes of Diane Tarver to impede his descent. "You need her to understand?" he asked. "There's nothing to understand! He tried to rape you, Leah, what else does she need to know?" Then Ira looked at Diane. "What's the problem, Diane? You don't believe her?"

Diane didn't respond. She couldn't release her death stare on Matty's accuser to even hear Ira Marshall. She had thought she knew Leah. She'd never completely trusted her, it was true, but she at least thought she knew her. She knew Leah was a tireless self-promoter, somebody who was going to look out for her own interests if she didn't look out for anybody else's. And she'd play fair or she'd play dirty, but she'd get her way. But never, never had she known Leah to be a malicious liar, somebody who would be so consumed with herself that she wouldn't just hurt somebody else, she'd destroy him. It was a sobering realization, Diane thought, as she stared at the woman at the center of this storm, and she understood clearly for the first time why Matty had been so hesitant to open his heart to her. If she'd been through what he'd been through, in Chicago first, and now here in Floradale, thanks to Leah, then she would have closed up, too.

"Diane," Sam said, "my husband is talking to you."

"I need to talk with Leah," Diane said again, determined to hold her ground. Sam had always admired that about Diane, that unwavering faith of hers, and she knew trying to convince her of Pastor Jolson's guilt would be nearly impossible. But if anybody could pull it off, Sam felt, Leah could.

"Okay, ladies," Ira said, rising, prompting everybody else, except Leah, to rise, too. "Perhaps it is best if we leave."

"Agreed," Wanda said. "I'll call on you later, Sister Littleton."

"Thank you," Leah said. "Thank you all. And thank you especially, Judge Marshall, for taking time out of your busy schedule to come and see about me."

"You're welcome," Ira said without smiling, inwardly seething at Leah's carelessness. He placed his arm around Sam's waist, to blunt any suspicions she could have possibly had. But from the look on her cheerful face, he knew better. Sam idolized him. That was why he loved her. That was why he wasn't about to let Leah Littleton or anybody else break up his happy home.

"And don't you worry about a thing, Leah," Wanda said as they all made their way to the front door. "This is an awful tragedy. But Fountain Hope will stand by you through this whole ordeal."

Leah smiled. Fountain Hope had better leave her alone, that's what Fountain Hope had better do. She wanted them to forget this mess, not showcase it! She'd said what she said and that was all she was going to say about it.

Diane, however, had other ideas. It was apparent as soon as the house had emptied and she asked that all important question: "What happened?"

"At least sit down, Diane," Leah said.

"No, thank you. Just tell me what happened, please."

Leah smiled. "You are so naive. What you think happened? He wanted me, Diane. But I didn't want him. That's what happened."

Diane stared at her. "I don't believe you," she said.

Leah laughed. "And? Is that supposed to upset me?"

"What you're doing is dangerous, Leah."

"Dangerous? What I'm doing? What about what your boyfriend did? I know you don't wanna believe that he could be like that, but hey, that's not my problem."

"He's a preacher," Diane said passionately. "The pastor of our church. You can't lie on a man like that and expect no retribution."

"Number one, I'm not lying, okay? And number two, what kind of retribution? Matty better not try nothing with me because I got my connections, too. He bring goons my way, my uncles and cousins will be coming his way. They might just drop in on you, too, if you don't watch yourself."

Diane shook her head. The woman had no clue. Leah Littleton had no idea the firestorm she'd pulled herself into. "You're gonna rue the day you ever told this lie, Leah. I guarantee it. You may not feel it now, or even a week or month from now, but eventually you're gonna feel it. Eventually you will have to give account."

"We all got to give account. Ain't just me. All have sinned and come short. And as for your boyfriend he ain't no saint either, okay?"

"He didn't say he was. He'd be the last person on earth to claim perfection. But he's still a man of God. And you can't do what you're doing to a man of God, Leah. Think! Use your head for once in your life and think about what you're doing!"

Leah stood up. "You know what, I'm tired, I'm angry, and as far as I'm concerned this conversation is over. He tried to rape me and you're making me out to be the villain? Get out!"

Diane thought she knew Leah. But now, looking into her hard, cold eyes, her face almost gleeful in a twisted, demonic sort of way, made Diane realize the truth. She didn't know her at all.

She left. And it was a good thing, too, because Leah had been close to throwing her out. How dare she call her a liar. How dare she act as if Matty was all holier than thou and Leah was the big troublemaker. Matty had started this trouble. Matty was the one who humiliated her. What did Diane expect her to do? Take the humiliation the way she would have? Not on her life. Leah Littleton didn't crawl for anybody. They dig one ditch, they'd better dig two, as far as Leah was concerned, because just as sure as somebody did it to her, she was definitely going to do it to them. And love every minute of it. The aftereffects of this one were different, however. She didn't feel all that elated the way she thought she would, and the idea that Matty might do some time in prison wasn't something she cared to think about. But at least she got her revenge. At least Diane and everybody else would think twice before they ever again tried to handle Leah Littleton.

Chapter 16

The weeks following Leah's allegations were a blur to Matty. He prayed and fasted, sat on his porch and watched the cars drive by, walked around his house just to stretch his legs. They were long, lonely weeks. He felt as if his life were a careening ball of fire, heading straight over a cliff, and there was nothing he could do about it. Lie after lie had been told on him. As soon as he came up for air, as soon as he felt that he'd weathered the storm, another hurricane veered his way. And another lie was told. Now he was battle weary, and just about ready to call it a day. He was just about ready to interrupt production and stop this disaster movie they called his life, and get out. But that Sunday night, nearly a month after Leah first made her devastating allegations, proved calming. For the first night in a long time, Matty was able to sleep. As soon as he laid his head on his pillow, instead of tossing and turning, instead of wondering when it would all be over and whether he should resign or just wait until they fired him, he slept like a baby.

On that same night Diane, too, in her own bed on Clarion Avenue, was amazed at how easily sleep came to her. She had been worried all month, so devastated by the allegations and what she knew they had to be doing to Matty, that her life seemed to be turned upside down. She wanted to go to him every day and beg him not to shut her out, but she remembered that look in his eyes. He told her that he didn't want her help, that his battle was not her fight. He was upset, she knew it, and he may not have meant a word he said. But that look in his eyes, the disgust that was all over his face, made her think otherwise.

Bishop Owens came to town and preached every Sunday. Matty was nowhere to be seen. Diane was disappointed; she had hoped Matty would at least show up for service even if he wasn't allowed to preach, just to prove to those unbelievers that he was as innocent as she knew he was. But he didn't show. Bishop had told them to stand fast, that God was still on the throne and He had it all in control. Bishop didn't know what the truth was, he'd said, but he knew Matty. And he implored them to keep the faith a little longer, to not rush to judgment, and everything, he assured them, would be all right.

It seemed doubtful, Diane thought, when Matty didn't show up for church, despite Bishop's positive, upbeat sermons. And after service, when she tried once again to get Matty to open his door and talk to her, and he didn't even come to the door, her doubt increased. Matty was tired of fighting, tired of the lies and the rumors. And it seemed to Diane that he might have given up. Which only added to her stress and worry, and which also kept her on her knees. But on that Sunday night, nearly a month after Leah's lies shifted her entire world, she actually, remarkably, found rest.

Across town, however, on Juniper Street, Leah Littleton found anything but rest. She woke up in a cold sweat, her clothes drenched, her soul stunned with fear. The voice was so clear, so plain, and it would not stop. *Touch not my anointed,* it kept saying. *Touch not my anointed.* Over and over again. Leah looked around her room, and then she ran through her entire house. Ready to hurt somebody. Ready to cuss somebody out. What kind of joke did they think they were playing on her? But nobody was there. Just that voice. That soft, still voice that pierced her eardrums. *Touch not my anointed.* No more than that. No less than that. Just those four words over and over. Was she dreaming? Was she crazy? She stood in the middle of her hallway and jammed her hands over her ears. And then suddenly, just like that, the voice ceased.

Leah, at first, was skeptical. She looked from side to side, certain that she would hear those words again. Surely a voice that had tormented her all night, a voice that would not relent for a second, was just toying with her again. But a minute passed, then two, then five, and not a sound was heard. Leah, drenched in sweat, shaking in fear, decided that it was just the trauma of the week. It was just her imagination. That was it. It had to be. A bad, bad flight of fanciful imagination.

She did not return to her bed, however, but instead lay down on the sofa in her living room. But as soon as sleep returned, as soon as she had concluded that her good sense was back in check and drowsiness overtook her, she saw a hole, and she was falling into it, and it was never ending. She tried to break her fall, she grabbed for the side walls, grabbed for air, grabbed for whatever she could grab for, but she kept on falling. And falling and falling. And then that voice came again. *Touch not my anointed,* it said. Again and again. And then she heard children screaming, with the screams getting closer and closer to her. And then she saw the face. A form of a face she could not comprehend, a form of a face she'd never seen before. But the terror of that face. The horrific terror.

She woke up.

And ran.

She tore out of her house, and began running down the street in just her pajamas, running and screaming and pounding on neighbors' doors. Until she realized she had forgotten her car. She ran back into her house, grabbed her keys, and then jumped into her car and drove like a bat out of hell, drove as if her life depended on her speed, until she stopped in front of the Floradale Police Department. Sheriff Crane wasn't there. But his deputy was.

"Lady, calm down," the deputy said again, as he was unable to understand a word this hysterical woman who stood before him was saying.

"You've got to tell them to stop," Leah said, exhausted. Nobody understood her. Why wasn't anybody understanding her? "You've got to make them stop!"

"Make who stop?" the deputy asked her, baffled.

"Them. I saw it. I saw it. Make them stop!"

"Just hold on, lady. Now just settle yourself down. I can't help you if I don't know what you're talking about. Now, who's them? Who are you talking about?"

"It wasn't true," Leah said, ignoring the deputy's plea. "I lied. I lied on Matty Jolson. But he didn't want me, you see. He didn't want me. And I'm just as good as Diane Tarver. But he didn't want me. You should have seen the way he looked at me. He couldn't bear the sight of me. So I lied. He had humiliated me, you see. But he never touched me. Touch not my anointed."

The deputy frowned. "What?"

"He wouldn't. But what was I supposed to do? He had humiliated me! That's why you've got to help me now. They coming. They coming, I tell ya. And I saw them. I saw them! Jesus help me, I saw them!" Leah grabbed the deputy by his shirt as if only he could save her now. "Don't let them take me away. I didn't mean it. I swear I didn't mean it. Make them stop. Please make them stop!"

Leah began running around as if her feet were on fire. The deputy and two other lawmen tried frantically to restrain her, to get what they considered to be this pajama-wearing crazy woman to calm herself down, but her soul refused to be comforted. She kept on screaming, and lifting up her feet and running her hands up and down her silk pajamas, and asking them—no, *begging* them—to make them stop.

Matty did not break his fast with word of Leah's retraction. Deacon Molt came to his house to personally tell him the news, to tell him how Leah had gone mad with guilt and was now hospitalized claiming that demons were pursuing her. Every hour on the hour she was waking up and screaming, begging them to stop the demons from getting her, and the hospital staff said they'd never seen anything like it. They had to sedate her twice before she was anywhere near calm. "But even then," Deacon Molt had said, "every time she woke back up, she was screaming about them demons."

Molt's news didn't lessen the overwhelming burden Matty felt in his heart. Such strange news had, in fact, heightened it. But what could he do? He had warned Leah. He had told her to knock it off. But she was so offended. She was so certain that he was anything but who he claimed to be and she was going to prove it. Like his wife eleven years earlier who had left him without giving him a chance to explain. Like the woman in Chicago who had attempted suicide in his name when he barely even knew hers. They all thought he wasn't who he claimed to be and they all were going to cut him down to size.

And they all had, in their way.

It took nearly another week before Matty returned to the church. He hadn't been sure if he was going to return at all. But he did, even though he still had not recovered. His ability to trust anyone was near zero again. His exhaustion with life was all over his face and in his walk and talk and everything about his manner. It was not his bright idea to become a minister of the gospel, and it could never have been clearer than now. He didn't come back to his duties at Fountain Hope on the strength of his own righteousness, or on the romantic whim of some great love he had for his vocation. He came back because he had to come back. God had called him, God had ordained it to be so, God didn't make mistakes.

Diane went to see him the same day of his return. She arrived at the church and eagerly sent her request by Wanda Scott, who had become Matty's assistant, asking if she could have a word with him. He hadn't seen Diane since that day Leah made her allegations, and he'd desperately wanted to see her and hold her again, explain it all to her. But he couldn't. He cared about her enough that he couldn't. "Tell her no," he said to his stunned assistant. "I'm too busy and she'll only get in the way. Tell her no."

Those words confused Diane to such a degree that for the longest time after Wanda stopped talking, she just stood there. Matty wouldn't see her? The ordeal was over, but he still wouldn't see her? She looked at Wanda, searching for answers on her face, but Wanda was as perplexed as Diane. And almost as disappointed.

"He'll come around, Diane," she finally said, praying that somehow those words, those grossly inadequate words, could comfort her. Diane attempted to smile, as if she believed it, too, but the look on her face told Wanda differently. And Wanda felt angry with herself. If she had any spunk, if she had any backbone, she would tell Pastor Jolson about himself. Diane believed in him when no one else did. How could he turn her away?

But he had. And it was his right to do so. Wanda knew it and Diane knew it, too. That was why she left. That was why she thanked Wanda anyway for all of her kindness, and hurried out of the sanctuary.

Diane's flower garden, in the northwest corner of her parents' backyard, was surrounded by shrubbery and border grass. It was small and well maintained. After work most days lately she could be found on her knees at the garden's edge, digging and pruning and sprucing up. A week and three days after Leah's retraction she was in that very garden, this time potting plants, her mind oblivious to the world and all its contradictions, when Matty walked into her backyard.

She heard him before she saw him, but her body's reaction told her it was him. A chill ran down her spine. Her stomach muscles began to tighten. Her heart began to quiver. It was Matty.

She had her small trowel in hand as she began to upturn earth. She looked at his shoes first, shiny black and expensive. Then at his ash-gray pants and suit coat. And then, finally, his face. He had on dark sunglasses, his hands were in his pockets, and he stared down at her as if he were rooted where he stood. She wanted desperately to stop what she was doing and jump into his arms, dirt-smudged hands and all, and let him know how very pleased she was that Leah had finally told the truth. But she held her ground. He would not see her that day she hurried to the church to welcome him back, and it had broken her heart. Wanda had said it was just that he was busy on his first day back at work, but Diane knew better than that. This was the man she thought she was going to spend the rest of her life with. If he felt half the same for her, he would have found time to at least say hello. Besides, he hadn't allowed any contact with her since Leah's allegations, he wouldn't even talk to her on the phone, not one time during his ordeal. And his actions said it all to Diane. That was why she didn't move an inch.

"Good evening," he said to her in a voice that failed to carry much enthusiasm.

She squinted her eyes from the sun as she looked up at him, at those dark shades that were able to conceal whatever emotion might be visible in his eyes. "Good evening," she replied, and went back to grabbing chunks of dirt and stuffing it into her small pots.

Matty crouched down to her, and just the whiff of his fresh cologne, a smell she'd missed, made her heart pound faster. "This yours?" he asked her.

Diane looked around, at the garden she had begun the year after she returned from college. A garden that was fast becoming her own little place of refuge. "Yes," she said.

"Not bad."

"Not good. It's small."

"Nothing wrong with that."

"And my azaleas are all dying out and my trumpet creepers keep wanting to bend and break and I can't get those black-eyed Susans to act right for nothing in this world." Diane dug her trowel deep into the earth with an angry shove. "But what difference does it make?" she asked.

Matty stared at her, the pain and frustration so evident on her pretty face that it shattered any hopes of peace he had. He removed his shades. "Diane, I'm sorry," he said.

She looked at him, startled by his words, his dark gray eyes almost vulnerable in their sincerity, but she looked away from him and continued to upturn earth. "I was only trying to be there for you."

"I know that."

"But you shut me out." She said this with too much emotion, she knew, but she couldn't help it. It was how she felt. She looked at him again. "Why, Matty?" she asked him.

Matty exhaled. Then he tried to smile. "I could use a cigarette," he said, his shades swinging lightly in his hand, his eyes suddenly looking around the sizable yard. "Problem is,

I don't smoke anymore. I gave it up. You know why I gave it up? Because I finally reached the conclusion that smoking wasn't good for me. It was late in coming, but it came." He looked at Diane. "I'm not good for you, Diane. That's why."

Diane wanted to argue with him, to tell him he was perfect for her, what in the world was he talking about, but she didn't say a word. She wasn't good enough for *him,* that was the real reason, she felt. He didn't want to be bothered with her, was the bottom line. She would be yet another burden for him, yet another somebody he had to be responsible for, and he didn't care enough for her to want to delve that deep. So he decided not to delve at all.

"I just wanted to thank you," Matty said when it was clear she wasn't going to respond. "I want to thank you for not judging me. I want to thank you for your faithfulness. You're a gem, a precious child of God, and someday you're going to make a man mighty happy. I want you to forget about me and go on with your life, Diane. You deserve it."

Diane could not believe what she was hearing. He spoke as if he knew every inch of her most private thoughts. And she didn't like it. "I've already gone on with my life," she said with some degree of bitterness. "In fact, I never stopped going on with my life. My life didn't stop just because I met you, just because I thought it was my Christian duty to not judge you. So I don't know what you're talking about."

Her sternness surprised Matty, even though he knew he should not be surprised at all. People can take just so much. And the way he'd treated her, kissing her and caressing her one minute, then barring her from his life the next, was more anguish than any woman should be asked to endure. But she was strong and now, thankfully, a little angry, too. She'd get over him in a heartbeat, he felt.

He stood to his feet. Her heart dropped to her knees. "You take care, Diane," he said. She continued to pot her plants, without looking up at him again, and he lingered a little longer than necessary, but then he left.

She could feel the tears coming, but they never quite materialized. There was nothing really to cry about. God had blessed him through his ordeal with Leah. Bishop Owens and the national board of bishops had stood by him. Leah was now, hopefully, getting some much-needed help for her emotional problems, problems that had been manifesting long before Matty came along. Everybody, it seemed, was better off this way. Everybody, Diane thought as she fought back tears and grabbed another chunk of dirt, but her.

Chapter 17

Life moved on around Floradale as Fountain Hope slowly began to recover from the trauma of Leah's allegations. The scandal itself eventually faded into the woodwork of time and living and new distractions, and everybody who thought Matty could not possibly recover from such a momentous setback was wrong.

He continued to preach the word of God from the barrooms to the pulpit, enduring the stares and nasty whispers, going about his Father's business despite his own emotional exhaustion. He thought about quitting nearly every single day, but he didn't. He kept on pressing his way, praising God in his weariness, knowing in his soul that this was not about him, but God's name must be glorified. And he was determined to give God that glory.

He also continued to give the church leadership fits with his unwavering devotion to men and women of low estate, as he began a door-to-door ministry that brought so many lost souls into the church that the rolls swelled to the point of standing room only; to the point where the leadership had to begin daily meetings to see about expanding the sanctuary. It was a far cry from a few weeks earlier when Matty first returned to his official duties. As soon as word spread that he was back, nearly fifteen percent of the membership left the church in protest, insisting that they would not have a rapist as their spiritual leader. Molt was frantic for many reasons, but mainly because a great number of those members were some of Fountain Hope's most faithful tithers, and he sought to quell the exodus by making it clear to one and all that Leah had admitted she'd lied. But that didn't matter to them at all. Ever since Matty Jolson stepped foot in Floradale he'd done nothing but stir up trouble, they said, and this, to them, was the last stir.

Matty listened to the accusations. He stood in the pulpit or sat behind his office desk or walked around the church ground and heard it all. They were judge and jury and he was condemned without one of them, not one of them, asking him a single question. All they had to do was ask. *Are you guilty, Reverend? Is it true, Reverend? Tell us your side of the story, Reverend?* But not one of them bothered. Except Diane, of course, who believed in him through the entire ordeal. Only he had to keep her away. They'd devour her, too, if they could, if he broke down and allowed her into his hellish world. And that was exactly why he wasn't allowing it.

Some things he rejoiced in, however. He knew that the devil meant the membership drop as a curse, as yet another example of Matty's failed leadership, but God turned that curse into a blessing, and the results, Matty was pleased to see, bore it out. Fifteen percent of the old membership departed, but, by summer's end, nearly thirty percent new membership emerged. They were members starved for the word of God, desperately seeking a better life, and Matty aimed to lead them to the One who could give it to them.

He still kept Sister Inez on pins and needles, however, with his creative use of those new members. Such as the time when he allowed a blues singer to sing in the church choir. The woman wasn't even saved yet, from what Inez could surmise, and he allowed her to sing! Inez couldn't abide that. Or the time he had members of his recovering–addicts class conduct a car-wash detailing business on church grounds, washing cars not to benefit the church, but to feed their families. The only requirement Matty had was that they pay their tithe, and he wasn't making them do even that. "Half don't pay, Pastor," Inez was quick to point out, "and the other half don't know what a tenth mean. They pay what they wanna pay, which is usually mere pennies on the dollar."

But Matty didn't change his approach at all. He didn't believe in legislating Christian conduct and he wasn't about to start. If people aimed to do right, they would, he believed. And if they didn't, then their decision was between them and God. Inez, beyond frustration with her leader, left his office shaking her head.

Diane kept on keeping on, too. Church, choir rehearsal, helping Pam with her kids, bailing Frank out of one jam after another one, chauffeuring her mother around town. It was her very life before she met Matty. A good life. A contented life. And happiness wasn't the issue.

It was true that Diane had hoped time would change Matty's mind but he seemed more determined than ever to keep his distance from her. At first she couldn't deal with it. She'd go home and pray for God to tear down the wall of protection Matty had erected around himself. But as the weeks came and went she grew weary, too. She thought about leaving Fountain Hope, to lessen her own pain, but she wasn't about to let some man run her away from God. Fountain Hope was her home. And she loved it there. And if Matty Jolson couldn't see her heart, if Matty Jolson couldn't understand that she only meant him well, then that was his problem. But she wasn't leaving her home.

Leah's life went on, too. She was eventually released from the psychiatric hospital that had kept her for weeks, but instead of returning to her beauty salon in Floradale, she sold her interest and moved to Memphis. She was released from care and free to go but, according to Deacon Molt, she still wasn't right. She still saw demons. She still heard children screaming. She still would kick up her feet like they were on fire just when you thought she was coming around.

She asked to see Matty before she left town, to beg his forgiveness she had said, and when Molt set up the meeting it became anything but forgiving. Leah stood in Deacon Molt's office and lashed out at Matty, calling him everything but what he was, using the profanity of a sailor denied shore leave. Molt was stunned. He could not believe the hate that spewed from Leah's lips, and in the house of God no less. Matty, however, wasn't surprised in the least. He just sat there and prayed for her. She stood over him, yelling and pointing, but he prayed. Molt had to get three other deacons to get that Leah Littleton and her profane mouth out of the church. Matty, however, prayed without ceasing for Leah Littleton's soul.

Two months after Leah's retraction, when the one-time talk of the town was now barely even mentioned, Ira, Jr., and Alan were at home watching cartoons on television. Although they heard their parents arguing, and the occasional scuffling sounds from the room upstairs, they didn't move an inch from the TV. It was a typical Friday night at home for them. It didn't bother them.

At least it didn't bother Junior. He was a year older and much more adroit at tuning out. Little Alan, however, wasn't so blessed. It was his mother's voice that haunted him. She wasn't yelling at his father, she was begging him. *Ira, please don't. Ira, you know I wouldn't do that. Ira, for the love of God, let's just talk about it!* And on and on it went. Alan even cov-

ered his ears, to drown out the sound of his mother's plead-
ing voice.

But he still heard it. Heard it like firecrackers in his ears.
He looked at Junior, who was twirling around his toy mus-
cleman action figure as he stared unblinkingly at the TV. It
wasn't bothering Junior at all, Alan thought. Why was it
bothering him?

But when his mother screamed in that high-pitched voice
of hers, Alan didn't care why anymore. He jumped from his
chair and ran upstairs. His small hand held tightly on to the
fancy banister as one foot then the other hit down with each
stair he climbed. He could hear the commotion clearer and
clearer as he climbed. He could hear his father's terrifying
voice, and his mother's reassuring voice. He could hear what
sounded like chairs being moved around and other furniture being tossed around. He could hear the movement of
feet, as if his mother were trying her best to get away, but
couldn't. He moved faster. He pushed his glasses up on his
nose and moved faster. He had to get her out of there. But
how? he wondered, as he moved toward that dreaded room.
The door was closed, it was always closed, so he had to open
it. That's it, he decided. Just open the door. Then she could
escape. If only he could get that bedroom door open, then
she'd be safe.

He walked up to the huge white door that looked larger
than ever to Alan. He placed both of his hands on the knob
and turned it, his small shoulders pushing into the door. It
opened immediately. He released the knob so that his mother
would have room to escape. And as Alan had hoped, the door
did give her plenty good room, swinging widely. Only it
swung wide just as Ira Marshall, his father, grabbed a large
and expensive lamp from the nightstand, snatching it from
the socket as if he were Superman himself, and then violently
threw it at his wife with all the strength he had within him.
His wife, fortunately, ducked. Alan, however, didn't have time.

★ ★ ★

Wanda Scott was already at the hospital when Matty arrived. She was sitting alone on a bench near the entrance, her eyes red from too much crying, a well-worn tissue stuffed in her hands. When she saw Matty's tall frame come through the doors, she stood up quickly. Matty hurried to her.

"I'm so glad you came, Pastor," she said, as she fell into Matty's arms. Matty, who appeared as concerned as Wanda, pulled her back and looked at her. "What happened?" he asked her.

"It's just awful, Pastor. Just awful."

"You said on the phone there was an accident."

"Yes."

"Involving?"

"Sister Marshall's littlest boy."

"Alan?"

"Yes, yes, Alan. He's such a sweet child, Pastor. How could anything bad happen to such a sweet child?"

Matty exhaled. He had no answers either. "Now listen to me, Sister Scott. I need you to tell me exactly what happened."

Wanda shook her head. "I don't really know myself. I was out here at the hospital visiting some sick folks, just doing my Christian duty, when I saw Judge and Sister Marshall and little Alan was on the stretcher and there was blood everywhere, Pastor, it was just awful. I heard one of the nurses tell another nurse that Alan was in bad shape. Some kind of head injury."

"Good Lord. Was it from a car accident or—"

"I don't think so. One of the nurses seems to think he was at home or something. But it was all so confusing, what with everybody rushing the poor child to surgery, so I don't really know what's going on."

Matty stood erect and exhaled angrily. What would be the excuse this time? he wondered. "Where's Alan now? Is he still in surgery?"

Wanda, fighting back new tears, nodded. Matty rubbed her on the arm to comfort her. She was a good woman, a good, caring, Christian woman. "What about the parents? Where are they?"

Wanda sniffled and blew her nose with a tissue. "In the waiting room," she said. "It's so depressing, Pastor. I had to get out of there. But that's why I called you. Somebody needs to be with them, to pray for them."

Matty nodded. He was certain he would not have been the Marshalls' choice as prayer warrior, but he walked swiftly to the waiting room just the same. He was still their pastor, whether they liked it or not.

Ira Marshall was in the room, standing near the back wall talking calmly with Sheriff Crane, the same man who had arrested Matty, the same man who had seemed to take pleasure in handcuffing him. Matty could feel a tinge of bitterness just seeing Crane, but he quickly repressed it. This wasn't about him or his anger. It was about Alan and what had happened to him. That was why he stared at Ira Marshall. He couldn't seem to take his eyes off that man. Ira's charm offensive was in overdrive, as he easily had the sheriff's undivided attention. The sad part was that the sheriff was nodding as if he believed every word. The sad part was Ira's ability to tell a tale wrought with so much plausibility that it would be all the sheriff needed to hear. Something plausible. Something he could write down in his little notepad and go on home to his family. But it would take a lot more than plausibility to persuade Matty.

Samantha Marshall was also in the room, sitting in a chair with her older son, Junior, staring at a wall as if she were in a trance. She looked just awful to Matty, as if the poor woman had seen hell in session. Gone was the vibrancy. Gone was that great smile. Gone, he hoped, was that conviction in her soul that Judge Ira Marshall wasn't so bad after all.

Matty went to Sam and sat in the chair beside hers. She didn't move an inch in recognition, but given the circumstances, he didn't expect her to.

He decided to ask the tough questions right away, before her husband intervened. "What happened, Sister Marshall?" he asked her.

She didn't say a word.

"Sister, this is your pastor, and I know it's difficult for you right now. But I need you to tell me what happened."

After a moment, Sam exhaled. "The lamp hit Alan," she said, still staring, still seemingly unmoved.

"How did it hit him?"

"The lamp hit Alan." She looked at Matty. "He didn't duck."

Matty swallowed hard. "Who threw the lamp, Sister Marshall? Who threw it?"

"She's tired, Reverend," Ira's deep voice said suddenly and Matty quickly looked his way. The sheriff was closing up his notepad and Ira was walking toward Matty and Sam. Unlike Matty, who was at the church when Wanda phoned and therefore still in his suit, Ira was far more casually dressed in a pair of pants and a pullover shirt. He also wore the look of a man so tightly wound up that he could explode at any moment. Matty was hoping for that explosion right here, right now, for all to see. He stood up.

"Hello, Reverend," Ira said with his trademark smile.

"Judge," Matty replied, not even attempting to pretend any regard whatsoever for the man in front of him.

"She's still traumatized by this evening's events," Ira said. "That's why she's unresponsive right now. She's too worried about little Alan to answer your questions."

"She answered them," Matty said.

Ira stared at him, that explosiveness beginning to bubble to the surface. "I'm sure she's confused right now."

"I don't know," Matty said. "I didn't detect any confusion."

The door to the waiting room opened with a wild swing and Diane, in one of her rayon skirt suits, hurried in. Her face was so overwhelmed with devastation and bewilderment that just seeing her in such a state caused Matty to sigh in anguish. He wanted to go to her, and hold her, and tell her not to worry, honey, that by God's grace everything would be all right, but she ran to Samantha Marshall.

"Oh, Sam, I just heard," she said as she sat in the chair beside her friend, her voice cracking with grief. "Are you all right?"

Sam didn't even look at Diane. She continued staring at the wall in front of her. Diane looked at Ira, then Matty, with grave concern. "Where's Alan? Sister Scott said Alan was hurt."

"He's in surgery," Ira said dryly, as if it were nothing at all.

"Surgery?" Diane said, stunned. "Oh my God." She looked at Sam again. No wonder she was a basket case, she thought. Alan was so sweet, so precious. A child any mother would love to have. And Sam adored him.

"But he'll be all right," Ira added in a reassuring voice, as if to comfort her.

Diane looked up at him, unshed tears now in her big eyes, and Matty's heart thumped in despair just watching her. She began rubbing Sam's back, in an almost absent-minded gesture, but Matty could tell she was softly praying, too. And he knew the prayer. He'd prayed it after he got the call himself. He knew exactly what Diane wanted. She wanted Alan to be all right. She wanted Sister Marshall to be all right. She wanted this life to stop teasing with happiness, then taunting with despair. She prayed. She prayed fervently. She prayed as if it were her body, her flesh and blood, on that operating table. She prayed the way Matty should have been praying. But somehow he couldn't. Somehow he couldn't get beyond the anger in his soul. But Diane prayed.

"I'll check back with you later in the week, Judge," Sheriff Crane said as he moved closer to the group, behaving, prematurely in Matty's estimation, as if his work were done. "Hopefully your boy will be just fine."

"Thank you, Lucious," Ira said, shaking the sheriff's hand. "Thank you for everything."

The sheriff, a tall man with short, brown hair and those icy blue eyes, looked down at Junior, a boy who seemed bored by it all. "Counseling may help that one," he said. "He may not be showing it now, but this has got to be traumatic for him, too. Horseplay don't usually turn out this bad."

"That's the truth, Lucious," Ira said, as if to hurry him along. "And thanks for the suggestion."

"Any time, Judge, you know that."

"What happened, Sheriff?" Matty asked, unable to hold back any longer.

The sheriff looked at Matty, and then exhaled. He thought he'd seen the last of this guy when Leah's retraction forced him to drop the charges. But that didn't mean for a second he thought the preacher was innocent. "Good evening, Reverend Jolson," he said.

"What happened to Alan?" Matty asked. "Did I hear something about horseplay?"

The sheriff nodded. "You did. That's apparently what caused this accident. The two boys were playing around in their parents' bedroom. The older one, Junior here, knocks over a table, causing a lamp to fall and hit the smaller one. Unfortunately it hit him in the head."

Matty's anger flared. Now they were blaming the children, he thought. "And you believe that?" he asked the sheriff, unable to hold his tongue. The sheriff, stunned, looked at Ira.

"It's what happened, Reverend," Ira said. "Of course he believes it."

"Why wouldn't I believe it?" the sheriff asked Matty.

"What did Mrs. Marshall say?"

"I haven't spoken with Mrs. Marshall. As you can see she isn't exactly verbal right about now."

"She told me that a lamp hit Alan," Matty said. "She didn't say anything about it falling on him."

The sheriff stared at Matty. He was a hothead, he'd known it when he first laid eyes on him. One of those city slickers with his fancy suits and expensive shoes, shoes that probably cost as much as a month's pay for the sheriff. Somebody you had to watch. Somebody who would try to stir up trouble even when there was nothing to stir.

But the sheriff knelt down to Sam anyway. Just to cool off the hothead. Just to make it clear that he covered his bases well. His job was an elected one. The last thing he needed was trouble. "Samantha, this is Lucious Crane. Sheriff Crane? I want you to tell me what happened, dear. Can you do that?"

Sam looked at the sheriff. But she didn't respond. The sheriff looked at Matty. Matty kneeled down, too.

"Sister Marshall, you need to tell the sheriff what you told me. What happened to Alan?"

Sam looked into Matty's face. His compassionate eyes made her want to tell it all. Her dead-weight expression didn't change, but her lips began to move. "The lamp," she began saying, but stopped when Ira quickly sat down beside her and placed his arm around the small of her back. Diane immediately removed her hand, to allow him the privilege of comforting his wife. Only Ira wasn't comforting her at all. His big hand was squeezing her harshly in a warning grip she was all too familiar with.

"The lamp," she began again, "fell on Alan."

"You told me it hit him," Matty said, his frustration rising.

"It fell on Alan and hit him."

She had also told Matty that Alan didn't duck, which

seemed to Matty to be a description more consistent with a lamp being thrown than merely falling. But he didn't pursue it. The night was bad enough. There would be time.

The sheriff stood up. So did Matty. "Satisfied?" he asked Matty.

"What did Junior say?"

Ira exhaled loudly. "Will you please leave?" he asked. "My family doesn't need this aggravation tonight."

"Junior told me the same story everybody else told me," the sheriff said, in answer to Matty's question. "They were playing. The lamp fell on his brother. End of interrogation. Okay?"

Matty didn't respond so the sheriff shook his head as if mocking Matty, said his good-byes, and began to leave. Before he could walk out, however, the surgeon, still in his scrubs, looking exhausted, and the nurse, walked in. Everybody, except Junior, stood on their feet.

The surgeon looked first at Ira, who still had his arm around Sam, and then he looked at Sam. "I'm sorry," he said, and what seemed like a collective sigh of anguish went up into the rafters of the room. "The hemorrhaging wouldn't stop. He didn't make it."

The little life still left on Sam's face was gone. She screamed out *no!* in such a horrifying way that even the surgeon started to reach for her, to comfort her. She would have surely collapsed had it not been for Ira's protective arm around her. Alan was dead? It didn't have the ring of truth. It didn't seem possible. Alan? *Dead?*

Ira pulled his wife against him, bear hugging her, the stunned look on his face, as if he never even considered for a moment that Alan wouldn't make it, caused even Matty to pity him. But the pity didn't last long. Ira Marshall was responsible for this tragedy, Matty was convinced of it. Somehow his craziness, his need to control and dominate and beat the crap out of his own wife, caused the death of a fine little boy.

Matty looked at Diane. She was hurt beyond words. She stood there helplessly, as if she were dazed, and Matty moved over to her so fast, and pulled her so tightly into his arms, that he didn't even realize that she had, at first, resisted his pull. She didn't want to be comforted. Alan was dead. Why should she have warm arms around her, why should she feel loved and protected, when Alan Marshall was cold in a room somewhere?

He did not get any resistance from Diane when he told her to leave her car at the hospital and ride with him.

They walked somberly across the hospital's parking lot, Diane's arms folded, Matty's arm around her, attempting to comfort her on what had to be one of the saddest nights of her life. Wanda took it hard, too, crying profusely when Sam's deafening scream caused her to hurry into the waiting room and hear the news for herself. But when it was time to go, Matty knew where his responsibility lay. He was comforting Diane. He was praying for the Marshalls and praying for Wanda, but he was comforting Diane.

Diane sat down on the leather seat of his Jaguar and leaned her head back. She could still see the distraught look on Sam's face when the surgeon said those dreadful words, and she knew she'd never forget Sam's scream of agony as long as she lived. All she could think about was little Alan, that lovely child, and how in the world Sam would ever survive something like this. The doctors had to sedate her just to stop her screams, but how could she live, Diane wondered, knowing that poor Alan would never be a walking, breathing part of her life ever again?

Diane looked at Matty, who hadn't let her out of his sight since the news broke. He was now driving his Jaguar and smoking, a bad habit she thought he had quit, a tense edginess all over him. He seemed as angry as he was sad, it appeared to Diane, as if no explanation in this world was going to satisfy his deep-seated belief that this tragic accident had Ira Marshall written all over it.

"How does she live?" Diane asked him.

Those words stung Matty as he looked at her, at that devastating look still on her face. A look so distraught, so wrought with despair, that it was heartbreaking to see. He could have quoted her a Bible verse, or told her that Sam would survive if she learned to live *one day at a time.* He could have told her all kinds of brilliant clichés. But all of those catch phrases somehow didn't seem like an answer at all to Matty. Just something to say. "I don't know," he therefore said instead.

"She was so hurt," Diane said. "So devastated. Sam's family has always meant everything to her. She was reared in foster homes, you see, and not the best ones either. She's never had a family before Judge Marshall and those boys came into her life. Now this. It's so horrible. How does she live after something like this?"

Matty puffed on his cigarette and said nothing. It was just a sad, tragic mess, Matty thought. Just a mess. And he wasn't going to try and ease Diane's pain with wonderful sounding words of hope and encouragement he wasn't even sure he believed himself.

He didn't take her home. He, instead, drove across town to Haines Street, to his house, and helped her out of the car. He expected some resistance from her by now, although it would not have done any good, but Diane didn't say a word. She took his offered hand and walked with him across the lawn and into his dark home. She knew, as he did, that going home to Clarion Avenue, where her family wouldn't understand for a second the pain she was going through, wasn't a good idea. She could hear her mother now. *You're acting like it was your child,* she'd say. No, Diane thought, Clarion Avenue wasn't a place she needed to be right now.

After making coffee and handing Diane a cup, Matty sat down beside her on his sofa in the living room. He slouched down, exhausted. Diane slouched down, too, and moved closer to him, the sudden need to feel the warmth and comfort of his big body next to her almost staggering her. He didn't seem to mind the closeness, she felt, although he didn't encourage it either. Diane started to back off. What did she think she was doing anyway? But she couldn't.

He was practically chain-smoking tonight, she noticed, as he lit up yet another cigarette. They'd not spoken much at all to each other in weeks, not since he walked into her backyard and all but told her to get him out of her system, and seeing him again under these circumstances was trying enough. And Matty was absorbed with sadness. Reverend Cobb handled adversity so differently, she thought. He'd remain almost detached, praying for the family, listening to their cries of grief, but never, ever voicing any opinion or getting deeply involved. It was almost as if he'd felt nothing.

Matty, Diane suspected, felt everything, even down to anger over why it had to happen at all. The idea that he could detach himself from such a tragedy was too ludicrous to entertain.

"How did you find out?" Diane asked him.

"Sister Scott," he said.

Diane nodded. "Same here. But when she said Alan had been injured, my heart just broke in two. He was such a sweet, curious little boy, you know? He always wanted everybody to be happy and everything to be all right. Sam was always so worried about him."

Matty, still slouched down, looked at Diane, his long lashes nearly concealing his expressive eyes. "Worried about him how?"

"She didn't say it in so many words, but I got the feeling she didn't think he was loved enough."

"That she didn't love him enough?"

"Oh, no. Samantha adored little Alan."

"But Judge Marshall didn't?"

Diane sighed and leaned her head back on the sofa. "I don't know for sure but Ira, Jr., seemed to be his favorite."

"The child he now blames for Alan's death."

Diane looked at Matty. "That's why it doesn't make sense, Matty. He wouldn't put that burden on Junior if it weren't true."

"He would if it'd keep his behind out of prison."

"Prison?"

"Yes, Diane! You throw a lamp and it kills somebody, that's not an accident. You had no business throwing the lamp. It's manslaughter if it's anything."

Diane closed her eyes. "Manslaughter," she said. "I hate that word."

Matty studied Diane's now frowning face, a face that was growing on him with each passing day, down to the two little freckles on her small nose. She had him worried at the hospital. He thought she was going to pass out when she heard the tragic news. That was why he wouldn't let her out of his sight. He held her, he sat beside her, he stood outside the door when she excused herself to the restroom. And that was also why he wasn't about to let her go tonight. Her family may have been wonderful people beneath their harsh exterior, good Christian people. But she needed *him* tonight.

Diane opened her eyes, sensing that he was staring at her. And he was, his brooding dark gray eyes locked on to her. She didn't know what kind of look it was, if it was one of concern or contempt, but she knew she was in his house alone, it was late at night, and she was too drained to even entertain the thought of some emotional ride with Matty. She sat erect.

"Besides," she said, "even if Ira were trying to cover his butt, which I rather doubt, Sam would never go along with something like that. Not against her own son."

Matty leaned forward and tapped his cigarette ash into a tray. "It's complicated, Diane," he said.

"It doesn't make sense, Matty."

"You heard the sheriff, didn't you? He said he talked to Junior and Junior agreed with everything his father said. So don't tell me about Mrs. Marshall not going along with it. The boy himself is going along with it. They're probably terrified of Ira Marshall."

Diane exhaled and shook her head. It was too much to even think about. And poor Alan. And Sam. And Junior. Diane covered her mouth as a wrenching sob escaped and unshed tears began to appear in her eyes. She looked at Matty; she didn't know why, but the pain was searing her. Matty quickly doused his cigarette in the ashtray, and then pulled her into his arms.

He removed her shoes and put her in his bed. He didn't care how it looked. He didn't care what the neighbors would think if she stayed all night with him. He didn't really care what she thought was best at that moment in time. He wasn't letting her go. Not like this. Not when her pain was so shattering that it was tearing him apart.

He lay beside her, unmindful about wrinkling his perfectly fine suit, as she continued to sob in his arms. The love Diane had for the Marshall family was so genuine, so *Christian,* that it calmed Matty's heart. He could count on one hand all the selfless, kind-hearted, not-a-malicious-bone-in-their-body people he'd met in his lifetime. He was beginning to think now that Diane Tarver might be one of them.

She cried for hours, it seemed to Matty, and he did not try for a second to stop her or pray that she'd just go to sleep, or tell her that everything was going to be all right. He didn't know if it was or wasn't. But he knew, as long as Diane was with him, that she would be all right.

He closed his eyes and prayed, instead, for Ira Marshall.

He prayed that God would intervene and touch that black heart. He prayed that Ira would own up to his misdeeds like the man everybody took him for, and stop blaming Junior. Of all people. It was clear to Matty that Junior already had some serious emotional issues that were bound to lead him down a road of hate and destruction. The last thing he needed was to be blamed for something he didn't do. He might never recover from that. Ira was the key. Change Ira's heart, Matty believed, and that family might just stand a chance.

Diane's crying and restlessness finally stopped after midnight, when she succumbed to the sleep she had been fighting, her body now so closely cradled against Matty that he had to use considerable skill to break free of her. When he did, when he slid his body out of bed without disturbing her much-needed rest, he went into his parlor, his arms stiff as a board from holding her so long and so tight, his entire body drained by the constant activity of a life too full.

But the parlor was his sanctuary, his closet, his upper room. And once he was in there he could barely make it to his desk. He fell on his knees at his chair, and cried out to God. For hours he prayed. He prayed until he couldn't pray anymore. Then he prayed even more. And it was the same prayer over and over. He wasn't praying for the Marshalls, or Diane, or even poor Alan, whose soul, he knew, would rest in peace. He prayed for truth. Bare, simple truth. If truth reigned, if everybody removed the veils and accepted the harsh reality of truth, then no devil in hell could prevent the renewal that they all so badly needed. And Matty included himself at the top of the list. For if Alan's death had served any purpose at all, it served as an opportunity for eyes to open, hearts to change, and lives to be finally set free. Let truth, Matty kept praying as the dusk turned to dawn, set us free. Because then, he knew, they would be free indeed.

★ ★ ★

Diane's eyes opened to a quiet room. The sun was coming in through the closed curtains and the coldness of the night was giving way to the warmth of the day. Although she didn't remember everything vividly, she knew that her head was right now lying on Matty's chest and the arm draped around her belonged to him. She looked up at his beautiful face. He was still asleep, his long eyelashes pressed down against his soft brown skin giving him a peaceful, angelic look. And Diane smiled. She loved Matty. There was no denying it. She loved the way he had taken her in his arms last night and allowed her to mourn Alan's passing without judging her, or trying to stop her. He simply comforted her.

And to have him sleeping next to her wasn't a shock at all. She was happy beyond words to have him next to her. Still holding her in his arms. Still protecting her. She was right where she wanted to be and she was not interested in pretending that she wasn't. Alan was dead now. Fate had struck a harsh blow to a wonderful little boy. Life was too short, it could have never been truer than last night. She wasn't playing it safe anymore.

Matty began to stir as Diane lay her head back on his chest and draped her arm around him tighter. His eyes opened and he could smell the lemony scent of her soft hair. He could not even remember getting in bed with her, but he had apparently; he was here. And when Diane lifted her head from his chest and looked up into his eyes, smiling as if she were deliriously happy, he knew instinctively that he'd made a horrible mistake.

"Good morning, sleepyhead," she said jovially.

"Good morning," he said, rubbing her hair.

"I want to thank you."

"I didn't do anything, Diane."

"Oh, yes, you did. You helped me through the night,

which was exactly what I needed. I was a basket case when we left that hospital."

"You're still a basket case," Matty said teasingly and Diane laughed out loud.

She sat up, completely relaxed although she was in bed with a man. "Okay, now, what do you want for breakfast?"

"You don't have to fix me breakfast."

"Oh, yes, I do. You cooked it for me once, remember? And you didn't even know me then. Let's just say I'm returning the favor."

"Honey, I'm fine. You don't have to do that."

"I want to do it. I want the man I love to get a good start to his day."

Diane looked at Matty after she spoke those words. He was staring at her.

"What would you like?" she asked, looking away from him. She wanted to discuss it desperately. But that look in his eyes, so grave and steely, made her afraid to proceed.

"I don't think I could eat a thing right now," he replied, knowing full well that breakfast was the last thing on her mind. She thought she was in love, in love with a joker like him, and he wasn't about to feed that misperception. He needed her, badly, and as for loving her, as for being in love with her, he was beginning to realize his own truths about that, too. But that meant nothing in this life. He wasn't putting her through pain for his own selfish needs, when the last person she needed was him. And his baggage.

But she was so stubborn. And, this morning, so happy, that how could he not feel happy for her, too? "What would you like for breakfast?" he asked her.

She smiled even greater, if that were possible. "That is so sweet!" she said. "You're more concerned about me than about yourself. But that's you, Matty, you know that? That's why I love you." She said it again, and again looked into his eyes. Only this time she did not back down. "I love you very much, Matthew Jolson, and I'm not ashamed to admit it. I love you with all my heart!" The emotion was in her voice, causing her to lie back down and throw her arms around him. Matty's heart squeezed as she held on to him, and he felt he had no choice but to hold her, too. But he still knew better. He had no business allowing it to come to this.

The silence of the room was not lost on Diane as Matty had not responded at all to her confession. He held her, which she loved, but he didn't say a word. She wanted to lift her head back up and ask why. Did he not love her, too? But she couldn't bring herself to do it.

She, instead, got out of bed and went into the bathroom, opting to remain as hopeful and upbeat as she possibly could. When she yelled and asked Matty if it was okay for her to take a shower while she was in his bathroom, he understood immediately what she was really asking. She needed some time away from him, to clear her head, to realize just how monumental her confession had truly been and, he hoped, how premature.

"Of course it's okay," he yelled back to her, anxious to clear his head, too, and within seconds he could hear the water running full blast. He smiled. He could get used to having Diane around like this, he knew, but he also knew that it was a bad idea to dwell on such a thought. They were both still carrying the emotional baggage of last night, as the sting of Alan's death still showed all over their faces, and the last thing they needed was to make any life-altering decisions right now. Matty understood it clearly. His prayer was that Diane did, too.

When the shower was finally switched off and the sound of running water was replaced by the sound of silence, Matty suddenly became aware that his doorbell was ringing. When he got out of bed and looked out of his window, he nearly panicked. "Good Lord!" he said aloud as he looked at Sister Inez's long, white Cadillac in front of his home.

"Who is it?" Diane asked from behind the closed bathroom door. Matty hurried and threw on his jacket that had been tossed over a chair, and began walking toward the door.

"Who is it, Matty?" Diane asked again.

"Sister Inez," Matty said. He didn't wait for Diane's response, which, he suspected, would be just as dismayed as his was, but he, instead, hurried into the living room and opened the front door.

Sister Inez, of course, was not amused. "It certainly took you long enough," she said.

"Good morning."

"Good morning," she said, her small pocketbook across her arm, her face stern and ready for battle. "May I come in?"

Matty hesitated, but then he stepped aside.

Inez walked in slowly, looking around, seemingly surprised that Matty would keep his house in such a presentable state.

"What can I do for you this morning, Sister?" he asked her, not at all interested in prolonging this visit any more than was necessary.

"I've got some bad news, Reverend."

Matty's heart dropped. How much more? he wondered.

"Some horrible news."

"What is it?"

"We just found out that Judge and Sister Marshall's youngest boy passed away last night."

Matty exhaled. Then nodded. It was still a shocking thing to hear. "Yes, I know. I was there. It's awful news."

Sister Inez, however, seemed more surprised than grieved. "You was there? You was where?"

"At the hospital last night. When the surgeon announced the boy's passing."

"Oh, I see. Nobody told us nothing about that. We didn't think you knew. Deacon Molt is over to the Marshall house now, along with some of the other members. He didn't think it would look right if our pastor wasn't there, too."

"I thought the hospital was going to keep Sister Marshall overnight for observation."

"She went home before day this morning."

"How's she holding up?"

"As well as can be expected, which ain't saying much. This is just terrible, and so tragic that it had to happen to such a good…to such a good…"

Inez's mouth was opened but words did not escape. Matty looked at her then looked in the direction that now had her enthralled.

It was Diane. She was out of the shower and was wearing one of Matty's robes as she stood in the living room, the happy look on her face making it clear that she didn't care who knew she had spent the night with him. The sight of it, the implications of it, threw Inez into a stupor. She was shocked. Beyond shocked.

Matty was shocked, too. Then he was angry.

"Hello, Sister Inez!" Diane said happily, as if it were quite normal for her to be in her pastor's robe coming out of her pastor's bedroom.

Inez, however, couldn't speak. She looked at Matty.

"Tell Deacon Molt I'm on my way," Matty said, still staring at Diane, still attempting to contain his fury by speaking as calmly as he could. "I'll meet you over there."

"What's going on here, Reverend?" Inez asked him.

"Nothing's going on, Sister Inez. Now if you'll excuse me I'll change suits and be right over."

Inez paused, looking from Matty to Diane, easily floored by this. But, with Matty's insistence, she did manage to leave.

When she was gone, when Matty had stepped aside and allowed her safe passage out, he turned his attention back to Diane. Didn't she realize what a foolish move like this could do to his reputation? Not to mention *hers?* Inez and her gossipmongers would make her out to be the biggest tramp in town when they got through twisting the facts and telling it their way. And Diane, Matty decided, didn't have a clue. She was happy in love, as if love conquered all and wasn't the big burden she did not need. This had gone way too far, and he knew it. And he also knew it was all his fault.

"What did she want?" Diane finally asked, when it appeared as if Matty were content just staring at her.

"Go put on your clothes, Diane."

"Now? I've got to fix you breakfast first."

"You aren't fixing me anything!" Matty said angrily. "Just go put on your clothes so I can take you to get your car." Diane, however, was too stunned by Matty's drastic mood shift to comply.

"Now, Diane!" he yelled.

Diane, mortified, confused, and beyond embarrassed, hurried and did as he commanded.

Chapter 18

There was a feeling of disbelief to Diane's life now. From Leah's allegations and nervous breakdown, to Alan's tragedy and Matty's anger, she felt almost numb, as if she were going through the motions of life without really participating. Matty had driven her to the hospital that Saturday morning to retrieve her car, but all the way there he hadn't said a word to her. She wanted to ask what she had done that was so terrible, but he was so tense, and seemingly so angry, that she dared not ask. She had been as happy as she'd ever been just hours before, when she had let it be known to Matty how much she loved him. Now she was devastated.

And her devastation didn't ease. The next day, Sunday, was the worst. She woke up that morning hopeful, still praying that she hadn't made as big a fool of herself as Matty's actions seemed to indicate. But it didn't take long for her to realize that she had. He ignored her as if he were still angry with her, even as she walked past him to go into the choir stand. And after church, when he stood on the steps to shake the hands of the parishioners, he treated Diane as if she were nothing special to him at all.

She was smiling as she approached him, trying her best to look as if that whole scene yesterday morning never happened. "Hello, Reverend," she said, lively.

He shook her hand, said hello almost dispassionately, and then, without even inquiring about her well being, something he had *always* done, turned his attention to the next parishioner in line. Her smile dropped like an anchor, and although his heart pricked with despair as she left, she never knew it. All she saw was more rejection. More anger. More bitter disappointment.

Yet, she still held out hope. All week she hoped. Monday came around, her day off, but not a word from Matty. Tuesday and Wednesday, days he almost always dropped by the library, came and went with no sight of Matty. Diane, in fact, didn't see Matty until that Thursday night, just after choir rehearsal had broken up, and he walked into the sanctuary.

She was talking with a small group of her fellow choir members when he approached them. He was obviously there for a meeting because Deacon Molt and Sister Inez came in with him. Diane looked at him, she couldn't help it, as he headed in their direction. He was dressed in his usual perfection, a dark blue suit and tie this time, and his stern look gave way to an easy smile. She braced herself and laughed livelier with her choir members, hoping that he was now ready to make amends, but her smile (and hope) faded quickly when he walked on by.

"Good evening, ladies," he said to them all as he passed. Although Diane saw him glance her way as he went by, it did nothing to help the sinking feeling deep within her. And to make matters worse, Sister Inez came up behind him and pulled Diane aside. Diane had to force herself to step aside with Inez. The last thing she needed right now, she felt, was a lecture.

"This is what happens," Inez wasted no time in saying, "when you let them get the milk for free."

Diane looked at the older woman with a sudden disbelief. "Excuse me?" she asked her.

"The way he's treating you now is what happens when you let them get the milk for free."

"I cannot believe you would even think such a thing, Sister Inez. He didn't get any free milk from me. You should know that."

"I know what I saw," Inez said in her best voice of censure. "I saw you at his house. I saw you in his bathrobe."

"He was helping me, that's all it was. Alan had just died. It was a devastating time."

"I saw a lot of things that morning, Sister Tarver, but devastation wasn't one of them. You looked happy, if you ask me. Happier than I'd ever seen you look."

It was true, Diane thought. She was truly happy that morning for one of the few times in her life. Truly happy because the man she loved had held her all night. "I don't know what you think you saw," Diane said, "but he didn't get any free milk from me."

"He got something," Inez said. "Why else would he be ignoring you all of a sudden? Why else wouldn't he want to have anything more to do with his, excuse my French, *favorite cow* all of a sudden?"

Diane just shook her head. Not because of her disgust with Inez's allegations, which was a part of it, but mainly because she didn't know why he seemed to hate her now either. All she gave him was her love, although, she was beginning to believe, that may have been the last thing he wanted from her. She looked at Inez again, who seemed so certain in her false belief, and then she left the sanctuary. She had planned to go and see Sam tonight, to make sure Sam and Junior were doing okay. But just seeing that coldness on Matty's face again, and that *I told you so* look in Inez's eyes, sapped what little energy she did have.

And it didn't let up. Not even at Alan's funeral, where Bishop Owens, at Ira's request, came up from Florida and officiated. Bishop gave what Diane thought was a rousing eulogy, about the innocence of youth and the virtue of being good, and Matty just sat there as if he were still stung by Alan's death. Sam cried quietly, a far cry from her screams in the hospital, and Ira held on to her as if she were the most precious human being in this world to him. Junior sat beside Ira, leaning against his father, and if he showed the least bit of emotion, Diane didn't see it.

The repast was held at the Marshall home as the backyard was filled with gaiety and mirth, as if a funeral had never taken place, as if little Alan would come running into their midst at any moment now, yelling *Aunt Di-tan!* and happy to see one and all.

Diane sat at a table near the back of the yard, talking quietly with a few friends. But when they grabbed their plates to go and get more food, Diane declined to follow. The last thing she could do right now was eat. She, instead, found herself looking around for Matty.

She finally spotted him with Bishop Owens. He was taking the older man around from one group to the next, still in his suit of clothes despite the heat, still looking uneasy even when everybody else was trying to move on.

But when they began coming her way, with Matty seemingly not at all thrilled by the decision, it was Diane who suddenly felt uneasy. She tried to smooth loose strands of her hair in place, and straighten her posture, as every fiber of her being seemed to quake with nervousness.

"There's my little librarian!" Bishop Owens said jovially as Diane stood to her feet.

"Hello, Bishop, it's so good to see you again," she said. Although she extended her hand, Bishop gave her a big bear hug and a peck on the cheek. At seventy-six, he was old enough and respected enough to take liberties with the females. He was also big enough, at six-three and nearly three hundred pounds, his cheerful face and warm, friendly demeanor no distraction from his towering presence. He pulled Diane back at arm's length and smiled. "Let me get a good look at you," he insisted.

Matty looked, too, at that plain, oversized black dress she wore, hiding, once again, every inch of that sexy shape he knew she had. Then he looked into her eyes. She was still devastated by Alan's death, and by his subsequent treatment of her, he could see it all over her face. But he would not be deterred. He had to keep his distance. Her reputation and that great esteem everybody held for her was not going to be ruined any more than he'd already ruined it. Everything he touched seemed to turn to controversy and turmoil. But not Diane, he'd decided.

"You look like an angel, Sister Tarver," Bishop said. "A precious gift from God."

"Thank you."

"So sweet and pretty. I'll bet every man in this church has been trying to get their hands on you."

Diane, as if by reflex, glanced at Matty.

"I'm sure you know your pastor here," Bishop said as if it were an introduction. He was old, he knew, but he was perceptive. And something, or somebody, was bothering Matthew, big time. Based on his reaction, or lack of reaction, to Diane, the Bishop was beginning to wonder if that somebody was right here.

Diane looked at Matty. He looked tense, as if the last place he wanted to be was near her, and that look alone broke her heart. "Yes, of course," she said nervously, fighting hard to disguise her pain. "Hello, Pastor."

Every muscle in Matty's body tightened as he looked at

Diane. "Sister Tarver," he said grimly, his face frowning and stern. He was no-nonsense, direct, speaking to her as if she never spent a second in his arms, or a night in his bed. What had she done that was so horrible, she wanted to know. *He* was the one who insisted she stay at his house. *He* was the one who put her in his bed. *He* was the one who made her feel as if she could trust him with her life.

But she was the one who put on his robe and paraded her half-naked self in front of Sister Inez. Apparently all the rest could be forgiven, but not that. Her action was a mortal sin in his eyes apparently, when all she was trying to do was be happy for once in her life. She'd never known pure happiness before, and feeling it that morning in Matty's bed made her clumsy with giddiness. She wanted the world to know that she belonged to Matty Jolson and she couldn't wait to get started telling it. But Inez had misinterpreted everything and Matty had, too, apparently, because it seemed he couldn't get rid of her fast enough. Now he couldn't seem to stand the sight of her. And that reality, that harsh, painful reality, was shattering Diane.

"Sister Tarver is one of Fountain Hope's most loyal members, Matthew," Bishop said, "as I'm sure you know by now. The thing I like about her is that she gives her all in stewardship and service. She's the personification of a good, Christian woman. If you need anything, anything at all, Sister Tarver will try her best to assist you. Won't you, Diane?"

Diane tried to smile, tried to fight against her desire to cry. "Yes, sir."

Bishop Owens, sensing the battle, smiled, too. "You still work at the library?" he asked her.

"Yes. Yes, I do."

"Good. I trust life has been treating you well then?"

"Yes, sir, it's been… And you?"

"Not bad for an old man. Not bad at all. I was so sorry to hear about your friend Leah Littleton and that awful mess.

Have you heard anything more about her and her condition?"

Diane shook her head. "No, sir. She left town is all I know."

"Shame," Bishop said. "Nothing but a shame. But we wrestle not against flesh and blood."

"Amen."

"Some folks say she just snapped," Bishop Owens continued. "Just lied on Matthew here, on Reverend Jolson, and snapped. I say it was a long time coming. I've known Leah Littleton since she was a child and she always held church folk in very low esteem. Although she claimed to be one herself, she always hated Christians."

Diane smiled. "She believes we're all hypocrites."

"And we are. We're human beings. But you don't try and destroy God's people, I don't care what you think about them."

"Amen," Diane said, meaning it.

"Well," Bishop said, tired himself of the depressing past, "God bless you, child, but I'd better move on. I'm gonna go on over and spend a little time with Brother Marshall. Matthew, you stay here and entertain Sister Tarver. You don't have to keep escorting me around. I'm old, but I'm not dead yet."

Bishop said this with a warm smile and left, without waiting for Matty to respond.

Diane tried to smile, too, to lessen the pain of their sudden togetherness, but Matty wouldn't cooperate.

"Matty, what's wrong?" she finally asked him.

"Nothing's wrong."

"Then why are you avoiding me? Why do you seem to hate me now?"

"I don't hate you, Diane."

"You won't talk to me. You treat me as if I'm nothing to you every time I come around. And I wanna know why."

Matty exhaled. He nearly broke down and told her why. He nearly admitted that she made him feel unlike any other woman ever had and he was so very tempted to take advantage of those feelings. He nearly told her that he was this close to throwing her reputation to the dogs and claiming her as his own, letting the chips fall where they may. His past, his baggage, would just have to be hers, too. But he couldn't do it. Not to her. For once in his life, he was not going to be selfish.

It would be better if she hated him, he decided.

"Matty, will you please answer my question," she said. "I need to know why you are so unhappy now?"

Matty drew in a breath of frustration. "Maybe it has something to do with the fact that I just witnessed the burial of a six-year-old child. Okay?"

"Oh," Diane said, suddenly feeling petty and ashamed. "I didn't mean to minimize Alan's death—"

"Maybe after a funeral I'm not in all that much of a jovial mood. Maybe, just maybe, my unhappiness, as you call it, has nothing whatsoever to do with you, Diane. Ever thought of that? But then it's always all about you, isn't it? Always all about Diane Tarver. That's why you showed yourself to Inez. Because it's all about you. So excuse me if I'm not dancing on the side of the road just yet. Maybe I don't feel like dancing." Matty said this and then walked away from her, his face flushed, not with anger, as she suspected, but with despair, regret, and deep-seated anguish.

Diane's face was flushed with all kinds of feelings, too. He was still grieving Alan's death and she was worrying about herself. That realization alone disgusted her. He said she was selfish, a label no one had ever placed on her, but that was exactly how she felt at that very moment. Selfish. Insensitive. Unable to fully experience the agony of Alan's unfortunate death for worrying about her petty little problems.

"What's wrong with him?" Wanda asked as she came up

to Diane. Diane, surprised by the sudden intrusion into her thoughts, tried to smile.

"With who?" she said.

"Pastor Jolson. Every time I try to say two words to him he's acting like I'm bothering him. And I'm his assistant! So I just been staying out of his way."

Diane nodded. "I know. He says he's still broke up over Alan."

"Oh, can you imagine? It's just such a tragedy. That sweet little boy! And you know Pastor. He's such a sensitive, compassionate man. It's got to hurt him."

Diane agreed, although he didn't seem to feel any sensitivity or compassion for her. She made an error. One little error in judgment that Saturday morning after Alan's death, when she wasn't even herself, when she was in the midst of an emotional ride she had never experienced before. Sad beyond measure Friday night, happy beyond words Saturday morning. And that one moment in time had caused Matty to change his mind about her. He might have been sensitive and compassionate with others, she thought. But he somehow lost those feelings with her.

Both Diane and Wanda stared at Matty as he roamed the grounds, his face so flustered that they both seemed perplexed. Then Wanda exhaled. "Where's Sam?" she asked.

"Ira said she went upstairs to rest."

Wanda looked at Diane. "Alone?"

"Yeah," Diane said, then looked at Wanda. And without saying another word they both hurried across the grounds and into the house.

She was not in her room, where they had expected to find her, but was in Alan's room. She sat by the window in his favorite little rocking chair, her small body moving back and forth as she looked absently at the people downstairs on the veranda. Wanda led the way, as they walked in, and when it appeared Sam was not alert enough to respond to the less-than-quiet opening of the door, she cleared her throat.

"Sam?" she said. "I hope we aren't disturbing you."

Sam turned slowly to the sound, but when she realized it was Wanda and Diane, she turned back.

Diane felt awful. She didn't know how to comfort Sam. How do you comfort a mother who's lost a child?

"We thought you'd like a little company," Wanda said.

"It's a nice day," Sam said. "Thank God it's a nice day."

"Yes."

"Alan would have loved a day like this. He was very much the outdoors man, you see." She said this with a smile. "Not like Junior. But Alan, he loved people and places and God's green earth." She looked at her two friends. "Do you know he once said he wanted to be just like me when he grew up."

Wanda smiled. Diane's heart dropped.

"Me of all people. Alan said he wanted to be just like me. Nobody had ever said such a sweet thing to me in all my life."

Wanda sat on the edge of the bed. She was far better at this than Diane felt she was. Because Diane couldn't move. "What did you say when he said that?" Wanda asked Sam.

Sam smiled. "I told him no, he had it all wrong. I wanted to be just like *him* when I grew up."

Wanda laughed. Sam smiled for a while longer, then the hurt reappeared on her face and she returned her attention to the world outside.

"You were a wonderful mother to Alan, Sam," Diane said. "Just wonderful. Don't you ever forget that."

Sam shook her head. "No. I wasn't wonderful at all. I was awful. He deserved so much better than me."

"Don't say that, Sam. You love your children. You have always been a very devoted mother."

"Yes, you have," Wanda said. "Very devoted."

"From the moment those two little boys were born you've been doting on them."

"Stop it."

They looked at Sam. "Stop what, Sister Marshall?" Wanda asked.

"I was not a good mother. Stop playing with me."

"Nobody's playing with you, Sister. You were a good mother. That's a fact."

"If I was so good, where's my boy?" she said angrily and looked at them. "Huh? Where's Alan? If I was this great bulwark of motherhood why is my boy in a box in the ground and I'm sitting up here healthy as an ox? Don't talk to me about goodness. Alan was good. Even Bishop said so in his eulogy. Alan was everything goodness is. I wasn't his wonderful mother. I was his misfortune."

"Oh, Sam!" Diane said with great anguish as she hurried to comfort her friend. The tears began to fall down Sam's face before she could arrive. When she did arrive Sam did not resist her affection. They embraced, and the real sobbing began.

Matty didn't see her. Not where he'd left her standing, not at the table where she'd been sitting. She was angry with him, and she had every right to be, but he didn't want her leaving this place upset.

He started to ask about her, to see if anyone had seen her lately, but then he saw her for himself. She was coming out of the back door of the Marshall home, and Matty sighed in relief. Only she looked emotionally spent to him, as she stopped to hold small conversations here and there as she made her way back to the most inconspicuous table in the yard. Far back in the yard. She'd lost weight, too, over the past weeks; he noticed that when he first saw her at the hospital. But she at least managed to project some sense of liveliness. Now, after coming out of that house, she looked drained.

Matty took a glass of lemonade from one of the picnic tables and began sipping his drink and walking around the yard. Bishop had long since gone inside the house with Ira, and Matty had been previously tied up in drawn-out conversations with Deacon Molt and Sister Mayfield. Now he was free to roam. And he did. Only he couldn't take his eyes off Diane. He was still determined to keep his distance from her. But he couldn't ignore the fact that it was killing him not to be able to be near her, to hold her, to kiss her. She wasn't the only one battling feelings. That night they spent together made him well aware of their growing closeness, too. But he was not about to let people like Sister Inez sully Diane's stellar reputation the way they'd been attempting to sully his. He caught that show before, back in Chicago, and just recently with Leah, and he wasn't interested in re-runs.

A young man, or at least a man far closer to Diane's age than Matty was, came over to the table where she was sitting and began what appeared to be a friendly conversation with her. Although the young man wasn't handsome in the way that many would view Matty as handsome, he had a charm about him that Matty could tell was appealing to Diane. She even smiled at some joke he told and laughed at some hand-flailing gesture he made. Matty watched with rapt attention. He couldn't help but wonder if this would be the outcome of his treatment of Diane. By keeping his distance, he had to know he was clearing the way for others to come along. Young men with less than honorable motives in mind. They wouldn't give a twit about preserving her reputation but would make it their business to remove that cloak of honor that allowed her to stay in her safe place. And once they saw the real Diane, the one who wasn't just loving and kind but full of passion and sexiness, then they'd realize the jewel they had and hoard it for themselves.

Like the young man at her side now. He kept leaning toward her, whispering in her ear. And Diane, so starved for affection, was allowing it, viewing it, undoubtedly, as the innocent gestures of a very nice guy. Too nice, Matty thought, watching him. But when he pulled out a card and began writing what Matty was certain was a phone number on it, and then handed it to Diane, his niceness had just gone too far. Matty hurried toward them.

Diane saw him coming before her friend did. She saw him moving fast and deliberately, that grim look that had been the trademark of his mood that day now replaced by a look of uninhibited rage. What now? Diane wondered, as she stood. The young man, who was in the middle of telling her another one of his jokes, saw Diane rise and therefore rose, too. He didn't see Matty, however, until he was upon them.

"What's the matter?" Diane couldn't help but ask. Matty looked out of control, she thought. Dangerous.

The young man turned quickly to see to whom Diane had addressed her question, and when he realized it was Matty, he smiled. "Hello, Pastor Jolson."

"Hello," Matty said, without smiling or softening his stern demeanor. The youngster obviously knew Matty, but Matty had no idea who he could be. And he didn't care. "Diane," he said, "will you come with me?" He asked this as he held out his hand to her. Although his words were framed in question form, they didn't have the ring of a request, Diane thought, but the harsh intonation of a command.

Diane felt trapped, tired of the emotional pull this man had on her, and she didn't know whether to go or stay. But Matty looked so determined, and so edgy, that she didn't feel she had a choice. She was too curious to know if all of these shifting, bad-to-worse moods of his really had anything whatsoever to do with her.

When she placed her small hand in his large one, he squeezed it tightly, not to be harsh or, on the other extreme,

romantic, but because his adrenaline was pumping fero-
ciously and he seemed unable to calm down. He walked with
her, hand in hand, toward the side of the house, the young
man who had been entertaining her still standing there,
seemingly annoyed. But Matty didn't care. He knew people
were watching them and whispering about them, and he
knew that all of his ironclad bravado about keeping the
sharks at bay, about protecting her reputation, had instanta-
neously gone up in smoke. But he didn't care about that either. He wasn't losing Diane, and especially not to the likes
of some adolescent, smooth-talking comedian.

But as they left the gathered crowd and ended up alone
on the side of Ira Marshall's home, Matty suddenly realized
that he didn't know why exactly he had behaved so rashly.
He couldn't commit to this woman, not in the way that she
deserved, and she couldn't survive a friendly, casual relationship with him, considering that she had already voiced
her great love for him. Now he was encouraging her, just by
this unthinking move. He was making her feel that he really
did care about her when that was the last thing he wanted
her to feel. But the idea of some joker trying to worm his
way into her life, trying to seduce her with laughs and innocent repartee, required more self-restraint than he could
handle.

He was no saint.

"Matty, what's wrong?" Diane asked, when he appeared
content to just stand there.

"Who was that?"

"What?"

"Who's the guy, Diane?"

"You mean Jake?"

"Who is he?"

Diane felt as if her head were spinning. What was he trying to prove?

"Diane?" Matty said. "Who is he?"

"He's just somebody I was talking to. He said he used to go to Fountain Hope. I don't even know him."

"Yet you let him whisper in your ear and gladly accept his telephone number."

Diane smiled. It seemed surreal. One minute he was ignoring the daylights out of her or, if he wasn't ignoring her, was accusing her of selfishness. Then the next minute he was jealous because some guy she had no feelings for whatsoever, some man she didn't even know, was joking around with her. The Twilight Zone wasn't this unbelievable.

"Well?" he said.

"Well, what? What are you talking about, Matty?"

"You don't know what I'm talking about?"

"No!"

Matty snatched from her hand the card Jake had given her. "Does this ring a bell?"

"That's Jake's business card."

Matty glanced at the card, particularly what was written on the back. "His business card with his home phone number on back. Yeah, I could see where you wouldn't know what I'm talking about." Then he exhaled. "Don't cast your pearl before swine, Diane," he said.

"What?"

"You heard me."

"But I don't know what you're talking about."

Before Matty could say another word the absurdity of his reaction began to weigh heavily on him. What in heaven's name was he doing? She had a simple phone number from a simple man and he was ready to accuse her of fornication! It was craziness gone berserk. He wanted distance between them. He wanted her to hate his guts. Now he was blowing a gasket because some guy gave her a phone number! He ran his hand through his crop of short, curly hair. He was lost.

He looked at Diane. She was lost, too. No doubt about it.

She took her cues from him and he was giving her so many different ones that she couldn't help but be concerned. He handed back the card.

"Sorry about that," he said. "Forget everything I said. It's probably just the stress of the day." Then he paused. "I'll see you around."

He was telling her to hit the road. He was telling her, in no uncertain terms, she believed, that if he did have any feelings for her they had vanished as suddenly as they had emerged. Just as it was when he closed himself to her after Leah's allegations. Just as it was that Saturday morning after Alan's death, when she had shed her protectiveness for once in her life and told him that she loved him.

She began to move away, fighting tears and confusion, but just as she was about to clear his space, just as she was about to finally resolve within herself that nobody deserved to be treated like this, his hand reached out and grabbed hers. She should have snatched it away from him, but she didn't. She looked at him.

He stared at her, his heart pounding with regret as he sought to somehow tell her he was sorry about everything. But the words just wouldn't come. "Been taking care of yourself, Diane?" he asked her.

She hesitated. "I think so," she replied.

"You've lost weight. And look exhausted again."

A frown creased her brow. What did he expect from her? "How did you think I was going to look? I may sound selfish to you, since you've concluded that I'm this selfish person, but this has been a very trying time for me, too, Matty."

She wasn't giving an inch. Not anymore. Matty hesitated. He didn't realize his fingers were rubbing across hers until he could feel her try to pull her hand away from him. He held on to her tighter.

"I really need to get going," she said.

"Going where?"

Diane rolled her eyes. "Matty, what are you doing? Why are you torturing me like this? You don't care anything about where I'm going and you know it. Why are you doing this?"

Matty's heart dropped. Why indeed? he wondered. "I'm sorry," he said. "You're right." Then he exhaled. "Good-bye, Diane."

Those words shook her to her core. Good-bye. It sounded so final. He'd never sounded so certain before.

And he let her go.

Chapter 19

The grounds of Fountain Hope were bustling with activity on a bright Saturday morning. Matty and some of the younger men of the church were playing basketball on the far side of the day-care center, the women were selling cakes and pies and frying fish in the parking lot, and the children were laughing and running and some were playing softball on the grass. Wanda Scott, who manned the refreshment stand, was smiling adoringly as she sat beside the stand and watched the swirl of activity around her, especially the men on the basketball court. Janet Brown, one of the newer members, an attractive, big-hipped woman not quite thirty years old, grabbed a can of Mountain Dew from the cooler and sat in the folding chair beside her. She wiped off the can's top with the hem of her blouse and then looked at Wanda.

"What on earth got you smiling like that, girl?" she asked Wanda.

"How you doing, Sister Brown?"

"I'm doing fine. Now who are you smiling at?"

"Pastor, child," Wanda said. "He's the oldest thing on that basketball court but he's outplaying every one of those young boys."

Janet looked toward the basketball game and smiled, too. "Best-looking one on that court, too," she said. "But I ain't surprised he's outplaying them. They say he's got the stamina of a horse, you know."

Wanda, knowing Janet's flare for gossip and stirring up controversy, glanced at her friend when she said that, and then looked back at the men on the court. "I wouldn't know about that."

"But you wouldn't mind knowing, would you, girl?"

"Child, please. What I'll look like wanting my pastor?"

"You'll look like all these other females around here. The man can't hardly turn around without one skinning and grinning in his face." Then Janet paused, took a sip from her Mountain Dew. "Like that Diane Tarver."

Wanda looked at Janet. "Diane? What about Diane?"

"I heard things about that chick."

Wanda hesitated. She shouldn't even pursue it, she knew it. But she couldn't seem to stop herself. "What things?" she asked.

"I heard she wanted the pastor something fierce. And she got him, too. For a night." Janet said this and returned Wanda's glare.

"I don't believe that," Wanda said, shaking her head. "*Diane Tarver?* And *Pastor Jolson?* I don't believe that for a second."

"Don't believe it then. But don't you think it's strange the way he don't be bothered with her no more?"

Wanda looked at Matty as he took a jump shot from the free-throw line, his gray T-shirt bouncing up and revealing hard, six-pack abs. She had wondered herself why Pastor Jolson treated Diane the way he did. Especially when Diane, like some of the other members, hurried to the church to congratulate him after Leah's retraction. He accepted all of the other members' welcome-backs. He wouldn't even see Diane.

"According to Sister Inez she used to be his favorite," Janet said, "but now he don't have nothing to do with her. I don't know about you but that sounds like giving it up and getting the shaft to me."

"That's crazy, Janet. Pastor Jolson wouldn't do that."

"I don't know, now. Pastor got it going on, even you can see that. He's the kind of man who could charm even the most devout into losing their religion for a night. Even good-girl Diane. I know what I'm talking about. And you heard about how she's changed?"

"Changed?"

"You haven't heard?"

"Heard what?"

"He's coming this way."

"What?" Wanda asked frowningly then, realizing what Janet had just said to her, she, too, looked toward the basketball court.

"And don't that man look good?" Janet said. "Uh-uh-uh. We got us a good-looking pastor, y'all!"

Matty was walking toward them in a slow, lumbering gait, his T-shirt pouring sweat, his shorts revealing muscular, hairy legs. His handsome face lit up with a smile as he came near, causing both women to smile, too.

"Who's winning, Pastor?" Wanda asked him.

"I think I am, Sister Scott, if I may be so forward."

Wanda and Janet both laughed. "The truth is the light," Wanda said, standing up. "What would you like to drink?"

"Water's good."

As Wanda searched the cooler for a bottled water, Matty looked at Janet and smiled. She had her legs crossed, their plumpness and smooth brown tone not lost on Matty. "You are Sister Brown, right?"

"Janet Brown, that's right."

"One of our newer members."

Janet smiled. "Yes, I am. I joined up after I heard you preaching a sermon on a street corner."

"Good for you," Matty said as Wanda handed him his drink. "Evangelism is alive and well."

"Amen to that, Pastor," Wanda said.

Matty twisted off the bottle top and drank nearly half of the contents with one swift swoop. Both Wanda and Janet stared at him. "So," he said, "what were you ladies discussing before I interrupted?"

"Just talking," Wanda said.

"We were talking about one of the sisters in the church actually, Reverend," Janet said.

"No problem I hope."

"I wouldn't call it a problem." Wanda elbowed Janet, but Janet ignored her. "We were talking about Diane Tarver."

Matty's heart squeezed at the sound of that name. Then he drank more water and looked over at the children playing softball. "What about Sister Tarver?" he asked.

"Do you know her, Pastor?" Janet asked, and Wanda, knowing full well that Janet already knew the answer to that question, looked sidelong at her.

"Yes, I know her," Matty said with some degree of sadness, as he seemed unable to look at the woman who brought up that name again.

"I don't exactly know her," Janet said. "I mean we talk after church, and I've hollered at her when I've seen her around town, but that's about it. But everybody said she was such a wallflower type, somebody who did her Christian duty but totally neglected her own life. But I heard that ain't so anymore. I just found it refreshing to hear, that's all."

Matty looked at Janet, unable to conceal his confusion. "I don't understand. What's refreshing?"

"How much she's changed. Of course, some man had to break her heart first."

"Break her heart?" Matty asked hastily before he could stop himself. At first he thought Janet was talking about some other man coming along and hurting Diane. But that was ludicrous, he realized. He was the man.

"That's right," Janet said. "I heard some brother broke her heart and she was so devastated that she decided to change her life. She got her own apartment and everything now."

"Really?" Wanda asked, surprised. "Diane doesn't live at home with her parents anymore?"

"She sure don't. Got her one of those apartments on Brady Road."

"Now that *is* surprising."

"I told you it was," Janet said. "But that's what a good-for-nothing man will do for you. Ain't that right, Pastor?"

Both Janet and Wanda looked at Matty. Matty looked toward the basketball court. "Which apartment is it?" he asked, unable to conceal his feelings any longer. It was obvious to him that Janet knew. It was obvious to him that everybody knew.

"Near the back," she said gleefully. "Number fourteen if I remember correctly. I went by there with Sister Inez. She wanted to know what was wrong with Diane. I told her nothing's wrong with her. A woman that age should be on her own. But Sister Inez still couldn't believe it."

"I'm sure she couldn't," Matty said with a tinge of bitterness as he set his now-empty bottle of water on the stand. "Well, I'd better get back to the game. You ladies take care." He said this as he walked away, not even bothering to so much as glance at them again. He was suddenly so concerned he could hardly think straight. Diane had changed her life, Janet had said. Diane's heart had been broken and she changed her life. Did she hate him now? he wondered. That was what he had seemed to desire, for her to despise him and thereby go on with her life. But was it true? Deep down he never thought it would be possible for Diane to hate him. Deep down he didn't want to believe it could be so.

But maybe it was so. Maybe she wasn't as immune to bad treatment as he had thought. Now she had moved on. Without him. *Because* of him. He began running to the court. The memory of that devastated look in Diane's pretty eyes that Saturday morning, when he didn't get it, when he rejected her decision to take a chance for once in her life and strut her happiness, was like a fireball of pain etched eternally in his brain.

Diane sat at her kitchen table reading a newspaper and sipping coffee. She wore a sleeveless yellow sundress with spaghetti straps that hugged her breasts, exposing all of her upper chest and shoulders. She'd purchased it a few days ago, on her own dare, but it fit so snugly and exposed so much that she was now resigned to wearing it only indoors. She wasn't planning to go anywhere today, anyway. Just finish her coffee and then finish her unpacking, something she should have done weeks ago, when she first moved into her new apartment.

She looked around at the white walls and oak cabinets, the standard-issue stove and refrigerator that came with the place, and an odd combination of triumph and sadness overtook her. She was starting her life, was what she told her mother, and when her mother laughed in her face it seemed almost expected. Even her father had reservations, telling her over and over that she was always welcome in any home of his. And she appreciated that. But this wasn't about her parents. This wasn't about taking the easy way out. This was for her.

The knocks on her front door didn't startle her; this was Saturday and the Jehovah's Witnesses were always out in force, but she did look out of her front window before she went to answer the knocks. And she was startled.

It was Matty.

Her nerves were suddenly like rocks in her throat, but she swallowed hard, put on the grandest smile she could manage, and opened the door. She knew it wasn't a good idea for him to be here. Just seeing him always got her hopes up, only to have him dash them again. But a part of her was still thrilled to know that he came.

"Well, hello there," she said gaily.

"Good afternoon," Matty said, unable to match her elation. If she were lovesick over him, he thought, she certainly wasn't showing it.

"What brings you all the way out here to Brady Road, Reverend? I didn't know you knew where I stayed."

Matty looked at her disapprovingly. "It's Matty to you," he said, hoping that it came out as a joke, but the intense look on his face, a look he'd been unable to shake ever since he heard about her new situation, made it sound more like a dictate than a try at humor. "And I came to see you. May I come in?"

That look bothered Diane, too. She thought the man would be over whatever it was that had him so disagreeable toward her, but apparently she thought wrong. He was still harboring a grudge against her, still unable to look her in the eye without giving her the distinct impression that she was evoking some kind of visceral reaction in him. The last thing she needed was to allow him to come into her new life, into her new apartment, with those bad vibes. But she opened the door wider and let him in.

He walked in, moving by her with enough closeness that the smell of his cologne alone caused Diane's heart to thump. Could she ever get over this man? Would he ever stop tossing her a bone here, a bone there, long enough for her to realize that those very bones were what was choking the life out of her?

Matty stood in the middle of her living room and looked

around. The apartment was spacious, with new-smelling, bright brown carpet, clean white walls, and furniture that appeared inexpensive but brand new. There were also a lot of department store bags and boxes around the room, which caused Matty to turn toward Diane as she closed the door. His breath caught when he looked at her again, at the beautiful yellow sundress that seemed to bring out the sparkle in her eyes. He looked down at her, at the dress that exposed so much, and he exhaled.

Diane had expected him to say something to her when he turned—it seemed as if that was going to be his intention—but he just stared at her instead.

She decided to ignore his stares and invite him to sit down. He crossed his legs as he sat on her small, pastel-colored sofa, his big hand rubbing across the sofa's material as if he were inspecting it.

"What would you like to drink?" she asked him.

"Nothing."

"Sure?"

"Positive. I've been over at the church playing some basketball and Sister Scott and Janet Brown's been shoving beverages down my throat all morning."

Diane smiled. It was no secret that both of those ladies adored Matty. Young, old, it didn't matter. Most every female in that church had their eyes on Matty. The only difference between them and Diane, as she saw it, was that they had enough sense to know they couldn't have him.

She sat down, in the chair near the sofa, and crossed her legs, too. "They had a fish fry over at the church today, too, didn't they?" she asked him.

"Yes. A bake sale, too. It's like a veritable carnival over there today. I shot a few hoops myself before going home, showering, and coming here."

He smelled freshly showered, Diane thought. He always did.

"So how have you been keeping yourself, Diane?"

"I've been keeping myself just fine," she said, still smiling, still upbeat.

And she had, Matty thought, as he studied her face. She looked just fine to him, too. Her cheeks were smooth and shiny with rouge, her perfectly proportioned lips had just a dab of some sort of creamy lipstick, her large eyes had been lined and highlighted, and her hair was loose and hanging down her back in waves of curls. She looked radiant to him. He was proud of how she was able to keep herself together. But a little part of him was also disappointed that she seemed to be looking and doing so much better—since he got out of her way.

"You look wonderful, Diane," he couldn't help but acknowledge as he looked from that beautiful sundress she wore to her beautiful face. "You've had a make-over."

Diane smiled. "Not really. Just a dab here and there. But I feel fabulous. It's amazing what a little makeup can do for your self-esteem."

"You're probably turning quite a few heads with this new look of yours."

Diane nodded. "Actually, I am. That's what's so great about it. Men have generally, for the most part anyway, overlooked me, you know? Leah and Sam always got all of that kind of attention. But now you wouldn't believe it. Everywhere I go I get stares and conversation and men telling me how attractive they think I am. It's unbelievable. All I did was put on a little makeup and let my hair down and wear clothes more befitting my age and station in life and you'd think I was a different person."

She was, Matty thought. Different and so excited by her differentness that she was an even easier target. Men could take advantage of her, could seduce her, and she wouldn't even know it until it was way too late.

"You have to be careful with adulation, Diane," he said.

"Many brothers don't necessarily have your best interests at heart."

"I know. Sister Inez told me the same thing. And Wanda and my father and everybody else. They seem to think I'm some naive innocent who'll fall for any Smooth Joe that comes along. But that's not how it is. I just like the attention, that's all."

She'd been starved for attention, Matty thought, watching her, and when he could have given it to her, when he could have claimed her as his own and thereby not have to worry about some other Smooth Joe in her life, he kept his distance from her instead. Now she had many comers, many admirers, and he was probably last on her list, if on there at all. He thought he had been looking out for what was best for her. Now he wondered. "Just be careful," he said and pulled out a cigarette. He only smoked nowadays when he was troubled, which he was now. Deeply.

"I will be very careful," Diane said. Then she looked at Matty. "So, how have you been keeping yourself?"

Matty couldn't smile, couldn't seem to hide his ever-growing distaste with the twists and turns of life. "Mind if I smoke?" he asked her.

"I don't mind," she said. "I'm still praying for you."

"Good," he said, lighting up. She got up, placed a saucer from the kitchen on the coffee table in front of him, and sat back down.

"I'm sure you know that the reason you haven't quit isn't because God cannot help you," she said as she sat down. "You have to want to be helped."

Matty nodded. "Yep," he said as he took a puff on his cigarette and then pulled it from his mouth and looked at it. "I know." Then he looked at Diane. "And in answer to your question, I'm keeping myself just fine also."

"You don't look so fine," Diane said. "I mean you look

good, you're a very handsome man, but you don't look so good."

Matty looked once again at the lit cigarette between his fingers. "Yeah, well," he said, "I guess I'm a little tired, Diane."

"I heard you've been very busy lately. Doing a lot more outreach and counseling."

"I have. My counseling clients have tripled."

"Because of what happened to little Alan?"

Matty nodded. "And Leah's situation, yes. It shook a lot of people's faith."

"I know. But that's why you can't put your faith in man, or in what happens in this life. You have to put your faith in God."

Matty stared at Diane. She was right. He was, in fact, counseling others on that very point, but he wondered if she meant it another way. "But they'll be okay," he said. "It's just a natural reaction when tragedy strikes."

"I'm sure you're right," Diane said, and then silence ensued. She looked around the room, at her furnishings, the walls. Matty looked at her. When she returned his gaze, he exhaled.

"Anyway," he said, feeling a great need to run somewhere and hide, "I just dropped by to say hello. To make sure you were doing okay."

Diane suddenly felt sad. "I'm glad you came by."

Matty nodded. He knew he should have stood and left, but for some reason he couldn't. "How do you like your new place?" he asked her.

"Love it."

Matty nodded, looking around. "Good." Then he exhaled, and began to rise. "Well, I'll see you in church tomorrow, Diane."

"Not tomorrow."

Matty, who was about to stand, sat back down and looked at her. "Why not tomorrow? You've never missed a Sunday service."

"I know, but a friend of mine invited me to church in Bainbridge."

Matty's heart dropped. "A friend of yours?"

"Yes."

"Who? Some lady you met at the library or…"

"Just a friend. I met him a few weeks ago."

Matty tried to smile, to mask the sudden dread that came over him, but he couldn't pull it off. "Who is he?" he asked her.

"We met at a hair salon in Bainbridge. He sells beauty-care products, including his own line, around Florida and Georgia. He's very nice. And yes, he's a born again believer in case you're wondering."

A *traveling salesman?* She was falling for a *traveling salesman?* Matty could not believe it. Those guys were notorious for their womanizing, for keeping themselves a different female in every town. Those guys were scrupulous for taking fresh, virgin meat like Diane and seasoning her to their own taste and liking. That man would destroy her innocence, her sweetness, her faith and belief in God and goodness. Matty wanted to take her by the arms and shake some sense into her. A *traveling salesman?* How could she be *that* naive?

And he had to put a stop to it.

"Tell him you can't make it," he said to her.

Diane, stunned, at first just stared at him. "Excuse me?" she finally said.

"Call him on the telephone," Matty said, this time unable to conceal his distress, "and tell him that you will be unable to go anywhere with him this Sunday or any other Sunday or any other day of the week!"

Diane sat straight-backed. She couldn't believe what she was hearing. "Are you trying to tell me that I can't see him anymore?"

"No, I'm not trying to tell you anything. I'm telling you.

I'm making it plain. A traveling salesman, Diane? You must be out of your mind if you think I'm gonna let you fool around with somebody like that!"

Diane actually smiled. This was Twilight Zone time again. "Herman and I are friends, Matty—"

"Herman?"

"That's his name. And I will see him if I want to see him. And I want to see him on Sunday. So, again, I'll see you next week, if at all, because I won't be at Fountain Hope tomorrow."

Matty exhaled angrily. "Okay, fine. Do whatever you want. But when the joker breaks your heart don't come running to me."

"I won't."

They stared at each other, both upset, both with their own reasons for hating this entire scene. For Diane it was the gall of him. The only person who ever broke her heart wasn't some traveling salesman, but a man she once thought was the answer to her prayers. And he was the one warning her? Please.

For Matty it was the regret. He regretted not solidifying his relationship with Diane. She was an angel sent from heaven and he was too blind to see it. He wouldn't be distracted, he said. He wouldn't drag her down into his world, he said. Now he'd lost her. She'd probably already fallen for that salesman and his denigration of the man was only drawing her closer to her doom. Or happiness.

"So," Diane said, knowing that she couldn't bear it if they were to part like this, "how did you know where I stayed?"

Matty took a final hit on his cigarette, then put it out. "Janet told me," he said. "And I must say I was shocked."

Diane smiled. "Why would it be shocking that a woman my age would want to get her own place? Everybody's acting like it's such a big deal when it's nothing at all."

"It's something, all right. But that's not why I was shocked."

"Then what's so shocking about it?"

Matty stared at her. "You didn't consult me," he said.

Diane couldn't believe she heard what she'd just heard. "Consult you?" she asked incredulously. "Matty, you haven't let me within two feet of you. How was I supposed to consult you?"

"So it's my fault?"

Diane frowned. "What fault? What are you talking about? This has nothing to do with you. I decided to get my own place. You make it sound as if it's something bad. My parents make it sound as if it's something wrong. My friends make it sound as if something awful had to have happened to bring me to this decision. Nobody supports me, but everybody's got something to criticize about me. Well, I say forget all y'all! I'm sorry that my decision to take charge of my own life doesn't conform with some image y'all have of me, but that's not my problem!"

Diane said this and stood up, ready to forget trying to end this amicably and Matty could go to the dogs for all she cared. But he stood up, too, and moved in front of her, effectively cutting off her path.

"Diane," he said, heartfelt, as he grabbed her by the arms. But she kept moving, thrashing her arms away from him, trying to get away. "Diane, I'm sorry."

That stopped her cold. She looked into his eyes, into those big, dark gray eyes that always had a way of making her want to believe every word he said. And tears tried to well up in hers.

He pulled her into his arms and held her there. She didn't cry, she didn't break out into some pitiful sob that she knew wouldn't do anything to help her sense of independence, of getting over this man, of her conviction that she could make it, just fine, on her own. She looked up into his face, the feel of his arms around her more intoxicating than she had thought possible. She needed his comfort, she knew it, and she missed having it. But what price did she have to pay? How much of her self-respect did she have to surrender?

"I can't please everyone, Matty. I've tried. I've tried to do my best but it's never good enough. No matter what I do it's never enough. So I've given up trying. It's selfish, yes, but I need to be selfish right now."

Matty smiled. She never expected to see that beautiful smile of his again. He placed his hand on her chin and lifted her face to his. "Good for you," he said.

Then his smile slowly vanished as he stared at her. He seemed torn, perplexed, unable to make any kind of move without weighing all consequences first. Then he kissed her. It had been so long since she felt his lips on hers that she immediately threw her arms around him and returned his kiss. They kissed long and they kissed passionately and the way Diane was feeling they could have stayed this way all day.

Matty, however, knew it couldn't be. He could feel the temperature rising and his body too close to the brink. But instead of pushing Diane away, he pulled her closer and closer until she was as willing as he needed her to be. He could take advantage of this situation. He could seduce her so easily that she wouldn't know what hit her before it was all over. He was just that close, he felt, to possessing her completely, and relieving this burden he'd carried ever since he told Bishop Owens that he would come to Floradale and pastor Fountain Hope.

But the voice in his head was clear. What about Diane? it said. *What about Diane?*

And his lips quickly parted from hers and his arms relaxed their death grip on her body, and he let her go.

Diane felt cold when he released her. Her body, which had been burning with passion, was now aching with chill. She wanted to throw herself back into his arms. She didn't care anymore. She was tired of hiding her feelings. She was tired

of unfulfilled passion that was forever keeping her heart
tormented. He didn't have to love her. That was too much
to ask anyway. He loved God and she loved him dearly, and
that would be enough. It would have to be enough.

"What were you doing before I got here?" Matty asked,
as if their passionate love clutch had never occurred.

"Reading today's paper," Diane replied, trying to modu-
late her erratic breathing. "I've still got to unpack."

Matty looked around. "You've been shopping."

"Yeah. Everything in here is practically new. I pretty well
exhausted my savings."

He looked at her. "Need anything?"

"No, I'm fine."

He looked down the length of her. "That dress you're
wearing is new."

Diane looked down at the sundress she wore, and then she
looked at Matty. He was heavy-lidded now, the passion he
was trying to conceal still very much engrossing him. "Yes,"
she said. "I left my old clothes at my parents' home."

"Why's that?"

"I don't know. They just didn't seem to be my style anymore. I bought me all new ones. Ones that fit this time."

Matty smiled weakly. She was moving on, all right. Without him. Which was the best thing for her, he knew. "I guess
I'd better get going," he said, knowing that if he stayed a moment longer he might not be able to pull away from her.

She walked him to the door, feeling so painfully alone.
She rubbed her bare arm, the arm he had grabbed when she
thought to get away from him, the arm that was now aching
to feel his touch again. She was about to open the door, to
let him out of her life once more, but he placed his big hand
over her small one as it held the knob.

"You're a virgin, Diane," he said, looking deep into her
eyes, asking it not as if it were a question, but a fact.

Diane's heart dropped. He seemed disappointed about

that, too. She was a Christian, had been since she was four-teen years old. Of course she was a virgin. But he didn't like it. She could tell. That made her some kind of chump in his eyes, some kind of unsophisticated lady. She decided to smile. "Me? A virgin? I'm twenty-nine years old. How many twenty-nine-year-old virgins have you ever known?"

Matty stared at her. Had he done this to her? he wondered. Had he turned her into somebody so spooked by rejection that she no longer could appreciate the diamond she truly was? She hadn't been happy when he first met her, but at least she'd been content. At least she didn't have to depend on somebody else to validate her worthiness. The more he looked at her, the more she tried to smile and deny some-thing as special as her virginity, the more he knew Janet was right. Diane was heartbroken. And he was the reason.

"Well?" she asked, still smiling, still hurting. "Do you know any virgins in my age group?"

"I guess not," he said. "I had no business even asking it. Forgive me?"

Diane would forgive him anything. And she hated her-self for it. "Yes," she said.

Matty smiled weakly. Then he exhaled. "Have dinner with me Monday night, Diane," he said. Wrong move, he knew, but he had to make it.

Diane, however, could not believe her ears. "Dinner? With you?"

"Yes. I wish we could get together tonight, but I've got some witnessing to do, and tomorrow night I'm having a meeting with Pastor Demps, the pastor of the Fountain Hope church in Bainbridge. So how's Monday night around seven?"

Diane didn't know what to say.

"Diane?"

"Yes?"

"Around seven?"

"Yes," she said, realizing that it was no dream. He was actually asking her out on a date. "Yes, seven's fine."

Matty nodded. "Good. I'll pick you up. And I will also see you in church tomorrow."

He looked at her again, as if searching for some reaction from her, some confirmation that he'd done the right thing, and then he left. She stood there, too transfixed to move, wondering what in the world he was trying to do to her. One moment she didn't meet with his expectations at all. He needed a sophisticate, not some country bumpkin like her. Not some inexperienced neophyte who could actually confuse a man's lust for love.

The next moment he was inviting her to dinner.

She closed the door and leaned against it. The tears didn't hesitate to release as she looked around at her new house, her new clothes. Her new life. A life that she had thought just moments before was certain to not include Matty Jolson. Now, was it possible again?

She prayed to the Lord to make it possible again.

Chapter 20

Samantha Marshall arrived in seemingly uplifted spirits as she dropped off Junior at Fountain Hope Academy. It was his first day back since his brother's death but, unlike his mother, who was a master at putting on the mask, he could not conceal for a moment his displeasure with being there. Sister Inez saw it immediately. Junior, she always knew, wore his emotions on his sleeve. Some of her teachers used to call him a moody child, one of the moodiest little boys they'd ever seen. But Inez disagreed. Junior wasn't moody at all. His bad mood didn't come and go in shifts, it never left. And today, as he walked to his little desk, his arms folded, his lips stuck out, was no exception.

Sister Inez looked at Sam. Considering her tragedy, she appeared to have held up well. "You're looking prosperous, Sister Marshall," Inez said with a smile, prompting Sam to smile, too.

"Thank you," she said.

"I'm glad to see it. You have to go on with your life. It's

hard, I'll be the last to pretend it's not, but you don't really have a choice. Do you?"

"No, you don't. Ira said so, too. He said we can't neglect Junior. We still have to be there for him."

"And that ain't nothing but the truth. Judge Marshall is a wise man."

"Anyway, I'd better go. Junior is still a little upset about everything so please don't expect too much from him."

"I understand completely, Sister Marshall. I'll let his teachers know that he's just gonna be a little more ornery than usual. If that's possible."

Sam laughed, although she was crumbling inside. It took all the strength she had to even stand there. That was why she started getting away, as fast as she could. "Yes," she said, "if that's possible. Have a nice day, Sister Inez."

Sister Inez wished her well, too, and Sam quickly left. Unfortunately for her, however, it wasn't a clean getaway. Pastor Jolson, the last human being on earth she wanted to see right now, was in the parking lot leaning against her Mercedes.

She almost rolled her eyes. But she didn't. She merely began smiling as if nothing whatsoever was wrong with her life, but she slowed in her walk toward him.

"Good morning, Pastor," she said as he pushed away from her car and met her halfway.

"Good morning. You brought Junior back."

"Yes. I think it's time."

"Good move. He needs to be around other children."

"I agree."

"Judge Marshall agrees?"

Sam hesitated. "Of course."

"I didn't think he would want to have anything more to do with Fountain Hope."

"Why? Because you're here? Please. People like you come and go. The Marshalls will always be a part of this church family."

"Is he in counseling?" Matty asked, ignoring her putdown. Sam sighed her displeasure. "My husband doesn't need counseling, Pastor Jolson."

"I think he does. But I wasn't talking about your husband. I'm talking about your son."

Sam exhaled, feeling foolish and unnecessarily defensive. "No, Reverend, he's not in counseling."

"He certainly needs it, Sister Marshall. Desperately."

"He's okay."

"He's okay?"

"Yes."

"You can't believe that."

"I can believe it, Reverend. And I do."

"What really happened that night, Samantha?"

Sam briefly closed her eyes, as a flash of that night, of Ira throwing that lamp, tore threw her memory. Then she quickly looked at Matty again. "You already know what happened," she replied.

"No, I know what you and your husband said happened. I want to know what really happened. Who threw the lamp, Sam?"

"Nobody threw anything. I told you that."

"But did you tell me the truth?"

Sam shook her head. "I don't have time for this," she said, trying to move away, but Matty caught her by the arm. She looked at his hand on her, then she looked at him. The concern in his eyes made her want to confide in him, to unload this horrible burden once and for all. But she couldn't. She knew better. Ira had already told her to keep it zipped. He had already warned her to watch herself.

"Let go of my arm, Reverend," she said.

"You'll blame your own child for what that monster did?" he asked her.

Sam's heart dropped. He just didn't understand. Nobody understood. This was her family he was talking

about. Not some strangers up the road. Ira was all she had.
Ira and Junior. And she aimed to hold on to them with
all the strength she had within her. That preacher was just
mouthing words as far as she was concerned. He didn't live
on her street.

She snatched her arm away from him and began walking
away, her decision to just ignore his accusation the only one
she felt she could make.

Matty, however, sensed her anguish. It was deeply em-
bedded and eating her alive. "Your family is an illusion, Sister Marshall," he yelled after her, and she stopped in her
tracks. She turned around and looked at him.

"What?"

"This idyllic family you've been dreaming about all your
life isn't real. Ira Marshall is no knight in shining armor and
Junior has more problems than any seven-year-old should
ever have to deal with. You're fooling yourself if you think
living a lie is going to reap happiness and security for you.
All a lie can do is keep you tangled up in new lies to cover
old ones until you don't know what the truth is anymore.
Until you actually start to believe you have a happy family."

The emotion began to swell deep within Sam, but she
wasn't about to let him see her cry. She never pretended to
have a happy family, the Reverend was wrong about that.
Happiness wasn't meant for her, she found that out long ago
when she traveled from foster home to foster home and saw
the frowns on the faces of her new family as if a burden were
coming into their lives. She wasn't counting on a happy family. That would be too much for somebody like her to hope
for. Just to have a family, an attachment to somebody to ver-
ify that she wasn't all alone in this world, was about as good
as she could ever hope to get.

She turned back around, got into her car, and drove away.
She could barely see the road for her tears.

★ ★ ★

Matty didn't have to knock. Diane was already standing at the door. All day he had strongly considered revoking his invitation to take her to dinner. To avoid not only the talk, but the emotionalism that was becoming a by-product of being with her. But when he saw her at the door, looking at him with those sincere almond eyes of hers, he was glad he had resisted those urges. She looked lovely to him, in a sleeveless dark purple dress that hugged her body perfectly. He smiled when he saw her. There was definitely something about this one that could still warm his heart. "Good evening," he said, not gaily, but with some degree of joy. Diane, however, was flustered.

"I tried to reach you," she said as she stepped out of the door, "but the church said you had already gone for the day."

Matty sighed. He had hoped for smooth sailing tonight, a little R&R that he knew they both could use. But they hadn't even gotten started before the curveballs were being tossed. "What's the matter, Diane?" he cautiously asked her.

"I can't go."

Matty stared at her. And then he folded his arms in a defiant pose that didn't help her already frail nerves. "And why not?"

"I can't."

"Okay. Now answer my question. Why not?"

Diane didn't like his tone at all. She was high-strung enough. "I have to babysit," she said.

Matty frowned. *"Babysit?"*

"Yes. My sister Pam left her kids over here and I've got to watch them."

Matty unfolded his arms and shook his head. "Diane, didn't I ask you to have dinner with me tonight?"

"Yes, Matty, but she—"

"But she nothing, Diane! I've already made the reservations. Why would you agree to babysit for somebody when you knew you had to be with me?"

"I didn't agree to babysit. I told her I couldn't do it but she wouldn't listen. She said she had something to do."

"I see. Your plans didn't matter."

Diane didn't respond. It was already clear that they never did.

Matty sighed and shook his head. "Some family you've got, I'll tell you that," he said.

Diane looked at him with a sudden flash of anger. He had her life upside down for months, now he was angry because she couldn't go out with him? Because everything wasn't falling into place for *him?* She shook her head. "My family's fine," she said defensively.

Matty looked at her. His anger wanted to flare to greater extremes, it was certainly capable of it, but he maintained his cool. "Where is this sister of yours now?"

"She's not here. She's gone."

"Gone where, Diane? Now, you know what I mean!"

Diane paused before responding in an attempt to not allow this man to get a rise out of her. Not tonight. "I don't know," she said.

"Where do you think she might have gone?"

"I'm not sure, Matty, all right? She might be at Luther's house, but I can't be sure about that."

"Who's Luther?"

"Her boyfriend. Her babies' daddy."

"Does this Luther have a telephone?"

"No. He stays in a trailer over in Bainbridge."

"Where are the children now?"

"They're inside."

"Get them and let's go."

Diane hesitated. "What?"

Matty let out a heavy sigh. He was hoping to relax tonight,

Lord knew he needed it. This, he certainly did not need. "Just do it, Diane," he said.

Diane did not know why he would make such a request. But she did it. She got Pam's three kids and hustled them, along with herself, into Matty's Jaguar.

Luther lived in Bainbridge, in a single-wide, rundown trailer surrounded by woods, and Matty drove fast to get there. He looked so upset to Diane, like somebody sick and tired of life's derailments. Ever since the night of Alan's death there was an edginess to him, and it was still there, tensing every inch of his big body. She wondered if he somehow blamed himself for what happened to Alan, if he thought he should have done more about his suspicions. But how could she ask him? He had such a short fuse with her lately, was so frustrated with seemingly just the sight of her, that she felt she was the last person on earth he would confide in. And this fiasco tonight, where once again she was the source of his dismay, didn't help.

She looked at him. He wore a dark suit and dark shades, both of which seemed to match his dark mood perfectly. "I'm sorry about all of this, Matty," she said. "I tried to tell Pam I had something to do but she wouldn't listen. And I couldn't very well just take the kids to my parents' house. They're too old to be fooling up with these children."

Matty, at first, decided not to respond. His anger was nowhere near abated and he was tired of unleashing his barrage of frustration on sweet Diane. But enough was enough. They hadn't spent any real time together in months, and he would have thought she would at least make sure this night, this planned night, was free. But not Diane. Not this pillar of goodness who let the world use her as they saw fit.

"Why don't you just take us back to the house and go on to dinner without me," Diane suggested when it was clear to her that his anger and frustration was going to make for an unbearable evening anyway.

Matty exhaled. "You've got to learn to say no, Diane," he said. "Your plans are just as important as anybody else's. And, quite frankly, you may not mind this nonsense but I don't need this aggravation." He said this and glanced at her as if it were a warning, his big hands tightening around the steering wheel.

Diane sighed and looked forward, as they entered Bainbridge's city limits and proceeded to Luther's place, Diane giving careful directions. It was getting dark now, as the sun was beginning to set, and she couldn't help but worry. She'd always seen herself as her man's helper, as somebody who would calm him down when the burdens of the day weighed too heavily on him. Now, for Matty, for the one man who could twist up her emotions so completely, she was the burden. She was the reason for his lack of calm. She was always the problem.

And now this. Driving all the way over to Bainbridge when Pam may not even be at Luther's. She looked at Matty.

"I don't think this is a good idea, Matty," she said.

"Tough," Matty replied.

Diane frowned. "Why are you so upset? Things come up. Plans change. I'm sure you can easily find somebody else to go out with you. Sister Scott would love to go."

Matty's big body shifted in his seat. Diane didn't think it was possible, but he appeared even more angry. "If I wanted Sister Scott or anybody else to go with me, I would have asked them. I asked you. And you're going with me." He gave her a sharp look.

"Even if I don't want to?"

Matty didn't say anything.

"What's the matter, Matty?" Diane asked him. "And don't tell me it's this sudden change in plans because that can't be it. There's more going on with you. Is it because of what happened that Saturday morning when Sister Inez saw me? Is that still on your mind? Or is it because I said I love you?"

"Diane—"

"No, Matty, let's get this out in the open once and for all. If you're still angry with me about what happened you're wasting your time. I said too much that morning, I realize it now, and I apologize for that. I didn't mean to put any pressure on you. You've got enough on you and I understand that. You couldn't possibly be any more disappointed in me than I am in myself. And as for Sister Inez, I told her nothing happened. She's gone on to complain about other things. She knows nothing happened."

Matty glanced at Diane, then looked back at the road. "I saw Judge Marshall's wife today."

"Sam? Where?"

"She brought Ira, Jr., to school this morning."

Diane sighed. "How is she, Matty? How's Junior?"

Matty shook his head. "Not good."

"She hasn't returned any of my phone calls. I went by her house last week but she told me she really wasn't up for visitors right now."

"You keep pressing her."

"I will. I did. Every day. I told her she could talk to me, anytime, anyplace, but she won't. It's as if she's upset with me."

"She's not upset with you. She's upset with herself. But she can't admit it, not yet. She's hunkering down right now. She sees the world as her and her family on one side, everybody else on the other. But keep pressing her. And praying for her. She'll eventually come around."

"Lord knows I hope so." Then Diane looked at Matty. "You don't blame yourself, Matty. Do you?"

"I blame Ira Marshall. He's the snake in the grass. But Samantha failed to protect Alan. She should have never allowed her children to stay in that situation. And yes, that angers me."

"But we don't even know if there was a situation. Sam denies it to this day. And Junior, too."

"They can deny it all they want, but I know what I'm say-ing is true. And it'll all come to light. I'll see to that. The sher-iff may be convinced, and you and all of Fountain Hope may be convinced, but I'm not sold at all. I will not forget what happened to Alan Marshall. His death will not be in vain."

"Turn here," Diane said. "But what can we do?"

"You just stay on Sam's case. Don't let her go into the co-coon Ira wants her in. Keep at her. I'll take care of him."

A right on Tharpe yielded a left on Brevard and Luther's trailer was just across the railroad tracks. Pam's car was in the yard, an early-nineties model Nissan Sentra, and Diane was at least grateful that her best guess didn't turn up blanks. But she was still concerned. "Come on, children," she said. "You can wait in the car, Matty."

Matty, however, ignored her suggestion and got out of the car. Diane sighed, and got out, too.

Matty walked behind her and the children as they walked up to the small attached front porch. Diane's knock on the door turned up nothing and she almost seemed content to turn around and leave, but Matty moved up beside her and pounded on the flimsy door, causing it to become slightly ajar. Luther Tate, angry by the ferocious nature of the knocks and the opening of his door, swung the door open wider and stepped forward. "Who knocking on my door like they the police?" he demanded to know. He was a big man, with a round face and belly, wearing jeans but no shirt.

"Hello, Luther," Diane said to him. "Is Pam here?"

Luther looked from Matty and Diane to the children. "Nall," he said. "She ain't here."

"I see her car in the driveway so I thought that maybe…"

"I said she ain't here."

Matty, already sick of this, took Diane by the arm and pulled her back. Then he gently pushed the three children up to the front door. "Here are your children, Luther," he said as the children moved forward.

Luther looked at Matty. "Now just a minute here," he said. "Who you 'spose to be?"

"This is my pastor," Diane said. Then she turned and looked at Matty. "We can't just leave these children, Reverend."

"Why not?" Matty said. "They're with their father. Let's go."

"But I got things to do!" Luther yelled, suddenly panicked.

"So do we," Matty said and took Diane by the arm and began walking off of the porch.

"Nall now, Diane, you know I can't be taking care of no children. Diane!"

But Matty wouldn't allow her to so much as turn around. She wanted to, she didn't like to leave a situation in turmoil, but Matty gripped her arm and pulled her body so tightly against his that she could do nothing but keep walking away.

"I'll be doggone," Luther said as he scratched his head and looked at those children. Then he yelled inside the house. "Pam! Pam! You better get out here and stop your crazy sister! She trying to leave these children here!"

Matty was just about to open his car door for Diane when they heard Pam's voice. They quickly turned around just as Pam had come out of the house and was running toward Diane. "What you think you're doing?" she asked Diane, stunned.

"Luther said you weren't here," Diane said and Matty smiled.

"He thought I was gone to the store," Pam lied. "You said you was gonna babysit for me, Diane, what you doing?"

"I didn't say I was going to babysit. You said I was going to babysit. But I can't."

"Why not?"

Diane looked at Matty then looked at her sister. "Because I have a prior engagement."

"A prior what?"

Diane smiled. "Good night, Pam," she said as Matty opened the passenger door of his Jaguar and Diane sat inside.

Pam just stood there flustered. She looked at Matty, who was walking toward the driver's side. "What I'm supposed to do?" she asked him.

"Stop taking advantage of your sister and raise your children," he said and got into the car. Then he cranked up, backed out, and left. The look on Pam's face was priceless, Diane thought. And, oddly enough, Diane couldn't help but smile.

He took her to a beautiful restaurant, Brandeur's, but given his attitude, she thought, he might as well had taken her to McDonald's. From the time they drove over there to the moment they sat down and ordered drinks, Matty had barely said two words to Diane. He had finally removed those dark shades but his dark mood hadn't lifted at all. She tried to make small talk, in the car, and as they walked into the restaurant, but he pretty much ignored her. She wanted desperately to ask him what was driving all of these moods of his, but she held her tongue. Because she knew. She was driving his moods. She was turning out to be more trouble than he apparently assumed she was worth, she felt. And he couldn't deal with that.

But Diane was no quitter. She tried again. She looked across the table at Matty, who was looking over the menu, and smiled. "Thank you," she said.

Matty, who had on his reading glasses, looked over at her. "For what?" he asked her, his face still too tense for what should have been a relaxing night out.

"Thanks for inviting me to dinner. For bringing me here. This is a lovely place."

Matty grunted something, it could have been *oh* or *you're welcome,* Diane wasn't sure which, then he continued to peruse the menu. She sighed. He invited her here. He was the one who came to her apartment and disrupted her life. Now he was acting as if she were intruding on his! She threw her napkin on the table and grabbed her clutch purse. "Will you take me home, please?" she said.

Matty, easily surprised by her words, looked up at her. "What?"

"Take me home."

He gave her a sharp look. Then he removed his glasses. "Why, Diane?"

"Because I want to go home. Now will you take me or do I need to find my own way?"

"Knock it off."

Diane blew out a breath of frustration as Matty stared intensely at her. His expression softened as he stared at her, and he even tried to smile. "What would you like?" he asked her.

She looked at him. "What?"

Matty didn't like her harsh tone of voice, and almost didn't respond, but he knew he had brought her to this. "Would you like the steak or would you prefer shrimp?"

Diane couldn't believe it. He regarded her so little that he wasn't even considering her request. Of course he wasn't taking her home. He wasn't ready to go yet.

She stood up.

"Diane?" Matty said, caught off guard by her display, but she did not hesitate. With clutch in tow she walked briskly away, maneuvering her way out of that restaurant as if she'd been there a thousand times. Matty had been toying with her too long. He'd been taking her feelings for granted on too many occasions. He'd pull her to him, then push her away. Back and forth, back and forth, over and over again. As if she had no say in her own life. As if she were born to serve his whims.

Outside she ignored the attendant's request for her ticket and began walking out of the parking lot. She'd walk all the way back to Floradale if she had to. Matty arrived outside shortly after she did and handed the attendant the parking ticket. Then he ran across the lot to Diane, grabbing her by the forearm as she neared the curb that would have taken her across the busy boulevard. It was a chilly night and she was not dressed for the weather, a fact that had been lost on her, however, until Matty grabbed her and slung her around, the stiff night air whipping her in the face, the sounds of cars speeding by heightening the intensity.

"So you're going to walk home now?" he asked her angrily, his face not at all humored by her little demonstration.

"If that's the only way I can get home, yes."

"This isn't funny, Diane."

"Am I laughing, Matty? Do you see a smile anywhere near my face?"

"What's wrong with you?"

"Nothing's wrong with me."

"What are you so offended by?"

The parking attendant, an eager young man, drove up in Matty's Jaguar and stepped out. Matty handed the boy a twenty then turned back to Diane. "Well?" he asked. "What is it, Diane?"

"If you have to ask—"

"Don't get cute with me."

"Then just leave me alone. I can manage just fine, thank you."

Matty shook his head. "Get in the car," he said with little patience. Diane, however, began to move away.

"No, thank you," she said.

Matty grabbed her, once again, by the forearm. "Get in the car," he demanded.

She politely but firmly removed her arm from his grasp. Who did he think he was? But she got into the car.

The drive home was torturous. Neither said a word the entire time. Matty would glance at Diane and Diane would take sly looks at Matty, but neither seemed willing to air out their differences. For Diane it was a question of self-respect. She was always the one bending, always seeking answers, always trying with all she had to accommodate Matty and his wild mood swings. It was his time to bend and bow, she decided.

For Matty the question was more rudimentary. Diane was trying to blossom, she was trying to come into her own. Would it be fair for him to stand in her way? He knew the answer, he'd known it the moment he met her, he just didn't like it.

When they arrived back at Diane's apartment, Matty, true to form tonight, didn't get out of his car to open the door for her, something he had never neglected to do. He, instead, just sat there, his hands gripping his steering wheel, his plan involving a quick getaway as soon as she stepped out.

But as soon as she stepped out and began walking across the sidewalk, walking as if she'd just lost her best friend, he made his decision. And he couldn't move. His heart suddenly started hammering with fear. Never in his life had he been so afraid. Not because of how his decision would affect him, but because of how dramatically it would affect her. How could he be so cruel? he wondered. How could he be so selfish? Why couldn't he just drive on off and leave this woman alone? But he looked at her again as she headed for her front door. And he knew why. More clearly than he'd ever known before, he knew exactly why.

Diane walked somberly across her sidewalk, her entire body weighed down in despair. When she arrived at her front door she leaned her head against it, unable to find the strength to put the key in her lock. *Oh, God,* her heart cried. What had she done that was so horrible? What was so detestable about her that she would turn a wonderful man like Matty so completely against her? She made her mistakes, but were they that unforgivable? All she wanted was a little happiness in this life. All she wanted was somebody to love. Her entire soul cried out to God where she stood. "What have I done?" she found herself saying out loud.

"Nothing," a strong, calm voice said behind her, and it gave her such a start that she turned quickly toward the sound. It was Matty. In her grief she hadn't even heard him approach.

"You haven't done anything, Diane," he said. He was a full ten feet away from her but it was still too close for her comfort. She was at her door. And if it had been unlocked she would have bolted. Her heart could not bear another emotional ride with this man.

"I don't want you to think for a moment that you've done anything wrong, because you haven't." He began walking toward her. Her heart began to pound. "It's not you. I'm the problem in this relationship, you understand me? Not you. You're the sweetest human being I've ever met."

Diane began to shake her head. She did not want to hear this. She did not want him ever again to draw her in with such beautiful words then reel her back out again, with no words at all, just frowns and harsh looks and bitter glances. She turned toward her front door and was about to unlock it when words she never thought he'd say, were said.

"I love you, Diane," Matty said in a tone verging on desperation, as the distance between them closed from feet to mere inches.

Those words stopped every movement in Diane's body. Even her heart skipped a beat. She turned back around and looked at him. His features didn't appear stern anymore but oddly, strangely, vulnerable.

"You love me?" she asked him.

Matty's eyes almost welled up in tears. It was the hardest truth he ever had to admit. He began to nod his head. "Yes," he said. "I have from the moment I saw you trying to sing in my parlor." He smiled at the image, and the memory of the off-key sound. Diane was confounded.

Matty's face turned intense again. This was no simple matter and he knew it, too. "I love you, Diane. I love you and I need you and God help me but I'm too selfish to let you go!"

Diane flew into his arms, the impact of her slamming against his body enough to stagger him. But he wrapped her in his arms and held her. She was crying now, crying openly, and tears began to fill his eyes, too.

He loved her. He loved her deeply. He'd been denying it for far too long. He had tried to protect his own heart, then he had tried to protect hers. But no more, he decided. His Lord and Savior would just have to protect them both.

He took the keys from her hand, unlocked her front door, and tried to walk her, but, given her emotional state, ended up carrying her, into her home.

Chapter 21

He hated these things with a passion, but he knew they came with the territory. He sat at the head of the table in the boardroom while Deacon Molt and Sister Inez and four other church leaders brought the problem to his attention. He, at first, thought it might be about his relationship with Diane. Maybe they wanted to keep him away from their favorite daughter. Somebody like him certainly didn't deserve somebody like her and maybe they wanted to remind him of that fact. But from the grave look on their faces as they sat glumly around the table, Matty slowly became convinced that his relationship with Diane had nothing to do with this little get together. Whatever it was, it was going to be monumental foolishness in the end, he suspected. Therefore, the graver they looked, the less worried he became.

"What did I do this time?" he asked them, unable to suppress a smile.

Deacon Molt, however, didn't find it humorous at all. "We received a visit from Judge Marshall," he said.

Matty nodded. It wasn't quite the news he'd expected, but he could handle it. "Okay."

"He was extremely upset. He said you've been harassing him and his family, Reverend. He said ever since Sister Marshall brought young Junior back to school you've been driving by their house or coming by the courthouse or showing up at the church just when you knew his wife would be there. He wanted to file a restraining order against you, but we talked him out of it. A restraining order against the pastor of Fountain Hope is something we just will not have. We'll get rid of the pastor first."

Matty smiled. "I'm sure you'll try," he said.

"What's that supposed to mean?" Inez asked.

"God is in control, Sister Inez. And if He wants me here, restraining orders or no restraining orders, I'll be here. If He doesn't, I won't."

"You can't be running around harassing our most respected member!" Inez countered. "Judge Marshall and his family have done so much for the church. And this community. He will not be disrespected."

Matty wanted to unleash. He wanted to call them out for their misguided belief in a monster like Ira Marshall. The same way they were so quick to believe Leah Littleton. But all things in time, he thought. "Is there anything else?" he asked.

"I don't think you understand the gravity of this, Pastor Jolson," Deacon Molt said. "Brother Marshall ain't just whistling Dixie, he's serious. He can make a lot of trouble for you. And if he pulls his financial support from this church it could devastate us."

"Ah, the point," Matty said. "Is there anything else?"

"Why are you bothering Judge Marshall anyway?" Inez asked him. "What has he ever done to you?"

Matty looked at her. "What did Judge Marshall say?"

"He said he don't know what your problem is," Inez said.

"And he don't care. He just want you to leave him alone. Although he did insinuate that you might have taken a liking to his wife."

Everybody looked at Matty when Sister Inez said this. Judge Marshall was good, Matty thought. He'd give him that.

"Is it true, Pastor?" Inez asked. "Have you taken some kind of ungodly liking to Sister Marshall?"

"No."

"Are you sure?"

"I should be."

"Then what's going on here?" Molt asked. "Why would Judge Marshall have the idea that you've been harassing his family?"

"I'll reserve my explanations for later. Now, if that is all—" Matty began rising to his feet.

"After that horrible time involving Sister Littleton you have to be careful, Pastor. That's all we're trying to say."

Matty nodded. "Understood. Now, if that's all—"

"About that car of yours," Deacon Molt said suddenly and Matty, not believing what he just heard, sat back down.

"My car?"

"Yes. We want to know what your plans are."

Matty burst into laughter. He couldn't help it.

Molt frowned. He couldn't believe the insult. "I'm glad you think this funny, Reverend Jolson."

"I'm sorry, I really am, but I want to make sure I understand you. Did you just say you wanted to know *my* plans about *my* car?"

Inez gave him a coarse look, remembering her conversation with him about this very topic, then she looked at Molt.

"Yes," Deacon Molt said.

"Well, I'll tell you, Deacon. I plan to drive my car as long as it gives me pleasure to do so, then I plan to get rid of it and get me a brand-new one. Now if that doesn't jive with your plans for me or my automobile, then I'm sorry. But I think I have the only vote on that score. Now if you'll excuse me, I've got work to do."

Matty stood up and, without even bothering to await a reply, left the cluttered room.

Members of the Fountain Hope church choir slowly began to fill the choir stands as the chitchat before rehearsal reached fever pitch. Even Maurice, the choir director, wasn't his usual *all right, people, quiet down* self, but was gabbing up a storm with the pianist.

Diane had come early, hoping, as she always hoped, to catch a glimpse of Pastor Jolson. Since that glorious Monday night when he confessed his love for her she'd been unable to stop thinking about him. He phoned her, every day actually, and most nights as well, but he'd been so wrapped up in starting a new prison ministry that he hadn't dropped by to see her yet. Now she was here and she desperately wanted to see him, but he hadn't shown his face.

His assistant showed hers, however, walking downstairs and smiling greatly as choir members greeted her. "Hey, Wanda, sing us a song!" one of them, Sister Riley, yelled out in jest.

Wanda laughed. "You don't want me singing, Sister Riley. I can't sing a lick!"

"That never stopped none of us," Sister Riley replied, and everybody laughed. "We can't sing a lick either. But we serve the Lord just the same."

"Amen," a few other members agreed.

"Well, y'all keep on serving Him," Wanda said, in her polite but firm way, "I'll do my part, too, but it won't entail singing. Hello, Maurice."

"Hello, Miss Thang," Maurice said to Wanda as he stopped his chatter with the pianist and looked sidelong at her. "I know you ain't trying to disturb my rehearsal session."

"You mean your noise session."

"What*ever*."

"No, Maurice, I'm not here to disturb anything. Pastor needs to see Diane."

Diane's heart slammed against her chest when Wanda spoke those words. Was it good news, or was it bad news again? she wondered. Was he going to tell her that he'd been thinking things over and decided that she really wasn't good enough for him? Was the blissfulness she'd been feeling all week about to come to a screeching halt?

"Diane!" Maurice yelled up into the noisy choir stand. "Pastor needs to see you, girl. But hurry back 'cause I got a rehearsal to run."

"You mean a noise session," Wanda said as Diane rose from her chair and began to descend the steps.

"What*ever*," Maurice said again and continued talking with the pianist.

Diane smiled nervously at Wanda and then followed her through the side door that led to the stairs. They small-talked as they walked, with Diane's mind too paralyzed with fear to even ask Wanda if she knew what this was about. She had told Matty that night, when he literally carried her into her apartment, that she couldn't take another heartbreak, nor another roller-coaster ride with him. He held her tightly against him then and promised her that she wouldn't have to worry about that. But now she wondered. Matty was the moodiest individual she'd ever met in her life, a man who thought too much and reacted based on inner conclusions nobody knew he was even contemplating. And now he wanted to see her.

Wanda smiled as she disappeared into her office just outside of Matty's, leaving Diane to enter his office alone. She knocked and waited for his word, which came in the form of a loud *enter!*, then she opened the door slowly. Matty's face, she felt, would tell the story. Based on that look upon his face she'd know if he was for her or against her; if he was in a good mood or a bad one. Matty's face usually told it all.

He was seated behind his desk reading over a stack of papers when Diane opened the door. When he looked up at her and smiled, her heart leaped for joy. He was for her, she decided, as she gladly entered in. He was still on her side.

"Hello there!" he said as he rose and hurried from around his desk, just as anxious as Diane to come together, the sleeves of his light blue dress shirt rolled up revealing thick, hairy forearms. They kissed on the lips as they met and he pulled her into those arms.

"I thought it was going to be bad news," she said as Matty held her, unable to suppress the relief in her heart.

"Why would you think that?" he asked her, pulling her closer.

"It's usually bad news," she replied.

Matty just stood there, his smile frozen into an unnatural smirk. He'd treated her badly. His clumsy attempts at protecting her from the upheaval that was usually his life had somehow managed to have just the opposite effect. He'd hurt her, not helped her, with his decisions. Now she was probably crippled with worry, wondering *what now* every time he called her name. He closed his eyes as he held her. He was sorry. "No, Diane," he said, "it's not bad news."

She pulled back from him, forcing him to look her in the eye. "Then what was so important that you would drag me out of choir rehearsal?"

Matty stared at her and began rubbing the long, soft hair she now wore down routinely. His hesitation unnerved her.

"What is it, Matty?" she asked him.

"I just wanted to see for myself that you were all right."

Diane's heart soared again. It was still a roller-coaster ride, but one of her own making this time. She could live with that. "I'm fine," she said gaily. "Even better now."

"Good," Matty said with a smile, "because I'll be mighty upset if you weren't."

"And what about you?" she asked him. "Are you okay?"

Matty smiled, the lines on the side of his eyes enhanced by the broadness of his smile. He wasn't accustomed to someone caring about him, someone with no ulterior motives or hidden agendas or just plain craftiness. "I'm good, too, sweetie," he said.

"No second thoughts?"

Matty's look turned serious. It would take some time, he knew, before she could fully trust him again. "None," he said with all sincerity.

Diane smiled and wrapped her arms around him again. He let her hold on to him, glad to know that he could still please her, as the faint sound of the choir finally singing began to echo in their ears. Diane, however, didn't seem to care that she was missing out. She was holding the man she loved, gripping him as tightly as she could. Her small body was pressing harder and harder against him, dangerously too hard, Matty thought, causing him to pull her back.

She tried to regain her position against him, smiling as she tried, but he wouldn't allow it. "Diane," he said.

"I just like being with you."

"I know that. But you've got a rehearsal to attend."

Diane, for the first time, paid attention to the sounds of the choir in the sanctuary downstairs. "I guess you're right," she said reluctantly.

"I know I'm right."

"May I see you later?"

Matty smiled. "You may."

Diane smiled, too, and kissed him on the lips again. "Maybe I'll just skip choir rehearsal," she said.

Matty physically turned her away from him and pointed her toward the door. "Good-bye, lady," he said.

Diane, still smiling, just stood there. "Do I have to go?"

she asked jokingly, having what was becoming the time of her life.

"You have to," he said, pushing her along. "Now get downstairs and add some high-pitched, off-key soul singing to that melodic choir." He then gave her a hard slap on her backside as his final shove. Diane, stunned, looked back at him. When she realized he was laughing, she laughed, too. And walked on air as she returned to her place in the choir.

She called for him five times. "Come and take your bath, Junior!" she kept calling. But he stayed where he was, in the den, watching television, staring at the screen as he usually did, his muscle-man action figure toy being twirled and contorted to his own pleasure. He heard each time his mother called. He heard her nauseating voice that was becoming harder and harder for him to listen to. Then he saw her, after the fifth time, coming into the den. He rolled his eyes.

"Junior, did you hear me?" Sam asked her son. But he continued to ignore her. "Junior? Junior? *Junior?!*"

"What?!" he yelled back at her. The strident tone of his voice wasn't new to Sam, she'd had to deal with that since the day he learned to talk. But his manner, so tense, so close to the edge, was new.

"Don't you talk to me like that," she warned him. "I'm your mother, in case you've forgotten, and you will not talk to me that way."

"No," Junior said.

"No what, boy?"

"No, you ain't."

Sam frowned. "No I'm not what?"

Junior responded, but he did so under his breath.

"What did you say?" Sam asked him. "Junior, what did you say?"

Junior wouldn't answer. Sam, so frustrated that she sometimes wished Ira would let her take a switch to that boy, hurried toward him. He needed a spanking, she felt. He needed some manners beat into him. But Ira didn't believe in corporal punishment. He could knock her around, even more so now that Alan was gone, but he wouldn't allow her to lay a hand on his precious Junior.

Sam grabbed Junior by his arms and turned him around to face her. "Boy, what did you say to me?" she asked him.

"Leave me alone!" he yelled.

"I'll slap the paint off you, boy! Now tell me what you said."

"You ain't no mommy of mine!" Junior yelled from the top of his lungs. "That's what I said! I hate you! I hate everything about you! I hate looking at you and talking to you and being anywhere near you!"

Sam was stunned. She stared at her emotional son. "What?" she said almost as a whisper.

"I hate you! If you would have left Daddy, Alan would still be alive! I would still have my brother! If you would have left Daddy, Alan would still be here with me!"

Sam nearly fell back in shock. Junior sat there, fighting back tears with all he had, the hate and anguish all over his beautiful face. And Sam couldn't take it. It was her fault? How could he say that? She had thought she was doing the right thing. She thought keeping her family together was the Christian thing to do. But even Junior knew better. Even little Junior could see, like Pastor Jolson had seen, that they weren't a family at all. Just people marching to the beat of Ira's tune. No matter what.

Sam grabbed her son and held him. For the first time since he was a lap baby, he allowed her to show him affection. And the tears clouded her eyes, too. But not her head. Not any longer. She immediately picked up Junior into her arms. He was heavy, but she was strong enough now. She grabbed her car keys and ran to her car. Her foolish inaction had caused her to lose one of her sons. But not this one, too. For once in her adult life she was going to take a stand. For the only real family she had left. For her son.

She placed Junior into the car, got into the car herself, and drove as if her life depended on it, to Fountain Hope.

Choir rehearsal was just breaking up when Sam, carrying Junior, came through the sanctuary doors. As soon as Diane saw her she left the choir stand and hurried to her. The terror in Sam's eyes was evident even from a distance. And it was a horrifying sight to see. And Junior was crying. Something Diane had never seen him do. Something was wrong, Diane thought, as she approached her friend. Something was terribly wrong.

"What's the matter, Sam, what happened?" she asked her.

"He said he hated me," Sam said.

"What?"

"I ducked."

Diane stared blankly at her friend. She had no clue what was wrong with her, or what she was trying to say. But it was serious, she knew that much. Serious enough that Matty needed to get involved.

She therefore wrapped her arms around Sam and walked her and Junior into the back rooms of the church, up the stairs, to Matty's office. Wanda wasn't at her desk so she knocked once on Matty's door and quickly walked in. He was sitting behind his desk. Janet Brown was there, sitting across from the desk, her short dress revealing way too much, her plump legs crossed. A twinge of jealousy pricked at Diane, but she quickly dismissed it.

Matty stood up when he saw her. Especially when he saw that Sister Marshall and Ira, Jr., were with her. "Good evening," he said.

"Sam needs to talk with you, Pastor," Diane said.

"Absolutely. Have a seat, Sister Marshall."

Sam looked at Diane. She couldn't very well discuss this in front of Janet Brown, who was becoming the church's biggest gossip. Diane looked at Matty.

"Janet, I'm sorry, will you please excuse us?" Matty said.

"Sure, Reverend," Janet said with a smile. Then she looked at Sam and Junior and especially Diane, and then walked on out of the office.

"I'll be going, too," Diane said, knowing that it was none of her business either.

"No," Sam said, desperately. "Please stay."

Diane agreed without hesitation. Sam sat down in the chair Janet had vacated and placed Junior on her lap. Diane sat beside her and smiled at Junior. He just stared at her, his eyes now red from so much crying.

Matty walked from behind his desk and leaned against the front edge. He folded his arms. "What can I do for you, Sister Marshall?" he asked.

Sam sucked in her breath. And then she let go. "You were right," she said. "Ira has been abusive. Very abusive. He beats me if I smile, he beats me if I frown, he beats me if I don't say exactly what he wants to hear. You were right all along, Pastor. We used to have a wonderful marriage, and I loved him so much. But when he turned forty-five everything changed. Everything. He thought I was cheating on him, he thought so many horrible things about me. He just changed so completely."

Matty exhaled. Diane sat stunned. "And the alcoholism?" Matty asked Sam.

"I don't even drink, Reverend. Never have. It became a convenient excuse for us, you see. I would lie, cheat, steal, do anything to keep my family together. And I would have continued that same way for the rest of my life. I honestly would have. But Junior said no."

Matty glanced at Diane, who was already near tears, and then he looked at Junior. "What did Junior say?"

"He said he hated me. He said if it weren't for me, if I would have left Ira, Alan would still be alive today."

"What happened to Alan, Sister Marshall?"

Sam stared at Matty. "Ira killed him," she said.

Diane covered her mouth in shock. Matty unfolded his arms. "How?" he asked.

"He was angry at me because I forgot to ask him how his day had gone. That, of course, meant I didn't care how it went because I was fooling around with some other man. Same theme, different variation." Tears began to well up in Sam's eyes. "He threw a lamp at me, in the midst of our argument. I ducked. I always do. I had no idea Alan had come into the room. I had no idea, Pastor. But he had. And he didn't see it coming." Sam shook her head. "Oh, God, what have I done? How could I have allowed my children to live like this? They were happy when they were babies, before Ira changed. But he changed. And I didn't do anything. I let it happen. I let Ira's rage cause harm to sweet little Alan. And we blamed Junior. Junior had nothing to do with it. But we blamed him to cover up for Ira. And it was wrong. I was so wrong, Pastor."

Matty nodded. "Yes, you were, Sister Marshall," he said. Diane looked at him, surprised that he would be so unforgiving. But he ignored Diane. He had to be tough. No love in this world was worth the death of a little boy and the emotional scars the other one had to endure. Samantha Marshall had to understand that. It had to be made clear that she couldn't allow something like this to ever happen again.

"But it wasn't your fault," Diane said, to ease Sam's obvious pain. Then she looked at Matty. "It wasn't her fault, Matty."

"It was Ira's fault," Matty said, more to ease Diane's pain than Sam's. "But she didn't help."

Sam nodded. It was true.

"Where's your husband now, Sister Marshall?"

"He's still at the courthouse. He works late most nights."

"Okay," Matty said and reached back and picked up his desk receiver.

"What are you doing?"

Matty looked at Sam. "What do you think I'm doing? I'm calling the sheriff. And you will tell him exactly what you just told me. And he will arrest Ira Marshall for the murder of his son."

The tears began to fall freely from Sam's eyes. She grabbed Junior and held him tightly. Matty's heart broke for Sam and her son, but there was no other way. It was a mess and that was all there was to it.

Matty dialed 911.

Chapter 22

Ira Marshall's arrest stunned Floradale, as nobody could believe that a man of such esteem could have been so brutal, and so brutal toward his own family. Ira denied the charges, telling numerous reporters that he would easily be vindicated because he was "completely, unequivocally innocent." Those words made the newspaper headlines. He even seemed to relish the knowledge that he would have his day in court.

His cockiness dissipated fast, however, when Junior started talking. And he told it all, from the abuse his mother had to endure to the maltreatments he and his father both reaped on his little brother, to the night his brother went upstairs to free his mother from his father's rage, only to be a victim of that rage himself. The presiding judge, concerned for Sam and Junior's safety and very concerned that Ira, a judge himself, blamed his own son for a crime he knew he himself had committed, refused to grant any bail at all. Marshall had to be held to the highest standards, the judge had said. It was a stunning indictment against a man many thought flawless.

But from where Matty sat it was the least the community could do for poor Alan Marshall.

But if Ira Marshall's arrest stunned Floradale, it devastated Fountain Hope. The members were, at first, so reluctant to believe the allegations that it sickened Matty. The man was a monster, his own child was saying so, yet they were still willing to idolize Ira, to disbelieve everybody and everything but the monster himself. It wasn't until Sister Inez came on board, making it clear that she believed Junior and Samantha and that Fountain Hope would not turn a blind eye to the truth, that other members of the congregation came around, too. To Matty it was incredible that it would take that much to get them to see the light. But Deacon Molt correctly reminded him that the point wasn't what it took for them to come around, but that they did come around.

The fall of Ira Marshall was a great blow to the faith of many members and Matty found himself with more and more counseling clients. You never really know people, one woman said, and Matty agreed. He also told her that this misfortune should be a cautionary tale to all, a lesson that we should always put our trust in God, and not man.

A month later, it was a busy day at the Tarver home. Although it had been packed solid with guests earlier, the last to leave was Sam. She picked up Junior as he slept peacefully on the Tarver sofa, after a day of running and jumping and playing gloriously with Diane's nieces and nephew. Willie James and Malveen had argued most of the day, as had Frank and Pam when they dropped in on the festivities, but none of their hysterics, none of their complaints about the food or the music or the people Diane chose to invite, mainly church folk, was about to rain on Diane's parade. This was her thirtieth birthday celebration, the first birthday party she'd had in years, and nobody was taking that away from her.

She walked Sam and Junior to Sam's Ford Explorer SUV, and after Sam buckled a still-sleeping Junior into the car seat, they stood outside the truck and talked. It was strange seeing Sam driving around town in Ira's truck, something she'd never done in the past, and Diane told her so. Sam nodded. She knew.

"He can't use it where he's at," she said with a smile.

It was a breezy night, as the fall night air blew briskly across quiet Clarion Avenue. Diane's hair blew, too, and she constantly had to push it out of her face. Sam looked at her, in her stylish jeans and pretty white cashmere pullover, smiling as if she hadn't a care in this world. Diane had changed so much, Sam thought. She had always been positive, always upbeat, but now she seemed happy, too. She wouldn't tell Sam why she was so different now, but Sam had heard rumors. According to Janet Brown, among others, Pastor Jolson and Diane were more than just friends lately. Sam couldn't believe it when she heard it. Not Diane, she had said at the time. But now, watching Diane, watching this one-time wallflower of a human being maneuver through life as if she were an old pro at it, she could see how it could very well be true.

"Have you heard from him?" Diane asked her, completely oblivious to Sam's train of thought.

"Who?" Sam asked without thinking. Then she realized who. "No," she said. "When I went to see him last week he made it clear he didn't want to have anything to do with me."

Diane looked at Sam. "You went to see him?"

"Unfortunately, yes. I wanted to see if there was forgiveness there, you know? A man sorry for what he'd done to his family."

"Was he sorry?"

"Not at all, Diane. Bitter, yes. Angry, definitely. But not sorry. He even tried to put a guilt trip on me, but I told him he could forget that. He was wasting his time. My son is dead because of that—"

"All right, girl, I feel ya," Diane quickly said. "You don't have to go there, I can feel where you're coming from."

"He just does something to me. Just thinking about how he used me and treated me. And yes, I blame myself for what happened. I should have left him a long time ago. Even Pastor Jolson blames me—"

"He doesn't blame you, Sam. He blames Ira."

"Oh, yeah, I forgot. He blames Ira but I didn't help the situation, according to him."

Diane swallowed. "You didn't," she said and looked at her friend. "But I know you did the best you could think to do at the time."

Sam nodded. She was out of fantasy land now, and she wasn't about to go back. "I know. Pastor once told me that this happy family I wanted so desperately wasn't real. He said it was just a figment of my imagination. And you know I left him crying after he said that? Not because I was angry with him. But because he was so right. And I knew I'd been too far gone to admit it."

Diane folded her arms. She understood completely. Matty once told her that she was confusing contentment with happiness and he was right about that, too. And just like Sam, Diane, at that time, wasn't ready to hear it either. He even said she was hiding in the safety of her parents' home, that was why she hadn't moved out since returning home from college. And Diane didn't believe that either, at the time. But it was true. She was hiding in plain sight. But she was hiding.

"You know what he said?" Sam asked her.

"Pastor?"

"Ira."

"What did he say?"

"First he wanted to know how Leah was doing."

"Leah? Why would he care how she's doing? She couldn't stand him and I thought the feeling was mutual."

"Don't you believe it. It was all a ruse. It was all a front."
Confusion showed all over Diane's face. "What was a
front? Leah's feelings for Ira?"

"Yes!" Sam said this and then hesitated. "They were lovers,
Diane."

"Go on! No way!"

"Yes."

"But that can't be!"

"Wanna bet? Ira told me so himself. Bragged about it right
there in jail! He was always beating on me and accusing me
of doing what he was out there doing himself. Can you believe it?"

"No, I can't. That's some shocking news you telling me.
I never would have put those two together in a million
years. She acted like she hated him. And she was your
friend!"

"It was all lies, Diane. Deceptions straight from hell. You
saw how that witch lied on Pastor, didn't you? Why would
she care if she hurt a so-called friend of hers?" Sam shook
her head. "I just thank the Lord He got both of those devils out of my life."

Diane exhaled. "Matty says—"

"*Matty?* Not Pastor Jolson?"

Diane smiled. "He insists that I call him Matty."

"You go, girl. Matty, is it?"

"Anyway," Diane said, as if it meant nothing to her, causing both her and Sam to break out in laughter.

"You have really changed," Sam said. "But what were you
saying about *Matty?*"

"Forget you. I was just saying that he seems to think Ira
may be looking at some serious time."

"He is. No doubt about it. And I will be right there to
gladly testify, too. I'm telling it and I ain't holding nothing
back. Every beating he put on me gonna be his own undo-
ing. Junior's gonna testify, too, he already told me he wants

to. Ira ain't getting away with this. He got away with it too long. He killed Alan, that changed everything. Now he's got to pay."

"Poor Junior," Diane said. "How's he handling all of this?"

"Better than he's ever handled anything in his little life. You saw it for yourself today. He was laughing and playing with the other children—I've never seen that boy so happy. Pastor Jolson's counseling him, you know."

"Really?"

"You didn't know that?"

"No."

"You mean *Matty* didn't tell you?"

Diane wanted to smile but didn't. "He never tells me much of anything about his ministry. That's just not Matty's style."

"Oh," Sam said, smiling. "Not his style, is it? So you know the man's style now."

"You need to quit, you know that?"

Sam laughed. Then she paused. She and Diane had never really delved into each other's personal business, which had been crucial during her time with Ira, but now Sam was hopeful for Diane even if her chance was blown. "Is it serious?" she asked her.

Diane nodded. "It is on my part."

"And Pastor Jolson's part?"

"Sometimes I think it is, yes. But other times, I don't know. He has so much on his plate."

"Is that why he wasn't here today at your birthday party?"

"I guess so."

"Disappointed?"

"I told you he's a very busy man."

"Disappointed, Diane?"

"Yes! Okay? I am a little. But I'm sure he would have been here if he could have."

"Yeah," Sam said, opening her driver's-side door. "You're

probably right. One thing about Pastor Jolson: he's a straight shooter. He doesn't mix words, does he?"

Diane smiled. "No, he does not."

"But let me get this boy to bed. He played his heart out today. See you in church tomorrow."

"That'll work. And Sam?"

Sam looked back at Diane before stepping up into her truck. "Yes?"

"Have you heard from Leah?"

"Not from Leah, but one of those ladies who used to work for her told me she was in Memphis now."

"Memphis? Why Memphis?"

"Who knows."

"Is she doing better?"

"Nope. She's still seeing demons and all that nonsense. But how you thought she was gonna be doing? She lied on a man of God."

"We have to forgive, Sam. We can't get down to her level."

"I forgive her, but I'm not gonna forget what she did with my husband. I never dreamed Ira was unfaithful to me. Never. He would beat my behind if I looked at a man too hard and *he* was unfaithful? And with *Leah?* It's unbelievable, I tell you. It makes you wonder if anybody's right."

Diane nodded. She understood.

When Sam left, when her big Ford Explorer SUV lumbered on down the road, Diane hesitated before going back into the house. She looked up at her bedroom window. Just a few months ago Sam and Leah were in that very room laughing and talking with her and trying to help get her prepared for what they thought was going to be her big night with Russell Scram. It seemed like a lifetime ago. Now Leah was recovering from a nervous breakdown and still running around seeing demons. Sam had to bury precious Alan and then watch Ira go to jail for his death. Little Junior was in counseling trying to deal with more issues than a grown man could probably handle, and Sam was a bundle of nerves, too. But Diane, of all people, was happy. Truly happy for the first time in her life. It seemed almost strange that she should be the blessed one. But if Matty had taught her anything, he taught her to stop making other people's problems her own. She deserved happiness, too, he said. She didn't know if she deserved it, but she was going to enjoy every minute of it for as long as God saw fit to allow her.

Inside, Willie James and Malveen were embroiled in yet another argument. This one, Diane soon learned as she began clearing the dining room table of party cups and plates, was about angels.

"You ain't telling me," Malveen said as she moved around anxiously on the sofa, looking as though she were ready to fight somebody.

"I am telling you," Willie James said, leaned back in his recliner. "What an angel look like foolin' up with you?"

"They walk with me and they talk with me, I don't care what you say!"

"They ain't angels then, if they walking and talking with you. Devils, yeah, I can see that. But angels? With you? You crazy, woman!"

And on and on they went. Diane, who used to get downright depressed when her parents went on like this, was actually laughing now. She missed the revelry since she had her own place. It was always quiet there. Kind of lonely, too. But here, on Clarion Avenue, it was as lively as a carnival sideshow.

The doorbell rang but Diane remained in the dining room, still smiling and clearing off the table, stuffing a big black plastic trash bag with discarded party ware. Her heart sang, however, when her father opened the front door and Matty's deep voice bellowed through. Diane wanted to run into his arms as soon as she heard that voice, but she didn't.

Not in front of her parents. Not when she knew Matty did everything in his power to keep their relationship very, very discreet.

But when he asked for her, almost as soon as he stepped into the living room, she dropped the paper cups in her hands and hurried out of the dining room. Matty was caught short when he saw her coming, in her white cashmere sweater and with her beautiful wavy hair swept in a nice under wrap around her pretty, narrow face. He found himself staring at her, his heart thumping against his chest in a beat too fast, his always cautious instincts screaming out and warning him that he would rue the day he made this decision, but he was too far gone to listen. All he knew was that he had to have Diane. That she was the one he wanted. And craved. And needed. And he would have her.

Diane's grand smile became a line of concern across her face when she saw Matty's expression. He seemed so tense, and so intense, that her once leaping heart was now a nervous, slow, grinding beat of anxiety. *Now what?* she wanted to say.

"Hello, Matty," she said instead as she stopped just short of being directly in front of him, her voice not warm, as she had hoped it would be, but flat and cautious.

Matty realized his blunder. He realized how just a look from him could change the entire trajectory of Diane's mood. He therefore quickly smiled, and released his tension. "Hey, sweetie," he said as he stepped to her, and his smile alone caused hers to reappear. And when he kissed her, in a warm, caressing kiss on the mouth, she blushed. "Sorry I'm so late," he said, holding her by the arms and looking deeply into her always eager eyes, pleased to see the happiness he now came to expect from her. "I had to go see a young lady who attends my recovering addicts class. She had a relapse last night and needed a shoulder to cry on, and more than a few words of encouragement."

"You think she'll be all right?" Diane asked with true concern.

"With the help of the Lord she'll be okay. She just needs to start depending on Him more, rather than on the momentary pleasures of some high. But I'll be praying for her. What about my sweetheart? How are you doing?"

Diane wanted to pinch herself. He had never shown such open affection toward her around others before. It was certainly a turning point. A welcomed turning point. "I'm doing great, Matty," she said. "I had a wonderful day."

"Willie James didn't scare away your guests?"

Willie James laughed as he moved past Matty and sat back down on his recliner. "They better be glad I let 'em come at all," he said. "All that noise. I thought Malveen was gonna fight a few of 'em, though."

"You's a lie," Malveen said, still unable to release her frustration from their angels argument. "I just told them to keep that noise down, that's all I did."

"It was a party, Mother," Diane said. "People are supposed to be noisy. Besides, you were the one who insisted I have it here when my apartment would have done nicely. But you didn't feel like going anywhere and you wanted to be here and my apartment was too small for all those people who might drop in. Then you couldn't stop complaining because we were having it here." Diane looked at Matty, still smiling, although her frustration with her mother was beginning to show. "No, Matty," she said, "Dad was fine. It was Mother Dearest who gave me headaches all day."

"That's all right," Malveen said. "Everybody beat on Malveen. But that's all right."

Matty smiled and looked at the older woman. She was as starved for attention as a whiny child. He squeezed Diane's arms and released them. Then he walked over to the sofa and sat right next to Malveen. She immediately stiffened her back. "They're giving you a hard time, Sister Tarver?"

"You better know it. Couldn't stop blaming me. All day long. But that's all right."

"Then why you keep bringing it up if it's all right?" Willie James asked and Matty immediately shook his head.

"Nall, now, Willie James, give your wife a break. She's doing the best she can. Let's not forget that she was the one who almost single-handedly organized this special day for Diane."

"Only after you asked her to and gave her all that money to buy whatever she needed."

Diane looked at Malveen. Matty was the one who bankrolled the party, when all week she kept asking her mother if she needed her to pitch in? She knew her parents were both on fixed incomes. They could barely afford ten dollars beyond their present budget. And Malveen hadn't said a word.

"Regardless of who asked whom or what money was provided," Matty said to Willie James, "she did it. She worked diligently to make this day a success for Diane. And if that fabulous smile on Diane's face is any indication, she succeeded wildly. That's all I need to know."

Malveen smiled for the first time all day, as she looked at Willie James with satisfaction all over her face. Diane smiled, too, because Matty knew exactly what it took. He knew when to press and when to back off. When to praise and when to correct. She used to think it was an art he had mastered, something he'd learned from his days as a high-powered Atlanta lawyer. But she was wrong. It was a gift. A gift, Diane was becoming to believe, straight from God.

He looked at Diane, as if he could sense her assessment of him. She looked away, but his voice, his deep, melodic voice, drew her back. "Did you get any gifts, Diane?" he asked her.

"Oh, yes," she said, "quite a few. Everybody seemed to want to give me clothes, though." She smiled. "I think they were trying to tell me something."

"Where are they?"

"The gifts? In the trunk of my car. I had the children help me put them away before they left."

Matty stood up. "Show them to me," he said.

"Now?"

"Sure," Matty said as he walked toward her. "Why not?"

"I just thought you might want to sit back and relax a little."

"I'm relaxed," Matty said as he looked down at her sweater.

"Okay," Diane said, suddenly feeling comfortable with his stare. "Let me get my keys."

Outside, it was still breezy as the wind put a nip in the air. But even with the sudden coolness Diane noticed something different as soon as she stepped onto the porch.

"What is it?" Matty asked as he closed the front door and walked up behind her.

"You bought a new car?" she asked him.

"What do you mean?"

Diane continued to look at the car sitting in front of her house. It was dark and she was not all that receptive to the sudden cool air, but she knew the difference between a Lexus and a Jaguar. And the car she was now viewing was a light-colored, maybe silver or white, Lexus. Not Matty's car at all. She glanced at him over her shoulder. "That's not a Jaguar, Matty. Is that your car?"

"No," he said. "It's not mine." Then he dangled a pair of keys bearing the Lexus emblem in front of her unsuspecting face. "It's yours."

Diane stared at the keys and then, realizing what he had just said, turned quickly to Matty. "Mine?"

Matty smiled. "Happy birthday, sweetheart," he said.

Diane fell into his arms. Forget the car, she thought, it was Matty she wanted. To think that he would do something this grand for her. That he would take his own money and buy her a car, a brand-new car, staggered her. Tears began to appear in her eyes as she laid her head against his chest. She'd never been treated this well in her entire life. Not all that long ago she would have settled for Russell Scram and all of his insults. She'd thought that he was the best she could do. But apparently, she was coming to realize, God didn't think so.

Matty placed his hand under her chin and lifted her face to his. Tears streamed freely down her face—she didn't care if he saw her cry—and he wiped her tears away. Then he whispered into her ear. "Since I don't have any means of transportation right at the moment," he said, "looks like you'll have to drive me home."

Diane laughed. That was the least she was going to do for him. "With pleasure, Pastor Jolson," she said.

Diane felt like a kid on a Ferris wheel as she drove her brand-new Lexus through the streets of Floradale. She couldn't stop smiling and commenting on the smoothness of the ride and the newness of the smell. Matty just sat back and listened, since she wasn't about to let him get a word in edgewise anyway, and if there was ever one single moment in time that he felt he was making the right decision, it was this moment. Watching Diane. Seeing her childlike joy and feeling pleased that he was able to be a part of it. She was so happy, so filled with giddiness, that he had to tell her more than once to watch that stop sign, or that boy on his bicycle, or that car she was tailgating. But all in all he let her have her way, smiling and laughing right along with her as he couldn't get over such a jewel in his midst.

Diane couldn't describe how she felt. She loved her Buick Skylark but it was losing steam fast, with a mind of its own and the miles to prove it. And the idea that she, Diane Tarver, the girl most likely *not* to succeed, would be the one in the catbird seat, the one with the gift from God, the one driving in her brand-new Lexus on a cool Saturday evening with the man of her dreams sitting right beside her, made her feel like an angel with wings. She felt like she could fly. She felt like an honored child of God with a special dispensation to love one of His truest servants.

She also felt a sense of validation. She couldn't help it. Nobody had ever cared enough to give her the very best. And that was what Matty had done. He'd given her the best. Her. Of all people. She couldn't wait until Sister Inez saw her now, and Janet Brown, and all those others who never gave her any credit. They couldn't fathom in a million years how somebody as beautiful, as wealthy, as blessed by God as Matty could ever want to have anything to do with somebody as plain, as unaccomplished, as seemingly not favored at all by God as Diane. It didn't make sense. Matty's ex-girlfriend in Atlanta, that feisty Vicky Avery who was so sure of herself that she actually came to town to take him back, was more his speed. They wouldn't be surprised at all if he had a woman like her. But to cast his lot with Diane Tarver seemed impossible. She didn't think she had anything to offer a man like him. But God thought so. And that was all she needed to know.

She stopped her car in Matty's driveway and parked behind his Jaguar. His car may have been more expensive, and more elegant, but he could not have given her a nicer gift. She looked at him and sighed. How do you thank a man who's given you the world? "I don't know what to say, Matty," she said.

"Just enjoy it, Diane. Don't say any more. You've said enough, trust me." He said this with a smile. She leaned her head back and laughed. "I just want you to stop thinking about it, trying to figure it out; just enjoy the ride. We only get one, you know." He said this in such a heartfelt way that she wanted to cry again. But she didn't. His smile wouldn't let her.

"Well, good night," she said.

Matty's smile quickly disappeared, as if she'd just slapped him. It was all an act, for he was just as giddy as she was, but she didn't know it. She became immediately concerned. "What's the matter?"

"What's the matter?" he asked her. "You just said good night to me."

"Right."

"No, Diane. No good night yet." He said this and un-buckled his seat belt. He looked at her. Only he wasn't kid-ding anymore. He was intensely serious now. "You aren't getting away from me that easily," he said. "You're coming inside."

Diane sat stunned as he got out of the car. She was liter-ally unable to move a muscle. Did he mean what she thought he meant? Was there a high moral price she had to pay for this so-called gift he'd given her? Could Sister Inez be *right?*

Matty could sense her uneasiness as he led her out of the car. The girl seemed so suddenly terrified that he smiled and placed his hand around her waist, to help her keep her bal-ance. She was so green it was unbelievable, he thought. These backwood boys hadn't taught her a thing. But he was going to teach her, and enjoy every minute of it.

His mind, however, wasn't so much on Diane's lesson as it was on his decision. He'd never felt so certain yet so ner-vous about his certainty in his life. But he was determined to see this through. He had to do something that would bind Diane to him, that would take away any reason she might have to leave him when the storms that were surely to come tried to drown them. This was a purely selfish act he was about to commit with Diane. He knew it and he made no pretense about it. He loved this woman and was going to have her. And if those devils in hell didn't like it then that was tough. She was going to be his. And that was all there was to it.

She had a say in the matter, however, and he never thought
for a moment that she'd say no. But when they made it inside his house and he immediately closed the door and
pushed her against it, ready to do it and get it over with, he
realized for the first time that she might very well be frightened enough to not allow it. To just say no. His breath
caught by that realization, and his heart slammed against his
chest. He felt as if he would die if she said no.

He kissed her, long and lovingly, to calm her back down,
and she didn't resist him, which, he thought thankfully, was
a good sign. Then he looked at her, studied her, before he
spoke. She looked as if she wanted to break down that door
and escape from his grasp. But he couldn't allow it. She was
going to hear him out, even if she did turn him down.
"Diane," he said so softly, so vulnerably, that just his voice
helped to calm her down. "What I'm about to ask you is
probably going to shock you. But I've got to ask it. I've never
been a man to play games and you know it, and I'm not
about to start now. This is all about me, Diane. This is all
about my needs, my desires, my wants. For many years I've
fought against this day. And after what happened to me in
Chicago I knew I would never get this close to anybody
again. Then I get to this little backwater town, this place that
I was supposed to rescue, and what happens? This little slip
of a girl named Diane Tarver, this meek and mild librarian
no less, rescues me." He smiled and shook his head. Diane,
however, looked puzzled.

"I rescued you?" she asked.

"Oh, yes. Not with anything you said or did. But just by
being yourself. Just by smiling when I needed a smile and
praying for me when I needed, like I needed air to breathe,
your prayers. And all I did was shut you out. Especially when
Leah's allegations hit and after Alan Marshall's death. Those
were the worst times. The times I needed you most, Diane.
And you were there. I just couldn't use you like that. But

now I've come to the realization that I'm not that strong. I can't shut you out of my life a moment longer. I want you completely, Diane. I love you completely. And if you'll say yes, if you'll afford a fool like me this one act of selfishness, I want you to be my wife."

Diane's knees buckled, and she would have fallen if Matty had not grabbed her and pulled her back against the door. *Wife?* Did she hear *wife?* She looked at him to see if he were mocking her, to see if this whole day and night had been nothing but a great big hoax at her expense. But he wasn't smiling or sneering. He was hoping. She could see it in his eyes. He wasn't bold. He wasn't self-assured. He was as scared as she was.

"Did you say," she started asking but had to stop momentarily and place her hand on her heart to regulate her breathing again. "Did you say that you wanted me, *me,* to be your wife?"

Matty was so nervous that he had to wrap his arms around her, for his own balance. "Yes," he said, praying to God that she wouldn't think it so far-fetched that she'd laugh in his face.

Diane wanted to ask why. She wanted to ask, as she knew every female in Fountain Hope was going to ask each other, why her? Why not somebody more suited to him?

But she didn't ask him a thing. She smiled her greatest smile yet, he thought, threw her arms around him, and told him yes. She would be honored to be his wife.

Matty's heart soared. "Thank you, Jesus!" he yelled. Then he took her in his arms in an embrace that could have squeezed the life out of her. But she didn't feel the pain, just the euphoria of finally seeing what a perfect day looked like. And felt like, as he would not let her go. Both of them felt elation. Both of them felt it was the dawning of a new day. A day when two shall become one. A day when Matty Jolson would never again have any more reason to hate every hour of every minute of every second of his odd life.

Chapter 23

The following week was hectic as word traveled fast about Diane and Matty's impending matrimony, and by week's end, at the Saturday morning bake sale, Fountain Hope was all abuzz with the incredible news.

Diane arrived early, since the Pulpit Aid Board was sponsoring the event, and as soon as she drove into the parking lot in her brand-new silver Lexus a throng of females surrounded her and her car. If they weren't congratulating her about her engagement, they were congratulating her about her car. Everybody was excited, some even elated for her, but most were just plain astonished.

Matty watched this maddening scene from his upstairs office window, looking intently as his wife-to-be stepped out of her new car. She was dressed smartly in a pair of white cotton pants and a light blue button-down blouse he had purchased for her earlier in the week, and she stepped out unable to conceal her joy. She wore shades, also a Matty purchase, which astounded many since Diane was never a flashy person, and they assumed immediately that all of this sudden stylishness was all Matty's doing.

But it wasn't. Diane had changed long before he worked up the nerve to propose to her. She had, in fact, discovered her own uniqueness during the time when he had all but told her to take a hike. He knew the real deal. That woman he couldn't take his eyes off, who was strutting around that parking lot like a guinea hen on display, was as much her own woman as he was his own man. She was as precious as life itself to him, as he watched her show the ladies her big, empty trunk as if they'd never seen a brand-new, unused car trunk before, and he also watched the menfolk watch her. He was going to hold on to this one, he thought. His first wife had gotten away from him. She heard rumors and she ran. But this time it would be different. He was going to smother Diane Tarver with so much affection that she wouldn't have a chance to even think about leaving him. He was desperate and he knew it. He was sealing her fate to his and he knew it. And it was scaring the life out of him.

"Have you ever seen Diane so happy, Pastor?" Wanda Scott, whom he didn't even realize had come up and stood beside him, said. She, too, was looking out of the window at Diane in all her triumph and glory.

"No," he said bluntly as he glanced at Wanda, who'd been nothing but wonderful since the day he met her. He wasn't blind. He knew that Wanda had feelings for him and probably would have loved to have been his choice of wife herself. But she was a good, Christian woman through and through, a wonderful woman, and she had accepted Diane's good news as if it were her own.

He looked back out of the window. Wanda sighed in admiration of the woman who was soon to become the First Lady of Fountain Hope. "Diane was always a happy person," she said, "always would give her last to help her fellow man. But this is different. She's joyous now, like a burden has been lifted from her life. I remember when she told me that you had bought her a brand-new car, and not just any old car but a *Lexus,* and she said it just like that, a *Lexus,* and Pastor, you should have seen the look in her eyes. It was a look of wonderment, like she couldn't believe it herself. Yep, Pastor, you picked a good one. She's special."

Matty nodded his head. "That she is," he said with a sudden surge of pride. But he couldn't shake that feeling, a feeling deep down in the pit of his gut, that trouble, like every other time there was a good turn in his life, was on its way.

He shrugged and then turned from the window quickly, deciding without reservation that his future with Diane was in God's hands now, and he got back to work.

Matty and Deacon Molt stood on the steps of Fountain Hope and greeted their parishioners as they came out of the sanctuary. Among the first to appear were Sam and Junior. Junior, on seeing Matty, smiled greatly and leaped into his arms. Matty held him in his arms and looked at the happy boy. "How's my favorite Junior?" he asked him.

"I got me a brand-new PlayStation," he said.

"Did you, now? Got any new games?"

"Yes, sir. Plenty. Mommy bought me three new games. Will you come over to my house sometime and play them with me?"

Matty smiled. "I'd be delighted."

"Really?"

"Really."

"All right, son," Sam said as she walked up, too, "don't put pressure on Pastor."

"No pressure at all," Matty said, looking at Sam now. She looked gorgeous, he thought, in her beautiful bright red skirt suit. "Don't you look pretty," he said.

"Thank you, Pastor," Sam said. "And congratulations."

"Thank you, thank you."

"Diane is so sweet," Sam said with all sincerity. "She'll make you a great wife. She's been a perfect friend to me."

"How have you been holding up?"

"Good. Just thrilled to see Junior happy again. He makes it all worthwhile, you know?"

Matty knew.

"I'm about to take him over to Bainbridge now to visit a friend of mine. She has a son his age."

"Good. He needs to be around kids his age as much as possible."

"Agreed."

"Okay, buddy," Matty said, putting Junior down, "I'll see you in our next counseling session."

Junior, after being released by Matty, began to cry. His mother couldn't believe it. "Ira, Jr., I know you aren't crying. The pastor can't hold you here all day."

Junior burrowed into his mother's skirt, trying desperately to hide his face. "It's okay, Sister Marshall," Matty said to her.

"He cries so easily, Pastor," Sam said. "I told him he's got to be strong now. I told him he's the man of the house now."

"No, Sister Marshall," Matty said firmly, "he's not the man of the house. He's a seven-year-old boy. Let him laugh and play and be a carefree kid for a change. He's carried around enough man-of-the-house burdens and chips on his shoulder to last a lifetime. He's not the man of anything. He's a little boy who needs to stay in a little boy's place. You understand me?"

Sam nodded. She'd never seen Reverend Jolson so firm. "Yes, sir," she said.

"You're the woman of the house," Matty said. "That will have to do."

Sam understood. She picked up Junior, picked up her little boy, and left. Deacon Molt, who had his customary position beside Matty, looked at her as she left. "That boy's got a long way to go, don't he?" Molt asked Matty.

"Yes," Matty said. "But he's come a long way, too."

Molt agreed, as he and Matty greeted more parishioners. By the time Diane came out of the church after being detained by fellow worshipers who still couldn't get over her good news, his hand was red from so many handshakes. At least greeting this one, he thought, as he watched her approach, would require more use of his lips than his hands.

"Hello, Sister Tarver," Deacon Molt said grandly, showing her, like many of the parishioners, more respect and courtesy than he'd ever shown her before. Being attached to Matty had its privileges, she thought.

"Hello, Deacon Molt," she replied to him. "How are you?"

"I'm wonderful now that you're here," he said and Matty held back a laugh. "Congratulations."

"Thank you so much."

"And good afternoon to you, Pastor Jolson," Diane said as she extended her hand and behaved as if she were the epitome of propriety. Matty smiled and pulled her into his arms.

"Matty!" she said in horror, looking around to see who was witnessing this out-of-character display. But Matty kissed her on the cheek and pulled her closer against his chest. He just wanted to feel her in his arms again, and he didn't care who saw it. But Diane was determined. She managed to pull herself away from him without appearing to struggle out of his grasp, which was exactly what she had to do. Matty laughed.

"It's not funny," she said, straightening herself, unable to suppress a smile of her own.

"Sorry I didn't give you a call last night, but by the time I got home it was late."

"I was up."

"I doubt that."

"Where were you?"

"Sister Brown had some problems."

Diane's heart dropped. Not that hot mama, she thought. "Janet Brown?" she asked.

"Yes. I had to go over there and calm that situation down."

Diane looked over at Janet Brown, who was dilly-dally-ing around the doors to the sanctuary as if she were posi-tioning herself to be the last person to shake Pastor's hand. Diane looked at Matty, and he could sense her jealousy. He could have reassured her, but he didn't. She was going to be the wife of a pastor. And not just any pastor but one ac-tively involved in the lives of his members. She had to get used to that.

"Well," Diane said, when it appeared Matty had nothing more to say to her, "I guess I'd better get going." She was his bride-to-be, she was the woman who had pledged to com-mit her life to him, but she still didn't feel comfortable enough to ask him to spend some time with her. Matty was wonderful to her in every way, but he still had that air of un-approachability about him that had kept her off balance much of the time she'd known him. Being betrothed to him changed a lot in her relationship with Matty, but not every-thing. "You take care, Deacon Molt," she said, looking past Matty, suddenly feeling unnerved by the thought that Janet Brown, Fountain Hope's resident seductress, was waiting to touch his hand.

"You, too, Sister Tarver," Deacon Molt said.

Diane smiled one more time at Matty, wishing to God she could just tell him exactly how she felt, then turned and began to walk away. She felt a warm hand slip into hers be-fore she could get away, and she turned and looked at Matty.

"Where do you think you're going?" he asked her, his face now seemingly disappointed by her behavior. She didn't know what to say. She was going home, that was obvious, but he was acting as if she had offended him. *What?* she wondered. She had to get permission now to leave his pres-ence?

Matty gently pulled her until she was standing beside him, his hand refusing to let go of hers. He had sensed the regret in her heart as she began to walk away, and he was upset that she didn't just come out and tell him that she didn't want to leave him. He sighed in frustration as he glanced at her and held her hand. She was one woman who was going to require a lot of patience, when patience, he thought, was never one of his strong suits.

Janet Brown indeed was the last parishioner to step before Matty. She seemed put off that Diane was still there, and that he was holding her hand as if she were really his woman, but Janet assumed he would easily misinterpret her glum mood for the depression she faked last night. She thought wrong.

"Hello, Sister Brown," Matty said as he shook her hand.

"Hello, Reverend," Janet said.

"I'm glad to see you in church today."

"Thank you. I told the devil he was a liar if he thought he was gonna keep me from serving the Lord—amen, hallelujah!"

Matty just stood there, without responding to her burst of holiness. Diane smiled and extended her hand, however.

"Hello, Janet," Diane said and Janet reluctantly shook her hand.

"Diane."

"Matty—I mean Pastor Jolson—told me about your ordeal last night. I trust you're doing better today?"

"Not really. But I came on to worship the Lord anyhow."

"Good for you."

"I was wondering, Pastor," Janet said, looking away from Diane, "if you could come over this evening. I feel that depression coming back on me worse than before."

"I don't know what Pastor can do about that," Diane said, suddenly emboldened, suddenly tired of Janet Brown and her little antics. "Depression is an illness. And like all illnesses, having the right attitude is crucial. You have to want to get better, to get better."

Matty looked at Diane. He knew her intentions better than this.

"What you trying to say?" Janet asked her.

"God don't like ugly," Diane said. "That's what I'm saying. He don't like people playing with Him."

"Playing with Him? Who's playing with Him?"

"A liar will not tarry in God's sight."

Matty quickly released Diane's hand and grabbed her by the arm. "Excuse us, Sister Brown," he said stiffly as he all but dragged Diane into the now-empty sanctuary, the few onlookers still standing outside the church watching them intensely as they hurried inside. Matty, so beside himself with fury, found a bench near the back and slung Diane down on it.

"What do you think you're doing?" he asked her.

Diane, once emboldened, was now afraid that she had gone too far. "She was lying, Matty," she said. "She just wanted to get you back to her house."

"So?"

"So? So I just wanted to make you aware of that."

"Do I look like I need you to make me aware of anything?"

"You were acting like you believed her and I was just letting you know that she wasn't being truthful."

Matty exhaled. "Diane, I will not tolerate jealousy from you."

"Jealousy?"

"It is unbecoming, it is fruitless, and I'll not stand for it. You hear me?"

"Who says I'm jealous?"

"Did you hear me?"

"Yes! But I don't know what you're talking about."

"You think this is a game with me, Diane?" he asked her.

"Of course not."

"You think I'm preaching the gospel, day in and day out,

from the street corners to the bars, for my *health?* God has ordained me to take His word to the people, an awesome appointment. I don't do this because I want to do it, I do this because I have to do it. And you will respect that!" He said this with a thrust of his finger into her face.

"Oh, Matty. I do respect that. You know I do."

"Then don't you ever again publicly ostracize a member who is in dire need of getting her soul saved. I knew that woman was lying. I knew she was scheming. But I also know she needs Christ in her life. And if my listening to her lies will get her into this church on Sunday mornings to hear the word of God, then I'll listen. And wife or no wife, you will not interfere with that. Do we understand each other, Diane?"

Diane nodded quickly. Her little bit of boldness had gone so wrong. What had she done? she wondered. And would this be all Matty needed to change his mind about her? She looked into his intense eyes. He exhaled again, but then his entire look softened. "I know I sound harsh, honey," he said. "But you have to trust me completely, and that includes my interaction with lost souls. All I want is to get them saved. I'm not interested in anything else. You're my woman. You're all I want."

"But she's so devious, Matty."

"Diane!"

"Okay! I'm just... I'm new to this, all right? You've got to be patient with me."

Matty knew it was true. He knew he was expecting too much too soon from a woman who had just begun to come into her own. He looked at her, at the love and anguish in her glorious eyes, and his heart told him to pull her into his arms and show her how much he understood. But his head told him to walk out of the sanctuary and leave her where she sat. And so he did. The world was shooting darts and arrows at him left and right, suspicious of every move he made, and year after year he'd tolerated it. But it would be a cold day in hell, he thought as he walked back out of the church, before he tolerated such rancid distrust from Diane, too.

The very next day, however, when Inez Flachette was just beginning to come around to the fact that a kind, sweet sister like Diane Tarver could fall for that snake-oil salesman disguised as their pastor, a letter, like manna from heaven, landed in her hands.

She was sitting behind her desk finishing up her secretarial duty of going through all of the church mail and preparing to respond to the invitations or solicitations, when she stood up to take a much-needed break. And that was when she saw it. It caught her attention because it had no return address and wasn't addressed to anyone in particular at the church. She stood behind her desk and decided to open it up before she took her break, and the contents inside, newspaper clippings and photographs, literally knocked her off her feet. She sat down so abruptly, in fact, that it took several more minutes for her to regain her composure. But when she did she flew to her feet and hurried to find Deacon Molt.

This was it, she felt. This was finally it. That imposter would be exposed for the scoundrel he was and Fountain Hope could get back to being the church it used to be: a respectable, quiet establishment that didn't try to ram anything down anybody's throat. No more feeding the hungry every day the way he insisted. No more drug-addict support groups or job-skills classes. No more witnessing by paid moochers and no more detailing cars on church grounds. They would continue to do education functions and Vacation Bible School, but that was it. The rest of those wild and crazy and wholly unholy activities would subside immediately.

Deacon Molt was not in his office, which disturbed her no end, but she did manage to find him in the downstairs bathroom repairing a busted pipe. When Sister Inez saw him, when she finally made her way from his office to every other room in the church and found him kneeling down underneath the bathroom sink, she couldn't wait to tell the news.

"What news?" he asked and then, pointing toward his tool box, said, "Hand me that wrench."

Inez reluctantly grabbed the greasy tool, and then sighed a great sigh of anticipation. "It's about the pastor," she said. "And it's bad."

Molt smiled, still working rather than bothering to look at her. "What has Maverick done now?" he asked her.

"Oh, it ain't nothing to laugh about, Head Deacon. You ain't gonna believe this one. It's from his past and it's a shocker."

Molt, however, was still unconvinced. Whatever flaws Matty had, and he had many, he also had the full support of Bishop Owens and the national board of bishops. Fighting a man with that kind of clout behind him was ludicrous, he felt. Besides, he'd seen Matty in action. He was beginning to respect the man. "Oh, come now, Inez," he said. "That mess that went on in Chicago old news now and you know it. I agree there's a lot more to that story than we've been led to believe, but Bishop don't care. None of the bishops care. Why should we?"

"They gonna care about this. This ain't no idle talk. I got the newspaper clippings to prove it!"

"So what? Bishop Owens don't care nothing about newspaper clippings. Chicago is in the past, far as he's concerned."

"This ain't about Chicago," Inez said and Deacon Molt, for the first time, looked up at her.

"It's not about Chicago?"

"It most certainly is not. That's what I'm trying to tell you. This went on in Atlanta, Molt. Not Chicago. And I'm telling you it's something else. It'll make Chicago look like chicken feed!"

Molt, seeing the unbridled elation in Inez's eyes, as if triumph were just a meeting away, dropped his wrench and stood.

Chapter 24

Matty stopped his Jaguar at the apartment on Brady Road and stared at the old Chevy Chevette hatchback pulled up across the sidewalk in front of Diane's door. He knew who owned the car, which gave him a sudden surge of uneasiness, but he also knew that such an inevitable confrontation was going to happen sooner or later and today, given the cool, calming wind and the beautiful, cloudless sky, was as good a day as any.

He grabbed the big, gift-wrapped box on his front seat and got out of his car. Diane's new car was parked proudly in the small, narrow driveway allotted her, and he still smiled inside when he remembered that look in her eyes when he had given her the keys. That car had cost him thirty grand and he hadn't thought twice when he wrote the check. No wife of his was driving around in a car old enough to be her mother's, even though it was just like Diane to own such a car.

She was one of a kind, he thought, as he walked across

the sidewalk and headed for her front door. Yesterday, after church, he had been tougher on her than he should have been, making it clear that the pastor of a church could not have a jealous wife. Too many females would be in his face. Too many opportunities to seethe in envy would present themselves. Diane had said she understood, but seemed more taken aback by his reaction to her behavior than by her behavior itself. Especially after he decided against spending time with her and sent her on her way. She fought back then, angrily protesting that he was overreacting. He wasn't—he'd seen too many marriages devastated by that green-eyed monster—but he was coming to her today with a peace offering just the same.

He barely got two knocks on the apartment door before it swung open. Frank Tarver, looking even more desperate than Matty had seen him previously, stood inside with one hand on the doorknob and the other hand rubbing his arm. He couldn't wait to get his hands on some junk, Matty thought, staring deep into his wild eyes. And it angered Matty, not because Frank wanted to get high—a junkie was a junkie—but because he was coming around Diane with his dangerous self-destructiveness. A man who didn't give a hoot about himself, Matty had long since learned, couldn't possibly care about anybody else.

"Hello, Frank," Matty said as he walked on in, his arrogance seeming to peak every time Diane's brother was near.

Frank could see it, too, as he mumbled some choice words under his breath and closed the door. The man was just walking on in like he owned the place, he thought. Then he wondered how much he could get for that Rolex Matty was wearing.

Matty looked around but did not ask where Diane was. He sat down on the sofa instead and crossed his legs, setting his box beside him. Frank just stood there, then let out a bitter exhale. "May I help you?" he said to Matty harshly, his gruff expression making it clear that he didn't like Matty's rudeness at all.

Matty couldn't care less what Frank Tarver didn't like as he remained silent and stared at him. His refusal to get into it with Frank, however, caused Frank's anger to flare again.

"You think you God's gift to Floradale, don't you?" Frank asked, staring at Matty. "Don't you?!" he yelled.

"So you say," Matty said.

"That's right I'm sayin' it! Always wearin' a suit like you too good to dress common. Always got on them Italian shoes and that Rolex watch and driving around in that Jaguar and you think you ain't nothin' but the man!"

"Frank, who are you talking to?" Diane's voice yelled from the back bedroom.

"Yeah, I know Leah supposed to be all crazy now," Frank continued, ignoring his sister's voice, "and everybody talkin' about the devil in her, but I'll bet you any amount of money that Leah told the truth! I can look at you and tell you ain't righteous."

"Frank, who are you talking to?" Diane asked again as she came into her living room. When she saw Matty sitting on her sofa, she stopped short. They had exchanged harsh words the last time they'd met. She hadn't expected to see him at all today. "Matty," she said, unable to hide her surprise. She was secure enough in her relationship with him now to believe that a little spat wouldn't be the end of it, but she still didn't handle upheaval well. She hadn't slept a wink last night.

"Yeah, the big man's here, sis," Frank said.

"That's enough, Frank."

"Nall, now, he sittin' up there like the king of the world; maybe we should bow down or somethin'!"

"I said that's enough. You will not disrespect Pastor Jolson in my home."

"Then give me the cash and I'll get out of your sanctified home," Frank said and Diane pulled out the money she had gone into the bedroom to retrieve. She hurried toward her brother, anxious to keep the confusion down. But Matty wasn't so easily persuaded.

"Diane," he said softly, almost nonchalantly. Diane looked at him.

"Yes," she said.

"You aren't giving him anything."

Diane exhaled. This was all she needed. "He's got a job interview out of town, Matty," she said, trying her best to explain, to get him to back down, "and he just needs—"

"Diane?" Matty said this and looked at her. And his look was clear: he didn't want to hear it. "You aren't giving him anything."

Frank shook his head. He couldn't believe it. If there was such a thing as an angry smile, he was displaying it. "This is my sister," he said, pointing at Diane. "You got that, Reverend?"

"Frank!" Diane said.

"My sister! And if she wants to give me her last dime, she got a right to do that. This ain't got nothin' to do with you!"

Matty didn't respond. He just continued to stare at Frank as if he were staring through him. His silence, however, angered Frank more than if he would have tried to slice a knife through his heart. He hated guys like him. Just hated them.

"Give me the money, sis," he said, talking to Diane but still staring at Matty.

Diane sighed. It was no use. Satan was busy today. "I can't," she said.

Frank looked at her. "What you mean you can't?"

"My husband says I can't."

"He ain't your husband yet!"

"He will be."

"I don't believe this. You gonna mess me over, your own flesh and blood, over some cheese-eatin' joker like that?"

"Just leave, Frank, all right?"

"Just give me my money!" Frank said, quickly moving up into Diane's face. Matty stood up just as quickly and positioned himself between Diane and her brother.

"You heard her," Matty said, staring down the taller man. "Now leave."

Frank stared unblinkingly at Matty. Then he looked at his sister with equal passion. He turned to leave, as if resigned to the fact that his gravy train wasn't stopping this way anymore, but it was no resignation at all. For he turned around hurriedly and swung a punch that was intended to cold-cock Matty. But Matty caught the blow with a grab of Frank's wrist and flipped the younger man to the floor, his back slamming down hard.

Diane, by now, was hysterical, screaming for them to stop, for Matty not to hurt Frank, but Matty wasn't listening. He got down to Frank's level, holding him down with a knee to his chest, and spoke plainly. "If you ever get in Diane's face again," he said, "I'll hurt you. You understand? Don't let the Reverend in front of my name fool you. I'm still Matty Jolson. And nobody has ever laid a hand on me and remained upright. You get my meaning, Frank?" Matty pressed his knee down harder in Frank's chest. "Do you get my meaning, Frank?"

"Yes!" Frank yelled, his chest twisting in pain. And Matty immediately stood up.

Diane went to help her brother, but he jerked away from her. He looked ridiculous, sprawled on the floor, but he was determined to take his pretty time getting up. Matty pulled out a handkerchief and began slowly wiping his hands. He hated going there with Frank Tarver, and he knew he would probably be up half the night in prayer of repentance, but it was done now. Nothing he could do about it now.

Frank eventually stood up from the floor and began dusting himself off.

"Are you all right, Frank?" Diane asked him, her compassion for her brother overwhelming her.

"What do you think?" Frank responded angrily. Then he looked at Matty again. Looked at that money in Diane's hand, money he was this close to possessing before Rambo showed up. And then he left.

Diane's heart ached for her brother, as she watched him leave, and she began heading for the door as he walked out of it. "I'll be back, Matty," she said, not looking at him, her every intention to run behind her brother and give him the money anyway.

"Diane," Matty said calmly, knowing full well her intention.

"Matty, he's my brother," she pleaded as she stood at the door, her hand on the knob.

"He's your brother on crack, Diane. I don't mind you helping your brother, but I absolutely mind you helping him feed his problem. You aren't going to do that."

Diane leaned against the door. "How can I help him?"

"Pray for him. Talk to him. Be honest with him. But don't enable him."

She knew Matty was right. She knew she was doing nothing to aid her brother's recovery. But he was still her brother. Her only brother. If she could ease his pain a little, she felt it was her duty to try. Didn't Matty understand that?

"Come here," he said, as if he could feel her anguish. She hesitated, then walked to him, her heart still heavy, her soul praying that her brother wouldn't do anything rash.

When she arrived in front of Matty, looking down, he stood there as if willing her to look into his eyes. She finally lifted her head and did just that.

"It's up to Frank, Diane," he said. "You can't make this all better. Your baby brother isn't a baby anymore. And you've got to understand that."

Diane nodded, fighting back tears. Then she leaned

against Matty. Matty hugged her tightly and squeezed her against him, then he looked at her again. "I got you something," he said.

Diane looked at the box on the sofa, her heart still thinking about Frank. "What is it?"

"A dress. Here," he reached over, picked up the box, and handed it to her. "Go try it on."

"Now?"

"Yes, now."

Diane exhaled. But she went to try it on. Matty smiled. She was going to be all right after all, he thought, then he sat down and crossed his legs. His cell phone rang before Diane could make it back into the room. It was Deacon Molt.

"We need to see you, Reverend," he said. "We need to see you at once."

Matty hesitated. "What is this about, Horace?" he asked.

"We need you here at the church immediately, Reverend," was all Molt would say and Matty's heart squeezed. Something was up. Something different. He could feel it.

"I'm on my way," Matty said and flipped shut his cell.

"This is way too tight, Matty," Diane said as she stepped out of the back room in the new dress he had purchased for her, a sleek, dark brown, body-hugging, beautiful dress. What she saw as tight Matty saw as a perfect fit.

She started to twirl around, to show him what she meant, but when she saw his face she stopped in her tracks. "What's wrong?" she asked him.

"That was Deacon Molt. They want me over to the church," he said, still holding the phone, still with that worried look that worried Diane.

But she managed to smile, to minimize that stern look of his. "Another one of their meetings?" she asked lightheartedly.

"Perhaps," Matty said, not even attempting to minimize

his sudden concern. It could be foolishness again, as Diane was implying, but for some reason, this time, it didn't feel like foolishness to him.

Matty was slightly behind Diane when they walked into the boardroom of Fountain Hope, prompting Sister Inez, who sat at the table along with Deacon Molt, to wave her hand. "Not now, Sister Tarver," she said. "We can't see you right now."

"She's with me," Matty said as he moved up beside her, his hand on the small of her back as he did so. "Honey, have a seat over there."

Diane moved quickly to the chair against the wall. She wasn't comfortable being there; she had, in fact, urged Matty to let her wait in the sanctuary. But he wouldn't hear of it. If they were out to crucify him, as he suspected they were, then he wanted somebody on his side when the allegations flew. "You're my woman now," he whispered in her ear as they made their way to the boardroom. "You need to know what's going on."

Only problem was, Matty didn't know. And as he took a seat at the head of the table, his usual position at these so-called emergency meetings, a hundred possibilities flashed through his head. Was it something he said. Something he didn't say. Something he did. Something he didn't do. Some program he started. Some program he should have started. The possibilities were endless. And given the pettiness his church leadership sometimes displayed, he could go insane trying to figure out what trump card they thought they had this time.

Deacon Molt kept looking at Diane as Matty sat down. He had at first decided to keep his mouth shut, but looking at Sister Tarver in all of her wide-eyed innocence, he changed his mind. "Pastor," he said, leaning toward Matty, "I really don't think this should concern Diane."

"She's okay."

"But I really think it'll be better if she waited downstairs."

"She's okay. Now what is this about, Deacon?"

Molt looked at Inez. She shrugged her shoulders. Molt shook his head then opened the folder that sat in front of him. "This is really a very painful position we're in, Pastor Jolson. A position we wish we weren't in. But right is right."

"Amen," Sister Inez said firmly.

"And we, as the leadership of Fountain Hope, has got to do what's right. As you can see, we are gonna try to keep this thing quiet. We haven't even notified Bishop Owens yet. We thought it was only fair that we present this information to you, hear your side of things, and then decide what our next move should be. I do hope, however, that once you realize the proof we have you won't hesitate to do the right thing. If not for yourself, at least for the sake and reputation of Fountain Hope, Bishop Owens, and everybody else who believed in you."

Diane looked from Deacon Molt to Matty. What in the world was he talking about? she wondered. And why didn't Matty look the least concerned? His reticence, his calmness, was the only thing that kept her calm.

Deacon Molt looked at Sister Inez. "Sister Inez, if you please."

Sister Inez sat erect. Diane braced herself. She knew Inez well. She knew that look that was now on her face, a look that was serious but in a gleeful, expectant way. Matty, too, looked at Inez. "Tell us about Atlanta," she said.

Matty stared blankly at her. "What about Atlanta?"

"Dena Johnson. That's what about it. Does that name ring a bell?"

Matty's heart dropped. His entire serene expression immediately turned into a ghostly stare, the same expression he'd worn back at Diane's apartment. This new look of his caused Diane to suddenly become concerned, too.

"Well?" Sister Inez asked, knowing full well that she was on to something. "Have you ever heard of Dena Johnson?"

"You know I have."

"What happened?"

"Nothing happened."

Inez looked at Molt. "Didn't I tell you? I told you he wasn't gonna admit to nothing! We should have called Bishop and washed our hands of this. You can't help nobody like this."

"We need to know the truth, Pastor," Deacon Molt said. "Tell us what happened between you and Dena Johnson."

"I told you the truth. Nothing happened."

Molt sighed. Diane nervously looked at him. He pulled out a newspaper clipping, slipped on his reading glasses, and read it. "Famed attorney Matthew Jolson accused of molesting twelve-year-old." Molt looked up over his glasses. Matty glanced at Diane, who was suddenly mortified. When their eyes met, his heart squeezed in agony. If he could only take her aside. If he could only explain to her. But it seemed so hopeless. So very, very hopeless.

"Now I need you, Pastor," Molt said, "to tell us exactly why you were accused of child molestation. And don't tell me nothing happened because something obviously did."

Matty ran his fingers through his soft, curly hair. When would it ever end? he wondered. This had happened so long ago. Before he was even saved. Lies and innuendo that caused his wife to leave him, his friends to desert him, and his soul to cry out to God. So long ago. Seemingly years ago. Now right back in his face again. When will it all end!

"Pastor, we're waiting," Molt said. His heart was aching, too. Because he wished to God it wasn't true. He wished to God Matty would say the right words, show the right degree of contrition and maybe, just maybe he could survive this nightmare. But Molt didn't see it. Matty had that same old arrogant look. That same old unaffected, ironclad look that turned Molt's stomach. If he weren't a Christian he might actually relish the man's fall. But he was a Christian.

"Pastor," he said again.

"A young lady and her mother did accuse me of improprieties, Deacon Molt, yes, they did. The allegations were untrue. The charges were dropped. And that's all. That's it."

"Huh!" Inez said, turning around in her seat. "Where there's smoke there's fire or fire done been there!"

"According to this news story I have here," Deacon Molt said, "the prosecutors dropped the charges, not because they didn't believe them, but because the little girl wouldn't testify. And without the little girl's testimony they didn't have a case. But that don't mean the allegations weren't true. In fact, according to this information we have, a private investigator did some checking and he concluded that the little girl had indeed been raped and the only reason she wouldn't talk was because she was threatened by some gangster friend of yours."

Matty leaned back in his chair. It was hopeless, just as he had thought. He could proclaim his innocence until he was hoarse, he could stand on rooftops and bridges shouting the truth, but they still wouldn't believe him. Some investigator who was investigating an eleven-year-old case for God-only-knew what reason said the girl didn't lie and that was all they needed to hear. Matty's word meant nothing to them. It never had, it never would. And he was done defending himself against people whose minds were made up before they ever had any proof.

"Is that true, Reverend?" Inez asked him. "Was the little girl threatened?"

Matty looked at her with such a harsh stare that she immediately took offense.

"Don't be getting all hot with us," she said, defensively. "We ain't just making this stuff up. It's right there, in black and white. You've been accused of being a child abuser, a child rapist. We can't just sit back and let this go on in our church. Them other churches might not mind it, but we ain't having it. Now you can get mad at us and wanna shoot the messengers all you want. But where there's smoke there's fire or fire done been there and I'll believe it until my dying day!"

Matty stood up, stunning everyone in the room. Diane was too shocked to stand. "Believe whatever you want," he said.

Molt stood up, too, dumbstruck. "Pastor, what you think you're doing? You can't just leave! These are deadly serious allegations here. Somebody saying you raped a child and got away with it. Leah Littleton accused you of the same thing. We can't just sweep this under a rug."

"Nobody's expecting you to."

"Then you'd better tell us more than you telling us now because just saying it ain't true ain't enough."

"Right. So why should I waste my breath? I can't prove a negative. I can't convince you or anybody else that I didn't do something when my word means nothing to you. So you take your papers and your private investigator and do what you have to do. I'm going home."

"You got to resign," Inez said, standing up. "There's no other way. You resign quietly, explaining to Bishop why, so he can explain it to the board of bishops and that will be the end of it."

Chicago once gave him that same choice. Resign or else. He resigned then. But never again. "Do what you have to do," he said, "because I'm not resigning." Then he looked at Diane. She looked as if she'd just lost her best friend. His heart broke. "Let's go, Diane," he said to her.

Diane looked at Sister Inez, who had always been her example of living an uncompromising Christian life, and Deacon Molt, who she had nothing but respect for. And then she looked at Matty. And she was torn. Any other allegation. Any other crime and he would not have even had to explain a thing to her. She'd take him at his word. But a child was raped. A *child*. And he was accused of it. Everything within her told her it couldn't be true. Everything within her asked her what if it was.

"Diane," he said again, terrified that she would desert him, too. He would explain to her. He had to explain to her. But not here. Not in this den of lies and made-up minds. He wanted her with him. Alone. She'd understand. She had to.

She didn't understand. He saw it as soon as they made it back to her apartment. He sat her on the sofa and tried to explain, painfully reliving those dreadful days. But she didn't understand.

"But why would a twelve-year-old lie like that, Matty?" she asked him, staring at him, searching his sincere eyes.

"I told you why. I was doing pro bono work on the side for a legal clinic at the time. There was a landlord-tenant dispute and I was asked to check into it. I did. The tenant was a woman named Jasmine Johnson and she had a twelve-year-old daughter named Dena. They lived in this apartment that looked good from the outside but had numerous problems inside. So me and the mother hit it off, we started talking. Dena, the little girl, enjoyed my company, too, she said we played off each other very well, joking around and stuff. She called us Johnson and Jolson, a kind of play on Johnson and Johnson. It was all good innocent fun."

"What about the mother? This Jasmine. What was your relationship like with her?"

Matty hesitated. "It was good. For a while."

"Was it sexual?"

Again Matty hesitated. "No."

Diane swallowed hard. "You said the relationship was good for a while. What changed it?"

"I found out that the mother wasn't this respectable school

teacher she had made herself out to be, but was actually a prostitute. So naturally, as an attorney, as an officer of the court, I couldn't hang out with a woman engaged in an illegal activity. I could have given her a chance to change, to stop what she was doing, but I didn't. I ended what was nothing more than a friendship anyway, and went on about my business. She apparently thought we were much more than friends because she became fiercely angry when I broke it off. She started calling me at home, making harassing phone calls to me at work. Then the next thing I knew," Matty said and then hesitated, as the pain ripped through every fiber of his being, and Diane could see the sudden agony in his dark gray eyes. "The next thing I knew I was being booked on suspicion of child abuse."

"But you never touched the child?"

"Never."

"But why would she say you did?"

"You'll have to ask her that. Her and her mother. Because I assure you, this incident had everything to do with that mother of hers."

Diane wanted to believe him. She wanted to believe every word. But there were so many accusations. So many different problems associated with this man. She didn't know what to believe. Before they had left the church Sister Inez had pulled her aside and told her not to be so gullible, that Matty might look good but Lucifer was pretty, too. "Christians have their crosses to bear," Inez had said, "but not as many as this man's been bearing. There comes a time when you have to say that maybe they ain't crosses at all but his own sins coming back to haunt him."

Those words stunned Diane, making Matty's words that much harder to comprehend. He could say what he wanted, but she kept coming back to the main point. Why would a little girl lie about something like that? The mother may have had a motive to lie, but the little girl didn't. She gave a state-

ment to the police. Out of her own mouth she accused
Matty. It was too much. Way too much. Diane stood quickly.

"Diane," Matty said, standing, too. His heart was in his
shoe. Not her, too, Lord, he prayed. Not her, too!

"I need some time, Matty," she said.

"But Diane—"

She removed her arm from his grasp and began walking
toward her bedroom. He just stood there, in the middle of
her living room. There was a reason he kept her at bay. Every
spiritual discernment he had told him not to bring her into
his loop of hell. But he pulled her in anyway. Now she was
tossed and turned because of his selfishness. Now she was
filled with pain and despair because of his need to have
somebody in this life on his side. And now she didn't believe him either.

She heard the front door slam shut as Matty left her home.
Diane laid on her bed, balled up into a fetal position. The
tears streamed freely from her eyes and she felt emotionally
drained already. She could forgive Matty anything, including all the sordid details of his past life with women, but an
allegation like this was too much. It was, to Diane, the sick-
est, most perverted of sins, and the idea that Matty, *her* Matty,
had been accused of such a crime was unbearable. The
charges had been dropped, he said, but there was no trial.
No vindication. And Matty never gave a real reason as to
why the charges were dropped. His explanation was simple:
they were dropped because they weren't true. Period. And
Diane was expected to trust his word on it. And she would
have. She wanted to more than she had ever wanted to believe another human being before. But a child was involved.
A child. Why would a child, Diane could not stop asking
herself, lie like that?

She stayed in her bedroom all night, praying, reading her
Bible, crying out to God for direction. Her entire body

ached to the core. Her very soul shook. Matty was the man she just knew was the man for her. Now she didn't know who he was. He should have told her long ago about the allegations. They were so traumatic, he said, that they led him to salvation. She had thought it was the breakup of his marriage that had caused him to give his life to Christ. At least that was the impression he had given her. Now she knew that it was the allegations that had caused his marriage to break up, and the allegations that caused him to beg God's forgiveness.

Why hadn't he told her, if those allegations weren't true? He had to know that his enemies, of which he had so many, would sooner or later uncover that part of his past. Why would he let her find out like this? In front of Sister Inez, of all people. Somebody who seemed happy to see Matty fail. His marriage broke up because of rumors, he told Diane that night at the truck stop café. But he failed to mention that those rumors concerned charges of child molestation. Now she felt betrayed. He should have told her a long time ago. Before she invested her heart.

Diane blew her nose with a tissue and sat back against her bed's headboard. It wasn't as if she had that kind of relationship with Matty. She didn't. He never really told her any details about his personal life. And when he did tell her a little here and a little there he fully expected her to just accept what he said without questioning it. Now all she had were questions. Questions he tried to answer—but not at all to her satisfaction. She needed proof of his innocence. She had hoped to spend the rest of her life with this man and have children with him. How could she ever trust him with a child with these kind of allegations hanging over his head? His word wasn't enough she concluded. She needed proof. God help her, but she had to know for certain.

Knocking was suddenly heard on her front door. Hard pounding. She knew it was Matty. She knew he was coming back to try and convince her again that he wasn't the monster those allegations tried to make him out to be. She got up, not to hear him out—she didn't want to hear any more right now—but to tell him to please leave her alone. She needed time. She needed to be certain.

But it wasn't Matty. Frank's voice could be heard calling her name before she opened the door. All she needed was his begging for money right now, she thought. She therefore sniffled and blew her nose in a lame attempt at hiding what was obviously her horrific emotional state. But when she opened the door, Frank, who had come here hoping Jolson would be gone and he could then easily wrangle that money out of her, immediately frowned. "Dang, Diane, what's wrong with you?"

Diane looked at her brother. He couldn't help her. He never helped her. "What do you want, Frank?"

"Is it that preacher? That preacher got you crying like this?"

"Good night, Frank," Diane said, not about to stand up there and see him gloat, too. She was about to close the door, but he placed his hand on it.

"Okay. Goodness. Forgive me for being concerned."

"What do you want?"

"It's not what I want. I need that money, sis. I need it bad."

"I told you my..." She started to say her husband said she couldn't give him a dime. But it now seemed like a lifetime ago when she first uttered those words. Now she couldn't see herself married to Matty any more than she could see what the next moment was going to bring. She exhaled. What difference did it make anyway?

She opened the door further and went into her bedroom. She pulled money out of her purse, she didn't know how much and she didn't care. When she returned Frank was inside her living room, his body screaming for a fix, his eyes resting on the cash in Diane's hand as if it were pure gold.

"You'll get every dime of it back, sis, I promise you," Frank said as Diane gave him the money.

"Just go," she said with little enthusiasm as she opened the door for him. Frank looked at her. She was usually so upbeat, even when she was scolding him about the error of his ways and how he needed to be saved. Now she looked like a disaster, a ghost of who she used to be. She looked at him. He had the money, he had what he wanted. Why didn't he just leave, just give her some privacy in her pain?

But he just stood there staring at her.

"What?" she finally said with a twinge of anger. The last thing she needed right now was his judgment, his opinion, his *I told you so.*

"What, Frank? What are you staring at me for?"

Frank exhaled. "He's worth it, Diane."

She frowned. "Who's worth it?"

"The preacher. Pastor Jolson. He's a good man."

Diane almost smiled. Was this Frank talking? She couldn't believe it. He *hated* Matty. He hated him. Now he thinks he's a good man? Diane shook her head. "I'm not buying whatever you're selling, brother."

"He always tries to do right by you. I been noticing that. I let my own needs get in the way of the truth, sis, but the man is different. He looks out for you. Like that car out there he bought. How many brothers we know would do a thing like that for their woman? They too busy buying for themselves. He's a righteous dude, I'm tellin' you."

"He was unrighteous before I gave you that money. Now he's righteous? Good night, Frank."

"Okay. I'm going. And you can say what you want but I'll bet you any 'mount of money you ain't gonna find another man like him. He's worth it, Diane."

Diane just wanted him to leave. She couldn't hear that right now. He didn't know what had happened. He didn't know that this man he now thought was so righteous might very well be a pedophile. A pedophile, Diane thought as Frank finally left and she closed her front door. How could Matty be a pedophile?

She plopped down on her living room sofa. And the tears returned. She felt so torn that she could almost feel her very life seeping out of her. And all she could think to do was get down on her knees again.

And pray.

Early that next morning Matty's Jaguar stopped in front of her apartment. He had to explain himself again. He had to beg her, if necessary, to please believe him. He'd prayed all night, prayed without ceasing, not for Deacon Molt or Sister Inez or even the board of bishops to believe his report. He didn't care what they believed. He prayed that Diane believed him. That was all he needed. Her belief. Her faith. *Her.*

But her car was gone. He knocked on her door, banged on her door, but he received no response. He started to whip out his cell phone and call around, but he was too afraid it would scare her away before he could get to her. He therefore drove over to the library, to see if in her grief she went where she was probably most comfortable, but the library was closed and her car was nowhere to be seen. He drove over to Clarion Avenue, to her parents' house, but neither Willie James nor Malveen had heard a thing. He drove over to the church, just to see if she might be in the sanctuary praying. But she wasn't there. He drove over to Sam's house, who was busy getting Junior ready for school, but she hadn't seen or heard from Diane either. Matty smiled and thanked her, patted Junior on his head, and went and got back into his car. When he drove around the corner, he stopped.

It was certain now, he thought. Diane had surely left him. She had heard those horrible allegations and couldn't take it. Just as he had thought all along. His life was too much for anybody to take. He could barely navigate through it himself. How could he have ever expected somebody like Diane to be able to do it, too?

His heart ached beyond any pain he had ever felt before as he shifted gears and drove away. He was now resigned to the awful truth. He was now resigned to a life of loneliness, trouble, and despair. A life where peace was as elusive as a falling star. A life that contained no happiness for him.

Chapter 25

It took an hour of sitting and waiting before she would even see Diane, and even when she did allow her into her office all she wanted to talk about was Matty and how he hurt her and how she would never believe that a man like him could ever be a preacher.

"The things we used to do together," she said as she laughed and leaned back in her big executive chair.

Diane just sat across from the big desk, looking intensely at Victoria Avery, trying with all the strength she had not to turn this into some kind of defense of Matty's piety. She hadn't driven all the way to Atlanta to defend Matty. She was there to find the truth.

"Do you know where she might be now?" Diane asked her.

"Again, what's it to you?" Vicky replied. She was being nasty and she knew it. But this female, this same female she had seen with Matty that day she drove all the way to Floradale, was undoubtedly now his new woman. How did she expect her to behave?

"I need to talk to her."

"Why?"

"I just do."

"Oh, so you don't care to answer my question?"

"You were Matty's law partner, weren't you, when it all happened?"

Vicky hesitated. "No," she said.

"You weren't?"

"No. Matty and I became partners six years ago. That happened ten, eleven years ago, before I even knew him."

"Oh," Diane said, standing, her heart dropping in pain. She had wasted so much time. "I'm sorry to disturb you. I thought you knew what happened."

Vicky looked at Diane. And she finally saw it. She finally saw what it was about her that could have attracted somebody like Matty. It certainly wasn't her good looks or great body. She was passable in both departments, but hardly in Vicky's league, if she could say so herself. But there was a genuineness about her, an almost unspoiled goodness. The disappointment of not being able to help Matty was all over her face as she stood there. And Vicky felt sorry for her, although she was certain Diane didn't want her pity. But that was how she felt. Diane Tarver, this meek and mild little woman who was probably in way over her head, was pitiful.

"Sit back down, Diane," she said to her.

"But if you weren't there…"

"Do you want my help or not?"

Diane paused. Vicky Avery seemed so sure of herself as she sat back in her big office and wore her beautiful clothes, a woman so beyond Diane's humble background that Diane couldn't help but feel even worse. Why would Matty want her when he could have somebody like Vicky Avery? she wondered. And all those old doubts, the absolute last thing she needed right now, began to settle right back into yet another burden for Diane to bear. She sat down.

"It's true," Vicky said. "I wasn't there during his arrest and the subsequent dropping of the charges, but he told me all about it."

"He told you?" Diane asked, again unsettled.

"Yes. He told me everything about his life."

"I see," Diane said. Matty hadn't told her much of anything about his life. And it pained her to wonder why not.

"Dena Johnson is still here in town," Vicky said and Diane looked at her.

"Can you tell me where I can find her?"

"I doubt if she'll want to talk about it."

"I know. But I've got to try."

"May I ask why?"

Diane didn't hesitate. "Because he's worth it," she said.

Vicky looked at Diane with a searching glare. Then she exhaled as if she'd made up her mind, and stood up, causing Diane to stand, too. "Her mother owns a small company here in town."

"Her mother? But I thought she was, Matty said she was—"

"A prostitute? She was. But she got married to a Realtor who later died and left everything to her. Instead of returning to her old life she decided to make do with her new one."

"Do you know her?"

"No. Don't want to either. But Atlanta is like a small town sometimes, Diane. Everybody knows somebody who knows the person you might want to know about. I heard about her, that's all. I also heard that her daughter, now twenty-three, I believe, works for her. I'll take you to see her."

Diane's heart soared. But then she thought about it. Why would Vicky Avery, of all people, suddenly want to help her?

"Why would you do that for me?" she asked her.

"Let's get one thing straight," Vicky said, putting on her suit coat. "I'm not doing anything for you. I'm doing it for Matty."

"For Matty? I thought you said he hurt you."

"He did."

"Then why do you want to help him now?"

She hesitated. "Because he's worth it, Miss Tarver. Now do you want my help or not?"

Diane smiled. Yes, Lord, she wanted to say.

It was a small storefront office in downtown Atlanta. Parker Realty was written on the plate-glass window in small, semicircle lettering. Dena Johnson, a cute young woman with catlike eyes and large lips, was in the office making copies. Her mother, the owner of the small realty company, wasn't there. Dena listened to Diane's plea to understand exactly what had happened, to get her to tell the truth, but Dena seemed more content to listen than to talk. So Diane kept talking, explaining everything to Dena, how Matty was now pastor of Fountain Hope in Floradale, Georgia, how those allegations could cost him everything, how she loved him herself and had to know the truth. Even Vicky tried to get Dena to spill the beans, to let them have it even if it turned out that the allegations were true after all.

But Dena wouldn't say a word. For nearly an hour they badgered the young woman, especially Diane, who was begging her to talk. For nearly an hour she told them she didn't have anything to say. It was crippling to Diane when they finally left, when they finally realized that this woman, this seemingly heartless woman, would probably take the truth to her grave.

Diane thanked Vicky again. Vicky told her that she didn't want Matty to know that she had anything to do with this little excursion of Diane's, believing that she was the last person Matty wanted helping him. Diane agreed not to say a word. It was an easy pledge to make. She doubted seriously if she would ever have anything more to say to Matty herself, anyway.

★ ★ ★

Matty was staring out the window of his office when Deacon Molt and Sister Inez arrived. He'd been expecting them all day. He had planned to teach his classes earlier but they had all been canceled by Deacon Molt. He didn't argue with it; he didn't have the energy to argue. He just went back into his office and stayed there. He felt beaten down. He felt as if the world had dragged him through the mud one time too many now and he couldn't come up for the count anymore. He was embarrassed and he was humiliated. He was angry and he was bitter. He was *tired*.

And Diane had left him. That was the hardest of it all. He expected abuse from the world. He expected its doubts and admonitions. But he had always thought, somewhere deep inside, that when all the dust cleared, when all the lies had been aired for all the world to hear, she'd still stand with him.

He didn't blame her for not being there. Any fool could see he was a marked man. But that didn't lessen his pain. That didn't make him feel less alone than he'd ever felt before.

Sometimes he wished he was never born.

He declared he felt that way sometimes.

Deacon Molt and Sister Inez didn't bother to knock when they arrived. Even Wanda didn't bother to warn him of their arrival. And when he turned around and faced them, it was obvious why.

"This is the hardest thing I've ever had to do," Deacon Molt said, the anguish showing all over his face. Then he couldn't do it. He looked to Sister Inez, who had no such problem with fulfilling her duty.

"We have been in consultation with Bishop Owens all morning," she said, still unable to suppress her glee. "Bishop Owens has been consulting with the board of bishops all day. And based on the nature of the charges they don't see how they can allow you to remain in your current position."

"It's the liability, Reverend," Molt said, still upset. "If word got out about these allegations the church could open itself up to all kinds of lawsuits, people claiming left and right that you abused their children, too."

Matty's heart dropped. He'd never harm a child if his life depended on it. Why couldn't they understand that? Why couldn't they see it, too?

"You see what happened with the Catholic church," Molt continued, "when their leaders were accused of molesting children. And they got all kinds of money to settle lawsuits. Well, Reverend, one lawsuit could wipe out Fountain Hope. The bishops don't see how they can risk that."

Matty nodded. Those same bishops hadn't stood by him in Chicago either. They couldn't risk it there either. But he was still disappointed to hear it.

"Besides," Inez said, still determined, still so lacking faith in Matty that it sickened him, "you ain't been nothing but trouble for this church since you got here. All them drug addicts hanging around, and prostitutes. Turning the house of worship into I don't know what. We don't need your kind of leadership here. We want a pastor who knows how to be a pastor. Not some social worker. And the board has agreed that this time we get to choose our new pastor. This time we get to have our say in this matter. We didn't choose you. They did. And today I'll have you know they're sorely sorry they did."

Molt swallowed hard. "You have one hour, Reverend, to get your things and leave this building. If you don't leave peacefully, they have instructed us to contact the sheriff."

Matty smiled weakly. He didn't doubt their resolve for a minute. They wouldn't hesitate to have deputies throw him out of the house of God.

Without packing a thing, without saying a word, he left right then and there.

* * *

He was sitting on his front porch when Diane's Lexus drove into his driveway. He appeared so aloof, so distraught that she wondered if he even noticed that a car had suddenly stopped at his house. He looked solemn, she thought, in his jeans and sweatshirt, his legs gapped wide open, his head slumped down, a lit cigarette between his fingers. The front door of his house was open and the sounds of laughter and talk from his television blared out across the yard. It was late evening, the neighborhood was settling in for the night, and Matty, it seemed to Diane, was in a world all his own.

She got out of her car slowly, still drained from that useless trip to Atlanta, a trip she'd driven nonstop to and from and kept on driving until she made it here, to Matty's house. She stared unblinkingly at him as she walked across the yard, up the steps, and onto his porch. He didn't move a muscle. He looked so broken, so tired, so unlike the tough fighter she'd always known him to be that she had to struggle to choke back the tears. "Matty," she said to him. And just her voice, just the sound of that voice again, caused him to look up at her.

Her heart slammed against her chest. He looked so helpless, so very, very helpless. "Are you all right?" she asked him, her face ripe with worry.

He stared at her longer. Then he shook his head. "No," he said.

Diane lost all reason then. She ran to him, fell on her knees and threw her arms around him. She thought she had come to tell him that she couldn't marry him, that she couldn't live with a man who might have harmed a child. But she did love him. She loved him to the depths of her soul. And she had to believe him. She had to.

"I'm so sorry, Matty," she said, her face buried into his chest as she cried out loud. "I should have believed you. I should not have let it get to this."

Matty closed his eyes. "It's not your fault, Diane," he said dryly. He didn't hold her, he didn't comfort her, he didn't touch her in any way. She was better off without him. And nothing she said now could change that for him.

She knew it, too. That was why she didn't say anything. She just stayed where she was, holding him tighter and tighter, her tears subsiding as her head rested on his chest. She was as drained as he was, and almost as tired, and as the minutes ticked away so did her fears. God's got it all in control, she said to herself, over and over and over again. And then she fell asleep.

Matty looked at her, as she snored against his chest, and he could not believe it. He was a monster, didn't she realize that? He'd been labeled the worst kind of monster. How could she fall asleep? How could she trust him enough to lean on him? He couldn't even hold himself up; how in the world did she expect him to hold her up?

But that was exactly what she expected. He knew it. He slowly began to rub her hair. Diane wouldn't turn her back on him. She wouldn't point fingers at him and sneer at him and treat him as if he were the lowest of the low. She was too sweet to do that to any human being. She was too kind to throw him to the dogs the way the world kept trying to do. She was too Godly to judge him.

She opened her eyes as she felt his touch in her hair. She looked up at him and smiled. "I guess I fell asleep," she said but he quickly shook his head.

"No, Diane," he said. "I did." He ran the back of his hand along her cheek. Then he grabbed her by the hand and stood up. "Come on," he said as she stood, as he began pulling her along with him.

"Where are we going, Matty?"

"Where we should have gone a long time ago," he said.

And he meant it, too. He drove Diane's car, since it was the closest to the street, and didn't say another word to her until they were pulling up into the parking lot of the Fountain Hope Baptist Church of Bainbridge, Georgia, the next town over from Floradale. He got out of the car, got Diane out, and walked briskly into the sanctuary. It was Tuesday night and no one was in the church except the pastor, Jeffrey Demps, and his wife, Patricia. He was sweeping around the pulpit and she was collecting fans from the pews. When they saw Matty and Diane, they both smiled.

"Pastor Jolson," Demps said as he walked down the aisle to meet them. "What a welcome surprise."

"Hello, Pastor Jolson," Sister Demps said also as she followed her husband to meet them.

"Pastor," Matty said. "Sister Demps. You know Diane Tarver."

"Oh, yes," Pastor Demps said. "And how are you, Sister Tarver?"

"I'm…" Diane didn't know how she was. She was still wondering why they were there at all. "I'm fine," she managed to say.

"Good, good. And if you aren't, don't you worry about it. God is still in the blessing business."

"I take it you haven't heard," Matty said, although he suspected otherwise.

Demps exhaled. "We heard," he said.

Diane felt crushed. Would they judge him, too?

"But we don't believe it," Demps added. "You, harming a child? A man who cares so much about those poor folks around Floradale? No. I've seen a lot. I've been around that corner more than a few times and I've seen a lot. But I ain't seeing that."

Matty and Diane both smiled. Matty extended his hand. "Thank you, Pastor," he said.

"So what brings y'all out here to Bainbridge?" Sister Demps asked Diane. Diane looked at Matty.

"A favor," Matty said.

"Name it," Pastor Demps replied, meaning it.

Matty looked at Diane. And then he smiled. "I need you to marry us, Reverend," he said.

Diane stared at Matty, and a smile that could brighten any day brightened his. "Yes, Reverend," she said, her eyes glued to Matty's. "Will you marry us?"

"Y'all got a license?"

"Yes, sir," Diane said happily. "Will you do it? Will you marry us?"

Sister Demps clasped her hands together. She knew two people in love when she saw them. Then she looked at her husband. He smiled, too. "Without a doubt, Sister Tarver," he said. "Without a doubt!"

Chapter 26

The very next day Deacon Molt convened the first meeting of the committee formed to begin the search for a new pastor of Fountain Hope. As chairman he was determined that they were going to get it right. And Sister Inez, as co-chairman, agreed. The committee also boasted seemingly every member of the major auxiliaries of the church, including Sister Baker, Sister Mayfield, and Deacon Benford. Molt called the meeting to order at eight a.m. By ten-thirty they had narrowed their list to five names. All older, wiser preachers, all men they just knew wouldn't try to change a thing.

"Excuse me, Deacon Molt," Wanda Scott peeped into the boardroom and said. Sisters Inez and Baker sighed with unbridled frustration. They didn't like interruptions at all.

"Yes, Sister Scott," Deacon Molt said, not too fond of them either.

"A woman is here to see you."

"Not now, Sister. I'll have to see her this afternoon."

"It can't wait, sir."

Inez looked at Wanda. "And why's that?" she asked, displeased by Wanda's sudden brashness.

"Her name is Dena Johnson and she came all this way from Atlanta to see y'all."

Inez looked at Molt. Molt stared at Wanda. "Dena Johnson? Isn't that the little girl…"

"She ain't little anymore, Deacon Molt. She's a grown woman now. And she says she's got to talk to you."

Inez began to turn around in her chair. She had known something was bound to happen. Everything was going too smoothly. "Well, you tell her she just gonna have to come back," Sister Inez said, hoping to keep on going the way they were.

"Send her in," Deacon Molt said. He wasn't about to keep going. If there was more to the story than what those newspaper clippings and investigator reports had to say then he wanted to hear it.

And Wanda didn't disappoint, sending the quiet Dena Johnson in as soon as Molt gave the word. Wanda herself stayed, too.

After simple formalities that Inez didn't seem to care for, Dena didn't waste any time. She became as talkative now as she was quiet before. "He didn't do it," she said without hesitation.

"Who didn't do what?" Molt asked her although he surely knew who and what.

"Matty Jolson didn't touch me. He never did."

"Oh, please," Sister Inez said. "Why should we believe that?"

"Because I thought you was a Christian. I thought you wanted to hear the truth."

"And you supposed to know the truth?"

"I'm the one he was accused of molesting. I should know!"

"How do we know you Dena Johnson anyway?" Sister Mayfield asked, feeling, like Inez, that sleeping dogs were better left alone.

"I checked her driver's license before I brought her up," Wanda said. "She's Dena Johnson and she has an Atlanta address."

Mayfield exhaled. Then she looked at Inez.

"What business you had knowing him at all?" Inez asked the stranger, her tone decidedly dismissive. But Dena didn't even care. She had come to tell her story. She was going to tell it and leave. If that wasn't enough to save Matty's position, then there was nothing more she could do about it.

"He was a friend of me and my mama's when I was little," she said. "He did a lot for us then. He paid our rent, he made sure we never went without, he was a Godsend to us."

"That's all?" Inez asked. "He just gave you and your mama all this money and asked for nothing in return?"

"That's right."

"Him and your mama were just friends then?"

"That's all."

"See!" Inez said, as if her worst suspicions had been confirmed. "I know she's lying now!"

"When he found out that my mama wasn't the good little schoolteacher she claimed to be," Dena went on, ignoring Inez, "he broke off the friendship. He stopped coming around, everything. And my mama couldn't take it. She was depending on his money, she depended on him for so much. She was stalking the man it got so bad. Then she became obsessed with bringing him down. Late one night she came up with her plan. I'll never forget it. She dragged me out of bed and told me the story. Made me repeat and repeat it until I knew it like I knew my name. Then the next morning we went to the police. And I told my story. But it was all lies. Every word of it. Matty Jolson never touched me. My mama had so many different men coming in and out of our home, it was like a train station the way they came and went. I ain't joking. It was pathetic. And that's why it's so ironic now. Of all those men, all those horrible, horrible men, Matty Jolson was the only one who never touched me. And I mean the only one."

When Dena finished talking Molt leaned back in his chair. Inez, for once in her life, sat mute. And Wanda Scott, already excited, shouted hallelujah from the top of her lungs.

Diane was grabbing clothes and tossing them into her suitcases as if she couldn't pack fast enough. And she had company. Her entire family, in fact. Willie James and Malveen, Frank and Pam, and all three of Pam's children. They looked like they'd just lost their best friend—except for Willie James, who seemed happy for her—but the rest of her family was livid.

"You can't just leave town like this," Pam said as her children ran around her skirt.

"Watch me," Diane said, packing feverishly. She couldn't wait to leave town.

"But this don't make no kind of sense," Malveen said. "A traveling evangelist. I thought he was a pastor. Now he gon' be a traveling evangelist? Whoever heard of such nonsense? Why can't he just leave you here and go traveling on his own?"

Diane didn't even respond to that. She wasn't about to let Matty leave her here. Not on her life.

"Diane, listen to me," Malveen said, grabbing her daughter's arm.

"I have listened to you, Mother. And listened and listened. I'm sorry if you think it's strange that Matty wants to hit the road, but I don't think so at all. I'm his wife now, we were legally married, and he's going to preach wherever souls are lost and I'm gonna be right by his side."

"But this don't make no kind of sense."

"Maybe it doesn't," she said as she began taking her luggage into the living room. Frank, who'd been pretty much silent the whole time, helped her carry the luggage, and Willie James, inasmuch as his bum leg would allow, helped, too.

When Diane and Matty had arrived back from Bainbridge last night, Diane was walking on air. She could not believe how grandly her fortunes had turned. Even when Matty surprised her by sending her home, carefully explaining that he did not want to consummate his marriage here, in Floradale, in this place and time where too much pain still lingered, she did not hesitate to comply.

But she didn't go home. She couldn't. She was too excited. She, instead, went to her old friend Samantha Marshall's house and they stayed up half the night celebrating Diane's great news. From Russell Scram to Matty Jolson. They could not believe it.

And now her family was trying to dissuade her from holding on to her new beginnings as if it were possible to turn her around. Her mother even went so far as to bring up those horrid allegations.

"They're lies," Diane said bluntly.

"I heard they the truth. I heard he did some time in prison and everything."

Diane rolled her eyes. "You heard wrong, Mother."

"First Leah Littleton and now this. How could you marry somebody like that?"

"It was the easiest thing I'd ever done," Diane said proudly. "The smartest, too."

"It was foolishness. Pure and simple foolishness."

"Okay," Diane said, not even caring to convince her or anybody else otherwise.

Malveen stopped her again, stopped her in her tracks. She just looked at her daughter as if she didn't know what to say. Who was going to take her to bingo if Diane left? Who was going to run errands for her and take her to the supermarket and take her over to Edna's for dinner every now and then? That was why she felt so panicky. That was why she felt such a sense of urgency. What was going to happen to *her*?

Pam also worried, as she picked up her daughter and held her. What in the world was she going to do? she wondered. Diane was her babysitter. A person she could always count on. Who was going to help her now?

Frank had similar thoughts as he helped carry Diane's luggage. She would always come through for him when he needed a quick buck, and when he, in truth, needed a quick fix. He couldn't imagine not having her around.

"What about me?" Malveen finally said, the only one to voice what they all had been thinking.

Diane set her luggage down and looked at her mother. "This isn't about you, Mother. Or about Pam. Or Frank. Or anybody else. This is about me. And I'm going with Matty. I'm gladly going. Now if you don't like it or you can't deal with that, then I'm sorry. I already submitted my resignation at the library. I already notified my landlord of my departure. I'm out of here. And you might not want to hear this, but I can't wait to go."

Malveen stared at the daughter she thought she knew so well; the daughter who, not very long ago, would do anything she wanted her to if she complained long enough. And she didn't recognize her.

Matty was loading his last suitcase into the trunk of his car when Diane, with her father in the front seat, drove up. Matty stood beside his car and smiled. Diane was back. He'd never felt more relieved in his life. And when she got out of her car, in her tight jeans and T-shirt, her hair bouncing as she walked, his heart sang.

"You look like a breath of fresh air, woman," he said lovingly as her walk hastened. She couldn't seem to get to him fast enough, and her heartbeat quickened as she nearly started running. Her father was just getting out of her car when she jumped into Matty's arms. They hugged and he kissed her and then he just held her.

"You okay?" he asked her.

"I'm great," she said with a smile.

"I see you brought Willie James along."

"I told him what you said about the car. He's very excited."

"Yeah, he would be," Matty said and then allowed Diane's feet to touch the ground again. He looked at Willie James as he walked with his cane up the driveway. "Hey there, old man."

"Who?" Willie James said. "I ain't old yet. Speak for yourself. I'm a blessed man, that's what I am. A blessed man with a Lexus!" Willie James laughed when he said this. Matty placed one hand around Diane's waist and shook his hand.

"Thanks for the opportunity, Matty," Willie James said in all sincerity.

"Take care of my wife's car and you'll have no problem with me."

"Don't you worry 'bout a thing. I'll guard it with my life. Drive it with it, too."

Matty laughed. "And remember Malveen."

"Malveen?" Willie James asked suspiciously.

"Yes, Daddy," Diane said. "You've got to take her around, to bingo and Miss Edna's, and all those places she likes to go."

"I know. Just jivin'. I'll take care of the witch."

"Daddy!"

Matty repressed a smile and then began walking toward Diane's car to get her luggage out of the trunk. Diane pressed the key pad for him and the trunk popped open. Then she handed the keys to her father.

"Um um um!" Willie James said, staring down at the keys. "Me with a Lexus." Then he looked at his daughter. "Never in my wildest dreams, baby girl."

"It was Matty's idea. He respects you, Daddy."

"That's a smart man."

Diane smiled. Then her look turned more solemn. "Daddy, treat Mama right."

"Don't worry about that."

"Just do it, please. I know she's a handful. I know she gets on your nerves no end. But you're all she's got."

"Don't you worry about no Malveen, Diane. She's stronger than you think. We all are."

Diane hugged her father. "I know *you* are," she whispered in his ear. Then she went and helped Matty with her luggage.

They had just finished loading her luggage into Matty's Jaguar, and Matty had just locked up his house, when a big, white Cadillac turned onto Haines Street and stopped in front of that very house.

Matty knew the car as soon as he saw it and he walked slowly back to his Jaguar, where Diane and Willie James stood. As soon as Sister Inez and Deacon Molt stepped out of Inez's car, Matty felt a tingle of anxiety in the pit of his stomach. Those two affected him viscerally now.

"Good evening, everybody!" Molt said with nervous cheerfulness as he and Inez walked up to the threesome. Diane and Willie James returned his greeting. Matty's entire demeanor was too intense to speak.

"Nice day, isn't it?" Molt said, trying to lighten Matty's mood.

"What can we do for you, Deacon?" Matty asked, not interested in lightening up.

"You right. This ain't no time for chitchat." Molt stood straight back. "We got a visit from a young lady this morning."

Matty's heart dropped. Diane shook her head. "Now what?" she asked bitterly.

"No, no, Sister Tarver—"

"Jolson," Matty said.

"Excuse me?"

"Diane is my wife. Her name is Jolson now."

"Your wife?" Inez asked, stunned.

"Well, congratulations," Molt said nervously.

"What's this about, Horace?" Matty asked, his patience wearing thin.

"Dena Johnson came to see us, Reverend," Molt said.

Matty frowned. "Dena?"

"That's right?"

"She's in town?" Diane asked, more astonished than anybody.

"She was. And she had quite a bit to say before she left, too."

"Why would Dena, how would she know to come here?" Matty asked, completely confused by this turn of events.

Molt smiled. "Ask your wife. Miss Johnson said she got a visit from a lady named Diane yesterday."

Matty looked at Diane. "You went to Atlanta yesterday?" he asked, unable to conceive of such an act.

Diane nodded.

"That's where you were? In Atlanta?"

"I had to go, Matty. I couldn't just sit back and do nothing. But I didn't think it did any good. She wouldn't tell me anything."

Matty looked at his wife with renewed respect. She went all the way to Atlanta to find out for herself, to do what she could to get to the bottom of the truth. More than what anybody else had ever been willing to do for him.

"She told us all about what happened, Reverend," Molt said. "Everything. Including the fact that you never touched her."

Diane closed her eyes in relief, in a silent prayer of thanks.

"We owe you an apology," Molt said earnestly. "We acted too rash and we were wrong as we could be. You're truly a man of God and we are deeply sorry, Matty."

Matty nodded. He still felt devastated by his Floradale experience. Even with Molt's apology there was still that ache deep within him that no amount of words could heal. "Okay," Matty said.

"You accept our apology?" Inez asked as if she weren't expecting him to.

"Of course, Sister Inez."

Molt exhaled loudly. "Thank God. Inez didn't believe you would, but I was praying you'd understand."

"Oh, I understand fully, Deacon Molt," Matty said. Then he looked at his wife. "Get in the car, Diane," he said. "And you take care of yourself, old man." Matty said this affectionately and extended his hand to Willie James. Willie James gladly shook it.

"Me and that Lexus gonna be just fine," he said. "You take care of my little girl."

Matty watched Diane as she walked around to the passenger door. "I'll guarantee it," he said.

"Wait a minute," Molt said, confused. "You going somewhere?"

"They hittin' the road, Jack," Willie James said happily.

"But you said you forgave us, Reverend," Molt said. "You accepted our apology. How can you forgive us and still leave the church?"

"Because I can't stay!" Matty said with such a sudden burst of emotion that Diane stopped and looked at him. "Don't you understand that? I can't do it anymore, Deacon. I'm sorry but I can't. I'm tired of people gunning for me, people who should be helping me and supporting my ministry. I'm tired of sitting around waiting for the next shoe to drop. I'm going to be about my Father's business, forget the games.

Forget the rumors and innuendos and all of this foolishness
I can't abide anymore. I'm taking my message on the road
until God tells me otherwise. So yes, Deacon, I accept your
apology. But I can't stay." Then he looked at his wife again.
"Get in, Diane," he said, and got in, too.

Molt and Inez stared at each other as the Jaguar backed
out of the driveway. They could not believe he was really
leaving like this. They had apologized; what more did he
want? Inez saw the whole thing as a slap in the face, as yet
another example of that preacher's stubbornness. But Molt
knew better. Matty Jolson was like an eagle, he felt. Hanging around Floradale wasn't meant for him. A man like that
was meant to fly, to soar, to be free in the house of the Lord,
not caged and hampered.

Diane knew it, too. That was why she couldn't stop smiling as the car drove away. She didn't know where they were
going or what to expect when they got there. And it didn't
matter. For once in her orderly life it didn't matter. She was
with Matty. Her *husband*. The man God had ordained to
preach His gospel.

That was all that mattered to her.